D1008373

"This awesome paranormal mystery stars a terrific heroine." —Genre Go Round Reviews

Secondhand Spirits

"Juliet Blackwell provides a terrific urban fantasy with the opening of the Witchcraft mystery series." —Genre Go Round Reviews

"An excellent blend of mystery, paranormal, and light humor, creating a cozy that is a must read for anyone with an interest in literature with paranormal elements." —The Romance Readers Connection

"It's a fun story, with romance possibilities with a couple hunky men, terrific vintage clothing, and the enchanting Oscar. But there is so much more to this book. It has serious depth." —The Herald News (MA)

THE HAUNTED HOME RENOVATION MYSTERIES

Dead Bolt

"Cozy fans will want to see a lot more of the endearing Mel." —Publishers Weekly

"Cleverly plotted with a terrific sense of the history of the greater Bay Area, Blackwell's series has plenty of ghosts and supernatural happenings to keep readers entertained and off-balance." —Library Journal

If Walls Could Talk

"A riveting tale with a twisting plot, likable characters, and an ending that will make you shudder with how easily something small can get totally out of hand. Juliet Blackwell's writing is able to mix paranormal experiences with everyday life. [It] leaves you wondering what you just saw out of the corner of your eye . . . a good solid read." —The Romance Readers Connection

"Ms. Blackwell's offbeat, humorous book is a fun, light read. . . . Mel makes a likable heroine. . . . Overall, a terrific blend of suspense and laughter with a dash of the paranormal thrown in makes this a great read."—TwoLips Reviews

"Kudos and high-fives to Ms. Blackwell for creating a new set of characters for readers to hang around with as well as a new twist on the ghostly paranormal mystery niche. I can't wait to see what otherworldly stories Juliet has in mind for us next!"   —Once Upon a Romance

"A wonderful new series. . . . There's enough excitement to keep you reading until late in the night."   —Fresh Fiction

THE ART LOVER'S MYSTERIES
BY JULIET BLACKWELL
WRITING AS HAILEY LIND

Brush with Death

"Lind deftly combines a smart and witty sleuth with entertaining characters who are all engaged in a fascinating new adventure."   —Romantic Times

Shooting Gallery

"If you enjoy Janet Evanovich's Stephanie Plum books, Jonathan Gash's Lovejoy series, or Iain Pears's art history mysteries . . . then you will enjoy Shooting Gallery."   —Gumshoe

"An artfully crafted new mystery series!"
        —Tim Myers, Agatha Award–nominated author of
                                        Key to Murder

"The art world is murder in this witty and entertaining mystery!"
            —Cleo Coyle, national bestselling author of
                                    Murder by Mocha

Feint of Art

"Annie Kincaid is a wonderful cozy heroine. . . . It's a rollicking good read."   —Mystery News

Also by Juliet Blackwell

WITCHCRAFT MYSTERIES
Secondhand Spirits
A Cast-off Coven
Hexes and Hemlines

HAUNTED HOME RENOVATION MYSTERIES
If Walls Could Talk
Dead Bolt

IN A WITCH'S WARDROBE

A
Witchcraft
Mystery

Juliet Blackwell

AN OBSIDIAN MYSTERY

OBSIDIAN
Published by New American Library, a division of
Penguin Group (USA) Inc., 375 Hudson Street,
New York, New York 10014, USA
Penguin Group (Canada), 90 Eglinton Avenue East, Suite 700, Toronto,
Ontario M4P 2Y3, Canada (a division of Pearson Penguin Canada Inc.)
Penguin Books Ltd., 80 Strand, London WC2R 0RL, England
Penguin Ireland, 25 St. Stephen's Green, Dublin 2,
Ireland (a division of Penguin Books Ltd.)
Penguin Group (Australia), 250 Camberwell Road, Camberwell, Victoria 3124,
Australia (a division of Pearson Australia Group Pty. Ltd.)
Penguin Books India Pvt. Ltd., 11 Community Centre, Panchsheel Park,
New Delhi - 110 017, India
Penguin Group (NZ), 67 Apollo Drive, Rosedale, Auckland 0632,
New Zealand (a division of Pearson New Zealand Ltd.)
Penguin Books (South Africa) (Pty.) Ltd., 24 Sturdee Avenue,
Rosebank, Johannesburg 2196, South Africa

Penguin Books Ltd., Registered Offices:
80 Strand, London WC2R 0RL, England

First published by Obsidian, an imprint of New American Library,
a division of Penguin Group (USA) Inc.

First Printing, July 2012
10 9 8 7 6 5 4 3 2 1

PUBLISHER'S NOTE
This is a work of fiction. Names, characters, places, and incidents either are the
product of the author's imagination or are used fictitiously, and any resemblance
to actual persons, living or dead, business establishments, events, or locales is
entirely coincidental.

The publisher does not have any control over and does not assume any responsibility for author or third-party Web sites or their content.

If you purchased this book without a cover you should be aware that this book
is stolen property. It was reported as "unsold and destroyed" to the publisher and
neither the author nor the publisher has received any payment for this "stripped
book."

ALWAYS LEARNING   **PEARSON**

To Sergio,
the brightest star in my galaxy.
Thank you for bringing such precious light into my life.

Acknowledgments

Thanks are due, as always, to my editor, Kerry Donovan, and all the artists, copy editors, publicists, and typesetters at Penguin for all their hard work.

Special thanks are due to Luci Zahray, affectionately known as "the Poison Lady," for her advice and suggestions about henbane and other poisonous plants. I've made a note never to get on your bad side! And to Victoria Laurie, for her friendship, support, and warm invitation into the supernatural writers' club. To the Pensfatales, each and every one of you. Thank you for being there to celebrate, as well as commiserate. And I'm so glad we now have the naughty and delightful Nicole Peeler in our midst!

To Carolyn Lawes, JC Johnson, Sharon Demetrius, and Suzanne Chan for reading early drafts and providing helpful insights, ideas, and constructive criticisms. As always, thanks to my father, who is a constant source of support in my life and never fails to urge me to "be good and work hard," and to my sister, Susan, for her unflagging encouragement. And to Mom, whom I miss so much.

To my wonderful, close circle of friends, who put up with the constant deadlines and angst and whining—and occasional euphoria—common to those of us who write. I am more grateful than I can say to each and every one of you. My life would be so poor without the riches of friendship.

And finally, to Oscar. Thanks for the laughs, little guy.

There be none of Beauty's daughter
With a magic like thee.

—LORD BYRON

Chapter 1

Not being a necromancer, I can't see ghosts. Normally.

But tonight felt like a different story. The brightly lit streets of downtown Oakland were host to a sea of women wearing beaded flapper dresses, glamorous 1930s-era gowns, and vibrant swing costumes. Men clad in tuxedos with tails, white bow ties, and shiny black shoes accompanied the feathered and spangled partygoers.

A black Model T Ford, polished and gleaming, glided to a stop in front of the magnificent Paramount Theater, and the couple that emerged could have stepped right out of the pages of *The Great Gatsby*.

Sprinkled among these apparent spirits-from-another-time was a handful of witches.

"The top hat is all wrong," murmured one such witch, Aidan Rhodes. His blue-eyed gaze flickered over the formally attired man who opened the theater door and welcomed us to the Art Deco Ball.

"Top hats are elegant," I replied. "They're *never* not right."

"But it's not authentic. Top hats were already out of

style by the twenties. And, my dear Lily, you of all people should know: The devil's in the details."

"I hope you don't mean that litera—"

I stumbled, shoved from behind. Aidan's strong arms caught me before I toppled off my unfamiliar high heels and plunged down a short flight of stone steps.

"Oh! I'm so sorry!" exclaimed a young woman as she steadied herself. "It's these dang shoes!"

"Miriam, you okay?" asked her gray-haired escort, wrapping a beefy arm around her shoulders.

"Fine. Just clumsy. I'm more of a barefoot gal."

The woman named Miriam had hazel eyes that echoed the sea-foam shade of her dress, and her honey-colored hair was covered by a glittery beaded cap. Unlike many of tonight's guests, who had clearly modified or sewn their dresses, this young woman's gauzy number was authentic. A diaphanous flapper dress, it was beaded and fishtailed and hung loose on her creamy white shoulders. My vintage-clothes-dealer sensibilities kicked into high gear, leaving me wondering where she had found such an incredible gown in mint condition.

"I know the feeling," I commiserated. "No harm done. Your dress is exquisite."

"Why, thank you! Yours too." When she smiled, I noticed her expression was warm yet strangely . . . vacant. Off-kilter. Though undeniably pretty, her face appeared flushed but pinched, as though she were feverish.

And from the vibrations she gave off I could sense . . . something was wrong.

Wrong and yet familiar to me. One of my magical skills was the ability to sense vibrations from clothes and sometimes from people. But I was certain I hadn't sold her the flapper dress she was wearing. I would have remembered obtaining such an exquisite antique gown for my shop.

At the moment the young woman stumbled into me I had been distracted by Aidan's touch—which had, as usual, sent an annoying yet intriguing *zing* through me. So I couldn't tell whether the disturbing vibrations emanated from Miriam's garment or from the woman herself. I'd have to find a reason to touch her again.

As she turned to continue up the steps, I reached toward her bare shoulder.

"*Leave it*," Aidan whispered, resting a white-gloved hand on my arm. "It's not that kind of night."

I hesitated, and the young woman and her escort disappeared into the crowd.

"I suppose *you* wouldn't offer to help until you'd run a credit check on her," I said, miffed at his interference.

Aidan sold his magical services. Many talented witches did. We're human; we need to eat and pay rent just like everyone else. Still, the practice galled me. It seemed so crass to cash in on our special abilities. Which was one of the many reasons I had opened Aunt Cora's Closet, my vintage clothes store, where I earn a legitimate living the old-fashioned way—just like every non-witchy merchant in San Francisco's Haight-Ashbury neighborhood.

Usually, anyway. Vintage clothing is a cutthroat business, and I might, from time to time, utilize my witchy wiles to gain an ever so slight edge. But I kept it to a minimum. It seemed only sporting.

Aidan, unfazed by my criticism, smiled and led me into the grand lobby of Oakland's Paramount Theater.

I paused, taking it all in. The 1920s Art Deco extravaganza was the ideal locale for the annual Art Deco Preservation Ball. A massive carved glass "Fountain of Light," over thirty feet tall, dominated the entrance, casting a rich amber glow throughout the room. Overhead a vitreous green panel was bordered by labyrinthine fretwork and diamond-shaped gold patterns.

A sight more interesting than your average multiplex.

In one corner a man with slicked-back hair stood near a grand piano, singing a lilting tune from the twenties. And the crowd was, to a person, dressed to the nines in outfits from the heyday of the Art Deco movement.

It didn't take a wild imagination to feel as though we had just stepped into a ghostly reenactment of a high-society soiree from days gone by.

"Do me a favor?" Aidan asked.

"Hmm. That depends. . . ." With a powerful witch like Aidan, an offhand promise could lead to something one didn't intend: a lifetime of servitude, for example. It paid to be cautious.

"Relax and enjoy yourself tonight? As a woman, not as a witch."

I laughed. "The woman part I've got down. It's the dancing bit that's making me jittery."

"Surely you've been to a formal dance before. What about your senior prom?"

"Closest I came was a hootenanny when I was eight." That was before the good people in my Texas hometown decided to shun me.

Aidan raised one eyebrow. "Is that right? Well, then, this *is* a special occasion. Chin up, my dear. You're making an entrance."

"I'm as nervous as a long-tailed cat in a room full of rockers."

"You shouldn't be. You're stunning," he whispered. "Just look at yourself."

I scoffed but glanced at my reflection in the mirrored wall.

Land sakes. I *did* look nice. I often tell my customers that when their clothes change, *they* change. No reason this transformation wouldn't apply to me.

I had chosen the dress carefully . . . or perhaps it had chosen *me*. I had been planning to wear a peacock blue cocktail gown from the 1930s when I received a call from an elderly woman who had two generations' worth of fine, formal garments in her crammed walk-in closet that she wished to sell. The moment I picked up the tea-stained silk chiffon, I fell in love. The fabric was embossed with beads and flat gold leaf sequins in a twisting vine pattern. Simple spaghetti straps led to a deep V neck, and the bottom was trimmed in a sassy beaded ruffle. Two handmade silk roses sat on the drop waist along with a velvet sash.

Best of all, the vibrations from the dress gave me courage. The gown had been altered so it fit me perfectly: loose, as a flapper dress should, but accentuating my figure. The fine fabrics brushed against my legs as I moved, making me aware of my skin.

Bronwyn and Maya, my friends and coworkers, had tortured my straight hair into a wavy Marcel style, then gathered it into a chignon at the nape of my neck and decorated it with a glittery beaded hairnet. My lipstick was a brilliant red, and I wore matte makeup, eyeliner, and a bit of powder.

My only complaint was the shoes. Bronwyn and Maya had nixed my usual comfy footwear, insisting the shoes be appropriate to the event. Thus tonight I wore reproduction heels that looked great but made me miss my Keds with each uncomfortable step.

Still, the reflection in the mirror showed the effort had been worth it. I fit in here, with these other would-be spirits from the roaring twenties, the elegant thirties, and the swinging forties . . .

Until I saw something else in the mirror.

A frisson of . . . *something* passed over me. I'm not a

sensitive and have no special gift of sight. Even my pre-
monitions are vague and generally useless, arriving as
they do mere seconds before they come true.

But this time, I could have sworn I saw the image of a
woman sleeping amid vines and briars and roses. As I
watched, she reached out to me. . . . I raised my hand to
the mirror. . . .

"Lily?" For the second time that evening, Aidan laid
his hand upon my arm to stop me. His voice was low but
adamant. "What are you doing? You should know it can
be dangerous to place your palm against a mirror. Especially in a place like this."

"I . . . I thought I sensed something. Do you see anything in the mirror?"

"I see you. And you do look lovely."

I looked around for a logical explanation for the strange
reflection. But all I saw was the faded gold gilt and chrome
of the theater's popcorn stand, the jade green of the bas-
relief sculptures that ringed the ornate lobby, and a throng
of costumed people milling about.

"I could have sworn I saw . . . a woman sleeping
among vines. Remember the fairy tale of Briar Rose, or
Sleeping Beauty?"

The corner of his mouth kicked up: "Relax, Lily. Old
theaters are full of ghosts. You probably caught a random, rogue glimpse of an old stage production."

"But—"

"Lily! Yoo-hoo! Over here!"

Susan Rogers sprang up from her chair at one of the
many round tables that ringed the grand lobby and
waved. Some time ago, Susan had written an article
about Aunt Cora's Closet for the Style section of the *San
Francisco Chronicle*, when she was helping to outfit her
niece's wedding party in vintage attire. In no small part

because of that article, business at Aunt Cora's Closet had boomed. Since then, Susan stopped by the store often, and we had become friends.

After a round of introductions, I noted Susan's handsome blond escort was at least a decade her junior. Age differences seemed to be slipping away, changing like everything else in the open-minded Bay Area.

"You look amazing," Susan gushed, holding my hands in hers and assessing my outfit with a practiced eye. "Absolutely smashing. How about me?"

She did a little pirouette, the shiny satin skirt of her 1930s full-length gown fanning out as she twirled. She wore feathers in her hair and a deep pink boa around her neck, which wasn't at all appropriate to the era but looked just right on a woman as vivacious as she.

"You are gorgeous, Susan. I knew that dress would suit you once it was tailored," I said.

"Champagne, ladies?" Aidan asked.

Susan and I nodded and took our seats at the table as our escorts set off toward the bar.

Near the grand piano, a petite woman in a beautiful crimson gown had taken control of the microphone and was speaking about the importance of preserving Art Deco buildings and "our way of life." Meanwhile, a full orchestra was tuning up on the exposed mezzanine that overlooked the entry hall, and there were loud cries of delight as guests greeted friends and *oohed* and *aahed* over one another's costumes.

It was a glittery, cacophonous bash.

I strained to hear what all the woman in red was saying, then watched as the tenor who had been singing tried to take over the microphone.

"What's going on?" I asked.

"Theatrical types," Susan scoffed. "I never bother listening to these speeches. I mean, I think it's important to contribute to the preservation of historic buildings. But, frankly, I'm here for the dancing. Aren't you?"

I smiled, inwardly doing my best not to panic. All last week, after we'd closed, Bronwyn had tried to teach me ballroom dancing in the aisles of the shop. I was a singularly unimpressive student. Dancing, I had decided one day as I flopped down in an overstuffed chair near the dressing rooms, was like math or music—either one had a talent for it or one didn't, and I definitely did *not*. Maybe I forfeited the dancing gene in favor of one of my witchy talents: brewing magical potions, calling on my ancestors to affect reality, communicating with the occasional non-human creature. After years of solitude, I was only now coming to realize just how challenged I was when it came to normal activities, such as dancing or making small talk. I didn't have much of a singing voice, either, as my ersatz witch's familiar was more than happy to remind me.

"I thought I might just sit and watch," I said. "I'm not well versed in the dances from this era." Or any other.

"I'm sure Aidan knows them."

Of course he did. Aidan knew everything.

Susan fixed me with a look, her eyes narrowing. "You can't sit out *all* the dances, Lily. We're at a *ball*. It's kind of the point."

I must have paled because Susan's insistence turned to concern.

"Lily, honey, are you all right? Where's that champagne? It'll help you relax. Liquid courage and all that."

"I'm not what you'd call 'gifted' in the rhythm department," I confessed. The only real dancing I'd done was drumbeat-inspired stomping around the fire while spell casting. Somehow I didn't think that counted. "I can't dance. I mean, at *all*."

"Don't be silly. Everybody can dance, Lily. Just follow your partner—and what a partner he is."

The band started up a 1940s West Coast Swing, and couples poured onto the dance floor, jitterbugging and foxtrotting. Big and small, old and young, they smiled and glided and laughed.

"Here they are, back with drinks," Susan singsonged as our handsome escorts wound their way through the costumed crowd.

I pasted on a smile. *Suck it up, Lily,* my inner voice lectured. *You've done a lot more embarrassing things than dance in public and you're still here. Need I remind you about the time you went camping with those students in the Swiss Alps and—*

"Gentlemen!" I said brightly. I took the champagne flute Aidan handed me, took a big sip, and placed the glass on the table. "Let's dance, shall we?"

Susan threw me an "atta girl" grin, and Aidan, looking bemused, held out his hand to lead me to the dance floor. Happily for me, the swing dance had ended and the tenor was now crooning a slow, romantic ballad.

But when Aidan held me . . . the singer, the dancers, even the decorations faded away. Aidan softly counted out the beat as we moved in unison: "One, two, rock-step." Squeezing my hand ever so slightly when I was supposed to turn, he guided me around the dance floor.

"You're doing wonderfully," he murmured, and steadied me when I stumbled. "I had no idea you were so graceful, Lily. You're a natural."

"I am *not*," I replied, though his flattery succeeded in relaxing me a tad.

"You know I never lie . . ."

I raised an eyebrow.

". . . about dancing," he amended with a crooked grin.

"Anyway, there's no such thing as a woman who doesn't know how to dance. Only men who don't know how to lead."

"I like that philosophy."

"I thought you might. On the dance floor it's the man's job to make the couple look good. The woman has to do only two things: enjoy herself and look pretty."

I laughed. "Bold words to utter in the Bay Area."

He shrugged and his smile was dazzling. "I would never suggest such were the case elsewhere in life."

I relaxed a little more and started to enjoy myself. My hands tingled where they touched Aidan's, and the rest of my body . . . well, that seemed to be responding to more than desire. Was Aidan doing more than leading me through the dance steps? Could he be assisting me with some kind of magic? Or was I simply so keyed into his energy that the steps seemed effortless, natural? Either way, it took my breath away.

Though I trusted Aidan not at all—for good reason—an undeniable attraction flowed between us. It was a revelation to be with someone who wasn't afraid of my powers—someone who admired them and, if anything, desired to meld them with his. But then I reminded myself that I didn't know Aidan well, not really. Among other things, I still hadn't figured out what happened between him and my father years ago, beyond the fact that they had once worked together. Which, given the little I knew about my father, boded very ill indeed.

"You see, Lily?" Aidan said, gazing down at me. "You just have to have a little faith. This sort of thing suits you."

"Thank you," I said, and I meant it. Being here among these revelers, dancing in a man's arms, felt like a step toward the well-adjusted life I craved—as long as I ignored the fact that Aidan and I were powerful witches. "By the way, I need to talk to you about Sailor."

"Who?"

"Very funny." Sailor was a friend—sort of—and a very grumpy psychic who had recently gone out on a limb for me. In return, I had promised to try to free him of the Faustian deal he had made with Aidan years ago.

"You really want to spoil the mood by talking business?"

"You need to release him from his obligation to you. He's miserable."

Aidan chuckled and shook his head.

"Why do you keep him beholden to you? He wants his freedom."

"Sailor doesn't know what he wants."

"And you do?"

"Better than you. Better than he knows himself. Without a focus, Sailor's the type to get into serious trouble. You should have seen him when I first met him. Why do you think he was so easy to influence?"

That had never occurred to me.

"And don't be afraid that I'll exert total control," continued Aidan. "He's not my puppet, Lily. Have you forgotten about the charm he has, the one that limits my power?"

"You know about that?" I asked.

"Of course."

"And it's okay with you?"

"It's essential. It would be disastrous for both of us if I had complete power over him. Much too tempting." He smiled, and his voice dropped. "I'm no saint, as you know well."

I took a deep breath. Aidan smelled of pine needles and earth. Not Christmas tree pine, but more something from an ancient primeval forest, the kind inhabited by woods folk: faeries and brownies and elves. He was tall enough that even in heels my eyes were at the height of his jaw, which sparkled with a hint of golden five-o'clock shadow. I was tempted to rise up on tiptoe and brush against those whiskers, to see if they were prickly or soft.

But that beautiful face held secrets. Too many secrets.

His face came close to mine. Then closer . . .

The music stopped. I stumbled.

Aidan smiled. "Would you like to sit out the next one?"

He laughed at my vigorous nod, and we returned to the table. But before I could sit, Susan stood, grabbed my hand, told the men, "Gotta run and powder our noses— girl talk!" and pulled me after her.

We headed toward the stairs.

"I adore the ladies' lounge on the lower level. Let's go there. Isn't this place incredible? It was built back when people really knew how to design things." Susan's conversational style often did not require a response. Some people probably found it annoying, but I thought it was charming. "Back in the day, a restroom was a place where a lady could actually *rest*—to escape the menfolk and gossip, I suppose. Speaking of which . . . are you and Aidan an *item* now?"

"Of course not." I gripped the rail as we descended the great sweep of stairs, worried about my heels and distracted by the swirl of beautiful gowns all around us.

Attending the Art Deco Ball was not an easy gig for someone in my line of business. I was beginning to feel like I had Vintage-Clothes-Related Attention Deficit Disorder.

"Check *this* out," said Susan when we reached the ladies' lounge at the bottom of the staircase. The outer chamber was a large yet intimate room encircled by gilt-framed mirrors, each with a narrow glass shelf and delicate wrought-iron chairs in which to sit and apply makeup. In each corner sat a pair of upholstered armchairs, and along one wall was a brocade chaise longue. A doorway led to the actual lavatory, with stalls of gray-and-white marble, hung with mahogany doors.

There was a line of women waiting for a stall to open up, so I sat down before a mirror to fuss with my hair. I took my comb from my vintage Whiting and Davis mesh purse before realizing that the complicated chignon made combing my hair impossible.

"Excuse me . . . would it be too much to ask if I could borrow that?"

It was Miriam, the young woman I had met on the front steps. Her dark gold tresses had escaped their pins and half tumbled to her shoulders.

"Oh, of course. Here, let me help you."

I caught her hair up in the comb as best I could, but I was clumsy—I didn't grow up playing "day at the hairdresser" with friends. Still, I did what I could with the heavy mass, twisting and gathering it. As I fussed with the long silken locks, I took the opportunity to concentrate on Miriam's vibrations. They felt chaotic, as if detached from their source. It was decidedly odd. Once again, I felt a strong sense of familiarity, though I still could not recall our ever having met.

"Are you feeling all right?" I asked.

Her gaze met mine in the mirror. "Of course." But her words rang hollow, and her eyes were too shiny.

"You're Miriam, right?" I asked.

After a brief moment of hesitation, she nodded.

"I'm Lily Ivory. You seem so familiar. . . . Have we met before?"

"I don't think so. . . . Oh wait! On the stairs earlier?"

"Yes, but I meant another time, maybe."

"I don't think so." She shook her head and gazed at her reflection, patting her new chignon. "Thanks for the help."

"You're welcome." As I dropped the comb into my bag I noticed a few strands of Miriam's hair were entangled in the teeth. I didn't bother removing them.

Just then a stall opened up, so I grabbed it. As I was washing my hands, I overheard women speaking in the outer room.

"Now, that's what I call lounging. You think she's all right?"

"Probably just had too much champagne. Girls today never eat."

"Excuse me—are you okay?"

With a sense of foreboding, I rushed out to the lounge.

Chapter 2

Miriam lay upon the chaise, her eyes closed, the silk dress splayed out around her. She had the odd stillness of one who wasn't merely sleeping.

"Wake up, sweetheart." An elderly woman gently shook Miriam's shoulder. "Are you all right? Would you like us to find your escort?"

The women stood back when I approached, as though I were a physician who would know what to do.

I knelt beside her. "Miriam?"

My heart caught in my throat at the sight of her. Bright red flags of color on her cheeks stood out against an unnatural, ashen pallor. I placed a hand on her brow and felt her neck for a pulse. It was weak, thready. But it was there.

"Call nine-one-one," I said over my shoulder.

As one of the women pulled a small cell phone from her beaded purse, Susan appeared.

"Lily? What can I do?"

"See if they have anyone on duty—a first-aid person, maybe. Oh! And tell Aidan I need him."

"Aidan has medical training?"

"In a manner of speaking."

As I brushed Miriam's hair away from her face, the orchid corsage pinned to her collar caught my eye. Lovely pale pink flowers tinged in violet formed a perfect contrast to the sea green of her dress. A few trumpet-shaped flowers formed a pale background. But as I looked closer, I spied beneath the foliage a bit of black ribbon, the glint of needles, and an ugly tangle of black thread. And I smelled . . . cigarettes?

This was no normal corsage. I concentrated on editing out the perfumes of the women in the lounge and detected the slightest hint of something putrid. Masked by the fragrant orchids, it was a subtle aroma no normal person would notice.

I was reaching to unpin the corsage when a commotion at the door announced Aidan's arrival.

"Lily, come away from there," he commanded.

"She needs help," I said.

"The EMTs are on their way," he said. "Come. It's none of our affair."

"But—"

"Miriam!" The woman's gray-haired escort appeared in the doorway before running in to kneel beside her. "What's wrong with her? Miriam? Talk to me, sweetheart."

Just then a plump, middle-aged woman carrying a first-aid bag joined the fray. She checked Miriam's pupils before applying a blood pressure cuff to her arm.

Miriam's escort passed large callused hands through his hair. "Is she all right?"

"We don't know anything yet, sir," said the woman, who seemed overwhelmed. I had the sense she was more prepared to provide Band-Aids for blistered heels than cope with actual medical emergencies. "Her blood pressure is low. . . . The paramedics are on their way."

Gripping my arm, Aidan pulled me out of the lounge

and urged me down the corridor. He guided me behind a red-and-gold velvet curtain marked PERSONNEL ONLY.

"What is *wrong* with you?" I demanded, yanking my arm out of his grasp. "I might have been able to help her."

"What is wrong with *you*? You saw that cursed corsage. I know you did," he said. "This sort of thing can cast serious suspicion on a witch, Lily. What do you think the Oakland PD is going to make of something like this? This isn't San Francisco, where you can call on your buddy Carlos to protect you."

"Oh, please—you really think the Oakland cops are going to accuse me of witchcraft? In this day and age?"

"I doubt they have the imagination. But they might suspect you of poisoning her, Ms. Botanical Specialist."

"That's absurd. I've never met her before in my life."

"Never underestimate the folly of the average cowan," said Aidan, using the derogatory word for nonmagical humans.

I shrugged. "Besides, I have you to protect me."

He gave me an enigmatic smile.

"Hey, you're supposed to be the Grand Poobah of Bay Area witches. Do you recognize Miriam or the hex? What do *you* think is going on?"

"I'd say she got on somebody's bad side or ran afoul of a witch."

"I have to help—"

"You 'have' to do nothing of the sort."

"Aidan—"

He held up one hand. "Tell you what: I'll look into it if you'll agree to let the authorities handle things. You don't need to involve yourself. The hex isn't strong enough to kill her. At least not right away."

"Did you even get close enough to make that sort of assessment?"

"Trust me. I'll look into it. Scout's honor."

"You don't strike me as a Boy Scout—in any sense of the word."

"I'll have you know I'm always prepared," he said. His gaze drifted down my body and back up to my face. He shook his head. "It is astonishing, you know. You truly appear as though a spirit from another time and place."

I wasn't sure how to take that. "I'm not. I'm me."

His gaze softened. "Do you ever think about . . . ? Do you believe in past lives?"

"Why do you ask?"

"Some people think that we travel through each life seeking the companions of our past lives and that they continue to play important roles, no matter how much time may pass."

"I . . ." Suddenly the idea of knowing someone from one life to the next made all kinds of sense. It would explain the sense of familiarity I had with Aidan, the inexplicable pull I felt despite my reservations about him. But I wasn't sure I truly believed such things. The only thing I *really* knew, at the moment, was I had to be cautious of thinking along those lines. Aidan and I had once shared a kiss . . . and the combined heat we threw off had quite literally melted metal.

He caressed the line of my jaw with his thumb. "And here we are, just the two of us, in a secluded corner of a fancy dress ball, as though in a different time and place. . . ."

"Bad things happen when we kiss, remember?"

"I wouldn't say 'bad' as much as . . . 'powerful.' Anyway, I've been working on my control."

Speaking of control, it took all my willpower to place my hand on his chest and push him away. "Maybe another time. Right now, I want to see what's happening with Miriam and make sure she's okay."

"This wasn't exactly how I saw the evening going."

"Apparently seeing the future isn't one of your gifts."

"Why are you so interested in this stranger? Because you bumped into her on the front steps? That's not a significant social bond." Aidan clenched his jaw, clearly irked. "Stay out of it, Lily. I haven't been around as long as I have, and been as successful as I have, by interfering in witches' squabbles."

"Are you saying Miriam's a witch?"

"I have no idea yet what she is. But please, leave this alone. I told you I'd look into it."

After a moment, I nodded. "All right. Thank you."

We emerged from our private corner just as the EMTs wheeled the gurney carrying Miriam down the corridor. Her tuxedoed escort jogged alongside, distraught. He may be too old for her, I thought, but it was clear he loved her. I caught whiffs of dread and fear as he hurried past, and watched until the gurney rolled around the corner and out of sight.

After a few moments of subdued hubbub, the orchestra started back up and the crowd returned to the festivities. I could almost feel the communal sigh of relief. Aidan was right—whatever had happened to Miriam was none of my affair. I didn't know her, and as much as I might want to, I simply can't help everyone. Sometimes I have to protect myself.

Still, I felt at a loss. The thought of dancing away the evening now seemed impossible. Carved, gold gilt faces seemed to watch me from the walls, waiting to see what I'd do. The Paramount Theater was stunning, but at the moment it felt chock-full of ghosts.

"Oh wait. I left my bag in the lounge," I said.

"Want me to get it?" offered Aidan.

"It's a women's room, remember? I'll be right back."

The crowd suddenly swelled as a song came to an end

and people rushed for the lounges and bars. I squeezed into the ladies' room, and with a sense of relief, spied my beaded bag sitting on a glass ledge.

And behind it, something in the mirror.

An odd flicker. I looked more closely.

Miriam.

Her face appeared before me, her big hazel eyes, clear as day, reflected in the shiny glass.

I glanced over my shoulder to see if by any chance she or someone else—her doppelganger, perhaps?—was behind me. I'm a witch, yes, but I'm also human and as prone to an overactive imagination as anyone else.

But there was no Miriam and no Miriam-look-alike standing there. Just a small crowd of women milling about, heading to and fro.

When I turned back to the mirrored walls, the image was gone.

I was about to give up, to blame the vision on nerves, when I glanced up at the mirrored glass chandelier—and saw Miriam's flickering image.

This time there was no mistake about it. Although her body was strapped to a gurney, en route to the hospital, Miriam's spirit was trapped in the reflective surfaces of the Paramount Theater.

She was here. Displaced. Distraught.

Dang it all.

Chapter 3

I needed help. I hurried out of the lounge and up the stairs.

"Have y'all seen Aidan?" I asked as I returned to our table to see my escort wasn't there.

"What—did he ditch you?" Susan teased. Seeing my concern, she suggested, "He's probably in the men's room, Lily."

"Good idea," I said, and hurried off in that direction.

I stood outside the men's room, calling Aidan's name, but got no reply. An obliging young man agreed to check the stalls for me. No luck.

Next I discovered he wasn't at either of the bars, and he wasn't on the dance floor. Surely by now he should have sensed that I needed him, was calling to him. Although neither of us is psychic, our intuitive connection, our "witchy premonition," is strong enough that he should have responded. Unless he had left the building or was ignoring me on purpose.

Climbing up to the balcony, I edged in by the orchestra to get a bird's-eye view of the party below. I scanned the crowd, looking for Aidan's golden hair, trying to locate his brilliant aura. Nothing. He wasn't here.

Susan had been teasing, but now I wondered—*had* Aidan ditched me?

I returned to the ladies' lounge and loitered in the outer chamber, waiting until it emptied.

"Miriam?" I whispered. "Are you here?"

I caught quick flashes of her, glimmers so fleeting that if I hadn't known better, I might have thought my imagination was running amok or that I needed an eye exam. Finally, I knelt on the floor, bowed my head, took my medicine bundle from my evening bag, and centered myself.

I'm not psychic and I'm no necromancer. Although ghosts seem drawn to me, I had never been able to communicate with them. But Miriam wasn't dead—at least so far as I knew—which meant what I was seeing wasn't a ghost. . . . It was something else. Maybe if I tried hard enough, concentrated enough, I could read Miriam's aura. If she was still alive and her soul was caught in the mirror, perhaps I could learn something from her reflection.

A few women walked in and out of the lounge, casting interested looks my way, but I ignored them and continued chanting softly under my breath. *To hell with keeping my powers under wraps—a woman's life is at stake.* I wouldn't be able to do a full conjure under these circumstances, but I called to Miriam with all the strength of my mind and my magic.

When I opened my eyes, she was there. I saw her in the gold-framed mirror as clearly as though she were standing behind me, looking at herself in the glass.

I stood. My own reflection was over hers, almost as though we were melding.

"*Raew mah I?*" she said. "*Pleh eem! Pleh ime eebabe, zeelp. Zeelp pleh eem.*"

Her words were garbled, nightmarish.

She raised her hand, placing her palm to the mirror, holding my gaze. Her hazel eyes shone brightly; her color was still high, flushed. She licked at chapped lips, blinking repeatedly.

"I don't understand. I'm so sorry." I spoke a smattering of languages, but linguistics wasn't my strong suit. Still, Miriam hadn't spoken with any kind of accent earlier tonight. It made no sense.

Could this be a language of the underworld . . . some sort of demon tongue?

A pair of women who had been using the toilets strode past, heads bent close to each other, whispering as they glanced over at me. But they didn't seem horrified or scared as they surely would be if they saw Miriam. Just giggly and snickering, as though they thought I was deranged.

I placed my hand flat against the mirror and felt the energy of Miriam's palm meeting mine.

"Uth pill mawb," she said. *"Pill mawb?"*

"I'll be back, Miriam," I whispered. "I promise. I won't leave you there."

When I pulled my hand away from the mirror, there were foggy traces of two handprints: mine and one with longer fingers.

I watched while the handprints faded away.

I paid the cabdriver a small fortune, let myself into my store, crossed the darkened shop, and climbed the rear stairs to my second-floor apartment.

Through the door I heard screams.

"Oscar?"

As I opened the door, I braced myself. I expected Oscar, my pseudo-familiar, to be waiting up, wanting to hear about my evening. Oscar had tried to talk me into letting him accompany me tonight, not understanding why a shape-shifting potbellied pig might have been out of place at an Art Deco Ball.

In his natural form, Oscar is a mix of goblin and gargoyle, a greenish gray fellow covered in scales with big bat ears, a monkeylike snout and hands, and clawed feet. While other witches had reasonable familiars, such as black cats or croaking toads, I had Oscar. When he was around non-witchy folks, he shape-shifted into a miniature potbellied pig, which was only slightly easier to explain than his gobgoyle form.

Truth be told, Oscar isn't a very good familiar. A gift from Aidan, Oscar's loyalties were divided. Usually a witch's familiar was her staunchest ally, but Oscar slipped occasionally and called Aidan "master." Still, he was entertaining as all get-out.

I found Oscar sprawled on the couch in my cozy living room, a huge bowl of popcorn on his lap, his big green eyes fixed, wide and unblinking, upon the screen of the old television set Bronwyn had passed down to me.

I always felt bad about leaving Oscar alone, so I had set up a DVD player and taught him how to use it. And how to make popcorn.

I approached, but he didn't look up, mesmerized by the movie. On screen, creepy-looking twins in matching blue dresses were inviting little Danny to come play with them *"forever, and ever, and ever."*

I had to smile. *The Shining* was one of the few movies I was familiar with. I remembered watching it in high school at a film festival, sitting by myself in the darkened theater while my fellow students used the macabre tale as an excuse to cuddle and scream. Personally, I found the story unsettling but not all that frightening; I've accepted that there are other entities sharing this space with us, seen or not. To me, that was normal life.

I leaned over the back of the couch, my face very

close to one batlike ear, and whispered: *"Heeeeere's Johnny."*

The bowl of popcorn went flying, scattering kernels to all corners of the room. Oscar jumped so high he hit the ceiling, fell back onto the couch, and trampolined into my arms.

"Mistress! You scared me!"

"Sorry, Oscar. I didn't mean to give you such a fright." I chuckled, patting his quivering form. "I *told* you not to watch these scary movies. Especially not all by yourself."

I had supplied Oscar with a dozen wholesome film classics, including one I thought he'd particularly enjoy: *Charlotte's Web*. But my familiar had decidedly ghoulish tastes.

"Where'd you get these movies, anyway?" I asked, noting a stack of DVDs on the salvaged steamer trunk that served as a coffee table. The movie at the top of the stack was the cult zombie classic *Night of the Living Dead*.

A shrug was my only answer. Oscar craned his neck to look around the apartment.

"Where's Aidan?" he asked as he crawled out of my arms to stand on his own two sets of talons. "Why didn't he come up?"

"Long story." I went into the kitchen and handed Oscar a small broom and dustpan. This was my utilitarian broom; I kept the ceremonial one in my bedroom closet.

Taking a seat at one of the painted wooden chairs at the kitchen table, I kicked off the wretched high heels and rubbed my sore toes. My liberated feet relished their freedom.

"I like long stories," Oscar said, halfheartedly brushing popcorn kernels into the dustpan. "Plus, I got all the time in the world. My kind live a long time."

"Aidan . . . had to attend to something."

"Like, at the ball?"

"No, not at the ball."

"Then where?"

"Oscar, please. Give me a moment. I just got home."

"Yes, mistress." I saw him sneak a couple of glistening buttered morsels from the floor into his mouth. And two seconds later, he asked again, "Where's Aidan?"

"He had to leave early."

"Leave *early*? Leave the ball? Why?"

"I don't know why."

"He didn't tell you?"

Why couldn't I just lie to Oscar to quiet him? Living a life of integrity, as I'd sworn to do, had its drawbacks. "Not in so many words."

"How many?"

"What?"

"How many words?"

I sighed. "None, actually."

"You mean he *ditched* you?" said Oscar, grizzled mouth agape.

"He didn't *ditch* me," I insisted, despite the fact that I had indeed been abandoned at the ball, as though in some twisted version of the Cinderella fairy tale. But I had other things to worry about: I couldn't stop seeing Miriam's face in the mirror. Her final words sounded like "Pill mob." Was she taking pills of some sort? Is that what had sickened her? But pills wouldn't explain how she ended up in the mirror. . . . That smacked of magic.

I slumped in my chair, feeling beaten. I had lost my princess status, and more than my wrist corsage was wilting. A lank lock fell from my chignon; its precious Marcel curves now a distant memory.

"Where'd he go?" Oscar persisted.

"If he didn't tell me he was leaving, how would I know where he went?"

As Oscar puzzled over this conundrum, I went into

the bedroom to change. I slipped out of my finery, hanging the lovely silk-chiffon beads-and-lace concoction on a padded hanger and giving it a wistful pat. Then I shrugged on a comfy oversized white cotton dress from the thirties, which I had bought at auction as part of a lot that included two wonderful 1940s cocktail dresses and an assortment of pillbox hats like Jacqueline Kennedy used to wear. I had almost tossed the white dress because it was irreparably stained, but realized it was perfect for the messier aspects of my work.

"Does this mean you won't watch the rest of the movie with me?" Oscar asked when I returned to the kitchen. He recognized my work dress.

"Not just now. Time to brew," I said, reaching for the musty, red leather-bound Book of Shadows I kept on a high shelf in my kitchen, above mismatched jars of dried herbs, fungi, honey, and powders.

"How come?"

"I met a woman at the ball named Miriam, and she . . . needs my help."

"Pretty name."

"It suits her." I flipped through the Book of Shadows until something caught my eye. "It's as I thought: says here her soul's been displaced, which makes sense. Mirrors capture souls adrift."

Oscar's big bottle glass green eyes were full of trepidation, but also fascination.

"The only problem is," I continued, speaking now to myself more than to my familiar, "her soul shouldn't have been adrift, since she's not dead. Yet."

"Sounds like witchcraft. Your kind of magic, mistress."

"There's more: She was wearing a cursed corsage."

"Is that why Aidan ditched you?"

One thing I can say for my familiar: He gets to the crux of matters.

But why would Miriam's collapse prompt Aidan to leave so abruptly? Or had the two occurrences been coincidental? Maybe Aidan was called away to mediate an unrelated dispute or to intervene with something on someone's behalf. But wouldn't he have said something to me? Aidan was many things—a lot of them questionable— but his manners were impeccable. Ditching one's date was never polite.

I was highly aware that I had agreed, sort of, to let Aidan try to figure out what was going on with Miriam before I became involved. But a little extra protection never hurt. And given my relationship to Aidan . . . well, it made sense to have a backup plan.

"That is the question, isn't it?"

"Whatcha gonna do?"

"The only thing I'm really good at."

Grabbing my wicker basket and *boline*, the special knife I use for cutting herbs, I passed through the living room and out a pair of French doors onto my terrace garden. A verdant, serene little urban oasis, the terrace was chock-full of tubs and planters containing lush magical and medicinal herbs and plants.

I started snipping. Nothing like work to focus the mind and calm one down.

"Watcha doin'?" asked Oscar as he trailed me around the terrace. When I stopped to gather Saint-John's-wort he plowed into the back of my legs. "My bad," he said by way of apology.

"I told you: I have to brew tonight."

"Did the woman in the mirror hire you to do a spell?" Oscar rubbed his big hands together in anticipation. "Oooh, how much is she payin' you?"

Oscar was always interested in the paycheck. I never understood his avarice. I bought all his food, and he didn't wear clothes or pay rent. What did he need cash for?

I cut bits of Hecate's Sword and stinging nettles, adding them to the sprigs of lavender and rue in my basket. "You know I don't charge for my witchcraft."

He crossed his skinny arms over his scaly chest and tapped his foot. "Don't forget, her type would have burned you at the stake not so long ago."

"I'm *not* going over this again, Oscar. I *like* regular people. And no one's getting burned."

I hoped.

I brought my basket into the kitchen, set it on the tiled counter, and put my cauldron on to boil. I wished I had thought to take Miriam's corsage before the emergency medical personnel arrived. If I could examine it more closely, there was a slight chance I could recognize who had made it. Some witches were so distinctive that their work was unique, like a signature. And very occasionally, I could recognize that signature.

I didn't have the corsage. But I did have time. As Aidan had reminded me, witchcraft seldom worked quickly. Unless someone died of a heart attack due to the stress and strain of confronting a curse, or in the case of the infamous choking curses, witchcraft took a while to take effect. Which is how a lot of witches — like Aidan — made money. Removing curses was big business. Almost as lucrative as casting them.

The spell that cursed Miriam seemed to have initiated a long-term fading, giving me time to come up with a cure. It wouldn't be easy, but I remembered I did have one advantage: a sample of Miriam's hair. I took the comb out of my beaded purse and extracted the two strands.

"Whose are they?" Oscar asked, wide-eyed.

"Miriam's. The woman I met at the dance."

"The one in the mirror?"

"That's right."

His bottle glass eyes grew even bigger. "You're going to curse her?"

"Don't be silly. I'm trying to help her."

"How'd you get her hair?"

"She borrowed my comb."

He gasped.

To witches, hair and fingernail clippings are powerful. Originally parts of our body, they maintain a connection with us even when they are shed and, like DNA, contain a little bit of the magic that makes each of us unique. My grandmother Graciela taught me as a little girl to gather my hair and nails and burn them so they couldn't be used to cast a spell on me. To this day, simply walking by a beauty salon could make me hyperventilate.

"Why'd you keep 'em if you didn't wanna cast a spell on her?" Oscar asked.

"I just . . . I don't know, actually."

"When I first knew you, you didn't want to admit what you were to anyone, especially to cowans," he said. "I liked it better when it was just us. It was safer. Strangers can be dangerous."

"Most people aren't dangerous, Oscar," I said, wondering, and not for the first time, about his past. For such a garrulous fellow, Oscar was close-muzzled about his experiences before he came to me. Only recently I had learned that he was searching for his mother, a woodscreature who suffered under a curse that transformed her into a gargoyle. But who he had been with before me, and how he came to be in Aidan Rhodes's debt . . . it was all still a mystery. "If I think I can help someone, especially if I might be the only one who can help . . . well, I feel obliged."

I crushed rosemary with my mortar and pestle, then sprinkled it into the bubbling cauldron, starting to chant and mumble under my breath. "The brew will help pro-

tect Miriam from further harm, which will give me some
time to find the perpetrator and force her—or him—to
retract the curse."

"How ya gonna find her—or him?"

He had me there. I was plum out of ideas.

After finishing the brew, pouring it into a glass bowl
with a pair of talismans, and setting it out on the terrace
under the moonlight, then washing my cauldron and
magical tools, I slumped onto the couch to watch the rest
of *The Shining* with Oscar. I was exhausted but too riled
up to go to bed. Good thing I didn't need much sleep.

Chapter 4

The next morning, I was anxious to discover what had happened to Miriam.

But first things first: I had made a commitment to my friend Bronwyn's coven. The coven sisters were helping women from the Haight-Ashbury Women's Shelter to set up job interviews. Today a group of shelter residents was coming to Aunt Cora's Closet to pick out new clothing so they could be well dressed for the interview process.

Before people started arriving, I began the day as I always did: by sprinkling saltwater widdershins—counterclockwise—around the perimeter of my shop, then smudging deosil—clockwise—with a sage bundle. This cleansed the shop of any lingering negative energy, and started the day afresh. Finally, I lit a white beeswax candle and mumbled a quick incantation of protection.

As soon as I'd finished, my assistant, Maya, walked in, clutching two cardboard cups from the café down the street.

"Morning, Lily." She handed me a Red Eye—coffee with a shot of espresso—and blew on her own soy chai latte. Today Maya's multitude of black locks were decorated with vivid orange beads, which contrasted nicely with the bright blue tips of her hair. The pleasant clacking of the beads as she moved had become a familiar, favorite sound of the normal workday in Aunt Cora's Closet. "Today's the big day, huh?"

"Yep. Ready for the onslaught?"

"You bet. I think it's a great idea."

Within minutes of my opening the front door, a long caravan of cars arrived. They pulled up one by one in front of the shop and deposited small groups of women, from their late teens to early sixties, at the door. A pair of coven sisters covered a card table with a brilliant orange tablecloth and laid out a selection of homemade baked goods along with cider and coffee. I provided orange juice and peanut butter cookies.

As I had come to learn, no one went home hungry after a coven gathering.

When Bronwyn approached me with the idea for today's event, I had immediately agreed. I loved being able to help out women going through tough times. Still, I wondered how much of the clothing that crowded my shop would be suitable for job interviews: My inventory leaned more toward the funky than the corporate. Then again, this *is* San Francisco, where the average convenience store worker is adorned with multiple tattoos, ear plugs, and piercings and favored offbeat vintage clothing. In this city, I imagined a stockbroker could wear a frilly corset to the office and fit in just fine.

Still, as I watched a couple of women giggling near the rack of 1950s-era prom dresses, I wondered what kind of job would consider powder blue chiffon to be proper attire. But if nothing else, at least today's outing provided the women a rare chance to relax and enjoy the absurdities of past fashion trends.

"Oscar," I called out sternly. *"Stop."*

Oscar had taken on his potbellied pig form, as he always did around nonmagical folk. But while people attribute a fair amount of intelligence to pigs, they tended to underestimate this particular critter.

At my reprimand, he withdrew his snout from under the velvet curtains of the shop's communal changing room and batted his pink porcine eyes at me in an attempt to appear guileless. I wasn't fooled.

"Pillow," I ordered, holding my arm out and pointing. Oscar trotted over to his purple silk pillow near Bronwyn's herb stand and settled down, grumbling just a bit.

"So, tell me *everything*," Maya said, elbows on the glass counter, ready to listen. Though when it came to romance Maya was much more cynical than the average twenty-three-year-old, I'd noticed she always wanted to hear about *my* experiences. "How was the ball? Was Aidan amazing? The way he moves, I'll bet he's an incredible dancer. Are you two, you know, an *item* now?"

"No, we're not an *item*. We're friends." Sort of.

She frowned. "You told me no more than two days ago that you and Max Carmichael were 'just friends.' You keep moving smart, employed *hetero* men into the 'friend' category and you'll run out before you know it. This is San Francisco, lest you forget."

"Mmm," I said. "I thought you didn't believe in romance."

She shrugged. "I'd like to be proven wrong. So? What happened? Surely he kissed you good night, at least?"

"No, he was . . . called away."

"Away?"

I nodded.

Her eyes, dark as my coffee, widened. "You mean, he *ditched* you?"

"He didn't *ditch* me. It was unavoidable."

"What happened?"

"I really don't know."

She blew out a breath and shook her head slowly. "Can't *believe* that fine fellow ditched you. Geez. Sorry, Lily."

I could feel my cheeks burn. To distract myself, I took in the crowded shop floor. Aunt Cora's Closet was jumping. Bronwyn was helping a young woman try on a mustard-colored bolero jacket with a dark tweed skirt. Another coven member, Wendy, knelt by the overflowing lingerie chest, rooting through silk teddies and lacy, old-fashioned bloomers. A clutch of women was flicking through the racks of mid-1960s A-line "career dresses" appliquéd with flowers. Two other members of Bronwyn's group lingered near the communal dressing room, acting as gofers.

"So, I've always wondered," Maya said, tactfully changing the subject, "how can you tell which are witches?"

"Mostly we're green with warts on our noses. And then, of course, there's the cackle."

As if on cue, Bronwyn held up a 1970s-era white polyester pantsuit encrusted with rhinestones, and two of her coven sisters broke into loud peals of laughter.

"The cackling part, I believe," Maya said with a smile.

"Lily, we could use your help over here," said Starr, a coven sister who wore her hair in wheat-colored braids. She stood with a young woman who at first glance looked to be in her late thirties, but as I approached I could tell she was much younger—maybe late twenties. Her skin was sunburned and blotchy, her hair dry and untamed. There was a scar on her cheekbone, right near her eye, and another running from her upper lip toward her cheek. She had that wary, skittish look I had seen on too many people living on the streets. No matter what country, what city, that look was the same: beaten or abused, as though waiting for someone to yell or do much worse.

"This is Monica," continued Starr. "She thinks she'd like to find a job in a café or maybe a diner."

"My mom was a waitress," Monica said with a shrug. "She always said it was hard work, but the tips were okay. I think I'd like it better than a desk job. Plus, I'm not so good with writing. I'm better with math. I could do bills okay."

"It's nice to meet you, Monica." I held out my hand to shake.

Monica glanced over at Starr, who nodded. As though unsure, Monica took my hand, her own resting limply in mine. I noticed that her nail beds were red and inflamed, as though she chewed on her cuticles.

I smiled, held her hand with both of mine, and concentrated. She was fragile. She'd seen hard times, violence. Her vibrations felt heavy, as though weighed down by responsibility. Probably had children, and wore the shame of being unable to provide for them like a shroud.

I knew exactly what she needed.

"Have I got an outfit for you, Monica," I said and led her to a 1940s cream linen skirt suit with cocoa-brown piping around the edges culminating in a squiggly design on the jacket lapel. I had acquired it recently from a garage sale; it was unusual to find an outfit this nice in such a setting. I had the rare opportunity to speak with its original owner, a woman in her nineties with a ready laugh, despite hands gnarled from arthritis. The woman told me she had left Alabama during World War II to work across the bay in the shipyards of Richmond. "I had me some times in that suit," she'd said, a mischievous twinkle in her deep brown eyes. She didn't elaborate, but she didn't have to. The clothes told their own story: of having adorned an independent, spirited young woman. Their vibrations were bold, strong, and striking.

Starr unearthed a mocha silk shell to wear underneath the suit, and a pair of stylish yet comfortable walking shoes to complete the outfit.

Monica looked doubtful. "It seems kind of . . . bland."

"Go on, give it a try," I urged her. "If you don't like it, you don't have to take it."

With a sigh of resignation, Monica disappeared behind the curtain. When she emerged again, she gazed at her reflection in the antique three-sided mirror. For a long time she said nothing, her expression flat. Finally, she smiled, looking shy but delighted.

"Oh my dear *goddess*," said Bronwyn, clapping her hands over her chest. "Monica, I swear you look like a whole different person. A few tucks around the waist and it'll fit like a glove."

"One more thing," I said, as I brought over a scarf printed with orangey red lip prints, like a dozen kisses. It added a surprising dash of color to the outfit. As I tied Monica's tangled hair loosely at the back of her neck, I wondered if the coven sisters intended to prevail upon a local salon for hair and makeup help.

"I like that," said Monica. She smiled and instantly looked a decade younger.

"Come look at these talismans," I said as I led the way to the display counter. Maya opened the sliding door in the rear of the display and brought out a maroon velvet-covered tray that held a selection of hand-carved necklaces. Each was charged with magic.

"Those are cool," Monica breathed, looking at them almost reverently.

"Would you like to choose one?"

She looked up at me in surprise. "Really?"

I nodded. As other women gathered around, I passed

out the necklaces. I don't normally give away my merchandise, but these women needed every ounce of strength they could muster to get back on their feet. Their pleased, surprised faces were more than sufficient payment.

I made a note to remember to carve more talismans during the next full moon.

One of the women from the shelter noticed a cardboard box full of baby clothes behind the counter. She started pawing through them.

"Oh, I'm sorry. Those aren't for sale yet," I said. "They haven't been washed or sorted."

"I don't mind," said the woman. "And there's a washing machine at the shelter."

I hesitated, stymied. The other day Maya had bought the box of children's clothes, which was out of character for her, not to mention pointless since we don't carry children's clothes at Aunt Cora's Closet.

But that wasn't what was bothering me. There was something wrong with the clothes, a disturbing sensation I had sensed immediately but hadn't had time to investigate. I should have tucked them out of sight but had been so focused on getting ready for the Art Deco Ball that I had forgotten all about them.

"I'm truly sorry," I said as I closed up the box and lifted it. "I'll be happy to bring them to you at the shelter. But I wouldn't feel right until I've had a chance to go through them. . . ."

"She's a stickler that way," said Bronwyn, coming to my rescue. "Professional standards, don't you know?"

The woman looked a bit miffed, and I sensed her rolling her eyes at me as I struggled to carry the overflowing box into the back room. I set it upon the jade linoleum table—an exact replica of the one in my mama's kitchen in Jarod, Texas—and picked up the outfit on top, a cute

little red-and-white-striped onesie, complete with foot-
ies. It would be adorable on a baby.

Too bad there was something wrong with it, something almost ... dangerous.

The murmur of the crowd drifted through the heavy
velvet curtains that separated the back room from the
shop floor. I preferred to do this sort of thing alone, but
a sense of urgency washed over me, a compulsion to look
through the clothes *now*.

I hugged the red and white striped onesie to my chest.
The vibrations were shrill, vacant, and disturbing.

Miriam. I had felt these very same vibrations last
night when I touched Miriam. I would bet my cauldron
on it.

No wonder the young woman had felt familiar—I
must have been remembering the sensations from these
clothes. But how were the garments connected to Miriam? Had she brought them to the shop and sold them
to Maya? Did the poor woman in the mirror have a
child, and was that baby in peril?

If I had felt compelled to try to help Miriam before, I
now felt doubly so. I returned to the front of the store to
find out what my assistant might know.

"Maya—"

I felt a whispered tingle of premonition. Sure enough,
moments later the bell over the front door tinkled as
SFPD homicide inspector Carlos Romero strode into
Aunt Cora's Closet.

He stopped, taking in the good-natured melee, before turning his grim, dark eyes on me. As usual, his
aura was guarded, tense, humming with determination
and grit.

What was *he* doing here? Had Miriam ... passed
over? Could my intervention, meager as it was, have
made me a suspect, as Aidan had warned?

My heart hammered within my chest like a bird's, robbing me of speech.

"Carlos! It's been a long time," said Bronwyn with her signature warm smile as she handed a lace blouse to a client.

"Good morning, Inspector," said Maya with a big smile.

The other night, over a pitcher of margaritas, Maya had confided that she thought Carlos was cute . . . which I supposed he was, though I didn't usually think of him that way. He was short for a man, barely taller than I was, but with dramatic, dark features and a sense of purpose that made him seem much larger. A few years on the city's homicide beat could do that to a person.

Oscar snorted and made a big show of turning his back on the inspector, though I doubted Carlos noticed. My familiar wasn't fond of authority figures of any kind. His sentiments were shared by the women in the aisles, who, when they heard Maya greet Carlos as "Inspector," quieted down and avoided eye contact.

Not long ago I would have done the same, but now I was happy to count Carlos as an ally—maybe even a friend. He had surprised me by being open to the possibility of other dimensions, and not long ago had sought out my opinion in a case with supernatural overtones.

I swallowed hard and found my voice.

"Carlos, nice to see you."

"You too. You seem busy today."

"We're helping women from the local shelter in their job searches," said Bronwyn. "Lily offered to provide them with new clothes for their interviews and whatnot."

Carlos looked at me. "That's awfully nice of you."

I shrugged. "It's good to be able to help in a concrete way."

He stuck out his chin, nodded, and seemed to mull

something over. Despite the fact that we were on friendly terms, the inspector had a disconcerting way of making a witch like me feel guilty . . . of what, exactly, I didn't know. Must be an occupational hazard.

"Could we talk in private?"

"Of course." I led the way through the velvet curtains to the back room, where we took seats at the table. I moved the box of baby clothes—which were still humming maddeningly—to the floor.

"You carrying baby clothes now?"

"Not exactly, no. I'll probably give them away once they've been washed." And I would cleanse them, spiritually as well as physically, before I'd allow another baby to come near them. "What can I do for you, Inspector?" *Please don't be here about Miriam.*

"Do you happen to know a young woman named Tanya Kolchek?"

"Doesn't ring a bell."

"She also went by the name Tarra, short for Tarragon Dark Moon?"

I shook my head. "Is there a reason I might know her?"

"Not necessarily. She was found dead on Friday."

"Oh . . . I'm sorry to hear that."

He shook his head. "Damned shame. Twenty-two years old. About Maya's age." He handed me a photograph.

Tarragon Dark Moon had a short black bob and wore bright red lipstick and a shirt with a wide sailor's collar. She looked pixyish and retro at the same time, jaunty in a sailor's cap. I wondered if she'd ever been to Aunt Cora's Closet, but I didn't recognize the top . . . and I almost always remembered the clothes that passed through my perceptive hands.

"Not a natural death, I take it?"

"Hard to say. We're waiting on the medical examiner's report."

"I see. Why are you asking me about her?"

"Because she was big into the Wiccan scene."

"I'm not Wicca."

"I know that. But I thought you might be able to ask around, see what people knew about her. I'm hitting a wall every time I try to talk to them. They're not telling me anything I want to know."

Surprise, surprise. "What would you like to know?"

"Usual stuff: who her friends and lovers were, what she was into, that sort of thing. She was estranged from her family so they aren't much help, and all her work contacts have been dead ends. Far as I can tell, she worked several part-time jobs, did occasional child care, dog walking, flower delivery, that sort of thing. It seems the Wiccans were her life."

I stared at Tarra's photo. What a tragedy for her family, estranged or not. Perhaps, like me, her real family was her friends, or her coven sisters. But if so, why would they be secretive about the circumstances of her death? Or were they just naturally suspicious of the police, as I myself had been most of my life?

"Do you know which coven she belonged to?" I asked.

"I don't know anything, which is why I need your help."

"You said you were talking to some Wiccans who wouldn't tell you anything. . . . Who were they?"

He shrugged. "An occult supply store down on Mission was broken into. I thought maybe there was a connection. Somebody runs a store like that, they're probably Wiccans of one kind or another, right?"

"That's hard to say," I said. I wasn't up to speed on the local witch scene—my whole life I had tried to avoid local witchy politics. But at least I wasn't as clueless as most, such as the inspector. I knew that not all witches were Wiccan and not all those who dealt in the occult were witches. "What makes you think Tarra was Wiccan?"

"Her parents mentioned it—I got the impression they didn't approve. We also found paraphernalia in her apartment."

"Paraphernalia?"

He gave a crooked half smile. "The usual suspects: an altar to some goddess, pentacles, crystals. And she had a bumper sticker on her car that reads: 'Where there's a Witch, there's a Way.'"

"Cute," I said, writing down her names: Tarragon Dark Moon, née Tanya Kolchek. "I'll ask around. May I keep the photo?"

He nodded. "Just find out general stuff: the name of her boyfriend or girlfriend, if she had one, her friends, what she did with her time." Carlos fixed me with a serious look. "I don't want you to *investigate*, just ask around. Are we clear on that?"

"Got it." The last time Carlos had asked for my help, I went a little over the top in my zeal to unmask a murderer.

"Carlos, since you're here, could I ask you about something?"

"Shoot."

"I was at a dance at the Paramount Theater last night—"

A smile lit his dark eyes. "You went to that Art Deco Ball? Seriously? How was it?"

"You've heard of it?"

"Sure. It's supposed to be quite something."

"It was."

"Hard to imagine you going to a fancy dance like that."

I felt vaguely insulted. Was it really that hard to imagine me in elegant surroundings? Were my small-town West Texas roots showing? "Why *shouldn't* I go?"

"No reason," he said, backtracking hastily. "I guess it makes sense, at that. What with the clothes and all. At least you had the wardrobe, right? Who was your date?"

"A ... um ... friend."

"Come on; you can tell your uncle Carlos. You have a beau?"

"He's not my *beau*," I said, cheeks flushing. "Aidan Rhodes."

"*Rhodes?* The guy who operates out of the Wax Museum at the wharf? Supposed to be able to rid people of curses? Guy's a fruitcake."

"I wouldn't go that far."

"Why are you running around with him?"

"We're not in a *gang* together or anything."

"Allow me to rephrase. Why are you wasting your time with Aidan Rhodes?"

"He's an ... acquaintance who escorted me to the ball, that's all." *And ditched me*, I added silently.

"Guy's trouble, Lily. You want my advice, stay away from him. Especially since ..." Carlos paused.

"Since what?"

"You're already sort of on the edge."

"What do you mean by that?"

He leaned forward, his elbows on his knees, and clasped his hands together. When he looked up at me, sincerity shone from his dark eyes.

"Look, you know I've proven that I'm ... okay with your special abilities, right? But most folks aren't so open-minded, and that could mean trouble. You get a reputation as someone who thinks she's a witch, and ... well, a lot of people are gonna associate that with kookiness at best. Or worse: satanism."

Chapter 5

"That's ridiculous, Carlos," I protested. "It's not the same thing at all—"

"You think *I* don't know that? But a lot of people aren't as open-minded. I'm just saying, Lily, you might want to watch your back." He played with a piece of packing string that had been left on the table, winding and unwinding it around his thumb. "There's been some evidence that a group opposed to witches has formed recently."

"What? Who would do such a thing?"

"C'mon, Lily—you don't need me to tell you, of all people, that lots of folks are afraid of witches, especially when times get tough. You've never run into this before?"

It was certainly true. Throughout the ages, attacks against witches have increased in times of stress. We're a convenient scapegoat.

"Has something happened in San Francisco?"

"There have been a handful of incidents. That occult supply store in the Mission was vandalized, like I mentioned, and had a bunch of antiwitch graffiti painted on the building. And a record store—the kind that sells old LPs?—was ransacked and a bunch of the records were smashed. A note left at the scene said the records conveyed satanic messages when played backward."

"How do you play a record backward?"

"A lot of old phonographs play backward as well as forward. Some even recorded."

"Seriously?"

"*Anyway*, the mechanics of it are not really the point. I just want you to be on your guard."

I supposed he was right. "What did these alleged satanic messages say?"

"I haven't heard them."

"Who would even think to play a record backward?"

"Don't you remember the old controversy over the backward lyrics in rock songs?"

I shook my head. Rarely did a day go by that I wasn't reminded of how out of the mainstream my upbringing had been. I loved old *Bewitched* reruns, but as for the rest of popular culture? I was clueless.

"How about the Beatles' 'I buried Paul' thing? Doesn't ring a bell?"

"Not really."

"It doesn't matter. The point is, these folks have gotten themselves all worked up, and they're taking action. I hear they call themselves DOM, which supposedly stands for Defenders of Morality. They seem to find the . . . 'openness' of the Bay Area to be a threat. They're upset about a lot of things, but their main target now seems to be New Age and witchy stuff."

"Are they a religious group?"

"Could be anything. You know how it is around here: Christians, Jews, Muslims, Buddhists . . ."

"I find it hard to believe *Buddhists* would be involved in something like this."

"I find it hard to believe people of *any* faith would be involved in something like this. In my religion, as in most, the core belief is 'love thy neighbor.'"

It surprised me to hear of Carlos speaking of faith, though when I took a moment to think about it, it made a certain kind of sense. He was steadfast and unflappable, which often reflected a deeper belief system.

"I didn't know you were religious," I replied.

"Catholic."

"Catholic," I repeated, taking care to keep my tone neutral. It was a long time ago, but the European church-led witch hunts rode high in every witch's collective memory.

"And before you make reference to the witch hunts, the Inquisition, *or* the Crusades," Carlos continued, "I would like to point out that those shameful incidents had to do with the fallible, power-hungry men in charge, not with God. In my version of Catholicism, we love our neighbors."

I smiled. "Well, then, I like the Carlos version. So, do you think Tarra Dark Moon's death could be linked to this DOM group . . . ?"

He shrugged and blew out a breath. "I hope not. She wasn't a leader in her coven, as far as I can tell, so I can't see why she would have been singled out. But like I said, I haven't been able to find out much about her."

"Most Wiccan groups aren't hierarchical; it might be hard for an outsider to identify who the leaders are, assuming there even *are* any."

"Maybe you could check that out for me, as well. See if Tarra was a high priestess, or whatever they're called."

I shivered a little. "Scary to think there's actually a group organized to do harm to witches."

"Watch your back, Lily. Whenever people come together through shared intolerance or hatred . . . well, they can be very bad news." He sat back in the chair. "So what were you going to ask me about the ball?"

"Pardon?"

"You started to say you went to the Art Deco Ball . . . ?"

"Oh, right. There was a woman there, Miriam . . . something." I realized I didn't know her last name. "She lost consciousness and was taken to the hospital. I don't suppose you heard anything about it?"

"No, but there's no reason I would. That's in Oakland—not my jurisdiction. And someone passing out at a dance wouldn't be deemed suspicious unless there was more to it. So, *was* there more to it?"

I hesitated. When I'd first met Carlos, he'd suspected me of murder and had dug up part of my past, at least the part I'd spent in my hometown of Jarod, Texas. It was something I had been trying hard to keep under wraps, making a fresh start in California. But instead of condemning me for my witchy ways, he'd come to me for help. It had astonished me, another in a series of lessons I was learning about friendship and faith. Still, old habits of mistrust died hard. And my feelings about the cursed corsage . . . Even to my own ears, it sounded weak with no other evidence. Not to mention no corsage.

"I'm not sure."

"If it's assault and you have any evidence, tell me. If not, well. . . . even then, unless she died under suspicious circumstances, there would be no reason to bring in homicide. Did she die?"

I stroked the medicine bag I wore around my waist and intoned a quick message of protection. "I hope not. Would there be a way to find out?"

His eyebrows lifted. "Call the hospitals, for a start. Why are you so interested? Doesn't sound like you knew her well."

"I didn't. I met her at the ball. I was just . . ." I thought of the corsage and the strange vibrations from her dress.

"Just what?"

"I was just concerned about her, that's all," I said with a shrug.

"Is there something you'd like to tell the investigating officers, presuming there are any? Do you know something about what happened to her? Was it a witch deal of some sort?"

"All I know is that she seemed a little . . . off. Something felt fishy. But I don't have anything more to go on."

His cell phone chirped. He checked the readout, texted something, then stood. "If you want, I can make a few phone calls, see if anyone in the Oakland PD knows anything."

"I would appreciate that. Thank you."

"No problem." Carlos rose and headed back through the velvet curtains. "I'd better be going."

Out on the shop floor, Bronwyn had given in to temptation and was traipsing around in a reproduction 1930s jet-beaded backless cocktail dress, showing off. The contrast of the sleek gown with Bronwyn's fuzzy mane—entwined with fresh flowers, as usual—made me smile.

Carlos let out a low whistle as he passed. "Can't arrest you for lookin' good, ma'am, but if I could . . ."

Bronwyn gave Carlos a deep curtsy.

"Why, Officer, ah do declay-are," Bronwyn said in a lousy imitation of my Texan accent. "Ah like to *swoon* at such words."

Carlos chuckled. The bell tinkled with finality as he shut the door and disappeared onto the crowded Haight Street sidewalk.

"Everything okay?" Maya asked softly as I joined her at the counter, where she was jotting down the final choices of the women from the shelter. Though we weren't charging for the clothes, we keep careful books and track inventory.

"He wants me to ask around about a woman named Tarragon Dark Moon. You wouldn't happen to know her?"

"No, but with a name like that I'll bet Bronwyn does."

Bronwyn was still surrounded by women, so I decided to talk to her about it later. In the meantime . . .

"Maya, what can you tell me about the woman who brought in the box of baby clothes?"

"I'm really sorry about buying those, Lily," Maya said. "I just . . . The woman seemed so upset. I thought she might need rent money or something."

"I probably would have done the same thing. But what did the woman look like?"

"Sort of ordinary? Pretty. Light brownish blond hair, medium height . . ." She shrugged. "She was distracted, a little breathless. She seemed to be in a hurry, but then she bought a capelet—that little zebra-striped one that used to be on the stand in the window?"

"So she couldn't have been that desperate for money." I searched for inspiration. "Did she say anything? Ask about me or the store?"

"She asked if I was the owner," said Maya. "I told her you'd be in later in the day, and she said she might come back."

"Was she interested in Bronwyn's herb stand?"

"Not that I noticed. Why?"

"No special reason."

If the woman had been Miriam, it was possible she had come in because the Art Deco Ball was on her mind. I hadn't recognized her dress, but perhaps she had bought something else from us, a piece of jewelry or headdress or even undergarments . . . something other than a zebra-striped capelet. I'm pretty sure I would have noticed that.

"You didn't happen to write down her name?"

Maya shook her head. "I'm sorry. I'll be more careful next time."

"No worries," I said. "I think I may have met her at the ball last night, and she became sick. I'd just like to know if there was a reason she came here, a reason I met her."

"A reason like what?" asked Maya.

I shrugged. I wish I knew.

I flipped through today's paper but didn't find anything about untoward events at the Art Deco Ball. Might as well try the Internet. Lately, though, whenever I came near the computer it popped and sizzled. I wondered if this meant my powers were increasing . . . or if it was time to go computer shopping.

I grounded myself by stroking my medicine bundle, then looked up the local paper's Web site, hoping it might have been updated recently. I found a brief article with a photo from the Art Deco Ball, but nothing about Miriam. Carlos was right: A woman getting sick wouldn't rate a newspaper story unless there were obvious signs of foul play, or unless she had died. While I was online I looked up Oakland hospitals, scribbled down their phone numbers, and called the one nearest the Paramount Theater.

Since I didn't know Miriam's last name, all I could ask was if a young woman had been admitted last night, and the operator I spoke with in Admissions wasn't willing to admit even that much. I *hate* telephones. If I were speaking to her in person, I might be able to use my powers to influence her response. Looked like a field trip was in order. Chances were good that Miriam was at Summit Medical Center, which was the closest emergency room to the Paramount. If I didn't find her there, I'd try the other medical centers in circles radiating out, like ripples in the surface of a lake.

First, though, I had to finish up my business with the women from the shelter. It was another hour before the last one left, new clothes folded neatly into recycled paper bags with AUNT CORA'S CLOSET stamped on the side.

I ran upstairs and decanted the brew I had made last night into a wide-mouthed mason jar, my favorite device for mobile spells. Then I slipped the prepared talismans into the side pocket of my satchel, along with two black silk bags filled with healing herbs. As I came down the stairs with the packed bag over my shoulder, Bronwyn's astute eyes swept over me.

"Going somewhere?" she asked.

"I . . . uh . . ."

"Want some company?"

Not long ago I would have refused. But lately, little by little, I was coming to trust and value the assistance of my friends.

"I'd love it."

As we headed across the Bay Bridge, I told Bronwyn about what had happened at the ball—all except my fears that Miriam's soul was trapped in the mirrors. That kind of information was best kept to myself.

"And how can you help?"

"I have no idea. But I want to see her, make sure she's all right."

"Is this what Carlos was talking to you about earlier?"

"No, actually. That was about another young woman, a Wiccan named Tarragon Dark Moon? Have you heard of her? Her birth name is Tanya Kolchek . . . not sure why she changed it."

"A lot of us change our names."

"Why?"

"To reflect our new belief system."

"Is it like . . . a born-again situation?" I asked, relating it to the kind of religion I had been raised with in rural West Texas.

"No, not like that. But it's not always easy to embrace Wicca or any other kind of pagan faith. Many of us are raised with other beliefs, so turning to the worship of nature can feel like a betrayal to our families. Taking on a new name isn't so much a rejection of the past as an embracing of our new selves, our inner selves, our true selves."

The Wiccans in Bronwyn's coven, the only one I knew well, were usually so friendly and happy and lighthearted that it never occurred to me that this had been an important, difficult decision for many of them.

We fell silent for a moment, our thoughts accompanied by the rhythmic *thump thump thump* of the wheels running over the joints between each segment of the bridge. I liked the sound; it reminded me of a heartbeat.

"The name sounds vaguely familiar, but I'm not placing it," Bronwyn said. "You might ask Wendy—she's been working on a witch directory, kind of like a witchy yellow pages. She calls it Moonstruck Madness."

"Cute."

"Want me to make a few calls and see if I can track down your mystery woman? *Oh*, I know who to call! My friend Bliss knows just about *everyone*. The name's Tarragon Dark Moon?"

I nodded. "Originally Tanya Kolchek. I'd really appreciate it, thanks."

We exited the freeway and made our unfamiliar way to Summit Medical Center, which, as its name suggested, sat atop a hill and was surrounded by acres of doctors' offices, labs, pharmacies, and health consultancies. Even the grand old homes on this hill had been turned into medical offices and clinics.

We parked at a meter and headed toward the hospital.

Before entering the building, I girded my defenses, stroking my medicine bag and mumbling a quick incantation. As difficult as it can be for normal people to go into hospitals, it's much harder for someone like me. I can't see ghosts, but I can feel their shivery presence. And there are a lot of them wandering the halls of medical centers. In addition, every surface I touched telegraphed anxiety and pain. And with my sensitivity to textiles, hospital gowns were especially harrowing.

The only exception is the maternity ward. There is pain there, too, but it's tempered with joy and celebration. In some parts of the world there are special maternity hospitals, which makes sense to me. I find perplexing the custom of mixing the happy arrival of life with the anguish of trauma and loss in a single setting.

We approached the information desk and I asked an elderly woman wearing a HOSPITAL VOLUNTEER badge if a Miriam had been admitted last night.

"Last name?" she asked.

"I don't know her last name."

"I'm afraid we can't help you without more information," she said in an oddly satisfied tone.

"She fell ill at the Art Deco Ball, at the Paramount Theater? She was brought in by ambulance last night around nine thirty?"

"Are you family?" the volunteer asked.

"If I were family, I'd know her last name."

"Can't help you, then."

I felt my blood pressure spike, but before I could say something I would regret—or make something crash— Bronwyn intervened. "Could you point us toward the emergency room?"

As the volunteer placed a xeroxed copy of the hospital's floor plan on the counter and circled the ER with a bright red Sharpie, a man hurrying past caught my eye: Miriam's escort at the ball.

He was dressed casually today, his finery replaced by worn jeans and a plaid shirt buttoned over a white tee, a stubbly beard shadowing his ruddy cheeks. . . . and he carried a baby on his hip, with a diaper bag on the opposite shoulder. The child looked to be about a year old, with bright red cheeks and the soft golden curls unique to the very young. But she was frowning, and her face was tearstained. From the dark circles under the man's eyes, I would wager he hadn't slept a wink.

I tugged on Bronwyn's arm and gestured with my head.

"Thank you!" Bronwyn grabbed the map.

"Come again!" the volunteer chirped.

We followed the man through the twists and turns of the hospital corridors, dodging medical personnel and gurneys, until we reached the Intensive Care Unit. We paused outside, watching through the windows as he entered a curtained area.

"Go on in," Bronwyn whispered, glancing at the nurses' station a few yards away. "I'll be your lookout."

"Do you think that's really necessary?"

"If you hear the signal—the hoot of an owl—cheese it."

Bronwyn had a dramatic streak. I went with it.

"Okay, I'm going in. Cover me."

"Got your back, sister."

I slipped into the ICU quietly, not wanting to disrupt the patients, and halted next to the curtains where Miriam's escort had gone. Through the parted drapes I glimpsed him gazing down at the figure in the bed, holding the fussing baby out to her and murmuring softly. I paused, eavesdropping for a moment.

Chapter 6

"Miriam Rose, your baby needs you. Luna needs you, honey. You need to wake up. I'm trying my best here, sweetheart, but she needs her mother."

There were tears in his voice. He cleared his throat, trying to pull himself together.

"Excuse me?" I said softly as I approached.

He looked up, a questioning look on his face.

"I don't mean to interrupt," I said. "I . . . I was at the ball last night. Do you remember? I called in the paramedics when I realized something was wrong with Miriam."

He ran his hand through his disheveled salt-and-pepper hair. "Oh, yeah. I'm Duke. Duke Demeter."

"I'm Lily. How is she?"

"I don't know—nobody knows. The docs can't figure out what happened to her. They're still running tests."

Miriam lay absolutely still, an IV dripping slowly into one arm, wires connecting electronic sensors to her chest and finger. With her silky gold hair fanning out around her on the pillow and the remnants of last night's makeup on her eyes and lips, she looked like a character in a fairy tale, waiting to be awakened by a kiss.

"They suggested I bring in Luna and some familiar things to remind her of home . . ." Duke said as he pulled items from the diaper bag and placed them on the nightstand: a hairbrush, a couple of small pots of lotions and salve, a book of fairy tales. "Don't see how they can help, but . . . I guess they can't hurt."

"Has Miriam been sick recently?"

He shook his head. "She hasn't been feeling herself for the past week or so. I knew that. She looked tired. Miriam was always such a bundle of energy. . . . I could tell there was something wrong. But she told me she was fine."

The baby fussed, and Duke patted her awkwardly. He stared at the heart monitor, which showed a steady blipping line. The machine's monotonous sound was strangely comforting, each regular bleat a sign that Miriam's heart was still active, keeping her alive.

"She's a single mother," Duke continued. "I thought maybe she was just overwhelmed taking care of little Luna, here. And then her boyfriend turned out to be a scumbag, so I offered to accompany her to the dance. She'd been looking forward to it, even altered her own dress. I don't . . . I just don't know what to do. Her mother passed away years ago. It's just been her and me, and now little Luna."

"You're her father, then?" I asked.

He nodded. "You a friend of hers?"

"We met last night, at the dance. . . ." I trailed off as his eyes slewed back toward his daughter, as though he could barely pay attention to my words. "Duke, where did Miriam get the corsage she was wearing last night?"

"It was delivered." He shrugged. "I guess it was an apology from her so-called boyfriend."

"What's his name?"

"Why—you think he had something to do with this?" His gaze turned back to me, a thousand questions burning in his tired hazel eyes. "Don't get me wrong. Guy's an ass—'scuze me, a grade-A jerk. Still, I don't think he'd hurt her." As if the oddness of my presence finally registered, he asked, "Why are you so interested?"

"When I met Miriam last night, well . . . I don't know. I just really liked her. I wanted to see if there's anything I could do to help. Would you mind if I talked to the boyfriend, see if I can figure out anything about what's going on?"

He looked unsure and didn't answer. I don't cast casually, but in this case I felt the need to expedite things. I placed my hand on his arm and felt his vibrations. Duke had no guard up—in fact, quite the opposite. He was desperate to help his daughter recover from this crisis. I would just give him a nudge to accept my offer of help. I looked into his eyes and concentrated.

"You can trust me."

He stared at me, as though in a mini-trance. After a long moment, he shrugged.

"Why not? His name's Jonathan Penn. He runs a gaming shop called MJ's—sells collectible cards, memorabilia, that sort of thing." He blew out an exasperated breath. "Like that's a job for a grown man. Downtown Oakland, on the corner of Washington and Ninth."

I made a mental note of his name and the location of his store.

"Was Miriam on any kind of medication, any pills?"

"Not that I know of."

Above the electronic boops and beeps of the hospital, I heard an owl hoot.

Seconds later, a nurse came in and bustled about, checking Miriam's IV bag and the various electronic monitors and entering some notes into a handheld device. Her eyes raked over us, disapproval writ upon her features.

"Visitors are restricted in the ICU. She needs her rest. You can come back later. One at a time, please."

Duke nodded, gave his daughter one last look, and we stepped into the corridor, where Bronwyn was waiting. The baby kicked and pushed away from Duke's chest, whimpering, her distress ratcheting up as though she was working up to a good cry. Duke passed his free hand through his hair one more time, looking harassed and defeated.

Bronwyn placed her hand on his shoulder. "When's the last time you ate?"

Duke's expression remained blank. "What?"

"Food. Have you eaten?"

He shook his head. "No time."

Bronwyn glanced at me. "How about this? Lily will stay with Miriam while you and I and the baby go down to the cafeteria and get you something to eat."

"I don't know . . ."

"You need fuel," Bronwyn said. She might not be gifted in the way I was, but when it came to making people feel safe and cared for, the woman was pure magic. "You can't help Miriam if you don't take care of yourself."

"I'll stay until you get back, in case she wakes up," I said.

"Um . . . who are you two, again?" Duke asked.

"We're friends," I said, once again placing my hand on his arm. "We just want to help."

After an awkward moment, he nodded and allowed Bronwyn to lead him away.

The nurse gave me a dirty look when I returned to

Miriam's bedside, but I ignored her. Miriam needed me. The doctors clearly had no clue what was wrong. I was relieved that her vital signs were strong; still, I didn't have to be a witch to know that her spirit had flown her earthbound body.

The moment the nurse left, I opened the small wooden cabinet next to the bed and found a plastic storage bag holding personal effects marked DEMETER, MIRIAM. I riffled through it: There were the dress from last night, undergarments, and a small purse with a driver's license, compact, cell phone, and lipstick. I looked through the other two drawers. No corsage.

Clearly Miriam wouldn't be able to drink my brew, which was unfortunate. It could have helped her. But I placed the mason jar full of liquid on the bedside table, alongside the few personal objects Duke had left there. I noticed that the book's cover featured a full-color old-fashioned illustration of Sleeping Beauty. How ironic, I thought.

As I slipped a protective talisman under the mattress, I spotted something. Reaching in farther, I pulled out a handful of small wax conjure balls, about the size of marbles. They were deep red, the color of life. The wax had been rolled while still warm and filled with herbs and powders and little Mexican *milagro* trinkets of hearts and heads.

I recognized the vibrations: Aidan had been here. I had taught him how to make conjure balls not long ago. In my mind's eye I could practically see him rolling the soft, hot wax between his palms, chanting and mumbling.

Aidan was protecting Miriam now but had warned me off when we were at the theater. Why? What was going *on*?

I replaced the conjure balls, hoping the sight of these

and the talisman didn't frighten the poor housekeeping staff when they came in to change the sheets. Then again, I decided, they'd probably seen worse.

On the bedside table I laid out three stones I had washed in the brew: one clear crystal, one amethyst, one tiger's-eye. Normally I would have lit a white candle, but with all this oxygen around . . . suffice it to say that chemistry was never my strong suit. The magic of the candle wasn't important enough to risk blowing things up. What mattered most, as always, was a witch's intent. I whispered a protective incantation over Miriam, concentrating. Since her spirit had fled her earthly body, she would not heal, could not respond to my powers. But the protective spell would at least help keep her body from additional harm.

Finally, I laid my hands upon her—one on her brow, the other on her chest over her heart. I felt a pang of self-doubt and wished my grandmother were here. She was a master healer while I was still a novice in comparison.

I breathed deeply, trying to filter out the harsh fluorescent lighting of the ICU, the muted beeping of various machines, the faraway sounds of telephones from the nurses' station, the hustle of medical personnel hurrying past in the hallway. I cast my powers, reaching out to my ancestors, to the helping spirit that came to me when I brewed, appearing to me and opening the conduits to my magic.

I had a vision . . . or was it a memory? Miriam stumbling in to me, her pale face swimming before my eyes, a smile hovering, then fading as she reached out for her baby. She called out to me, wanting, yearning. She held a bouquet of roses, but pricked herself on a thorn, bleeding. . . . I felt bereft, empty, yet compelled to reach out to her in return. . . .

"What are you *doing*?" demanded Duke from the corridor.

"I'm sorry," I said, stepping away from the bed. I tend to lose track of time when I spell cast. It was difficult to explain in a public setting. "I—"

"Who are you people, anyway?" He looked from me to Bronwyn, then back again. "I mean, to each their own, but I don't go in for that crystal-gazing garbage."

I glanced at Bronwyn, who shrugged and gave me a resigned look. "Duke and I had a . . . discussion about the possibility of Miriam's affliction having a nonphysical origin."

"I don't mean to be rude, but I'd like you to go now," said Duke. "It's been one hell of a couple of days. I'm going out of my mind."

Luna let out a little screech and reared back so quickly that Duke barely caught her before she flipped out of his arms. He squeezed the baby to his chest, but that seemed to make her even angrier.

"Duke, has Luna been this fussy for a while?"

"For the past week or so. I don't know what's got into her," the weary grandfather muttered.

"Poor little love's probably colicky. Want me to hold her for a while?" Bronwyn asked. "I love babies."

Duke hesitated, then passed Luna to Bronwyn. I had seen my friend work her earth-mother magic more than once in Aunt Cora's Closet: She would cradle a fretting child in her strong arms, against her ample bosom, and the baby, accurately sensing it was safe, would settle right in.

Not this time. Little Luna continued to struggle, frowning and scrunching up her darling little face into an ugly scowl.

"She doesn't seem right to me," said Duke. "I asked Miriam about it, but she wasn't doing that well either.

I thought maybe . . . I don't know what I thought, maybe that they both had some kind of virus, something like that."

"And is she getting any better, or worse?"

"About the same, I think." Alarm entered his eyes. "Do you think Miriam could have something contagious, maybe passed it on to the baby?"

"It's possible," I said. "If it's not too pushy, could I suggest you take the baby to the pediatrician, explain what happened with Miriam? Just in case it *is* contagious." I was almost positive what troubled Miriam didn't have an organic cause, but it didn't hurt to be sure.

"I'll take her in tomorrow." Duke searched my face, his gaze perceptive. He was clearly an intelligent, focused man. "But you think it's something else?"

"Yes."

He nodded, sizing me up. I was accustomed to scrutiny, if not outright disdain. But Duke was looking at me with something else . . . skepticism, yes, but also something that looked like hope. Perhaps it was the spell I had cast—he was cynical, but felt he could trust me.

His eyes flashed over me and the talisman in my hands. "You're some kind of faith healer?"

"Not exactly . . . more like a . . . um . . ."

"Naturopath," said Bronwyn, bouncing and swaying to please the baby, who was not at all pleased. "Lily is a whiz with herbs and teas and the like."

"Miriam's into that sort of thing too. Always has been. I brought some of her special stuff here." He gestured toward the lotion and lip balm in pretty pots with hand-drawn labels. "I always thought it was a bunch of hooey, but . . . You really believe in this sort of thing?"

"Sometimes when Western medicine fails, traditional methods work," I said. "Scientists still don't know that much about patients when they're comatose—they might even hear us talking around them or be aware of loved ones nearby."

Duke nodded. "The doctor told me to bring Luna to see Miriam, said Miriam might respond to having her baby near. And that's why I brought her favorite book from when she was a girl. Listen, I guess . . . If you want to leave that stuff for Miriam, that'd be okay. It couldn't hurt, right?"

I nodded and muttered a brief incantation as I tucked the talisman under her pillow.

"If the pediatrician can't find anything further, I'm happy to help if I can. . . ." I handed him my card. "I'm in the Haight—but I could come to you, if that's better."

His gaze had returned to his daughter, weariness coming off him in waves. "Thanks."

"Please don't hesitate, if there's anything at all I can do." I put a hand over his, which rested on the snowy white sheet. He seemed to ease, just slightly, his big shoulders relaxing.

"And if you need any help with this little angel," Bronwyn said, "I love babies."

As Bronwyn came over to pass Luna back to her grandfather, the most astonishing thing happened. Luna held out her chubby little arms . . . to *me*.

"She wants you, Lily," said Bronwyn.

"I don't know anything about babies," I said. But what could I do? I held my arms out, and the tot practically jumped into them. She hiccupped, let out a little sigh, and laid her head on my chest.

"Would you look at that?" Bronwyn smiled. "Sometimes you don't have to know a thing about babies— sometimes babies know about *you*."

We had been ready to go, but now that the child was so content in my arms, we lingered.

Duke took a seat in the only chair and started to read

the legend of Sleeping Beauty to Miriam. His voice was deep and sonorous, his reading almost poetic.

I held little Luna, rocking slightly, softly crooning a song that I hadn't even realized I remembered from my childhood. Despite the baby's odd vibrations, she smelled of talcum powder and new life, bright green like the first blades of grass in the spring. I couldn't bear to think that she might be ill, might fall sick like her mother.

When Duke finished the story, I passed Luna back to him.

"I'd better get her home and feed her," Duke said.

"We have to go as well," I said. "Please call us if anything . . . Well, just call us anytime."

Bronwyn and I walked silently through the nicely decorated hospital hallways, painted in soothing hues of pink and mauve. The last time I had been in a hospital I remembered everything being a starkly sterile white.

Outside, the day was sunny and warm. Medical professionals bustled to and fro, wearing lanyards and scrubs. Cars circled the lots, searching for parking, shuttles picked up people in wheelchairs, and we heard the vivacious calls and laughter of children playing at a nearby child care center. A bustling group of workers swarmed over a large construction site, which promised to be a new branch of the medical center. Apparently the health business was booming.

"Hey, look," Bronwyn said, gesturing toward a brown shingle Arts and Crafts–era home that had been converted into offices and a supply store. "Nightingale Scrubs. The sign says they sell lab coats and stethoscopes!"

"Did you become a doctor while I wasn't looking?"

"Silly. I'm thinking of Halloween, of course." She turned to me, excitement shining in her eyes. Bronwyn loved a party. And a celebration that demanded costumes? Even better. "They have the real thing here. You never know when someone might be in need of something like this for an authentic outfit."

I smiled. "I think I could put together a costume from the offerings at Aunt Cora's Closet. Don't you?"

"We don't have much along these lines."

"True."

"And after today, our inventory's down, of costumey-things besides everything else. You might need to go out clothes hunting soon."

"Already planning to," I said as I unlocked the car and we both climbed in. "Now that Maya's out of school for the summer and available for more hours at the store, I'll dedicate some more time to scouting." The world of vintage clothing was highly competitive and getting more so all the time now that people realized there was so much money to be made in cast-off clothing.

"So, tell me: What did you learn from Miriam's father?" I asked as we headed toward the freeway entrance.

"Not much. He's a widower. Lives in Bernal Heights, in the same house where he and his late wife raised Miriam. And he's a fisherman."

"You mean, for a living? Really?" In the Bay Area—where almost everyone I met seemed to work in some aspect of the computer industry—such a traditional, hands-on occupation seemed exotic.

She nodded. "Like his father before him. He has one of the few slots for actual fishing boats down at Fisherman's Wharf."

"Seems ironic, doesn't it? That Fisherman's Wharf would have so little room for fishermen anymore."

"I'm sure the irony isn't lost on him—he's a pretty sharp guy. He's also a poet. He told me he works the tourist trade some, taking folks sightseeing on the Bay.

But he calls himself a fisherman, and he's got the calluses to prove it."

"He seems like a nice guy. Do you think he'll really let me help?"

"That's hard to say." Bronwyn was a wide-open, goddess-loving earth-mother type. It wasn't like her to be cynical, but recently she'd gone through something of a trauma and seemed rather more circumspect about her beliefs than she used to be. "I'm not sure how he might react to your attempts to help his daughter if they're any more . . . invasive than talismans and crystals."

"I don't even know if I *can* do anything for her. It surely would help if I had the faintest idea what is wrong with her. I've never seen anything like this."

I still hesitated to tell Bronwyn about the apparition in the mirrors of the Paramount Theater. Not that she wouldn't believe me, but . . . there was something undeniably creepy about it, as though Miriam now belonged to another realm. I didn't want to burden Bronwyn with such disturbing thoughts. She would want to help, but as far as I could tell there was nothing useful she could do.

But this much was clear: I had to go back to the theater, this time with someone who could make contact with Miriam's spirit. Figuring out what was ailing Miriam was the only way to help her and her daughter. I needed Sailor, the reluctant psychic who, at the moment, was a bit annoyed with me. I sighed. So what else was new?

"I can't believe Aidan ditched you at the dance last night," Bronwyn said as I forked over a five-dollar bill to the woman in a tollbooth at the base of the bridge.

News travels fast.

"He didn't *ditch* me, exactly," I said as I stomped on the gas to get up to speed as we ascended onto the bridge.

"Of course not," Bronwyn said.

"Okay, he ditched me. But it wasn't like I couldn't find my own way home."

"Of course not," Bronwyn repeated.

I cast her a reproachful look, but before Bronwyn could say anything more her cell phone rang with the Wicked Witch music from *The Wizard of Oz*. I'd never seen the movie—another gap in my upbringing—but I knew the tune. The kids in my hometown used to sing it whenever I walked by. One of these days, I vowed, I was going to lighten up enough to find it funny.

Bronwyn chatted for a few moments, then snapped the phone closed.

"That was my friend Bliss, of the Welcome coven over in Berkeley. I called her while you were in with Miriam," Bronwyn said. "I told you, Bliss knows *everyone*. She says Tarragon Dark Moon is with the Unspoken coven. They're a closed group, but they're holding open recruitment meetings this month at the Cherry Creek Design Center in Berkeley."

"The coven meets at a design center?"

"It's an old converted factory building; I think they meet in a yoga studio."

"Ah." I was old-school; I expected covens to meet in the thick of the forest under the full moon, or at the very least in an old, abandoned building. Then again, Bronwyn's coven had met several times at Aunt Cora's Closet and combined their worship of the Lord and Lady with a shopping party. As I was coming to learn, we all showed devotion in our own ways.

"I don't think they always meet there—it might just be for the public meetings. Anyway, their open gatherings are on Sundays—that's tonight!"

"Oh goodie," I mumbled. Even though I'm a witch— or perhaps *because* I'm a witch—I don't feel all that comfortable around covens. I'm not much of a joiner, and don't really understand group process. In addition ... I don't know what my magic will do when combined with the strength of a coven, and I hate not being in complete control.

Besides, after our hospital visit I felt jumpy and sore, as though my skin had been rubbed raw by a psychic grater of some kind. I wanted to rest, recharge my energies by being at home amid my things, absorbing their serene vibrations and warm energy.

Bronwyn glanced at me. "What's wrong?"

"Covens make me nervous."

"You're a witch, Lily."

"I know, but ... I've never been part of a coven."

"What about my group?"

"I'm lucky to count them as friends, but I'm nowhere near being a sister. Would you come with me tonight?"

"Wish I could, but I promised to sit with my grandkids. Rebecca and Gregory have a hot date." Bronwyn smiled and wiggled her eyebrows. Not long ago she— and I—had been instrumental in bringing her daughter, Rebecca, closer to her husband, Gregory. Bronwyn took this as proof positive that she was, indeed, meant to be a matchmaker. I feared I was her next project.

I tried to think of someone else who might go with me. Maya shied away from such things, and I didn't know Bronwyn's other coven sisters well enough to ask them at the last minute. I was tempted to skip it altogether, but felt obligated to provide Carlos some information about poor Tarra.

"I don't suppose there might be another time?" I asked.

"This is the last Sunday of the month." Noting my hesitation, Bronwyn reached out and squeezed my shoulder. "Be brave, Lily. Go draw down the moon and enjoy yourself."

"Any advice?"

"Bring a chalice for grog. Oh, and cookies to share. And most important: relax. They'll be glad to have you with them."

I wished I could be so sure.

Chapter 7

"Don't be nervous," said Oscar in the car that evening as we sat in the parking lot of the Cherry Creek Design Center.

It was the fourth time since we'd left San Francisco for Berkeley that he'd suggested I not be nervous. It was making me nervous.

"I'm *fine*," I insisted, all evidence to the contrary. I noticed a suspicious number of crumbs on his snout. "And stop with the lemon bars already. Those are for me to bring to the meeting. You already ate half of them in batter form, and another five fresh out of the oven."

I wished I could have asked Aidan for advice before attending this coven meeting. For that matter, I wished he would tell me if he'd found anything out about Miriam. There was no use trying to call him; if he had a phone number, I had no idea what it was. I had dropped by the Wax Museum earlier but had no luck. Not only had he not answered my shouted calls and knocks, but he had put a glamour on his office door so even a witch like me could barely see it.

"Oscar, why would Aidan have left the ball so suddenly last night? Do you know where he is?"

"When he goes dark, it's best to leave him be."

"I'd like to try to see him anyway."

Huge eyes stared at me, his muzzle clamped shut.

"Oscar, do it. That's a direct order."

"Do what?"

"Whatever it is you do to get in touch with Aidan. Let him know I want to speak with him."

In the past when I wanted to see Aidan, all I had to do was mention it to Oscar, and—voilà—eventually Aidan would appear, though usually at the most awkward moment possible.

"That's not a good idea, mistress."

"Oscar, you're my familiar. You have to do what I say." Most familiars don't have to be reminded of this.

He sighed and harrumphed.

"I'll take that as a 'yes, ma'am.'" To sweeten the deal, I held out the platter of lemon bars. There weren't many sure things in my life, but this I knew: Oscar's pout couldn't withstand homemade baked goods.

My gaze slewed back to the Cherry Creek Design Center. It was a two-story brick structure with the huge, multipaned windows common to historic factories. Faded paint high on the wall facing the street identified the building as the Simpsons' Chair Factory.

Munching, my familiar stared at me with a surprising level of understanding. "They're a group of witches, and you're a witch, ain'tcha?"

"It's just . . . I don't hang out with witches much. I know it sounds strange. . . ."

"Nah. You're just weird. For you that's kinda normal."

This from the creature with scaly gray-green skin.

"'Sides," Oscar continued, suddenly the philosopher,

"you'll be the most powerful witch there. So if they're mean to you, just zap 'em."

"There will be no 'zapping.' Even if I could do such a thing, which I can't."

"Sure you can."

"Well, I wouldn't. Hell's bells. What must you think of me?"

Oscar shrugged and picked at his talonlike toenails. "Master Aidan says most local covens are bogus. Buncha . . . whaddayacall 'em? Wiccans."

"Wiccans aren't bogus. They're . . . Wiccans. The ones I've met have been wonderful. Besides, you like Bronwyn, and she's Wiccan."

"Oooh, the laaady. I like the *lady*." Bronwyn babied Oscar, cradling him to her chest and carrying him around while he was in his miniature potbellied pig form. She called him her "Oscaroo."

"Anyway, curl up and get some sleep. I don't know how long this will take."

"Awww-ah," he whined. "Can't I explore the neighborhood or something?"

I hesitated. Oscar wasn't a typical familiar and could take good care of himself—had, in fact, managed to survive for centuries. I glanced around the neighborhood: The brick design center building had a grassy park on one side, but otherwise was surrounded by quiet, residential streets lined with trim bungalows and lush, flower-filled gardens. Several yards showed signs of children: tricycles, swing sets, and strollers.

"I doubt there are any gargoyles around here . . . but all right. Just be careful. And don't go too far—if history's any indication, I'll be kicked out before they cast the circle."

I had scarcely finished the sentence before Oscar was

out of the car and trotting down the street. I looked to be sure no one was watching. But, like most of our kind, he was good at hiding his true self from strangers.

I took a deep breath, climbed out of my Mustang, and grabbed my chalice. The lemon bars that had been so neatly arranged on the blue Delft platter I found in a junk store last week now had conspicuous gaps. I rearranged the bars to fill in the holes, licking the sweetly tart filling from my fingers.

Mmm. Made from fresh lemons with my mother's old recipe. Delicious, if I did say so myself. No wonder Oscar was so tempted.

Since it was evening, most of the offices in the building were closed. A wooden directory outside the front door indicated the yoga studio was on the second floor. I followed a pair of women clad in flowing garments up an outdoor wooden staircase.

By the time I opened the door at the top of the stairs to reveal an interior hallway, the women had disappeared. I poked my head in the first open doorway and found a group of men, led by a shirtless fellow with — I couldn't help but notice — a well-muscled torso. Smooth olive skin, a dark tribal tattoo wrapping around one ample biceps. Fit, but more like a medieval knight than a ripped Bay Area gym rat. He had long dark hair that fell past his shoulders, was clean shaven, wore black drawstring pants and no shoes. Large, graceful hands caressed a set of bongo drums clenched between his knees.

He looked up at me and smiled.

"I'm . . . uh . . ." I stammered, suave as always.

"You're looking for the open coven meeting? They're right down the hall, Suite 117."

"Thank you."

"This is Apollo's circle — we're the men's affiliate to the coven. I'm Wolfgang, tonight's leader."

"Nice to meet you. I'm Lily. I'm sorry to disturb."

"No problem."

Our eyes held for a beat before I turned away.

I proceeded down the corridor to Suite 117 and paused in the doorway, taking it all in. Whoever had remodeled this old factory had taken full advantage of the broad-plank floors, high ceilings, and massive multipaned windows to create a warm and airy interior space. Along one exposed redbrick wall were large mirrors, and by the back wall were stacks of purple and green yoga mats. A low table in the center of the room held a statue of a woods goddess and Pan, bunches of flowers, several crystals and stones, and an open Crock-Pot filled with fragrant, steaming cider. In the four corners of the room the coven had arranged shrines to different goddesses, none of whom I recognized.

At least twenty women milled about, chatting. Most were clad in gauzy outfits or Indonesian batik or African mud cloths, though a few wore black hooded robes. I smoothed my hands over my vintage 1950s wool skirt suit and silk blouse. Out of place, as usual. I should have thought to borrow something from Bronwyn.

Bells on bracelets and metal pieces sewn onto clothing tinkled merrily as the women moved about the room. Their hair was long and flowing, or short and spiky, and they ranged in age from late teens to sixty-something. Many wore flowers in their hair, and all had kicked off their shoes upon entering the room. I followed suit, leaving my canvas sneakers next to a jumble of leather Birkenstock sandals, multicolored espadrilles, and sensible walking shoes.

I took a deep breath and crossed over to a long, thin table that had been pushed against one wall. It was crowded with plates of homemade cookies and cakes, to which I added the Delft platter of lemon bars.

"Welcome!" declared a young woman as she rushed up to me. She must have been in her early twenties, with long red hair and naturally rosy, full lips. In her romantic, gauzy gown she looked like the kind of fairy-tale princess that had peopled my childhood fantasy books.

"I'm Jonquil, apprentice priestess," the woman said, her voice breathy. "I'll be leading tonight's circle for the very first time. I'm so excited! What's your name?"

"Lily Iv—"

Jonquil took my hand and turned to face the crowd. "Everyone, we have a new coven visitor! Lily Ivy."

The women responded with a chorus of "Welcome!" "Blessed be" and "Merry met."

"Ivory," I said. "Not Ivy."

"Pardon?"

"Iv— Never mind. Thank you for the warm welcome. It's good to be here."

Two minutes with the coven and already I felt like a fraud: I wasn't here to learn more about the mystical world or the Unspoken coven. I was here for informa-tion about a crime. It dawned on me that this was why I could never be as open and wonderful as Bronwyn: When it came to dealing with others, I too often had ul-terior motives.

"Oooh, lemon bars!" someone exclaimed, and the women began to introduce themselves to me.

Morocca was in her forties, calm and serene and ex-ceedingly welcoming. Sienna reminded me of Maya, with her serious air, black hair in dreadlocks, and small, styl-ish black-rimmed glasses. Anise was boyish, her hair cropped short, wearing faded jeans and a black hoodie sweatshirt. She had Celtic tattoos ringing her neck and a vague air, suggesting she was either a touch confused or stoned. Then came Wildflower, Thistle, and Elm . . .

names I imagined the women had chosen, or perhaps it was the effect of living in Berkeley.

As someone named after a flower, at least on this score I fit in—for once.

There was a clutch of older women as well, dressed in flowing garb, their graying hair in long braids or piled on their heads. Several had flowers or ribbons twining through their locks. I felt a pang of longing for Bronwyn's bright energy. One of the downsides of growing accustomed to having friends is that solo endeavors such as this became that much more uncomfortable.

"I'm so excited to be part of this." Jonquil leaned in to me and spoke in a soft voice, as though confessing. Her vibrations were agitated and nervous, but that was no surprise, given that she was leading the coven tonight. "I'm only a level two witch!"

"What does 'level two' mean?"

"I'm still in training. Hey, do you live around here?"

I shook my head. "In San Francisco. I have a vintage clothing store at Haight and Ashbury."

"Wow! That's awesome. Anyway, I'm studying with Morocca and Fawn. They're amazing."

"Oh," I said, and hesitated. Would it be better to ask about Tarra now, or afterward? When was the socializing portion of the evening? I wondered. I would feel better if I could leave before the circle was cast—

"If everyone would please gather together," Jonquil called out, and stepped forward to proclaim herself one of the priestesses of the evening. She welcomed the newcomers and explained that there were several priestesses with the coven and that they took turns leading the chant and drawing down the moon.

She then urged us to form the circle, and I tried not to hyperventilate as I was enveloped by the crowd. I wasn't sure what would happen when my powers combined with that of the sisters around me—whether or not they had supernatural powers, the concerted effort of a group of believers could be powerful. I should have asked Oscar to stand vigil outside the window; he was useful in helping me to measure my magic.

"Starting with me," Jonquil said, looking straight at me, "we'll go deosil, taking the hand of the sister next to you, one by one."

"I—I don't suppose I could just watch?" I stammered.

"The circle is sacred and inclusive," said the priestess named Sienna. "There are no observers allowed. Please join us."

I closed my eyes, took a deep breath, and tried to center myself as the women joined hands, one by one, linking the chain as women had done throughout the ages.

My turn came, and I clasped the hand on my right and then on my left.

When the last hands linked, the circle closed and a shock ran through us.

I opened my eyes and could have sworn I saw actual arcs of light hopping from one woman to the next.

A chorus of "Ohs!" rippled around the room. Several women pulled their hands away in surprise, including the two holding mine. I read fear on their faces.

"What in the name of the goddess was *that*?" one woman asked.

"I'm . . . I think that was me." I could feel my cheeks burning. "I'm sorry."

It was Texas all over again. In the town where I grew up, variations on this scene had been repeated throughout my childhood. We didn't have covens in Jarod—at least none that were out in the open—but any sort of group activity that I took part in, from games of duck-duck-goose to square dancing, had ended the same way. My power couldn't be trusted in assemblies, especially those held in a circle. It always found a way to show itself.

I had to get away. I hurried out into the hall.

Wolfgang stood in front of the door to the exterior stairway. Blocking my way.

Chapter 8

I heard a voice behind me.

"Wait." It was Jonquil. "Lily? Are you all right?"

Steeling myself, I turned around to face the music.

"I'm sorry. I—I'm so embarrassed."

The other women streamed out of the room, crowding the corridor behind Jonquil and encircling me as Wolfgang disappeared. I felt hot, flushed. It was my own custom-made Lily-nightmare. Other people dreamed of showing up naked at school without their homework; I had anxiety dreams about things like this.

"Why would you be embarrassed?" asked one of the coven members, a silver-haired woman with a kind expression.

"I . . . I'm not used to this sort of thing."

"You've never been to a coven meeting?" asked Morocca.

"I . . . well, sort of." Every instinct told me to lie, to say I didn't feel well, anything to get *out* of here. But I was trying to be better than that, trying to be brave and open. "To tell you the truth . . . I came here looking for information."

"But, Lily, that's perfectly all right," said Jonquil. "That's why we hold these circles open to the public. So people can learn about us."

"No, not information about your coven, but about a member. Tarragon Dark Moon?"

"Tarra?" Morocca said in a shaky whisper.

Several of the women gasped or shook their heads.

Jonquil's big amber eyes filled with tears. "It was such a loss. I'm trying hard not to be sad, but I can't . . ."

"Wait. What's going on?" The young woman named Anise came up behind Jonquil and rubbed her shoulders. She looked bemused as she took in the scene. "Don't cry, Jonquil."

In a clear, strong voice, Sienna said: "Be of cheer, everyone. Surely the gods called Tarra to the celestial plane for some reason we can't fathom. And she will return, perhaps has already returned."

"How do you know Tarra?" Jonquil asked me. "Were you studying botanicals as well?"

"Botanicals?"

"Tarra and Anise and I were in the same botanicals group."

"I didn't really know Tarra," I said. "I'm . . . friends with someone who is looking into what happened. He's afraid there might be something suspicious about her death. . . ."

I trailed off at the look of horror dawning on their faces. But I figured since I'd come this far . . . "Is there anything you can tell me about Tarra? Was there anything going on, anything that seemed unusual at all?"

Morocca stepped up. "The police already came to speak with us. If you are here as their representative, you should have declared yourself, should never have taken part in our sacred circle. We value honesty and transparency above all. I think you should leave."

I looked around but saw only suspicion and coldness in their eyes. Jonquil's friendly face was now wet with tears, while several of her coven sisters comforted her. Chagrined, I turned to leave. Until something else occurred to me.

"What about Miriam Demeter? Do you know her?"

Anise nodded. "Miriam's in our botanicals group. She's a coven sis—" She cut herself off at a sharp look from Sienna.

"Do you think I could speak with whoever leads the botanicals group?"

"As I was saying," said Morocca, "I think you should leave."

"But—"

"Please go," said Sienna. "Now."

I hesitated another moment. . . . There was so much to learn, if only I could convince them to trust me. But finessing social interactions had never been my strong suit.

"I'm very sorry. For everything."

I turned, slinked through the doors, and headed down the stairs.

Halfway to my car I stopped, closed my eyes, and breathed deeply of the damp evening air. I felt bruised, my eyes prickly with tears I couldn't shed. Back in the day, when I was strictly a solo act, I kept my guard up and others at arm's length, so I wasn't particularly hurt by rejection or even outright hostility. These days, it was tougher. I wanted to be home, surrounded by my things. Or . . . I could use the healing vibrations of my plants right now. Yes. This would be a perfect night to attend to my garden. My plants needed feeding and—

"You okay?" asked a masculine voice behind me.

I turned to see Wolfgang at the bottom of the stairs.

"Yes, thank you. I'm fine."

There was a question in his eyes. "They're usually pretty friendly. Did they kick you out?"

"Not exactly."

"I'll see you to your car."

"There's no need—"

"Please, allow me."

Either his mama had raised Wolfgang with old-fashioned courtliness, or he was making sure I left. I nodded and together we walked the short distance to the Mustang.

I glanced at Wolfgang's inscrutable face. What the heck? I had already alienated the rest of the coven.

"Wolfgang, did you know Tarragon Dark Moon? Tarra?"

He nodded. Swallowing hard, he looked up at the stars, took a deep breath in through his nostrils and released it slowly.

"We believe that death is another step in our journey, that one's passing should be a moment of celebration, not sadness." He cleared his throat, and in the dim light from a nearby streetlamp I saw tears shining in his eyes. "But it's still hard to say good-bye."

I nodded. "Were you and she . . . ?"

"We were friends. She was my coven sister."

"Do you know if she had a boyfriend, anyone important in her life?"

There was a long pause. I fixed him with my gaze and urged him to tell me, playing on our almost palpable connection. There was something about him . . .

"Yeah, guy named Rex Theroux."

"Do you know where I could find him?"

"He works at Randi's Café in San Francisco, near the ballpark."

"Thanks."

"Do you . . . ? Why are you asking about Tarra?"

"I'm just trying to help."

He gazed at me again. I felt little whispery fingers of thought reaching out: He was trying to read my mind. Was he a psychic, or just highly intuitive? I wasn't worried about him gaining access to my thoughts—even Sailor, powerful as he was, couldn't read me. But it was worthy of note.

"Could you tell me anything else about Tarra?"

"She smelled like violets."

"Violets?"

"Yeah, she— Wait. Am I seeing things, or is that a pig walking down the street?"

I turned to see Oscar trotting toward us.

"It's a pig. He's mine. My, uh . . . pet. Guess he got out of the car. So you were saying? About Tarra?"

Wolfgang glanced up at the top of the stairs. I followed his gaze to where several women in flowing robes were watching us in silence, their forms outlined by the light behind them.

He shook his head. "It just seemed too soon, her passing."

"*Wolf*?" one of the women called out.

"I'd better go," he said.

I nodded. "Thanks for talking with me."

I hustled Oscar into the car, then climbed into the driver's seat and backed out of the lot. The women at the top of the stairs, Wolfgang with his hands on his hips . . . everyone seemed to be waiting, and watching me go.

"Who the heck was *he*?" Oscar demanded as I pulled up to the light at University Avenue and signaled for a left turn. "Take a right."

"His name's Wolfgang. He's a coven member. . . . sort of. And the freeway's to the left."

"Take a right. What do you mean, he's sort of a member?"

"He runs a men's group. Why do you want me to turn right?"

"They call this town 'Berzerkley.'" He turned the full force of his big glass-green eyes on me. "I hear tell the Normandy Village on Spruce Street has gargoyles. *Please*?"

Oscar was searching for his mother. It seemed like a long shot that she would be found somewhere in the Bay Area, but as Oscar pointed out, gargoyles lived a very, very long time. She could be anywhere.

I was spent. But how could I turn down a gobgoyle looking for his mother?

I turned right.

"Thank you, mistress," he singsonged. "What's a men's group do?"

"Get together and be manly, I guess."

"Why?"

"Not sure. Maybe it's a guy's version of a sewing bee or a coffee klatch." I thought about the various women's groups my mother had belonged to, the kinds that until recently I had never been part of. "Maybe they gossip and talk about their feelings."

"Why's he half naked?"

"I don't know, and I don't care."

"Maybe we should bring him a shirt from the shop."

"Maybe we should." I laughed. "Maybe we should, at that."

The gargoyle search was a bust, though it was wonderful to explore the grounds of Normandy Village, a fanciful apartment complex built in medieval style back in the 1920s, right off Berkeley's historic University of California campus. Unfortunately for Oscar, the only "gargoyles" we found there were whimsical creatures carved from wood. None of them smacked of kin to my dear gobgoyle.

By the time we headed west across the Bay Bridge, it was late. I was exhausted. But . . . I still needed Sailor. I couldn't think of any other way to communicate with Miriam's spirit. And I couldn't get the thought of her daughter out of my mind. Miriam, according to what I had just learned, was in the same botanicals group and coven as Tarra, who had died a couple days ago. Was someone systematically eliminating witches, like the group that Carlos had mentioned? Or could it be a simple coincidence . . . ?

Sailor wasn't always easy to find, but at this hour I was pretty sure I knew where to look: his favorite watering hole.

The Cerulean Bar was one of those insiders-only places with no sign. Only the glow of blue neon lights and the thumping of the bass alerted a keen-eyed hipster to its presence. It was up a steep side street, near the lively Italian neighborhood of North Beach. It was also only half a block from the city's famous strip of "gentlemen's" clubs and girlie shows.

I found a parking place outside the Lusty Lady and admonished Oscar to stay in the car, in his piggy guise. He stared out the window, goggle-eyed, as a few of the eponymous lusty ladies strutted outside the club.

I climbed up the steep street and pushed open the heavy wooden door to the Cerulean Bar. The joint was jammed, as usual, with a young, vibrant, chic clientele. I wasn't much older than many and was younger than some. But their bubbly, untroubled energy made me feel very old indeed.

Sailor sat in his regular booth, slouched down against the far end, one long jeans-clad leg stretched out on the vinyl seat.

The moment he caught sight of me he muttered under his breath and turned away. I couldn't hear what he said

over the crushing *boom boom boom* of the DJ's spinning, but I felt safe in assuming he was swearing and
bemoaning his fate. I had that effect on the man.

I forced my way up to the bar, ordered a shot of
Laphroaig, an expensive scotch, and then made my way
over to Sailor's booth. I took a seat on the opposite side
of the table and placed the drink in front of him, next to
a couple of empty shot glasses.

I waited. Sailor pretended I wasn't there, his attention
on a dim corner of the bar behind me.

"Back in my hometown, empty liquor glasses left on
the table were referred to as dead soldiers," I said.

Sailor avoided my eyes and remained mute.

So much for small talk. "I need your help."

"What else is new?" he said with a snort and an eye
roll. "Ever occur to you to come see me when you *don't*
need something?"

That took me aback. "I didn't think you liked me that
much."

"And yet you think I'm happy to hop-to every time
you need a favor?"

"Um . . . Not 'happy,' exactly. But willing." Sailor's
psychic abilities were rare, and he had proved to be
mighty useful from time to time. And though he denied
it, I was pretty sure he had a sneaking fondness for me. I
liked to think I was growing on him. "I'm here for you if
you need me."

Sailor took a sip of the drink I had brought him.
"Don't need you."

"Doesn't mean you won't one day."

"We made a deal, you and me, last time I helped you
out. You still haven't come through."

"I haven't forgotten. I promised to help you get released from your obligation to Aidan, and I will."

"Uh-huh." Sailor again glanced toward the corner of

the bar and frowned. "How's that working out, exactly? You two talk about it while you were doing the tango at the Fat Cat Ball, did you?"

"Hey, it's a tall order. I'm working on it," I said, peering over my shoulder to see what he was looking at. "Are you here with someone?"

He shook his head.

"What are you looking at, then?"

"A pretty woman in a short skirt. Nosy much?"

I settled back into the booth. "Anyway, Aidan's sort of making himself scarce at the moment. I haven't seen him since the ball."

"What, did you refuse to invite him into your lair afterward?"

"Never had the chance. He left early."

"He ditched you?"

I rolled my eyes. "*No.* He had a very good reason."

"What?"

"I have no idea. But I'm sure it was good."

Sailor chuckled and sipped the scotch. Sooty eyelashes fluttered down over his dark eyes as he lost himself in the smoky taste and aroma of the liquor. The strong planes of his cheeks were covered in dark stubble, as usual, and his mahogany hair was tousled. His eyes were dark and mysterious. He'd be darned attractive, if he weren't so . . . dour.

"What is it you want this time?" He set down the drink, arranging it in a straight line with the other shot glasses. When I didn't answer immediately, he added: "Out with it, already. Your time's almost up."

"That scotch is the good stuff. It should buy me at least fifteen minutes of your time. Besides," I said, ostentatiously looking around at the revelers in the bar, "I don't see anyone else vying for the privilege of sitting with you."

"Maybe they're smart enough to avoid witches," he growled. "Unlike me."

"Okay, here it is: I met a woman at the ball, and she seemed . . . odd."

"As in not human?"

"Oh no, definitely human. But her vibrations were off, although I couldn't figure out exactly how so. Later I realized they were similar to, or somehow connected to, some baby clothes she had dropped off at the store a few days before."

"You sell baby clothes?"

"No. Maya felt sorry for her and bought them. She might have sensed something as well."

"Don't tell me Maya's psychic now? She's the only sane one at that store of yours."

"I never said she was psychic. As you well know, all of us pick up on things from time to time, whether we're psychic or not."

"Whatever." He cast another glance into the dark corner. The scotch in his glass was two-thirds gone, as was my time. "So Maya buys some baby clothes, even though you don't sell baby clothes. Sounds like employee-of-the-month material."

"I thought you liked Maya."

"I *do* like Maya. Don't understand why she hangs out with your ilk, but to each their own."

"Getting back to the point: I ran into this woman, Miriam, at the ball, and something seemed off about her. Later in the evening I bumped into her again, in the ladies' lounge, and helped her with her hair."

Sailor made a snoring sound. "Does this story get interesting anytime soon? Maybe we could skip ahead to the good part before I fall asleep."

"Then she lay down on the chaise longue and didn't wake up."

"What, she died?"

I shook my head. "She's in a coma, completely unresponsive. No known cause. The doctors have no explanation."

"Sounds like a medical mystery, not a witchy one. And by the way—you've been pretty open about being a witch lately. I'd watch that, if I were you. My advice? Stay out of it."

"It gets worse."

"Oh boy."

"Her soul is trapped in a mirror."

He went still. "You're sure?"

"I saw it with my own eyes. But I want to go back and try to speak with her, which is why I need your help."

"Let me get this straight: Some woman you bumped into at a costume party falls into a coma, her spirit's trapped in a mirror, and you want me to help you speak to her? That about sum it up?"

"Pretty much."

Sailor was silent for a moment. One more glance over my shoulder, and then he met my eyes. "You ever heard of the 'ghost light' they leave on in theaters?"

I shook my head.

"Old theaters are so packed with ghosts, by tradition the staff leaves a light on for them."

He glared at me, and I wondered what he expected me to say.

"Is that a problem?"

"Not for me it isn't, 'cause I don't go to theaters."

"I'll buy you another scotch."

"Don't bother."

"Sailor, this woman needs our help."

"You always say that as though it's a big selling point. You don't seem to get what everyone else understands:

I'm a misanthrope. I don't like people. I actively *dis*like people."

"I know that's what you'd like others to think—"

"I'd like them to think that because it's the truth."

"I believe you're really quite decent. You're just invested in this off-putting image for some reason."

"You ever notice how, when you come in here, I'm sitting alone in this booth? The operative word being 'alone.' These folks understand me."

"Several of the young women seem to notice you. And even know you."

He gave a little half smile. "A man has needs."

"Fine. I don't need to hear about it."

"And you know how it is—women do love bad boys."

"I wouldn't know about that."

"Uh-huh." He gave me a sardonic smile and knocked back the last of the scotch. "Seems to me you're attracted to Aidan. The quintessential bad boy—am I right?"

"*You* are the quintessential bad boy, with your motorcycle boots and scowl. Anyway, I've had too much bad in my life. I don't go for that."

He snorted. "You might not go for it in my case, but don't fool yourself. You're attracted to the dark side."

"Are you going to go to the gol-danged theater with me or not?" I snapped, annoyed at the turn in the conversation.

"Not."

"She needs our help, Sailor. She has a little girl, a father, people who love her."

"Not my problem."

"*Fine.*"

As I surged up and out of the booth, the shot glasses blasted apart, one smashing into the back of the wooden seat, another skittering off the table and onto the floor.

This sort of thing sometimes happened when I got angry, which was one reason I tried to keep a lid on my emotions. I made an exception for Sailor.

As I stormed out, I glanced into the dark corner that had drawn Sailor's attention. I saw nothing more than a trio of pretty young women clutching pink drinks in martini glasses and clad in skimpy slip dresses completely unsuited to the chilly San Francisco evening.

Perhaps it was just as Sailor said, an attractive woman claimed his attention.

If only I could ignore the tingle that it was something more.

Chapter 9

Pushing my way through the crowded bar, I made it out the front door, then stalked down the dark side street toward Broadway. Bright restaurants and music-filled clubs beckoned. Couples crowded the streets: young women gazing up at their youthful escorts, elderly couples walking arm in arm, laboriously, down the sidewalk. Lovers and friends crowded into cafés, sipping lattes or Campari and soda while waiting for their Italian pastries or eggplant parmigiana.

Usually I soaked up the carefree happiness in the air as though it were mother's milk. But tonight Sailor had hurt my feelings. I kept thinking we were friends, all evidence to the contrary. Besides, I was grumpy lately. I couldn't deny it. I felt . . . Was it envy? I wanted to wrap my arm around a man, have him hold the door for me and watch me drink Chianti as though he couldn't get enough. Why wasn't that an option for me?

Jiminy crickets, Lily, get a grip. Less than a year ago I had been alone and friendless. Now I had a whole group of people who cared about me, and what did I do? I got greedy.

But there was no denying that I wanted the whole enchilada. Romance, as well as friendship and community. My one recent attempt at a love life, with journalist Max Carmichael, had been a bust because he couldn't deal with my witchy ways, and I couldn't deal with him not dealing. Aidan's power scared me, and Sailor . . . well, Sailor didn't like me.

I noticed a young mother with her baby strapped to her chest leaning down to kiss his fuzzy head in a gesture as natural and timeless as the warmth of the sun. I felt a pang for Miriam and little Luna.

As I unlocked my car door, a sleek champagne-colored Jaguar glided past. The license plates read MAL-WTCH, and the car sparkled subtly under the streetlamps, the light fading in and out, emanating from the glamour that disguised the car and its owner: Aidan Rhodes, male witch. Was that the witchy premonition I felt in the bar . . . ? Was he following me? Or had I interrupted a meeting between him and Sailor? And if so, why would he hide from me?

By the time Oscar and I got home I was beat. No gardening for me tonight, after all. But I had one last task before snuggling into my old brass bed: I picked up the phone and made a call.

"Romero." His voice was scratchy.

"It's Lily. Did I wake you?"

"Nah, homicide inspectors never sleep. What's up?"

"I struck out with the coven."

"Didn't win them over with your charm?"

"I think I'm fresh out of charm," I said. Unless we were talking about the magical kind. "Anyway, the only lead I have is that Tarra was participating in botanicals training."

"Botanicals—that's right up your alley, isn't it?"

"It is. The problem is that I wasn't able to get any information about the training—where it takes place, who's teaching it. I'll work on it."

"Speaking of botanicals: The tox report came back on Tarra. Are you familiar with something called mandrake?"

"It's a medicinal plant."

"Medicinal and/or poisonous. I Googled it. Famous for being grown in witches' gardens."

"I have a mandrake plant on my terrace, as well as wolfsbane and datura. They're all poisonous if not used properly."

A long silence.

"Carlos, a lot of people know about these plants: gardeners, run-of-the-mill botanists, anyone into alternative medicine. There was an exhibit about poisonous plants at the San Francisco botanical gardens just last month."

"I know that. I'm just saying, it's interesting. I'd like to talk to whoever's running that botanical group you mentioned."

"I'll try to find out more." Maybe Bronwyn's friend Bliss would know about the group, or Wendy with her Moonstruck Madness phonebook. "Another thing: It turns out Tarra and Miriam are—*were*—coven sisters."

"Miriam? The woman you asked me to look into?"

"Yes."

"That's a coincidence."

"Yes."

"I don't like coincidences."

"Neither do I. But in this case . . . well, I guess it makes sense, in a way. I think Miriam may have been seeking me out."

"You mean she bumped into you at the ball on purpose?"

"Maybe . . . I don't know. Maybe she was drawn to me?"

"I'm getting the feeling we're leading up to yet another discussion of witchcraft. Frankly, I'd rather skip it unless it has something to do with my case. Does it?"

"I'm not sure." I was going to have to work on that one. There were too many variables right now. "Miriam seemed off when I met her at the ball, even before she fell ill. There was another woman at the coven meeting, Anise, who's in the botanicals group as well. She seemed rather confused, too."

"Maybe she'd been smoking something."

"Covens come together to worship, and they take it seriously. I can't imagine they'd accept a coven member coming to their meetings under the influence."

"Well, what then?"

"Could there be something in the building where the coven meets, or something like that? You know, like some kind of Legionnaires' disease?

"If so, everyone would be affected. But it's worth checking out. Give me their information."

I gave him the address of the design center, and hoped the coven wouldn't hold it against me. Morocca mentioned the cops had already spoken with the coven, and she hadn't seemed happy about it. On the other hand, if Tarra had been murdered and the same person had gone after Miriam and was now targeting Anise, they should not only cooperate but *volunteer* to help.

Unless they had something to hide.

"All right. I'll check out the mass-poisoning angle. Maybe it really was an accident."

"Or maybe they were exposed to something in the botanicals group?"

"Sounds more likely. See what you can find out from your end, and I'll do what I can as well. Seems to me this coven was on our list of folks we interviewed, but they didn't give us any pertinent information. So think of it this way: You did better than the SFPD."

"Thanks. I appreciate that. One more thing: Tarra had a boyfriend named Rex Theroux. Did you know about him?"

"Yep, we tracked him down today through her neighbors. Doesn't look likely. He's got an alibi."

"May I ask what it is?"

"Medical examiner's timing suggests Rex was with a men's group when the poisoning would have occurred. And he was pretty consistent throughout a very long interrogation, seemed genuinely shocked and clueless about plants. Can't rule him out, but I don't think he's our guy."

"Would you mind if I spoke with him?"

"Yes."

"Not as part of the investigation or anything official," I assured him. "But now that I know Miriam and Tarra were acquainted, I'd like to ask him a few questions."

"Stay out of this, Lily. I appreciate you asking around for me, but that's all."

"I, uh . . ."

"Do not interfere with my investigation. Is that clear?"

"Very. Did you find out anything further about Miriam?"

"No. Sorry. I talked to a buddy of mine over there, but the Oakland PD wasn't called in on the case."

"Could you do me a huge favor? Have the toxicology report sent over to Miriam's doctors, to see if she's suffering from whatever killed Tarra?"

"She still alive?"

"As far as I know," I said, knocking on wood.

*   *   *

Aunt Cora's Closet used to be closed on Mondays, but increased demand, and the help of Maya and Bronwyn, persuaded me to change our policy. It was great to be able to offer shopping seven days a week, but it sure made it difficult to deal with the never-ending Sisyphean task of the vintage clothes dealer: the laundry.

This morning I opened the store as I usually did, cleansing it and intoning a quick protection chant.

My simple shielding spell wouldn't keep away all negative intent, but it served as a deterrent. I rarely had to worry about shoplifting or abusive customers. I did wonder, though . . . with what Carlos told me about DOM, the antiwitch group, maybe I should step up the level of magical protection. But, as with everything else in the world of magic, there was a price: Minimizing risk meant restricting thought and creativity. Automatons may not steal or vandalize, but neither do they add much to a conversation.

I sighed. I needed coffee. I grabbed my woven shopping basket and stepped out into the misty, gray morning.

On the curb sat a lanky, thin fellow in his late teens or early twenties. Conrad—he went by "the Con"—and I had adopted each other when I first moved to the Haight and opened Aunt Cora's Closet. He did small tasks for me and watched over the store. In return, I made sure he had breakfast and allowed him to use the bathroom.

"Duuude," he said by way of good morning. "Sweep for you?"

"That would be great, thanks. I'll be right back."

I hurried down the block to my favorite café, Coffee to the People. On the way I passed by several young men and women—many who looked more like children—loitering on stoops and curbs, some smoking or playing

music, others accompanied by dogs that looked as un-
kempt as they. Ever since the Haight-Ashbury neighborhood hosted the Summer of Love in 1967 it had become
famous for welcoming rootless young people onto its
streets. Many of them, like Conrad, slept in nearby
Golden Gate Park but spent the greater part of their
days panhandling along Haight Street. Some local merchants and residents had tried to oust them and had
gone so far as to champion a "no sitting" law to forbid
anyone from relaxing on the sidewalk.

I understood their perspective. But because most of
these kids seemed as lost as I had been for so long, I
couldn't help but sympathize with them.

"One garlic and two toasted sesame bagels with the
usual," I ordered when I reached the head of the long
line at the café, another throwback to the area's hippie
heyday. "Plus one Flower Power and a double nonfat
latte, easy on the milk."

"You got it," said Wendy. Bronwyn's coven sister
Wendy worked the counter with a sweet, multipierced
fellow named Xander. The two baristas were among the
coolest folks I knew, and the day they started recogniz-
ing me and my "usual" order I felt like I had taken a gi-
ant step toward acceptance in the neighborhood.

"Awesome event yesterday with the shelter, right?"
Wendy continued as she set about mixing drinks and
toasting bagels with a fluid, multitasking mastery. "Thank
you for donating the clothes, Lily. That was really generous of you. Now we're going to keep following up on
leads, try to help them all find job opportunities."

"I was glad to help. And I had the easy part—it's great
that you're carrying through with them."

Though we were friendly, I still found Wendy intimi-
dating. She didn't smile much. She was a large young
woman who wore lingerie as outer garments, along with

heavy black boots, dark red lipstick, and her black hair cut in a Bettie Page do, bangs straight across her forehead. She certainly had her own style: sexy and brash. When it came right down to it, Wendy was about ten points higher than I on the coolness scale.

Then I remembered what Bronwyn had told me about Wendy's project, Moonstruck Madness.

"Do you happen to know a woman named Tanya Kolchek, goes by Tarragon Dark Moon?"

"Sounds familiar . . . Seems like we carpooled to a pagan festival up in Mendocino once. A lot of them are Feris."

"Faeries?"

"F-E-R-I. It's a belief system, different from the Wiccans. They don't adhere to the Wiccan Rede, among other things."

"Really? You know, I just went to a coven meeting. Have you heard of the Unspoken coven?"

"Yep, they're sort of Feris, sort of not—they have their own belief system. . . . It's a little complicated."

"Would you be willing to talk to me about it?"

She eyed the customers behind me. The line here was always long, and it moved slowly. Coffee to the People was the sort of café where you learned to be patient because the baristas weren't inclined to rush, and "all good things come to those who wait." It said so on the hand-painted sign.

Still, a detailed discussion would be out of place.

"How 'bout I come over tonight after your shop closes? Cook me dinner and we'll talk."

"Oh, I, uh . . ." I felt pleased and nervous, as though the popular kid at school had just invited me to join her at the lunch table. Or more to the point, to cook for her. "That would be great. Thanks."

"Just so you know, I don't hold with this vegan crap."

"How about jambalaya? Or, if you prefer, I make a mean *étouffée*."

"Yes, please," she said. Guess I was making both.

I smiled as she turned to the next customer in line, a disgruntled vegan who tried to engage Wendy in a debate about the advantages of the nonmeat lifestyle. Wendy shut him down by shouting "Next!" and serving the person in line behind him. Wendy was the Haight's version of New York City's soup Nazi.

I loaded up my basket with bagels and drinks and headed back toward Aunt Cora's Closet. Along the way I nodded to a few familiar faces, reveling in the realization that despite everything—despite my past and the fact that I kept getting embroiled in local situations that were making it clearer to all that I was, in fact, a witch— I was making friends in this neighborhood. I was finding a sense of community; it was precious to me.

Near Aunt Cora's Closet was a shop called Peaceful Things, run by a woman named Sandra Schmidt. The items on display in the front window included a black mirror framed on only three sides, a variety of crystals, a reproduction vintage Janis Joplin T-shirt, a guitar supposedly signed by Led Zeppelin, and a variety of beaded medicine bags. Peaceful Things used to carry mostly nostalgic goods reminiscent of the 1960s rock-and-roll culture, but lately Sandra was selling an increasing number of magic-related items.

I hadn't planned to stop, but the door was open and Sandra waved to me from behind her sales counter, calling, *"Yoo-hoo, Lily!"*

"Good morning, Sandra."

"Look at this." She hurried out from behind her counter, a bright green paper clutched in her hand. She held it out to me. The flyer was signed DOM. "Someone slipped it under my door. Do you think it's a threat?"

I read the detailed message. It was essentially a manifesto to "clean up our city" and bring it "back to its roots." I thought about the so-called occult supplies shop Carlos told me had been vandalized by the antimagic group. I wasn't familiar with the store he was talking about, which was no surprise—in a place like the Bay Area there are plenty of such shops to choose from. Most of those that advertised themselves as "occult" or "magic," however, were expensive and carried items more for the curious than for the serious practitioner; I got most of my ingredients from my own garden, or the grocery store.

Sandra was shorter than I, but she hovered while I read, rocking up and down on her toes with nervous energy. "Did you get one?"

"Not that I know of. When did you find it?"

"This morning. Why didn't they go after you? You and Bronwyn are both *witches;* I'm just a shopkeeper. Do you think I should jettison the pentagrams and crystals?"

This was one of the reasons Sandra and I weren't closer. Though she carried a lot of what Carlos might refer to as "paraphernalia" for magical systems, Sandra was a tourist. She catered to the curious and the hopeful— the student who thought if she rubbed a crystal hard enough it would help her on a final exam, the lovelorn who hoped an enchanted rose would win them a soul mate—with little idea about what it meant to follow a belief system, much less a magical discipline.

Sandra also seemed more than willing to throw others under the bus.

"Do you think I should report it to the police?" she asked.

"I would, if I were you. Apparently several shops have been vandalized recently. Perhaps the police could step up patrols or something."

"Maybe your pet hobo could keep an eye on the shop?"

"Pet hobo?"

"That fellow Con."

"Conrad is no one's 'pet,' Sandra. Or a 'hobo,' for that matter."

She pursed her lips. "If you feed him, he'll never leave. Just like a stray dog."

I clamped down on my anger lest I cause something in Sandra's shop to explode. Every time I tried to engage with Sandra, convinced she didn't mean any harm, she went and said something awful.

"Conrad's a good friend. And I'll feed whoever I like, stray or otherwise." I handed her back the flyer. "I suggest you call the police and watch your back. Oh, and blessed be."

Fuming, I strode down the street. Why were some people so eager to judge others? Would having a little compassion really be all that hard? I found Sandra's attitude especially galling considering how, not long ago, she had fallen victim to a curse and I had busted my you-know-what to save her. And had almost gotten burned to a crisp for my trouble. Story of a witch's life.

Speaking of breaking curses . . . my thoughts cast back to Miriam. At least with Sandra, I had known all the players involved. But in Miriam's case, I felt at a loss. If Sailor wouldn't help me communicate with her spirit, and her coven sisters were less than forthcoming . . . where should I go next to find out something, *anything*? I couldn't stop thinking about the poor woman. There had to be something I could do.

Then it hit me: *the cursed corsage.* Even if I couldn't find the actual item, I could speak with the man who sent it, the ex-boyfriend Duke had mentioned, Jonathan Penn. And the botanicals class—I should pursue that avenue, somehow, as well.

When I arrived at Aunt Cora's Closet, I opened the door and invited Oscar—in pig form, of course—to come out and join us, then scootched down to sit on the curb with Conrad. Sandra stood outside of Peaceful Things, glaring at us. Happily, Conrad and Oscar seemed oblivious, focusing on the food.

We ate our bagels in companionable silence. Oscar scarfed down his favorite: a garlic bagel with cream cheese, avocado, and roasted jalapeño peppers. Made for interesting breath.

"Conrad, I wanted to let you know that some ... things have been happening lately."

"Dude?"

"A group that goes by the initials DOM has targeted businesses they consider 'occult' or magical."

"Duuuude." A frown wrinkled Conrad's brow. "Like vintage clothes stores?"

"Not vintage clothes stores per se, but ... you know Bronwyn's herbal stand sells a lot of items to Wiccans and others, right?"

He nodded and took another bite of bagel.

"And I'm, well ..." I trailed off. We had never spoken of such things.

"Dude, I hear you are a *righteous* witch."

"Who told you that?"

He licked cream cheese off his thumb and shrugged. "Heard it. Around."

I nodded. "Anyway, in case you see anything odd, I thought you should know. Oh, and maybe keep an eye out for Sandra's shop as well?"

"Dude, that woman, like, totally is *not* into the Con."

"She's not happy with anyone living on the street."

"I totally live in the park, mostly."

"She's not happy with anyone in the park, either."

Conrad paused. "She's not that awesome—know what I'm sayin'?"

I nodded.

After another pause, he shrugged. "Duuude, I'll keep an eye out. Rise above and all that." He gathered up our trash, gave me a little salute, and shambled down the street toward Golden Gate Park.

If only all the residents of our neighborhood were as civic-minded as Conrad.

Chapter 10

Aunt Cora's Closet opens at ten, but the first hour is typically quiet. I had taken to filling the time by sorting and categorizing the new inventory, tagging items, reducing the price on pieces that had been here a while, and other, similar housekeeping tasks common to every small business owner. Maya and Bronwyn usually arrived around eleven, which freed me up in the afternoons to scope out sources of new inventory at garage sales, estate sales, flea markets, auctions, and charitable stores such as the Salvation Army.

Or to track down the source of magical curses, as the case may be.

I tuned the radio to 89.1, KCEA, a little station I had happened upon recently. It played hits from the twenties to the forties, mostly big band and swing—and all commercial-free. The signal wasn't very strong, so there was static and some fading in and out, but that only added to its otherworldly charm. The broadcasting station was based at a local high school, of all places, and was one of those hidden gems I kept finding in the surprising Bay Area.

This morning the music only reminded me of the Art Deco Ball. In addition to thinking about Miriam, it brought me back to being at the dance with Aidan. Why had he ditched me? Was I fooling myself into thinking he was actually fond of me? Or did he just want to use me, as he apparently did so many others? I shook off the nagging questions—to which I had no answers—and forced myself to concentrate on the work at hand.

An hour later, I had just finished up with some paperwork for the city when Maya and Bronwyn arrived together, both weighted down by cloth tote bags. They brought their bundles to Bronwyn's herbal stand. Oscar ran around in frantic circles until Bronwyn picked him up, cradled him for a moment, told him he was "Bwonwyn's wittle bitty baby," and kissed him on the head.

Maya shook her head and let out a snort. "I tell you what, Bronwyn. It's a really good thing you don't live in the neighborhood I grew up in, is all I'm saying."

"No such thing as loving too much," Bronwyn quipped as she put the pig down, patted him on the back, and started unloading bags of herbs and powders.

Oscar, not easily daunted, went to stand next to Maya, leaning against her leg and gazing up at her until she gave him a reluctant hello. Bronwyn and I shared a smile. Maya didn't fool anyone with her "we eat pigs where I grew up" routine. We'd all witnessed her slipping Oscar leftovers, and even crooning old Motown hits to him when she thought no one was listening. "Ain't Too Proud to Beg" was a current favorite.

"Mercy me, Lily," said Bronwyn. "I went to that Chinese grocery you told me about and then to the Mexican *botanica* down in the Mission for supplies. You're right. They've got great stuff, and so cheap!"

I smiled. "So what's your plan, to repackage it and sell it for a profit?"

"That's what *I* asked her," said Maya.

"Oh, you two cynics! Some of it I'll process — I'm going to hang the fresh herbs to dry, then strip and grind them into powders. And some of it I'm going to mix into proprietary blends. My rose hip orange-rind echinacea tea has been selling really well. But . . ." She pulled a bright green piece of paper from one of the bags. "Look what someone left at the *botanica*. I asked if I could take it; I thought you should see it."

"I'm afraid I already have. Sandra got one too."

Bronwyn's concerned gaze met mine. "Do you think we should be worried?"

"We haven't received anything yet, but yes. I guess we should all be on the lookout. Just in case. So," I said in a more upbeat tone, hoping to change the subject, "it seems Aunt Cora's Closet has become quite the hotbed of entrepreneurship lately. First Maya's mom starts making vintage-inspired reproductions, and now you're in the tea business."

"Speaking of tea, I'm going to run down to the café. Anybody want anything?" Maya offered.

"No, thanks. I'm all set," I said.

"I'd love a mocha," said Bronwyn, handing Maya a five-dollar bill. As soon as the door closed behind Maya, Bronwyn turned to me with a conspiratorial voice.

"So, how was the coven meeting last night?"

"It was . . . well . . . awkward."

"Weren't they welcoming?"

"Oh yes, they were. But you know how I can sometimes lose control of my power in a group setting?" I shook my head. "Let's just say it didn't go well. And anyway, I was there for information, not to join their coven. So . . ." I could feel my cheeks burn. "They ended up asking me to leave."

"Lily, I'm so sorry." Bronwyn walked toward me with arms open. She was a hugger.

"It's okay, really," I said, returning her squeeze. "They were right. It wasn't fair of me to take part in their ceremonies when I was really just there to ask questions."

"Well, next time I'll go with you. I don't see why a person can't do both, draw down the moon with a bunch of wonderful women and ask questions at the same time."

I smiled. That sort of epitomized Bronwyn's no-limit philosophy of life.

"Speaking of questions, I invited Wendy over for dinner tonight. She's going to fill me in on what she might know about Tarra and the Unspoken coven. Will you join us? I'm cooking Cajun."

"I'd love to! Oh, and I've been meaning to ask," Bronwyn said. "Have you heard from Duke? About Miriam or the baby?"

"No, nothing. I called the hospital last night but wasn't able to get any information. Maybe I should try calling him today."

"I'm happy to do it, if you like," she offered.

"Really? That would be great. I'd like to know how the baby is." I wrote down the number for her.

"No problem. I'll give him a call." She tucked the scrap paper in the pocket of the long, oversized vest she wore over yoga pants.

There was something in her voice . . . I studied her for a moment. She avoided my eyes, and a pink flush appeared high on her cheeks.

"Bronwyn Theodora Peters, as I live and breathe," I said with a smile. "You've got a crush on the man."

"Oh, good *goddess*, no," she said, suddenly becoming mightily intrigued with the sparkly eighties tops she was hanging on the rack. "He's a worried father. I'm sure romance is the last thing on his mind."

"He's an attractive fellow," I said. "And just about your age. A workingman with the soul of a poet . . ."

"Oh, look! Imogen's here!"

The bell on the front door rang as Bronwyn's eight-year-old granddaughter entered, cradling her black cat, Beowulf. Upon seeing Oscar, the cat jumped from Imogen's arms and stalked across the shop floor, imperiously twitching her tail at the pig. Oscar obediently trailed behind the feline, trying to get her attention.

Recently we'd learned that the cat was a female, although Oscar had already dubbed her Beowulf—through me—and no one had the heart to change her name.

It was summer, so, like Maya, Imogen was out of school. She had become something of a fixture at Aunt Cora's Closet now that her mother, Rebecca, allowed her to spend time with her Wiccan grandmother. I could have sworn I spotted a pentacle around her neck on a silver chain.

I loved having Imogen here. She was a lot like the child's version of her grandmother, with warm brown eyes, unruly hair, and a wide-open heart. But like me, she had a neat streak, and I especially enjoyed the way she kept the scarf shelves tidy.

But she was also a math whiz, and today I spotted the dreaded algebra book under her arm. It was time for lessons.

Not long ago Bronwyn and Susan had discovered that I never finished high school and had made it their personal crusade to help me study for the GED. Personally I didn't see why a witch in my position needed a certificate from the state to prove I was literate, but Bronwyn had *tsk*ed and asked me what kind of role model I was for the children.

I never thought of myself as a role model before, but she managed to cow me.

I read a lot, so with some minimal guidance from Maya, who was well versed in history, sociology, and literature, I felt like I had a good handle on the basics of the humanities. But math . . . ? That was something else altogether. Especially algebra.

Give me noxious brews involving rare herbs from high Tibetan mountains, baskets full of snapping venomous snakes, or even old-school spells requiring body parts . . . I'd choose any of them over solving for the "x."

As my grandmother used to say: *Once a witch, always a witch.*

After an hour I managed to escape with the almost legitimate excuse of needing to visit the Salvation Army and Goodwill stores. Mondays were a big day for thrift shops, as so many people used the weekends to clean out their closets.

I packed up my things, left Aunt Cora's Closet—and Oscar—in the capable hands of Maya, Bronwyn, and Imogen, and pointed my vintage Mustang back toward the East Bay. Duke told me Miriam's corsage had been sent by her boyfriend, Jonathan, who worked at a collectible card shop called MJ's Games in downtown Oakland. I didn't know Oakland well, and truth to tell, it intimidated me. But once I got off the freeway and found my way to the downtown area, it was charming. Though there were a number of empty shop fronts, clearly it had once been a bustling downtown, full of ornate Victorians and Art Deco buildings, much like San Francisco. The curbs were crowded, so I parked several blocks away and walked past a historic hotel, a brewpub, and a Vietnamese restaurant to reach the corner of Ninth and Washington, where a large sign read MJ'S GAMES—COMICS, COLLECTIBLES, CRAZY STUFF.

Unwashed windows held a dozen posters of superheroes, but I recognized only the most obvious: Spider-Man and Batman.

The shop front was long and narrow, with a counter running along one side and the opposite wall holding racks of comic books. In the center were several substantial-looking card tables around which gathered scads of adolescent boys and teenagers. A soft murmur arose from the crowd, but by and large they were intent on the colorful cards splayed out on the tables in front of them.

The moment I walked through the door, the smell hit me. Not unwashed, necessarily, but distinctive of young males. Add to the mix those who hadn't quite discovered personal hygiene and a widespread penchant for strong, sprayed cologne, and the air at MJ's Games was pungent.

Two twenty-something men stood behind the counter. It was hard to imagine Miriam with either. One was short and stocky, with tattoo sleeves on his arms and *Tiko* emblazoned on his forehead. The other had a beard that hung from his chin in a braid. I tried not to stare ... Though upon reflection, I supposed maybe he wanted people to stare; otherwise why would he do something so unusual on his face?

"Help you?" asked the one with the braided beard, raising his chin at me.

"Hi," I said, and several young heads whipped around to look at me. I had the sense they didn't get a lot of estrogen in this place. "I was hoping to speak with Jonathan Penn?"

Just then a tall, thin man emerged from behind a bamboo curtain painted with a picture of a female superhero complete with exaggerated breasts and long, long legs. He wore a retro Frank Sinatra–type hat, had scraggly

facial hair, and a vest with silver rivets over a long-
sleeved vintage T-shirt with a Black Sabbath emblem.

His attention was fixed on a bright green flyer in his
hands.

"Get this," he said to his companions behind the
counter. "Says here that magic is damaging to society,
that it's connected to the devil."

"Magic as in *magic*, or like the cards?" asked Braidman.

"Or like pulling a rabbit out of a hat?" asked Tiko.

"Doesn't specify," said the man with the hat.

"You're saying they think the cards are connected to
the devil somehow?" I asked, though it was obvious I
was butting in.

"Guess so."

"Are they?"

He just gave me a look: a mixture of incredulity and
irritation.

"Why are they called 'magic' cards?" I asked.

"Magic, the Gathering. It's just the name of them; it's
like a fantasy-game-type deal. It doesn't have anything
to do with abracadabra, nothing like that."

"Who sent the letter?" I asked, though I already knew.

"It's signed DOM, Defense of Morality."

"Never heard of 'em," said Braidman. "What's their
deal?"

"Who cares? I'm gonna light up this here flyer and
show 'em what they can do with their magic." The man
with the hat pulled a silver engraved lighter from the
pocket of his black jeans and held the flame to the paper.

His companions laughed, and several of the young
boys looked up with awed smiles on their faces, a goodly
amount of hero worship in their expressions.

"Let them put *that* in their pipe and smoke it," he said,

then let the burning flyer fall to the glass display counter, where the black ash quivered.

"Yo, Jonathan," Braidman said, tweaking his head toward me. "Lady's here to see you, man."

So the tall fellow in the hat was Jonathan Penn, Miriam's boyfriend—or *ex*-boyfriend.

He raised his chin to me. "Hey, sorry about that. Listen, if your kid bought one of those collectible Iron Man comic books, I can't be giving refunds. I told the kids when they bought 'em they weren't licensed."

"It's nothing like that. I was hoping I could talk to you?" I began, trying to get a bead on him. There was intelligence in his eyes, a certain intensity that was easy to miss at first, given his slack posture. He looked me up and down, and I had to admit there was something appealing about him. If he took a bath and cleaned up a little.

He shrugged and placed his palms on the counter, leaning on his hands. "Sure. What's up?"

"I wanted to ask you about Miriam Demeter?"

At the mention of Miriam's name, he went still. "What are you, a friend of hers?"

"Sort of."

"Look, she said she didn't want to talk with me, so like, I respected that. I don't know what she wants from me, swear to God."

"When was the last time you spoke to her?"

"We went shopping for outfits for this dance she wanted to go to. It wasn't my thing, but I was, like, whatever she wanted. Know what I'm saying? If that floats her boat, then whatever."

His companions behind the counter nodded, in solidarity with a man trying to deal with the inscrutable whims of a woman.

"Where did you go for the outfit?" I asked.

"This vintage place down on Union Street, near Fillmore. She wound up getting a dress, but it was expensive and the lady told me I should just rent a tux instead of buy one, which I totally was gonna do until Miriam told me she didn't even want me to go with her."

"Why did she do that?"

A shadow passed over his eyes. "She's been wanting me to sell this shop to my partners. Says it isn't a grown-up job, and—I dunno—maybe she's right." He shrugged. "Hanging out all day with kids maybe isn't the best way to make a living, but it pays for itself and I like it. Guess Miriam . . . You know, we're the same age, but she's got a kid. So it's different for her. I guess I get where she's coming from."

His coworkers shook their heads, commiserating.

"And then what happened? She called off the dance?"

"Texted me, if you believe that. Said she was breaking up with me. Whatever. If that's the way she wants to play it . . ." He shrugged, looked at the boys hunched over their cards, then back to me. "So what'd she do? Send you here to talk with me? That's sort of effed up. Know what I'm saying? Communication is, like, the key to any relationship. If she wants to get back together, we, like, totally need to talk, and she should come here herself."

"She can't do that," I said. "She's in the hospital."

He went rigid, his nervous eyes finally fixing on mine. "Hospital?"

"They're not sure what it is. She fell sick the night of the ball."

"Are you serious? It seemed like something was wrong, but I never thought . . . Ah, maaaaan." He wiped his face with his hand. "I can't believe this. What hospital is she in?"

I told him where to find her, though I wasn't sure how Duke would react to Jonathan's presence.

"You might want . . . You should give her father a little room. He's sort of emotional right now."

"Her old man doesn't like me at all."

"He's a father. They can be protective."

"I wouldn't know about that," he said with bitterness. "I never knew my father."

"Me either," I said. "But Duke seems pretty close to his daughter. Anyway, he mentioned taking Luna to the doctor today so you could probably visit without a problem, if you want. Hey, can I ask you one more question? Did you happen to know Tarragon Dark Moon?"

"Yeah . . ." Realization dawned on his face. "Oh wait. No way. No effing *way*. First Tarra dies, and now Miriam . . . You think something's going on?"

"Maybe. It's quite a coincidence."

"Maaaaan," he breathed, shaking his head.

"Did you know Tarra well?"

"She was friends with Miriam."

"Do you know about the botanicals training they were both involved in?"

"Sure. Miriam couldn't stop talking about it."

"Could you tell me who ran it?"

"Name's Calypso something. She's way up in Marin, or maybe past that—not in the city, is all I know. But I don't have any details."

Darn. "One last thing: Did you send Miriam a corsage the night of the ball?"

He turned beet red, shrugging once more and glancing at his companions. "Yeah. Lame. Right? I just . . . I felt bad about it. I really sort of wanted to go. I wanted to be with her. Ah, *man*, I can't believe this." He took off his hat and ran a large hand through his dark hair. "I've got to go see her."

"Did you send the corsage yourself, or did someone take it for you?"

"What? Oh, girl works in a flower shop 'round the corner is a friend of ours. She gave me a discount, and I sent it through her."

"What's her name?"

Jonathan gave me an odd look. Now that I spent so much time snooping, I had come to recognize the signs: the moment when someone starts wondering why I was asking so many questions. The moment when a person stops talking.

His hands rested on the countertop. I covered one with my own and looked him straight in the eye. "I know it's a long shot, but I'm wondering about the corsage. Maybe there was something . . . wrong with it? I'd like to talk to the people who made it."

After a pause, he nodded. "Name's Anise."

"Like the flavor?" asked Braidman.

"It's a seed, I think, right?" said Jonathan. "Like in absinthe?"

He looked at his colleagues, eyebrows raised in question.

"I think so, yeah," said the tattooed one. "Some sort of spice."

"Like licorice."

"One more thing," I said to Jonathan, handing him my business card. "If you stop by the hospital, would you call me and let me know how Miriam's doing?" I had tried calling again earlier, but they refused to give me her status over the phone.

"Sure," he said, taking the card. "Aunt Cora's Closet? That's a vintage store in the Haight, right?"

I nodded. "You know it?"

"Nah. But it was on the list of stores Miriam had when we were looking for our outfits for the dance. If we hadn't found the dress at the other store, I guess we would have wound up at your place."

"My store was on your list?"

He nodded. "I remember the name, 'cause I actually have a great-aunt Cora. But like I say, we didn't get there. We stopped at a place on Union and found the perfect dress for her." Sadness entered his eyes. "She looked so pretty when she tried it on. Really great. I can't believe she's in the hospital. Dudes." He turned to his colleagues. "I'm totally gonna take off for a while, go see her."

"Go for it," said Tiko, patting him on the back in masculine solidarity. "Think you'll make it to drumming circle tomorrow night?"

Jonathan shrugged. "Dunno. See you when I see you."

We walked out together.

"So, why's a vintage clothes dealer asking about all this? You a member of Miriam's coven?"

"No."

"A friend of the coven?"

"Not really. I mean, I'm not an enemy or anything. I just don't know them very well. But I was at the dance when Miriam passed out. I think I can help her."

He gazed at me another moment, suspicion in his eyes.

"How?"

Good question. "I don't really know. But I want to try."

He studied me another moment, then shrugged his thin shoulders and loped off toward his car. I walked in the opposite direction, toward the flower shop.

Chapter 11

Lee's Flowers was easy to spot. Plastic tubs chock-full of colorful bundles of cut flowers spilled out onto the sidewalk in front of the store, which was no more than a tiny, fragrant box. After the aroma of the card shop, I was particularly appreciative of the flowers' gift of perfume, and took comfort in being surrounded by blossoms. If I weren't a witch, I could see myself owning a little stand like this one.

But then, knowing me, I would wind up filling it with medicinal plants rather than decorative flowers.

Inside, Anise sat on a high stool, her legs dangling and kicking, texting on her phone. Her short, light brown hair was brushed forward to fall almost over her eyes. She wore a navy blue hoodie and jeans, and had a chain hanging down with a bunch of jangly keys. She looked about twelve years old.

"Help you?" She looked up reluctantly from her phone.

"Hi, Anise. Good to see you again."

She looked at me, her expression confused. "I know you?"

"I met you last night, at the coven meeting?"

"Oh, right."

"I was just talking to Jonathan Penn, around the corner at the game store? He mentioned he sent a corsage through you to Miriam Demeter on Saturday?"

She nodded again, and brushed the hair out of her eyes. "Sure. Pink orchids, flax, Hyoscyamus, teal ribbons. I made it myself."

"Hyoscyamus?"

She nodded.

"Hyoscyamus niger? As in henbane? You're sure?"

"Special request."

"Requested by . . ."

She widened her eyes and gave me an annoyed, impatient look. "Uh, *Jonathan*?" The *duh* was implied. I recognized the tone from my sometimes less than mature familiar.

"Jonathan asked for Hyoscyamus by name?"

"He texted me while I was making it. What's all this about?"

"And you sent it directly to her address?"

"Yep. Didn't it arrive?"

"It did," I said, hesitating. Was it my place to tell the world that Miriam was sick? If Anise was a friend, as well, would she hustle on over to the ICU along with Jonathan, and at what point would Duke lose his patience with visitors . . . especially since he didn't seem thrilled with her current group of friends?

The phone rang. Anise looked over at it and blinked, as though she had forgotten how to respond to the ring.

"Are you feeling all right?" I asked.

She nodded, ignoring the phone.

"You're part of a botanicals group, aren't you? Along with Tarra and Miriam and Jonquil? Who else was in the group?"

She shrugged. "A couple of other girls not with the coven. And a couple foodie types. Some chef guy who works over at Randi's, near the ballpark."

"Can you tell me anything about the woman who teaches the class?"

"Calypso Cafaro," she said, animation finally filling her voice. "She's the best. She's, like, so awesome. Really. She let me stay there."

"Stay there, with her?"

She nodded. "When I first came here, to the Bay. I was, like, a runaway? And I stayed with her for a while until I got on my feet. She's done that for a lot of us."

"Sounds very generous."

"She's, like, awesome." She looked down at her stubby nails, where blue-black polish was chipping in spots. "I so want to be her when I'm, like, old."

"Could you give me her contact information? I'd love to talk with her."

"Who?"

"Calypso, the woman who teaches you about botanicals."

"Um . . . I don't think so. It probably wouldn't be smart."

"Why's that?"

"She's very private. People totally don't visit her without an invitation."

I'll bet. "Does Calypso grow Hyoscyamus niger in her yard?"

"She grows, like, *everything* in her yard. That's where I got the flowers for the corsage, 'cause they're not what you call standard. Usually I just use the business flowers, but since Miriam's a friend, I went above and beyond. Calypso taught me everything I know about flowers. That's how come I got this job."

I happened to know a thing or two about flowers myself. In particular, about the sort of flowers that can kill you.

If Calypso had taught Anise all about plants, I was surprised she hadn't mentioned that Hyoscyamus niger, otherwise known as henbane, is highly toxic, whether fresh or dried. The purplish flowers are rather pretty, though the whole plant is more aromatic of tobacco leaves than floral perfume.

When I'd seen Miriam's corsage at the ball, I'd been so focused on the needles and black thread—the obvious curse—that I didn't even notice henbane flowers. But thinking back on it now, I remembered sensing the subtle aroma of tobacco and assuming that someone nearby was a smoker.

"Did you include any black ribbon or needles in the corsage?"

Anise's delicate eyebrows narrowed. "Needles? Only, like, the pins to hold it on. And I just told you, the ribbon was teal."

"Do you remember that day? Do you recall actually sending it, or could someone have gotten hold of it and maybe changed it?"

She shook her head. "No way. I mean, I don't exactly remember—" She was cut off when two women came in, distraught over the wrong color of roses used in their wedding arrangements.

"This is an outrage . . . !" they began, and the discussion devolved from there. They started demanding that the red flowers be changed to rose-colored, and Anise strained to keep up with the shouted questions. It surprised me that such a small place would be furnishing whole weddings, but then I guessed they must be a small outlet while working out of bigger warehouses somewhere.

Then the phone rang, and a clearly distracted Anise

answered it, holding up a limp hand to the wedding planner.

Sensing I wasn't going to get much further with Anise today, I slipped out into the sunny afternoon.

Anise gave off no vibration of power, no indication of anything sinister. Her aura was young, innocent. Which was not to say that I couldn't be fooled, or that innocent souls couldn't get caught up in anger and jealousy. But she seemed so hapless I couldn't imagine her putting together a curse strong enough to harm—to put someone into a *coma*—from afar. And if she had understood the effects, surely she wouldn't be up-front about the henbane she put into Miriam's corsage?

One thing was sure: I needed to make the acquaintance of one Calypso Cafaro, the botanicals expert who'd supplied the apparently clueless Anise with poisonous flowers.

How could I track her down? I would need an address, obviously, and an introduction wouldn't hurt. I wondered whether she might be listed in Wendy's Moonlight Madness phone book—I could just call and ask whether we could get together and talk, one botanical enthusiast to another. On the other hand, if the "awesome," oh so private Calypso was a renegade poisoner, perhaps arriving unannounced might be the more productive way of going about things, though dangerous. Maybe I needed backup on this one. . . .

I decided to return to MJ's Games. I had a few more questions for Jonathan about his special request for henbane in his girlfriend's corsage.

Once again the smell of the boys hit me as I walked through the door; once again several stopped their playing for a moment to assess this alien female form before them.

"He left already to totally go see Miriam," said Braidman.

"I know—I walked out with him. But could I call him? Do you have his cell phone number?"

"Wouldn't do you any good. He lost his phone the other day."

"Oh, okay. So, you two know Miriam?"

"Sure," said Tiko. "She's real nice. Cute."

"But, dude, not right for Jonathan," inserted Braidman. "Kept wanting him to sell this place."

"Yes, he mentioned that," I said, turning toward the door. "Thanks."

"Anytime."

I considered tracking Jonathan down at the hospital, but reconsidered. The more I thought about it, I didn't really believe Jonathan had tried to kill Miriam. The flowers would be an unnecessarily obvious, risky thing to do. It was much more likely they were a message, or part of a curse. I imagined whoever killed Tarra had also assaulted Miriam, and why would Jonathan do that?

On the other hand, what did I know? There was only one way I could think of to get real answers—I needed to talk to Miriam's spirit, and fast.

I called Carlos Romero and got his voice mail. I left a message on it about the henbane and the text message sent by Jonathan—or at least through Jonathan's phone, now conveniently lost. At this rate, if Carlos followed up on all my visits like a specter of the SFPD, no one in this crowd would be talking to me by tomorrow. But I didn't want to keep anything from him, however trivial.

As I headed to my car, I realized that I wasn't far from Oakland's Paramount Theater, where the Art Deco Ball had been held. I walked the five city blocks, past Oaksterdam Museum, a convention center, and an old twenty-four-hour newsstand, and finally arrived at the theater, standing tall and proud with its colorful, intricate tiled façade. The marquee advertised the classic film

The Philadelphia Story, with Cary Grant and Katharine Hepburn, playing this Thursday night at eight.

I almost never went to the movies. But I remembered my mother watching this one on television many years ago. She had a crush on Cary Grant, and said life looked like it had been so much more beautiful back then; she seemed to yearn for the glamour and the wardrobe of a Philadelphia debutante. My mother was a country girl, born and raised in Jarod, and had left only for brief visits to relatives in Galveston and Houston. Being crowned Miss Tecla County when she was twenty had been the most glamorous moment of her life.

Idly, I wondered if I should send my mother a plane ticket to San Francisco. She cashed the checks I sent her every month but never called or wrote, and I wasn't at all sure she would relish the idea of a mother-daughter visit. We hadn't been in touch since I called to tell her I was settling in San Francisco. Mother's response to this news had been lukewarm; the truth was, she shied away from associating with witches, even one who was her own flesh and blood. My grandmother Graciela did not cotton to my mother's attitude at all, and insisted on remaining in contact. But then Graciela was so cantankerous she didn't care what people wanted, as long as she did what was right. Graciela was a force of nature.

According to people like Sailor, I'd started exhibiting some of those same tendencies. But so far I had respected my mother's wishes and left her alone.

Everything was locked up at the Paramount this afternoon; no one answered my knocks on the main doors. I walked around the side of the building and tried the stage door.

To my surprise, a woman answered. She was about Bronwyn's age and shared her coloring, but she was the suburban version—her hair was a neat close-cropped helmet, and she wore coral lipstick that matched her cardigan twinset.

"May I help you?" she said.

"Hi. I don't mean to barge in, but I was wondering if there's a lost and found I could check?"

"Of course, but they're closed now. What are you looking for?"

"A corsage I might have dropped during the Art Deco Ball. It had teal ribbons, pale pink and violet flowers. I know it sounds silly, but I wanted to keep it as a memento of the evening. I don't get to Oakland very often. Would it be possible to check while I'm here?"

She shook her head. "I'm sorry. I don't have access to that office. Tell you what. Why don't you leave me your address and I'll check in the morning. If it's there, I'll mail it to you."

"You would do that for me?"

"Of course."

I gave her my card, surprised that a perfect stranger would go above and beyond. But perhaps she was just being nice to get rid of me.

"One more thing," I said, though aware that my question might ruin my chances of her wanting to help me. "Have you ever heard of any ghost stories related to the Paramount?"

"Of course."

"Really?"

"There are always ghosts in theaters." Her response was so matter-of-fact that I was thrown off. I thought of Sailor's story about the ghost lamp. I half thought he'd been pulling my leg. "In fact, we offer a ghost tour once a month. I'm a docent. I give historical tours on Saturday mornings. But I hear the ghost tour leader is very good."

"But nothing . . . recent? Nothing new?"

She laughed. "Not that I know of, but I don't spend a lot of time here at night."

"Well, thank you for your time."

"It's no problem. I'll look for your corsage in the morning. Those can be such precious keepsakes. And I hope you come back for the tour. Saturdays at ten."

"Thank you. I'll try."

I headed back to the car, my mind filled with images of poisonous corsages and theatrical ghosts. But then it turned to much more prosaic demands—my stomach growled, reminding me that I needed to shop for tonight's Cajun dinner I'd promised Wendy.

I stopped in at a place called the Historic Housewives' Market. Independent stands sold everything from freshly butchered meats to condiments—the kinds of shops that offered a choice of ten different kinds of mustard, from classic yellow to organic stone-ground concoctions from France. I found sassafras file gumbo and some tasty-looking New Orleans hot sauce. Then I bought some beautiful sausage for the jambalaya and shrimp —they had crawfish, but it was frozen—for the *étouffée*. The seafood merchant even packed the shrimp on ice for me when I told him I was headed back over the bridge.

Finally, I purchased a loaf of crusty sourdough. A sweet boutard would have been more traditional, but in cooking, as in spell work, it was good to be flexible. The pride of the Bay Area bakeries, fresh sourdough bread was hard to beat.

At the last minute, I stopped to grab a bag of Ghirardelli chocolate chips to make dessert. Chocolate chip oatmeal cookies were Oscar's favorite.

The chocolate turned out to be a mistake. I had skipped lunch, and there was a backup at the tollbooth at the base of the Bay Bridge. That bag of chocolate chips was open before you could say *abracadabra*.

While I was inching along and munching, I noticed a billboard for DOM: JUDGMENT WILL BE CAST UPON THOSE WHO ADHERE TO THE EVIL OF MAGICK AND ALL IT ENTAILS. BROUGHT TO YOU BY DOM: PRESERVING OUR WAY OF LIFE.

The so-called Defenders of Morality were putting up *billboards* now? And leaving flyers in stores, warning them about their "wicked ways"? Well, if that didn't beat all. What kind of resources did these people have? And perhaps more important, exactly how far were they willing to go to impose their beliefs on others?

Once I got through the tollbooth, traffic moved along at a good clip. The first exit at the foot of the bridge advised drivers to get off for Union Square, reminding me that Jonathan had mentioned the vintage store where Miriam bought her dress was on Union Street. Suddenly I was curious about my competition. I pulled off and followed the signs to the shopping mecca.

After half an hour of fruitless searching, a very pleasant uniformed doorman outside the St. Francis Hotel informed me I had made a common outsider's mistake: Union *Street* was an entirely different trendy shopping district, clear across town, not far from the Marina.

Twenty minutes later I was searching for a parking space. Though not as upscale as the überchic Union Square, Union Street was nonetheless full of wine bars and pricey boutiques, art galleries and designer pet stores, soap stores and baby stores. I walked to the corner of Union and Filmore and spotted the shop: Vintage Chic.

On display in the twin bay windows were several mannequins clad in exquisite 1930s cocktail gowns in cream and gold. In fact, the whole motif was a symphony of cream satins and silks, with distressed gold gilt touches in the form of candlesticks and an antique French provincial vanity. An over-the-top distressed crystal chandelier hung overhead, and opaque cream-and-gold glass bubbles covered the floor so the mannequins looked as though they were surging out from a bubble bath.

I wasn't often given to feelings of professional inadequacy, but Aunt Cora's Closet would have to step it up a little if we wanted to compete with the likes of this place. On the other hand, Union Street set a different bar, chic-wise, than the Haight.

A bell on the door tinkled as I walked in. Though it didn't carry the scent of herbal sachets like Aunt Cora's Closet, Vintage Chic shared the pleasant aroma of clean laundry.

The shop was smaller than mine, less than half the size, but I could tell from a quick once-over that Vintage Chic carried a more expensive, exclusive inventory. There was a preponderance of silks and satins, and I didn't see any item—other than, possibly, jewelry—from later than the early sixties.

The cream-and-distressed-gold motif of the front display windows continued inside. It felt a bit like walking into a fashionable boutique in Paris.

I knelt to pet a little dog lying in an ornate gold pet bed topped with a crown—I had just seen the bed in the window of the designer pet store down the street. Good thing Oscar hadn't caught sight of this, I thought, or there would be no living with him.

A child sat cross-legged behind the counter, in an upholstered chair, reading a hardback novel. The big chair broke the subdued color scheme: It looked like something out of *Alice in Wonderland*, asymmetrical and covered in an orange-and-pink harlequin pattern.

"Hello, welcome," said the child, and I realized this was no girl, but a grown woman. "I'm Greta, the owner. Feel free to look around."

"Thank you." Upon second look, I realized the woman

was older than I, probably in her forties. Blond hair was cut in a wavy pageboy. She was super petite, not skinny but proportional. She was probably about the size and shape of the average American ten-year-old, as though she'd never really gotten that pubescent growth spurt. What must it be to go through life like that? I wondered.

What I couldn't understand was why she wasn't wearing her own vintage clothing. Unlike most modern women raised on plenty of protein and vitamins, she was small enough for even the tiniest-waisted Victorian numbers my customers always lusted after. Instead, she wore a matching cardigan and shell—rather like the middle-aged docent I met at the Paramount—and a skirt that was clearly modern, probably purchased from a nice mall store. Inoffensive, but uninspired.

"Nice dress," Greta said, looking me up and down with an assessing eye. I was wearing one of my favorite styles today: a sundress from the early sixties, sleeveless, with a fitted bodice and a full skirt. It had vertical stripes of shell pink and pale orange against a cream-colored background. I had tied my ponytail with a pink-polka-dotted scarf, and my Keds were a soft ginger.

The little dog started yapping the minute I stopped petting him. He was one of those expensive breeds, small and high-strung, with long glossy hair tied with a ribbon atop his head.

"Oh, ignore him. He's purebred shih tzu." Greta scooped up the dog and cradled it to her chest, cooing at him in baby talk. "Aren't you? Aren't you my purebred beauty?"

The dog licked her on the mouth, but she just laughed. Now I was doubly glad Oscar wasn't here to witness this, lest he get any untoward ideas about how the proper pet is supposed to act in public.

As I flipped through the merchandise, my suspicions were confirmed: Vintage Chic's prices were much higher than mine, but the inventory more selective. I had a hard time saying no to people who needed cash, or who brought in clothes that, while not spectacular, nonetheless carried lovely vibrations.

Still hugging her dog to her chest, Greta watched me like a hawk. I didn't want to feel like a spy, so I told her I was owner of Aunt Cora's Closet.

"I've heard of your store," she said. "There was an article about you a while back, about a vintage wedding?"

"Yes, when I first opened. Susan Rogers from the *Chronicle* came with her niece's wedding party. It was such fun."

"Must be nice. You know people over at the *Chronicle*?" There was a little sensation of envy, just a whiff. But in this business that sort of thing was hard to avoid.

"I do now, but originally it was pure chance. Susan happened on my shop one day. There are dozens of fabulous resale shops in the city, obviously."

Her smile froze, her head tilted to one side. "I'm not a resale shop. I'm a specialty boutique."

"Oh, of course. I, uh . . ."

Just then the phone rang, rescuing me. My lucky day. But not for the telemarketer on the other end of the line, to whom Greta read the riot act. She slammed the phone down and remained behind the counter, seething for a moment. Finally, appearing to remember she wasn't alone, she looked back at me and gave me a tight smile.

"Don't you just hate phone solicitations?"

I returned her smile and nodded. They did annoy me; that was true. But as they would say back in Jarod, Greta got her gussie up awful fast.

"You're more selective than I am," I said. "You have

some really fine things here. I have some items of this quality, but I also carry a lot of more ordinary clothes."

Greta seemed to warm under my compliments. "I know a shop owner near you on Haight Street, Peaceful Things? Sandra Schmidt?"

"Oh yes, of course. Sandra's my neighbor. She's a friend of yours?"

"I know her. I've seen her shop."

I nodded. She didn't embellish.

The dog yapped as a pair of giggling teenage girls entered the store, and the petite Greta fixed them with a challenging look. As a shopkeeper myself, I knew by instinct what she did: The girls were not here to buy, but to pass the time. Still, I always enjoyed having people roam the aisles of Aunt Cora's Closet, whether or not they were in the mood to buy. It seemed to me that the more people in the store, the more welcoming the atmosphere. I had the distinct impression Greta would not agree.

The girls ceased their giggling, browsed halfheartedly for a few moments, then left, seemingly chastened.

"Would you happen to remember a woman who bought a dress from you for the Art Deco Ball?" I asked after the girls left. I crossed over to the display counter and played with some colorful tangerine and pink Bakelite bangles hanging on a tiny mannequin. I slipped them onto my arm, admiring the way they picked up the pink and orange stripes on my dress. "It was sea-foam green, drop-waist, beaded, sleeveless. From the mid-twenties."

Many of us vintage clothing dealers remembered outfits better than the clients who purchased them. It made sense: We worked with those garments, unearthed them, vied for them, inspected them, cleaned them, repaired them, and sometimes lived with them for months. I imagined that even those who didn't have my special relationship to clothing might well feel as though they have an almost magical connection to the garments in their care.

"I remember her," Greta said with a small nod.

"Was there anything unusual about her, or her boyfriend, that you remember?"

Her big eyes narrowed with suspicion. "Why do you ask?"

"The woman who bought the dress, Miriam Demeter, fell into a coma the evening of the ball. I'm just trying to figure out what happened. . . . I thought if I retraced her footsteps in the days preceding the dance, something might occur to me."

"If she's such a close friend, how come she didn't buy the dress from *you*?"

"I wouldn't call her a close friend," I said, realizing that Greta was far too suspicious—some might even say cynical—to simply respond to my questions like most people. Witch or no witch, I didn't seem to inspire warm and fuzzy feelings in her. "I'm simply trying to help her father."

"Sounds like a problem for the doctors, or the police if you think there was foul play. I don't see how my dress could be involved."

"No," I said, holding her hostile, closed-off gaze. "No, you're right."

"Whatever happened to the dress?"

"Excuse me?"

"You said she was in a coma. I'll buy the dress back if she's not going to use it anymore. Not for full price, of course. This isn't a rental shop. Where's the dress now?"

"I, uh . . . I have no idea. It hasn't been a priority. Right now they're just trying to keep her alive."

"Okay," she said with a delicate shrug, scooping up her dog once again and kissing him on the head. "If you change your mind, you know where to find me."

"Thank you for your time," I said. "I appreciate it. You really do have a great place here. And if someone can't find the dress they need at my place, I'll suggest they look here."

She didn't seem particularly open to the idea, but what could I expect from my competition?

The dog yapped at me as I slipped out the door.

Chapter 12

"Whatever you do, do *not* drool in the food," I ordered Oscar.

My apartment smelled of sassafras, garlic, andouille sausage, and shrimp. The mouthwatering aromas reminded me of home.

Though the majority of my memories of Jarod were unhappy, a few still called to me. The food, number one. Also, the scent of chilies coaxed from the harsh red soil; the sound of a lone fiddle on a summer's night; the way a real "gully-washer" would sweep through, cleaning the air of the dust and heat, coaxing the children outside to play in the warm rain.

Until my guests arrived, necessitating his transformation into a potbellied pig, Oscar was serving as my salivating sous chef. He kept sneaking bites of spicy jambalaya rice when he thought I wasn't looking, and his enthusiastic way of stirring spewed ingredients all over the kitchen counters and the black-and-white-checked floor. Still and all, it was plain old fun to have a companion to cook with.

Far downstairs, we barely heard the bell ringing on the front door of the shop.

"They're here," I said, rushing to open the door of my apartment.

"Oh my *goddess*!" said Bronwyn as she mounted the stairs and enveloped me in a bear hug. "You can practically smell this meal all the way down the street!" She breathed in loudly through her nose. "Like heaven. I'm famished."

"Ditto," said Wendy.

"Good thing there's plenty," I said. Even though Bronwyn was one of my closest friends and I saw Wendy almost every day, I was a nervous hostess. To be on the safe side, I'd wound up making enough jambalaya and *étouffée* to feed an army, as well as stuffing the refrigerator with beer, wine, and watermelon *agua fresca*. Also cooling was the custard flan with *dulce de leche* for dessert.

In addition, I had scrubbed the small apartment to the cleanliness standards of the average operating room, then filled half a dozen mason jars with daisies, roses, and snapdragons and placed them all around the front room and kitchen.

"Would anyone care for . . ." I trailed off when I saw that Bronwyn was already peeking in the fridge. "Just help yourself to anything you like. There's beer and watermelon *agua fresca*—which is nonalcoholic, but is surprisingly good with a shot of vodka—or I've got wine, if you prefer."

"Wendy, look at this," Bronwyn said as she pointed to jars and bowls in my refrigerator that were labeled things such as "llama ear," "fresh spider silk," and "river water—smooth" and "river water—rapids."

"Um . . . the llama ear is a kind of tree fungus, not a real animal part . . ." I said in a small voice. Like many witches in my tradition, I used blood sacrifice from time to time, but avoided it whenever possible.

"And check *this* out," said Wendy, as she perused the jars on the shelf above the counter. "There are, what? Ten different kinds of honey here? What do you need so many kinds for?"

"Honey can be powerful, but it's a product of a third party — "

"As in bees?"

"Yes. And the bees extract the nectar at different times, from different kinds of flowers, so each honey has distinct properties. . . ." The intricacies of apiculture were hard to explain, and at the end of the day I was better at making things happen than explaining how things worked. "In short, they work differently in different brews, or in honey jar spells."

"Honey jar spells?"

"They attract sweetness and repel the negative. Like this." I gestured toward a jar that held a cored apple filled with orange blossom honey, topped by a rolled beeswax candle. Also in the jar were two cloves, a bit of bayberry root, two lodestones, a pinch of deer tongue leaves, and a square of rag soaked in camphor. "Honey's amazing. It never, ever spoils. Also, it has antibiotic and anti-inflammatory properties, so it was used in wound care long before modern antibiotics were developed."

"Really?" Wendy's darkly outlined eyes cast about the kitchen. "This is hella cool," she said after a moment, and I warmed under the praise.

While I finished up with the cooking, Bronwyn cuddled with Oscar and we chatted about my moon calendar and the most effective spells for romantic love. Finally we sat down to our feast at the kitchen table, and Wendy started to tell me what she knew about Tarragon Dark Moon, née Tanya Kolchek.

"I looked her up, and now I realize why she sounded so familiar. She goes by Tarra, and she's with the Unspoken coven. Remember, Bronwyn? A few of that group carpooled with us to the annual Pagan Festival up in Oroville last year, and then we saw Tarra at the craft retreats up in Humboldt County for Samhain."

Even now, after months in San Francisco, it made me dizzy to think how open people were with their witchcraft and pagan ways.

"Can you tell me about the Unspoken coven? You said they aren't Wiccan?"

She shook her head while pouring more hot sauce on a healthy serving of jambalaya. "I don't know that much about them. The Feri tradition is very different from Wicca, though, like us, there are probably as many different ways of worshipping as there are members. None of us are into hierarchical structures or edicts from above. But as far as I understand it, Feri is more an ecstatic tradition than a fertility group."

"I'm not sure I follow."

"In our group, for instance, we worship the Lord and Lady of the Woods and the beauty of fertility—whether it be creativity, or some other kind of fulfillment in life. The Feri tradition recognizes various gods that are fluid, both male and female, as well as dark and light. They value sensual experience and sexual mysticism."

"Sounds like fun," I said as I passed around the loaf of sourdough, which I had warmed in the oven, along with fresh butter from the farmers' market.

"They take it quite seriously."

"Sorry. I didn't mean to belittle it. . . . It just sounds like fun."

"There are some specific beliefs, like that of the Three Souls and the Black Heart of Innocence. But there are lots of splinter groups, too. I'm telling you, they aren't easy to categorize."

I was getting that.

"One more thing . . ." Wendy and Bronwyn met eyes across the table. "I don't know much about the Unspoken coven, as I said. They're a mystery religion, and unless you're a wand-holding initiate—which is no small thing—you can't know their secret names or anything like that. But they have a certain . . . 'comfort zone' with darkness."

"Darkness?"

"Becoming an initiate involves rigorous self-honesty, a willingness to delve into one's own darkness as a source of power and self-healing."

"That sounds a little like the tradition I was raised in. But . . ." I thought I heard something in her voice. "It sounds as though you're warning me off."

"It's not that," Wendy said. "I'm just telling you that they're not going to spill all over some jambalaya. Though this is pretty freaking good jambalaya, so I'm happy to spill all *my* secrets."

"I'm glad you like it." I, myself, had eaten so much I could barely move. "You should take some home when you go."

Oscar snorted his displeasure at my suggestion. He loved leftovers.

"Oh, by the way, Lily—I talked to Duke today," said Bronwyn. "He asked if we might come by tomorrow and visit with the baby. He hasn't been able to find anything new about his daughter's condition. Miriam's stable, so they moved her out of ICU. Duke had her transferred to San Francisco Medical Center so she'd be closer, and they have specialists in this area."

"How did he sound?"

"Oh, good, good. Given the circumstances."

"So anyway," said Wendy. "Bronwyn tells me you went to an open coven meeting last night. Didn't you see Tarra there?"

"No . . ." I realized I hadn't told either of them about Tarra yet. I looked at the faces of both these witches, these friends, and screwed up my courage. "I'm so sorry to tell you this, but the reason I was asking about her . . . I have a friend in the SFPD and he told me she was found dead last week."

"Are you serious?" Bronwyn gasped. "What happened?"

"That's what I'm trying to figure out. I went to their meeting yesterday, even took part in the circle, but it didn't go very well. When I told them I was looking for information, they clammed up."

"You joined the circle?" Wendy asked. "Before you told them what you were really doing there?"

I nodded.

"No wonder they were pissed. I would have been, too. You have to go into the circle with an open heart. You should know that."

I blushed. "You're right. I was . . . I felt awkward, wasn't sure how to approach it. At least it wasn't, you know, one of their private meetings, right?"

"You would never have been allowed to join that circle."

"I'm sure you're right. I screwed up. Do you know how to get in touch with them? I'd like to apologize."

Wendy shook her head. I sensed she was holding back, not that I blamed her. I guessed I was fulfilling all her fears about opening up to the likes of me. From the beginning, Bronwyn had been my backer in this community, while Wendy had kept some distance.

"How about a woman named Calypso Cafaro? She's

a botanical worker who was meeting with some of the young women from the coven to train them. Would you know any way I could get in touch with her?"

Wendy shook her head, looking down into her wine as though looking for inspiration.

"Sorry, Lily," Bronwyn said. "It's not as if we're all in the same group, or know each other. Some social circles overlap, but most don't."

"I'm just trying to figure out who harmed Tarra, and trying to help Miriam. I know I don't know all the rules . . ."

"You know," Wendy said, her voice thoughtful. "It's people like you who make what we do so difficult."

"Wendy—" Bronwyn began.

"No, Bronwyn, don't try to silence me on this. You know it's true." She turned back to me. "I mean, you weren't lying when you said you make a mean *étouffée*. But outside the kitchen, you're kind of a screwup. We were just starting to be accepted in the community when you came along and brought your 'friend' Aidan Rhodes, and suddenly there's this DOM group, people thinking we're all weirdos, mucking about with evil. And now Tarra's *dead*? Frankly, I don't want to be associated with the likes of—"

"That's enough, Wendy," Bronwyn said with uncharacteristic anger. "You owe Lily an apology."

"No, please," I said. "I truly am sorry if I caused you any difficulties; I certainly never intended to. I swear I'll—"

"Don't bother with promises," Wendy interrupted. She pushed back from the table, snatched up her things, and headed for the door. Before leaving, she turned back. "You're not the only one with family from the South, Lily, so let me phrase this in a way you'll understand: 'If promises were persimmons, possums could eat good.'"

She stomped down the stairs, and we heard the slam of the shop door.

Bronwyn sighed. "She certainly does know how to make an exit, doesn't she?"

I tried to return Bronwyn's smile, but couldn't. She wrapped her arms around me and hugged me tight. "Don't let it upset you, Lily. She's a little hypersensitive on this issue."

"Doesn't mean she's wrong about me."

Bronwyn stiffened. "That is ridiculous."

"Is it? I have a history of driving away everyone who cares about me."

"Well, now, that's simply not true. What about me and Maya?"

"How about my mother?"

"And you think that's *your* fault?"

I shrugged.

"Being a parent doesn't, by itself, create the capacity to love. If it did, there'd be no such thing as child abuse, now, would there? It doesn't mean there's something wrong with the child." She paused and slipped into her sweater. "I don't know what the situation is with your mother, Lily, and I can only imagine how painful that must be for you—and for her. Perhaps the two of you will still find a way to each other."

I nodded, though I didn't believe it in my heart.

Bronwyn helped clear the table and put away the food, but I insisted she leave the dishes to me. It was getting late, and I knew she wanted to return some phone calls and e-mails this evening. Bronwyn, no surprise, had more friends than she could shake a stick at. She spent a lot of time and energy maintaining such friendships, and I couldn't help but respect and admire that.

When I walked her to the door, Bronwyn gave me one last lavender-scented hug. "Wendy's upset. The news about Tarra, well, it's shocking. And none of us is without damage, Lily. Remember that."

After Bronwyn left, I started to clean the kitchen, but the music of the wind chimes coaxed me onto my terrace. I wandered out to stand amid the planters and pots that made up my urban witch's garden.

It was cool, veering clear round to cold, the way almost all San Francisco nights were, even in summer. The marine layer surged in off the ocean in most afternoons, covering the whole of the city with a thick mantle of fog and cooling off even the hottest summer's day — though no matter what, San Francisco's version of "hot" never came near that of steamy, sticky, so-hot-the-ice-cream-melted-before-you-started-licking West Texas.

The weather around here was crazy pleasant, but seemed somehow . . . dreamlike, even insincere. On my harshest, homesick days, such perfect weather, day in, day out, made me jittery. Seemed like maybe the weather should be better matched to the thorny realities of life.

Dang. I was in such a foul mood I should take care lest I brown the leaves just by standing near them.

I took a deep breath and let myself be soothed by my lush surrounds. The very first time I saw this terrace I knew how it would be. Though I've never had the gift of sight, I could envision it in my mind's eye as clear as though it already existed: abundant and green, overgrown with plants and vines and flowers. Though my grandmother had insisted a true witch's garden be grown directly in the earth, I brought in soil from the surrounding area, mixed it with my homemade compost, and compensated with frequent fertility spells and careful care of the plants.

Idly, I picked off a few dead sprigs from my bushes of lavender and mugwort. Then I noticed the rosemary was looking rather ragged, and there were weeds in the planters holding espaliered apple, pear, and pomegranate trees.

Before I knew it I had donned my gardening gloves and apron and was digging in the soft light of the gibbous moon.

The plants must be cared for, I remembered Graciela telling me, *and they will care for you in return. Tu las cuidas, y te van a cuidar a ti.* Sometimes I forgot that. It had been too long since I'd spent quality time with my photosynthesizing friends.

Graciela was a much better gardener than I, but almost all witches have a green thumb. It was the only part of "green-skinned witches" the legends got right.

"Watcha doin'?" Oscar appeared suddenly, hanging upside down from a small overhang that protected the French doors from the rain.

I jumped. I still hadn't gotten used to the sudden sight of a gargoyle-like face right in front of mine—especially when he smiled, which looked a lot like a grimace. The impression intensified when seeing him upside down.

"Gardening," I replied.

"It's late."

"And we're early to bed these days? I thought you were a night owl, like me."

He jumped down and crouched on the fresh patch of earth I had just dug up.

"Yeah, I'm a night owl. But . . . that works more for somethin' fun, like dancing or movies. Wanna watch a zombie movie?"

"No. You like dancing?"

He waved an oversized hand in my direction, shook his head, and cackled, as though I had said something hilarious. "Nah, not *human* dancing."

Whatever that meant.

The fruit trees now weed free, I moved on to pruning the rosemary. Oscar followed me.

"Master Aidan doesn't keep plants."

"And he's the poorer for it," I said, and meant it. It had never occurred to me to wonder where Aidan procured the herbs and powders for his spells. I knew he worked less with botanicals than I, but surely he needed a trusted source?

"What *are* all these plants?"

"This one's enchanter's nightshade," I said as I watered its pot thoroughly. "It likes it wet and swampy."

"Cool name . . . It's poisonous?"

"No, it's not deadly. It sounds like it should be, doesn't it? This one is belladonna, a pretty name for *deadly* nightshade—which is very poisonous. And here's rue, also called herb of grace. It was considered sacred to Diana, Aralia, and Mars. Used properly, rue can break the power of the evil eye."

As soon as I said it, I wondered whether little Luna might be helped by a cure for *mal ojo*. My grandmother treated the malady among the town children from time to time. *Mal ojo* can be caused inadvertently by someone with "strong eyes," whose admiration for a child can "heat up" the child's blood, resulting in colicky symptoms such as fever, inconsolable crying, aches and pains and a gassy stomach. Luna was so beautiful, *mal ojo* would make sense. There was a simple, straightforward diagnostic test I could try, involving an egg in a jar of water. I made a mental note to see whether Duke would let me perform it on Luna tomorrow.

"And this is one you might like: It's called witch's dust." It was a kind of club moss. "Its oily yellow spores explode when ignited, casting a miniature fireworks. Sometimes stage magicians—or witches for hire—use it for effect."

"Cool! Can we try some?"

"Some other time."

Weeds disposed of, plants trimmed and pruned, the greens put into my composter, I proceeded to feed the plants not only with the typical compost for the soil, but with sips of alcohol, sprinklings of powders, and dabs of enchanted oils, as I did my medicine bag.

I whispered to them of my hopes, my dreams, my fears.

Finally, feeling centered and confident, I turned my attention to my deadly, poisonous Hyoscyamus niger.

Otherwise known as henbane, or devil's eye.

Chapter 13

Henbane is a medicinal plant, but like most medicines, a tiny amount might help, while too much can hurt or kill. The "bane" refers to an Old English word for death. Apparently the plant did a real number on poultry.

I studied the pale tube-shaped flowers. By themselves, a few of these in a corsage could not have made Miriam so ill. But if they were enchanted, or their intent mixed with the curse indicated by the needles I had seen ... that would be a different story.

"Henbane was Circe's plant," I said absently to Oscar. "She enchanted it and used a tiny bit in wine to change Ulysses and his men into swine."

"Heh. I like that one," Oscar said.

"Yes, I thought you might," I said with a smile, stripping off my gloves and hanging my gardening apron by my little potting table. Wiping my hands, I held the door for Oscar, and we went inside.

I pulled a thick *Witch's Guide to Poisons* off a bookshelf crowded with sourcebooks and the classic novels I was plowing through, one by one, according to the reading list Maya had given me.

Setting the book on the kitchen table, I brewed myself a cup of peppermint tea, sweetened it with clover honey, and started reading about henbane.

Circe's tale wasn't the only one associated with the powerful plant. According to legend, the dead are crowned with henbane in hell. Its poison was poured in the ghost's ear in Shakespeare's *Macbeth*. Henbane was also used in Germany in medieval times—in minute amounts, I would wager—to enhance the inebriating qualities of beer. "Bilsen" is German for henbane, as in Pilsen. The ancient Greeks believed that people who ingested it became prophetic, and the priestesses of the Oracle of Delphi are said to have inhaled the smoke from smoldering henbane.

According to the book, the active ingredient in henbane, scopolamine, is used in modern medicines to cure motion sickness and a long list of other complaints. I read: *Scopolamine is a tropane alkaloid of the same group as those in jimsonweed and belladonna.* Symptoms of overexposure include dry mouth, dry skin, fever, blurred vision, dilated pupils, rapid heartbeat, excitement, dizziness, delirium, confusion, headache . . . and death.

I put the book down, feeling at a loss. Yes, henbane can be deadly and, yes, someone used it deliberately to harm Miriam. But nothing in this book was going to tell me the important parts of the mystery: who and why.

I brought my Book of Shadows off the shelf and flipped through recipes that called for henbane. There were quite a few. But the one that caught my eye was called "The Curse of Briar Rose." In it, henbane was combined with ointments and an evil charm to create memory loss and confusion; but if it wasn't carefully calibrated, it could lead to stupor and coma, or even death. It was a complex ritual, requiring sacrifice and a good deal of power.

Witch's curses weren't simply a matter of the right ingredients or combination of words; instead, they required the focus and conduits that some of us were born with and were then trained to control, while others strived to achieve them through study and practice.

All of which led me to believe I was either looking for a natural-born amateur witch, or a highly trained, experienced practitioner.

I wondered whether Aidan had found out what happened to Miriam. He was so much better connected than I, familiar with the local magical community—could he have discovered who cast the spell? The night of the ball he had promised me he would look into it. But, then, I had promised to stay out of it, and I guess I hadn't quite kept that pledge, either. Still, I wanted to talk with him.

With a jolt, I realized I had forgotten one very important task out in the garden.

Once again I donned my apron and gloves. Kneeling and digging with care, I unearthed a mud-encrusted cigar box from beneath the potted lemon tree.

Some time ago I had carved, bathed, and buried a section of mandrake root. Once the final steps were complete, it would be a mandragora, a kind of house elf. I didn't understand why Aidan wanted one so badly—he never seemed to be in need of a companion beyond his cat. But I had promised to make one for him in exchange for his help in another supernatural matter, what seemed like years ago.

I brought the nascent mandragora into the kitchen, unwrapped him, and set him on a clean cookie sheet I reserved exclusively for spells. Then I warmed him in the oven, surrounded by sprigs of lemon verbena.

"I don't like him," Oscar growled as he followed me around.

"No surprise there."

"I keep tellin' ya, you don't need more than one familiar. *I'm* your familiar. The one and only Oscar."

"I know that, little guy." I smiled and squeezed his scaly shoulder. "This is for Aidan, remember? I promised it to him some time ago. If you get in touch with him and let him know his mandragora is ready, this little fellow won't be with us long."

Once he was thoroughly warmed, I removed him from the oven, tucked the newborn little imp into his cigar box bed wrapped in black silk, and went to sleep secure in the knowledge that Aidan would be calling soon.

The next morning, I hung around Aunt Cora's Closet, taking Maya up on her offer to run to Coffee to the People. I had shared leftover jambalaya with Conrad and Oscar for breakfast and made a smoothie for Conrad. I wasn't ready to see Wendy yet, had no idea what to say to her.

She might have overreacted last night, but at core she was right: I had misled the Unspoken coven. I had done the wrong thing.

After Maya returned with our hot drinks, Bronwyn asked me: "Do you still want to go over to the hospital this morning?"

"Oh yes, of course," I said, embarrassed I had forgotten. I prided myself on an excellent memory, but I was running around so much lately I really should get myself an agenda. An old-fashioned one, made of paper. Somehow I couldn't imagine me and a smartphone getting along.

"Maya, can you handle the place on your own? We shouldn't be gone long."

"I think I can manage the madding crowds," she said, as we looked out onto a shop floor empty save for one woman quietly flipping through a collection of embroidered housecoats. "But don't forget my mom's coming in a little while to do the patternmaking deal."

Maya's mother, Lucille, was a gifted seamstress who did repairs and alterations on the clothes that came in to Aunt Cora's Closet. What she could accomplish with a needle and thread bordered on the miraculous. Not long ago, on a whim, Lucille used some leftover fabric to up-size a simple sheath to a size twelve, then added antique lace she had salvaged from a ruined garment. Before we could even hang it on the display rack, a customer pounced on it. Since then, Lucille had started deconstructing vintage garments that were falling apart, making patterns from them, and sizing them up.

Today she was coming over to demonstrate her technique and to teach patternmaking. I had put up a few flyers inviting customers to come and learn. There was so much interest we had to limit the number of RSVPs to twenty-five.

"I haven't forgotten—I'm looking forward to it. I even made extra lemon bars to offer to folks." Unless Oscar had scarfed them all down by now; I should probably check on that. "We'll be back in time."

We found Duke much as we had last time, holding a fussy Luna to his chest and looking down at his comatose daughter with haunted, sad eyes.

"Look, I'm sorry I sort of . . . At first I think I was sort of unfriendly when you mentioned you might be . . . that you believed in otherworldly things. I've never really been exposed to that kind of thing, except when Miriam told me she was studying witchcraft. Kind of freaked me out, to tell you the truth. But . . ." He trailed off with a shrug as he gazed at Miriam, still as death. Luna pushed at his chest and started to cry. "I'm willing to try anything at this point. It's been only a couple of days, but the doctors are at a total loss. They've tried everything they can think of. . . . Nothing has helped. I'll try anything. I can pay you."

"That's not necessary, Duke," I said. "I don't work that way. If I can help, I will."

I laid another newly charged talisman on her bedside and said a quick protective chant.

Bronwyn took Luna from Duke. The child's cries ratcheted down to a whimper as Bronwyn jostled her, doing that little bouncy sway people tended to do when they held babies.

The last time I was at San Francisco Medical Center was when Sandra Schmidt was laid low by a curse. And now I was here to see Miriam, also suffering from a hex.

How did Sandra know Greta, the owner of Vintage Chic? I wondered. My rival shopkeeper's reaction to Sandra seemed odd, but then everything about Greta seemed strange. Could she somehow be connected to all of this? I blew out a frustrated breath. At this point it seemed I was grasping at straws.

"Miriam's mother and I waited so long for a child, but she was never able to carry to term. We finally adopted a beautiful little girl, called her Miriam Rose. We couldn't believe she'd be so lovely, so sweet. Such a good child."

Luna started to cry again, pushing away from Bronwyn.

"You want to give it a go?" she asked me.

"Um . . . sure."

Luna whimpered and reached out for me, so I took her in my arms. I breathed in her fresh baby scent. She was beautiful, her blond curly hair and blue eyes on a delicate face made her look like a Renaissance-era cherub.

I looked down at her and she scowled up at me, but as long as she wasn't crying we all breathed a sigh of relief. Amazing how a baby's cry could jangle the calmest nerves.

Luna had several Band-Aids on her chubby legs and arms, and I noticed a small bandage on the tip of Miriam's finger as well. "What's with all the Band-Aids?"

"Luna's are from the blood tests at the doctor's office. Poor kid. And Miriam . . . It was just a splinter of some kind. I saw it when I was holding her hand—it looked a little inflamed, so I asked the nurse to dress it."

"Duke, does 'pill mob' mean anything to you?"

He shook his head.

"Did Miriam speak any other languages?"

"A little Spanish. Why?"

"I thought I heard her speaking another language, something not English or Spanish."

He shook his head. Duke stood with hands on hips, a picture of exhaustion and frustration. His eyes were rimmed in red, his gray hair was tousled, his chambray shirt buttoned wrong.

"What about the things you brought to Summit Medical Center, when Miriam was there?" I asked. "There was a comb and some homemade items?"

"I took them home—they're at her apartment. I've been staying there, since the baby knows it as home and all her stuff is there."

"Duke, I know this is going to sound strange," I said, placing a hand on his arm. "But I really think I might be able to help if I could take a look at her things. Do you think we could go to Miriam's place? Would you allow me to look around, see if I can find anything?"

He looked at me, assessing, as though deciding whether he could believe me. I concentrated on sending out comforting vibrations.

"You said you were willing to try anything," I said. "I can help. I know I can. But you'll have to trust me."

After another moment, he gave a curt nod.

Miriam's apartment was on a quiet street in Noe Valley. She and Luna lived in the attic apartment of a graceful old Victorian that had been painted in shades of purple, lilac, and gold.

Duke led us up two steep flights of stairs.

"Well, at least she gets her cardio every day," Bronwyn said as we arrived, winded, at Miriam's door.

The apartment was charming, sunny, and bright. The ceiling followed the crooked lines of the roof; there were window seats, flourishing potted plants, and a small fireplace. The walls were painted a soft pinky-white, and multicolored cushions adorned an old green velour sofa. Brightly colored paintings, goddess symbols, and pentacles adorned the walls.

"Since the baby was born, I offered to have her move back in with me, but Miriam's always been independent. We—" Duke cut himself off, shaking his head as he placed Luna on a blanket on the floor of the small living room. Upon being set down, the baby immediately started to wail. "I'm sorry to say that Miriam and I didn't always see eye to eye. Her mother used to say we were too alike; that's why we fought."

"Being a parent is never easy," said Bronwyn. "But what counts is that you love her, and you're there for her when she needs you."

"I hope it's not too personal," I began, "but where is Luna's father? Is he part of her life?"

Luna cried louder, sounding heartbroken. Duke seemed determined to ignore it.

"He's gone. He was bad news, took off before the baby was born. Miriam didn't bother going after him. . . .

Instead, she made a commitment to turn her life around. Started her own business, got serious. And then she met Jonathan, and he seemed like a good guy. He adored Luna. But . . ." He shrugged. "I dunno. I butted in, made things worse, I think."

"What did Miriam do for a living?" I asked, spying a paper-strewn desk with a computer set up with two screens.

"She had her own graphic design business, was doing pretty good. Her teenage years were tough, but lately she'd really pulled herself together. Her mom passed when she was a sophomore, and I wasn't always the best father—I might have been too strict. Maybe she rebelled."

Giving in to the inevitable, I picked up Luna. She tucked her head under my chin, snuggling in and quieting down, save for a long, shaky sigh and a hiccup.

"She looks so much like Miriam did at that age," said Duke, eyes on the baby. "The pediatrician couldn't find a thing. They ran so many tests, took so many blood samples. . . . Poor kid's like a pincushion. But, then, they couldn't find anything with Miriam either, and look what happened. . . ."

I wondered whether Grandpa Duke here, pragmatic man that he was, would allow me to perform my less than scientific diagnostic tests on the child.

But for now I wanted to look around the apartment to be sure there wasn't something obvious tucked somewhere . . . something like a curse.

"Would you mind if I looked around?" I asked him.

"Be my guest. Oh, could I offer you anything? I don't have much here, but juice maybe? Tea?"

"Tea would be lovely," Bronwyn said. "But let me get it. You sit right down and keep me company." Winking at me, she started opening cupboards to see what was available.

The apartment was full of signs of pagan worship: pentagrams, lots of crystals, bundles of herbs hung upside down to dry. Rosemary, lavender. Simple stuff, nothing dangerous.

One-handed, with Luna on my hip, I looked over the food in the refrigerator: butter, jam, leftover mac and cheese, expired milk, and organic yogurt. Nothing felt strange, no odd vibrations. Then I examined the cupboards—nothing there struck me as peculiar either.

"Have you thrown out any food items since Miriam's collapse?"

"Nothing," Duke said with a shake of his head. "I was thinking I should go through the fridge before garbage day, but hadn't gotten to it yet."

I proceeded down a short hall.

The apartment had only one bedroom, but the baby's crib was set up in an alcove off the bedroom. A mobile hung from the ceiling, and the walls had been decorated with cutout clouds and angels. I imagined Miriam cutting those out, applying them to the wall, humming a lullaby while she did so.

I placed my free hand on Miriam's neatly made bed and felt the vibrations I had sensed from her: vacant, scattered.

I spotted the plastic bag from the hospital. Though the dress had been removed and hung up, her small purse remained. I pulled out her cell phone.

And stared at it. Me and technology . . . we're not exactly a match. If only little Luna here were a year or two older, she could probably show me how it's done. I tucked it in my pocket—to get any clues from it, I was going to have to bring in a tech expert, like someone who owned a cell phone.

That reminded me. . . . I didn't have time to run back

over to Oakland. And I wanted to hear what Jonathan Penn had to say about the corsage.

I sat on Miriam's bed and used the phone on the nightstand to call MJ's Games.

"Nah, man, I don't know the first thing about flowers, or even which colors look good together," said Jonathan. There was a lot of noise in the background, several young male voices. "Jonquil suggested I send something to make amends, so I just asked Anise to put something pretty together."

"You didn't text her with a special request?"

"No. I lost my phone that day."

"You didn't ask for Hyoscyamus?"

"Dude, what? I don't even know what that is. I don't know anything about flowers."

"Could someone have stolen your phone and used it?"

"I guess . . ." I heard him saying something about the latest X-Men comic book to someone in the shop.

"Jonathan? When's the last time you remember seeing your phone?"

"What? Oh, at drumming circle the night before. I really gotta go. The movies just got out and we're swamped here."

I hung up and sat for a moment, thinking. Luna frowned up at me, and I smiled at her.

"Gah!" she said, patting me on the face.

I laughed and kissed her nose. She tucked her head back under my chin. I haven't been around babies much; they always made me nervous, with their vulnerability and need. But holding this child . . . it was easy to see how people fell in love with infants.

There were several framed pictures on the bedside: a few of Luna, one of Miriam with the newborn baby and her dad. And a cute one of Miriam and Jonathan, arm in arm, at a party.

She had broken up with him, but she kept this picture out? Or . . . Jonathan said she broke up with him through a text message. He had just denied sending a text message to Anise, which made me realize just how easy it would be to impersonate someone by using their phone. Could someone have pretended to be Miriam, sending the message to Jonathan in order to break up the happy couple? It was possible, though I had no idea why someone would do that.

What else? Clothes.

My arm started to ache, so I shifted Luna to the other hip and crossed over to the closet.

The lovely gown Miriam had worn to the ball was hanging on the outside of the door. Sea-foam green so suited to her honey-colored hair. A drop-waist, gauzy sheer dress worn over a simple satin sheath. Long strands of beaded fringe along the bottom. I brought the cloth up to touch my cheek, closed my eyes, and concentrated.

It would be better to take the dress home with me, if Duke would allow it. Offhand, it didn't seem to have any strong vibrations that could tell me anything, only what I'd sensed from Miriam when I saw her at the ball and what I'd felt on the bed: scattered, vague, confused.

I entered the small walk-in closet and hugged the hanging clothes with my one unoccupied arm. Some of them shared the same disturbing sensation. I noticed several wool skirts and winter clothes, which must not have been worn for a while. These had very different vibrations: upbeat, cheerful, and wide open. I blew out another breath of frustration.

Luna socked me in the jaw.

"Hey!" I said, but when I looked down I saw a fleeting

smile before the scowl returned to her face and she tucked her head back against my chest.

"No hitting," I said, though I couldn't work up much outrage. She was such a precious little thing. I patted her back and rocked a little, kissing the top of her head. "You need attention, sugar?"

The simple, natural act put me in mind of the young woman I had seen on the street in North Beach the other night, leaning down to kiss her baby on the head. I hurried to the bathroom. There on a small white-painted side table was a wooden box full of makeup. I snatched up several lipsticks, but felt nothing untoward.

But then I saw it: a jar decorated with a handwritten sticker: *Special Salve . . . for Miriam.*

I had first seen this pot at the hospital, with the other things Duke had brought from home for Miriam.

Reaching out with care, I picked it up. I felt it then, as sure as I knew my own name. It hummed with malice, with mal intent.

Slowly I unscrewed the top and brought it up to my nose: The scent was rose geranium. I touched it. It was hard and waxy, with a sheen of oil. Like most homemade salves without the preservatives and blenders used in the production of mass-produced lotions.

Olive oil. Beeswax. Essential oil for scent. And something more.

I closed my eyes and concentrated. I imagined Miriam rubbing a little of this over chapped lips and later leaning down and kissing her baby. This wasn't the sort of thing that would take you out by simple onetime exposure, but over time her energy would be drained, sapped. And then if one were to add a cursed corsage to the mix . . .

The scent of bread toasting brought me back to the moment. I tucked the pot of salve into my pocket and carried Luna out to the kitchen, where Bronwyn and Duke were sitting at the table, eating toast and jam and drinking tea. It never ceased to amaze me how Bronwyn transformed everyplace she went into a home.

"Duke, do you have any idea where Miriam got this salve?" I asked as I showed him the little jar.

He shrugged and shook his head. "I just found it out on her counter. I remember her using it for her lips, so when the hospital folks suggested I bring in a few of her things from home, I grabbed it. Why?"

"Do you mind if I take it, try to figure out what's in it?"

"Knock yourself out."

"Plus, I found her cell phone and—"

He threw up his hands. "Listen, as long as you think you can help, I don't care what you take."

"How about you let us take care of Luna for the day? Give you a break," Bronwyn suggested, handing the baby a tiny piece of toast. Little Luna gummed it happily.

"I really couldn't impose . . ." Duke said.

"How about this?" I suggested. "Why don't we all go back to my shop? You can bring your reading and relax there for a bit, while we take turns amusing the baby. Also, if you agree, I'd like to try a few healing techniques on her."

"You know what's wrong with her?"

"Not yet," I said. "But there are a few things I could try."

"I don't want the poor little thing to get stuck with any more needles."

"I promise, Luna won't need any more Band-Aids."

Chapter 14

By the time we arrived at Aunt Cora's Closet, two dozen women were milling about and chatting, waiting for Lucille's patternmaking class to begin.

One of them was Susan Rogers, who I hadn't seen since the Art Deco Ball. We said hello and she *ooh*ed and *aah*ed over the baby, then asked me what Aidan had said about ditching me at the dance.

"I haven't seen him since, to tell you the truth."

"Really?" She looked crestfallen. "Oh well, *fiddle dee dee*, as they say. Lots of fish in the sea, right?"

I smiled and nodded, not in the mood to ponder Aidan or his mysterious ways when I could focus on happier things.

I greeted a few women I knew from Bronwyn's coven, noting that Wendy's absence was rather conspicuous—she had RSVP'd the other day and had seemed excited about coming. There were several other women I recognized as regular customers at the shop and a few familiar faces from the neighborhood.

Duke took a seat in the big upholstered chair near the dressing room, silent but benign, observing but unobtrusive. He was one of those men who seemed able to let women gather without interfering or imposing.

"Looks like your mom's got a full house," I said to Maya, who remained behind the register and looked out at the crowd with a dubious expression.

"I had no idea it would be so popular," she replied. "I just hope we don't become a sewing shop. Not sure I can deal. I grew up with that."

Maya's mother, Lucille, joined us, laughing. "Maya has never liked sewing, no matter how much I tried. All she wanted to do was read and paint, but how could I fault her there? She's like her father, smart as a whip and so talented."

It was hard to tell, but I thought I saw Maya blushing.

Luna fussed and pushed away from me.

"Poor little love's probably colicky. Give her here. I can fix that." Lucille held out her arms. An ample, well-padded woman, Lucille was almost preternaturally calm and commanding, while being warm and welcoming. She made *me* want to curl up next to her. I handed over the baby, relieved to give my arm—and my back—a rest.

As soon as I handed Luna over, she started to wail. Lucille bounced and cooed at her. Luna screamed.

One of the young Wiccan women offered to take the baby. She had no better luck. Before long just about every woman in the shop had joined us.

"She must be teething," said one. "Give her a green onion to bite down on."

"My mama always held crying babies upside down, to shock them out of their mood."

"Maybe a healing ritual?" suggested another.

Luna's wails reached ear-piercing proportions. She pushed away from the sweet grandmotherly woman holding her, stretching toward me.

I opened my arms; she practically jumped into them.

And calmed, hiccupping and whining.

Oscar snorted and butted my legs. But the circle of women smiled in relief and admiration.

"You're a natural," one woman commented.

"Some women just have a way with babies," Lucille added. "My mother was like that."

"I really don't," I said. Still, I couldn't help but feel flattered. "But Luna seems to like me, for some reason. I may need an arm transplant soon."

"Wait. I've got this thing that Miriam used," Duke said, bringing a baby sling out of his bag.

"That's a great idea," I said. "First, though, I'd like to take her in the back and whip up something for her. It's not harmful at all."

Duke nodded his assent. "As I said, I'll try anything at this point."

Oscar glared at me, then harrumphed off to sulk on his pillow. If there's one thing I had learned about my familiar, it's that he doesn't like to share.

If *mal ojo* was the cause of whatever ailed young Luna, there was no need to consult my Book of Shadows. I knew what to do.

I asked Bronwyn to mix fresh ginger for upset tummy, chamomile for nerves, and a small amount of peppermint for heartburn into a tea sweetened with a spoonful of cane sugar. Meanwhile, Maya ran upstairs to my apartment for an egg and a potato as well as the lemon bars I had baked for the crowd, while I massaged Luna's back with warm almond oil.

When Maya returned, I laid the baby down on the floor on a soft blanket. I sliced the potato and held two pieces to her temples. Ignoring her renewed wailing, I swept the egg over her in the shape of a pentacle: top of head to ball of right foot, to the left hand, then the right, back down to other foot. I turned her over, facedown, and repeated the pattern. I cracked the egg and dropped it into a jar of water, then placed a pentacle made of broom straw on the top.

Then I spooned a little of the sweetened tea into her eager little mouth.

Finally, I chose a special amulet called an *azabache* from my display counter. It was a carved seed that looks like a deer's eye, or *ojo de venado*. I tucked it into the top of her diaper.

Luna had started fussing again. I brought her over to Duke, and he gave her a bottle. Within five minutes she was asleep.

"She hasn't gone to sleep that easily in ... weeks," said Duke, amazed.

"Let's put her down for a nap."

Duke tucked her into the portable crib we had set up in the back room. I placed the jar of water with the egg underneath the crib.

"What is it supposed to do?" asked Duke.

"After her nap it will tell us whether Luna is suffering from *mal ojo*. And if she is, I might need to sweep her a few more times with an egg, or with a sprig of rue, but I should be able to fix it."

Duke gave me an incredulous look. "You're saying you can fix what ails her by waving an egg over her?"

When he put it that way, it did seem rather dubious. But I had grown up witnessing the cure. It often worked.

"I know it seems strange. But as you said earlier, what could it hurt?"

Duke inclined his head and blew out a resigned breath. "I guess."

In the meantime, Lucille had called the women together and started to explain the process of patternmaking.

"Most dresses are made up of the same basic parts,"

Lucille said as she laid out a deconstructed dress, piece by piece. Earlier in the day, Conrad had helped place plywood over the glass counter, with a sawhorse supporting the other end. So we had one big surface plus three card tables for folks to work at.

"The magic is how the pieces are shaped and contoured, following the lines of the bust and hip, our bones. Sizing up means we take the shape and expand it. But before we start, let's talk supplies." She held up a piece of shaped plastic. "My French curve set. French curves mimic the curves of the body: armholes, necklines, hips. They arc on one end, then straighten out. Mine have ruler markings, very handy.

"Also necessary is a regular straight ruler. I like the clear acrylic kind, so you can see what's underneath. A protractor helps to transfer patterns and for marking the exact angles when putting in darts and shoulders and sleeves when the seam angles need to match."

I sometimes mistook Lucille's normally quiet demeanor for shyness. Now, in front of this large group of women, I saw how wrong I was. Lucille must belong to that "don't speak unless you've got something important to say" group. Now she had something to say, and she addressed the group with a natural ease.

"Tape measure, of course. Tailor's chalk to mark fabrics. Pen for marking the pattern pieces." She held up each item as she spoke of it. "Tracing wheel for making copies of garments and pattern pieces. Doubling seam allowances for quadrupling widths and shortening hems ... seam gauge and L square. And a calculator because there's so much math in dressmaking!"

The women nodded and murmured, some taking notes.

"See, Lily?" said Bronwyn. "This is a real-world example of using math, even algebra."

"Mmm," I said.

"And, of course, we'll need general sewing supplies: scissors, pins, cutting mat, and the like. Now, let's get down to work."

Lucille began by deconstructing several dresses that were beyond repair, though their original designs were lovely. She handed them to Susan and several other women to meticulously pick out the stitches, thread by thread, doing their best not to leave ragged edges. Though the dresses weren't worth anything, they were perfect to be used as masters.

"Here's another," said Maya, holding up a drop-waist "flapper" dress. Its lace had ripped away in spots, and the silk hung limp and "shattered," or shredded. There was no way to repair it, but it served as wonderful inspiration for a reproduction.

"I thought we could tear this one up, too," Susan said. "It's from my first marriage." Yards of white silk had been encrusted with seed pearls and hand-tatted lace, but it had yellowed significantly. "It kills me—I *paid* to have this dress 'preserved,' and now look at it."

At Aunt Cora's Closet we saw a lot of garments that had been improperly preserved. Plastic doesn't allow the cloth to breathe; therefore it causes yellowing and even encourages mold growth. The clothes would have done better simply left hanging in the closet. Or better yet, in a high-quality garment bag that provides protection from dust and insects, while allowing oxygen exchange.

Unwrapping the wedding dress, I thought back on when I first met Susan, outfitting her niece's wedding entourage. Max Carmichael and I still had a tentative date to attend her niece's vintage-style wedding together, though for all I'd heard from him lately I doubted he even remembered. Or if he did, he was probably trying to think of a way to get out of it. I realized I should call and let him off the hook. He was a wonderful man, but I was more certain with every passing day that Max was far too normal for the likes of me.

"This is fascinating, Lucille," said Susan as Lucille prepared to start making the actual patterns. "Thank you for letting us watch! Funny how I've worked with clothes and fashion my entire life and never knew the basic construction."

"You've never sewn?"

"Good heavens, no! And have no intention of starting. I like people to make my clothes for me." She smiled. "But it's still fascinating to learn about the inner workings of such things."

Lucille pulled out crinkly thin brown paper, almost like stiff tissue. This she laid upon the pieces and showed the women how to sketch the lines of the pieces of material, marking indents and darts with squiggles and triangles—a shorthand language of its own.

"We can use this bodice pattern for several kinds of dresses," said Lucille, "pairing it with different styles of skirt."

They began with a pattern for an early-1960s sundress. In much of coastal California, the sundresses were wonderful for almost every day, as they were so well paired with simple bright-colored cardigans for a coordinated outfit. I wore them all the time. They tended to look good on just about every body type, especially the plumper, full-breasted woman who was often difficult to dress in vintage clothing.

I looked over at Maya, who was studiously avoiding the sewing lessons.

"Guess I'd better get going on that Web site," she said, when she saw me looking her way. Maya was setting up a Web site for Aunt Cora's Closet to handle eventual Internet orders. We were starting small, but had decided to expand in response to demand.

"In all your spare time," I teased. In addition to work-ing part-time at Aunt Cora's Closet, Maya was attending the San Francisco School of Fine Arts and was conduct-ing an ongoing oral history project with elders in the community. She was young, but even the youth ran out of energy eventually. "Hey, speaking of high tech, could you help me with something?"

I pulled out Miriam's cell phone and explained to Maya what I needed.

"I swear, Lily, one of these days we're going to have to introduce you to the twenty-first century." She shook her head as she bent over the phone, both thumbs flying, and came up with Miriam's history of text messages, sent and received, in about four seconds flat.

"Thanks," I said with a smile, taking the phone. I scrolled through the messages and found Miriam's note to Jonathan saying it was over between them. I didn't blame him for being upset—I couldn't imagine caring for someone, then breaking up via this sort of short, imper-sonal messaging.

But then . . . several days previous to that message, there were several texts between Tarra and Miriam discussing none other than Wolfgang. In one, Tarra wrote: *OMG. M soooo in luv w Wolf. Will c him 2nite, cant w8!*

The bell tinkled over the front door, rousing me from my thoughts. Almost as though I had conjured them, two Unspoken coven sisters, Jonquil and Anise, passed through the doorway. Conrad had opened the door for them and was waving them in.

"Thank you, Conrad," said Jonquil. "So nice to meet you!"

Jonquil still had that excited, happy look, as though she was thrilled with a secret that she was about to im-part; she carried a large, flat package under one arm. Anise trailed behind her, seeming sullen and more interested in whatever she was texting on her phone than in her surroundings.

"Lily!" Jonquil called as she spotted me. "This is incredible! You said you owned a clothing store, but I never dreamed it would be this great. Check this out!"

"Hi," I said. I didn't know what to say. . . . Should I apologize for my actions the other night? But Jonquil didn't seem to sense any awkwardness. She gave me a warm smile and held out the package.

"You left so suddenly the other evening, you forgot your beautiful platter. I'm afraid the lemon bars went rather quickly. I didn't have a chance to make anything, so I'm bringing it back empty. I know it's crass—my foster mother used to tell me: Never bring back an empty dish. But here I am."

"Oh no, please don't worry about that. It was kind of you to bring it back. I . . . With regards to the other night, I—"

Jonquil waved away my concern. "Please don't worry about it. It was kind of a strange night, all the way around. I think we're all, well, grieving for Tarra. And sensitive about our privacy, of course."

"Of course," I replied. "Come in, please. I'd like you and Anise to meet my friends and colleagues: Lucille Jackson, her daughter, Maya, and you may remember Bronwyn?"

As they said their hellos, I studied Anise. Carlos hadn't found anything consistent with poisoning in the air at the Design Center, nothing that could explain her flat affect, and the other coven sisters seemed fine. Jonquil certainly didn't appear to be impaired.

"Can we look around?" Jonquil asked. "This place is amazing."

"Please do. Make yourselves at home."

Luna started crying in the back room. Duke went to

get her and brought her back into the front of the shop, but when Luna kept crying I offered to hold her again.

Jonquil held an ecru lace slip up to her body, assessing herself in the three-way mirror. "Wow, I bet you love getting dressed every day."

"I do. I have my own personal closet here . . . everything that fits, that is."

Luna kicked her legs and frowned.

Anise frowned back. "Why's she so grumpy?"

"She's been a little out of sorts," I said. If the baby did, indeed, have *mal ojo* she would need another sweep with the egg, called a *limpieza*. Clearly, she was still unhappy.

"Is that . . . Miriam's baby?" Jonquil asked.

"Yes, it's Luna." The baby turned her face into my chest.

"She's sick?" Jonquil's eyes widened with concern.

"I think so." Anise took a step back. "Nothing contagious, just a baby malady, probably. Or . . . it could be related to what's ailing her mother."

"Really? You think it could be the same thing Miriam's suffering from?" Jonquil asked, reaching out and smoothing Luna's golden curls. "I might have some herbs that could help her—I could ask Calypso about it."

"I'd love to talk to the famous Calypso myself, ask her a few questions. Could I get her contact information from you?"

"Oh, I don't think . . ." Jonquil trailed off and glanced at Anise. "She's pretty private."

"She's awesome," said Anise, not looking up from her phone. She had graduated from texting and was now placing a phone call.

Moments later a beeping sound came from Jonquil's bag. "Oh, sorry. That's my cell phone. I hate that. Anise, you should step outside to make your call. It's rude to

use phones in a place of business. Remember what Calypso said?"

"You're one to talk. You've got, like, an iPhone *plus* a
cell phone," said Anise.

"This isn't a competition," replied Jonquil in a patient
voice. She rolled her eye slightly and smiled in my direction. "It's a matter of basic politeness."

I wondered whether, even had I been a bit younger, I
would ever have become so smitten with phones or
other such devices. Their vibrations jangled my energy,
and by and large they broke when I used them. I didn't
trust them.

"He's still not answering anyway," said Anise.

"Okay, I simply *have* to try this on," said Jonquil suddenly, holding up a flouncy wedding dress.

"Of course," I said. I passed Luna off to her grandfather and gestured for Jonquil to follow me. "Right back
here."

I led the way to the large communal dressing room
and stayed with her to help button up the gown, which
had a long row of cloth-covered buttons and a diamond-
cut peekaboo panel cut out in back. Her auburn hair fell
down in long strands that contrasted with the soft ivory
of the gown, managing to look fetching rather than
messy.

"Jonquil, do you know Tarra's boyfriend, Rex, very
well?"

"Sure."

"Does he have a temper?"

"A temper?" She craned her neck to look at me. Her
eyes widened. "What are you thinking, that he had something to do with Tarra passing to the next dimension?"

I hesitated, but then confessed: "I just wondered. A
lot of times, these situations are domestic in nature. Rex

and Tarra were together, but . . . you talking about cell phones reminded me. . . . I found something that seems to indicate maybe Tarra was having an affair."

"An *affair*?"

I nodded.

"With who?"

"That fellow in the drumming group, Wolfgang?"

"No way." She shook her head and looked back in the mirror, swaying this way and that to see the skirt swish.

"Why do you say that?"

"She's not his type."

"Oh. Do you know him well?"

"We're good friends."

"More than friends, maybe?"

"Once. But we had an amicable parting of the ways. . . . He's really a good guy. A little obsessed with himself and his own development, though. I needed someone who could be there for me more, you know? That's why I say he and Tarra wouldn't have worked out. You didn't know her, but she was . . . needy. I mean, she was great, but I think that's why she was good with Rex. He coddled her, treated her like a princess."

"So she and Rex got along well? You wouldn't suspect him?"

"No, he worshipped her."

"Could she have been seeing someone else besides Wolfgang? Is Rex the jealous type?"

"We don't really do that." Our eyes met in the mirror. "Our coven doesn't believe in jealousy and possessiveness, everything that implies."

"Ah." That seemed laudable on many levels. Still, I wondered how realistic it was. Unless you were raised with the concept from childhood, it seemed a tough sell. Besides that, what we *want* to believe doesn't always translate directly to how we act; I was proof positive of that.

"Anyway, you could always ask the guys about it directly," Jonquil said. "They've got drumming circle tomorrow night, starting right at dusk. Up in Sibley Regional Park. Both of 'em'll be there."

"Sibley's in the East Bay?"

She nodded. "It's really beautiful up there, very spiritual. There are labyrinths."

Anise stuck her head into the dressing room, looking up from her cell phone but still punching buttons with her thumbs. "You look like a real bride. Awesome. You planning on getting married anytime soon?"

"Don't be silly," said Jonquil with a smile, looking at her reflection in the mirror. "You'll probably get married before I do. Hey, let's try it on you!"

Anise backed away, shaking her head. "I'm more the jeans type."

"You never know until you try," I said, then left the laughing young women to play dress up while I checked in on the patternmakers, and the results of little Luna's test for *mal ojo*

Chapter 15

I went into the back room, crouched down, and felt under the crib for the jar.

Finally I got down on all fours and looked. It was gone.

Then I noticed that a bunch of newly laundered and ironed dresses had been pulled off their hangers and left in a heap on the floor.

"Oscar!" I yelled. I had never seen a pig walk on tiptoe, but Oscar did so as he came in response to my call, remaining near the velvet curtain.

"What did you do with the jar under the bed?"

He snorted.

"Upstairs, now."

I followed him up. Once at the landing outside my apartment, he transformed.

"What did you do with the jar, Oscar?"

"Nothing."

"Are you suggesting it moved itself?"

He shook his head.

"Then what happened to it?"

"Baby took it."

"Baby Luna took the jar."

He nodded. "While you were talking."

"An eleven-month-old who can't even walk could not have taken the jar, Oscar."

He just gazed at me, bottle glass green eyes shiny and huge.

"Okay. *Why* would the baby have taken the jar?"

"To eat the egg."

"And what happened to the jar? Did she eat that too? And then she made a mess?"

He shrugged.

I blew out an exasperated breath, then sat on the top step. "Listen to me, Oscar. I know you don't like the baby. But we went through this not long ago with Beowulf, the black cat, remember? And then she ended up being one of your best friends."

"This isn't the same."

"I know it's not. This is a human baby. Human babies aren't able to get out of cribs and pull things off the rack."

Oscar picked at his talons.

"You made the mess yourself, didn't you, and now you're trying to blame the baby?"

"I told you! She did it when you were in the shop, distracted! And I couldn't tell you because *she* was here. She said if I told she would *get* me."

"You are treading on my last nerve, here, Oscar. Luna is too young to speak."

"Oh, I forgot to tell you. Aidan says he'll see you now."

"Now?"

"He says you should go over to his office."

I blew out a breath in frustration. I wasn't going to get any further with Oscar. "All right, fine. You stay away from the baby. You understand me?"

I cleaned up the clothes in the back room, fuming. Why would Oscar make up such a tale? But then I thought of him with Beowulf, an abandoned cat we had fostered for a few days. Oscar's behavior had been deplorable at first, his goblin nature coming out in nasty ways, wanting to deny the feline food and comfort.

I could only guess that Oscar came from a goblin-eat-goblin world.

The patternmaking class finally came to an end. We cleaned up the food—Oscar took care of the crumbs on the ground—pushed the racks back where they belonged, and dismantled the temporary plywood worktable.

Duke started packing up Luna's things, saying he had to get over to his boat and take care of a few issues, including filing new paperwork for the city. It sounded like a lot of running around, plus time on the boat . . . maybe not the best activities to attempt with a baby on your hip.

"Why don't you let me keep Luna with me for the afternoon?" I offered, placing my hand on his shoulder. "I know we've only just met, but she seems to like me, oddly enough. I have to run some errands, as well, but nowhere she wouldn't be welcome. I could drop her off later."

He held my gaze. He was still wide open, no guard up. I couldn't force people to do what I wanted, but I could influence them to trust me.

"If you really don't mind," he said.

"It will be my pleasure."

I swept Luna with another egg, just in case, then wrapped up the mandragora, strapped the baby seat into the back of the car, and finally conceded to Oscar's whining and let him come along. I was halfway across town when I realized I was heading toward a Wax Museum in a vintage Mustang convertible with a baby, a pig, and a mandragora in tow.

Land sakes. Was it me, or was I getting weirder all the time?

Luna shrieked.

I glanced in the rearview mirror to see Oscar casting a menacing snarl at the baby. "*Oscar*! Leave the baby alone."

"There's something wrong with it," he said.

"I know that. Poor child's ill. Anyway, you're just jealous."

"What would I be jealous of? It's ugly."

So says the creature covered in scales.

"She's beautiful. And even if she weren't, there's no such thing as an ugly baby. They're all little miracles."

"I don't think it's normal. Maybe it's a"—his voice dropped—"*demon*."

"*Oscar*. Do not intone that word around me, young man. She's a baby, not an evil creature. And anyway, demons don't inhabit babies. They're all about getting things done, and an infant is helpless."

I glanced in the rearview mirror to see a scowling Luna reach out and yank, hard, on Oscar's big ear.

"*Ow*!" Oscar gaped at me, his face a mask of outraged innocence.

Luna laughed, a loud, gleeful cackle that was, I had to admit, a fair imitation of a little demon.

Within moments Luna's laughter ceded, once again, to shrieking. I blew a strand of hair out of my eyes. I hadn't been caring for her very long, but I felt as weary as if I'd run a marathon, as jittery as if I'd drunk ten cups of coffee, my arms shaky as though I'd completed fifty push-ups. I was tired of the incessant whining and crying. Even Bronwyn had finally begged off when it became apparent I was the only one the child wanted, and even with me she squirmed and fretted. Luna had given me the kind of headache that willow's bark tea couldn't cure.

I felt a new appreciation for parents, teachers, and child care workers. Kids are a tough gig.

The streets of Fisherman's Wharf were full of dazed, jaywalking tourists, as usual. I drove around the block several times looking for a parking spot before breaking down and pulling a charm out of my glove box and concentrating on a huge SUV that took up more than its fair share of the street. After a minute, a confused-looking man came out of a nearby seafood restaurant and clicked the button on his key ring, causing the car to chirp and light up. He climbed in and left the spot, and I pulled in.

I tried not to use my magic for capricious ends, but on days like today I felt justified.

I got out, opened the back door, and unbuckled the baby seat.

Oscar shifted into his piggy guise.

"You're not coming, Oscar. I can only deal with one of you at the moment."

He shifted back, looking appalled. "You're taking *it* but not *me*?"

Automatically, I looked around to see if any passersby were witnessing my talking gobgoyle, but as usual he had made sure it was safe before shifting. Not once had I caught him not taking care to hide his real colors around nonmagical folks . . . unless he was saving my life.

"I'm sorry, Oscar. I won't be long. But I can't manage both of you."

"Then leave *it* here."

"I can't leave a baby alone, Oscar. Human babies aren't able to protect themselves."

His eyes narrowed. "How 'bout we leave it in the park? Kids like parks. Or let it go look around Pier 39. If it's still alive when you get back, it'll be, like, whaddaya-callit? Natural selection. I read about it once."

"Oscar, listen to me: Luna's not an 'it.' She's a helpless baby, and we will all pitch in to take care of her, no matter what. You hear me? Besides, it's only temporary. Now, hand me the mandragora."

"You won't take me but you're taking the *mandragora*?"

"*For crying out loud*, Oscar, I will *not* have this conversation." I slipped the mandragora into my satchel. "Now, stay here, and be good."

Oscar transformed into a pig, turned his butt to me, wiggled his corkscrew tail, and lay down in a huff.

I slammed the door, rather huffy myself. I was about to cross the street toward the Wax Museum when I heard my name being called.

"Lily!"

I searched the crowds and finally saw a man leaning up against the wall of a souvenir shop, eating a shrimp cocktail. He was tall with an athletic build, golden hair, and sparkling cornflower blue eyes. Aidan wasn't one to fade into the crowd, and as people passed him they made a wide berth, women and men gazing at him with undisguised admiration and envy. It wasn't just his looks. Aidan's aural spectrum was so intense that even the least sensitive human responded to its brilliance.

"Fancy meeting you here," he said with a crooked smile as I approached. "Shrimp?"

"No, thank you. What—"

"They make a nice crab cocktail, if you prefer."

"Thank you, no. Why—"

"You look good with a baby on your hip," he said, an assessing gleam in his eye. "Is she yours?"

"No, she's not *mine*," I said. "Where in tarnation would I get a baby?"

"Wherever you felt like." He smiled. "You're more than capable."

"She's Miriam's child." Baby Luna put a chubby hand on my cheek. I smiled down at her, but she scowled back. "She hasn't been well."

Aidan reached out and cupped the child's head in his large hand, stroking her hair and rubbing a few of the silky yellow strands between his fingers. "The faeries would love this golden hair. Perhaps she's a changeling."

"She's not a *changeling*," I said. Though, for a moment there, with the mess in the back room that Oscar denied making, it had crossed my mind.

"You sure?" he asked, eyebrows raised, a smile playing on his lips. "Want me to hold her? I love babies."

"She doesn't really like ..." I trailed off as the little traitor reached her pudgy arms out to him. Aidan smiled, hoisted her against his chest, and murmured to her softly. And then, wonder of wonders, she returned his smile and patted his face. Apparently *no one* could resist this man when he turned on the charm. The two golden-haired beauties looked good together.

"I need to talk to you," I said.

"I know. I promised I'd look into Miriam's curse, and I did."

"Is that why you ditched me at the ball?"

"I didn't *ditch* you," he said. But his eyes didn't meet mine, and he seemed somewhat discomfited. Rare for him. I savored the moment.

"Anyway, what did you find?"

"I—" he began, but cut himself off as a large group of children jostled past us.

It dawned on me: Aidan hardly ever lingered outside. "Should we go talk in your office?"

A thick blanket of fog was creeping toward us. It still hovered on the Pacific Ocean side of the Golden Gate

Bridge, but soon enough it would push toward the wharf and today's sunny midseventies would become a chilly midfifties with stunning speed.

We magical folk love the fog. It clarifies things, evens out the light. I glanced at Aidan. Could he be troubled, causing the fog either inadvertently or on purpose?

"Why are you out here?" I asked.

"I like to get out from time to time, enjoy the sunshine. You know what they say about all work and no play. Wouldn't want Aidan to be a dull boy."

"Uh-huh. I doubt dullness has ever been your problem." I studied him. His nonchalance was a ruse. "Something in your office you don't want me to see?"

"What makes you think that?"

"You standing out here eating shrimp cocktail amongst the tourists, that's what."

In general I'm fond of tourists. They're open to the world around them, excited by the newness and novelty. So normally I love coming to crowded Fisherman's Wharf. But today I wasn't in the mood.

"I want to show you something," he said as he tossed the near-empty cardboard container in a trash can and started strolling down the sidewalk.

He steered me into the Musée Mécanique, located in a cavernous old wharf building. The museum was jammed with historic arcade games and machines of all types, from old "movies" consisting of flipping photos of the 1906 earthquake, to painstakingly detailed miniatures of towns that came alive when you dropped a quarter into the slot, the train running and the dance hall lights ablaze.

Aidan paused beside a wooden box fitted with an intricate metal eyepiece and peered in. He had no need to drop a coin in the slot—it started as soon as he neared. He stepped back and let me look: Cards flipped rapidly to form a peep show of women in frilly Victorian attire slowly stripping off black stockings.

"Cute," I said.

"Why don't women dress like that anymore? Those black stockings drove men wild."

"Are you saying you're old enough to remember such things?"

Aidan looked to be in his late thirties. But recently I had learned that he was not at all what he seemed.

He made a *tsk-tsk* noise. "Impolite to ask a man his age."

"And perhaps women don't dress just to please you. Did that ever occur to you?"

"As a matter of fact, it didn't. But it does remind me that I haven't complimented you on today's outfit. You look like a breath of fresh air."

"Thank you."

I used to wear a lot of old jeans, and still do when I'm hunting for treasures by digging through musty attics and basements and moldy cardboard boxes. But otherwise I'd gotten used to using my vintage clothing store as a closet from which I could choose a new outfit every day. As Jonquil had pointed out, it was pretty amazing to have a whole inventory to choose from. Today's dress was a formfitting aqua cotton with a square neck, embroidered with tiny white and yellow daises. My long dark hair was pulled up in its usual ponytail, tied with a patterned turquoise scarf. A little mascara and pale pink lipstick was the extent of my makeup regime.

I told myself I looked hip, maybe even funky, though in times of self-doubt I still felt like a kid wearing dress-up clothes.

"That color reminds me of a mountain stream in the Alps," he said in a wistful voice. Aidan was never wistful.

"Are you sure everything's okay with you, Aidan?" I asked as we walked along one aisle.

The machines started up as we passed them, one after the other, so as we walked we left a cacophonous wake. I checked in with my vibrations—I was a bit jangled, true, but I didn't feel off-kilter enough to be causing all of this.

"Of course."

Luna let out a screech at the noise surrounding us. She gurgled, flapped her arms, and kicked her chubby legs. Aidan smiled down at her, again cupping the child's head in his large hand.

"Did you find out anything about Miriam?" I asked. "I found the conjure balls you left under her bed."

"I understand Tarragon Dark Moon was killed the other night."

I stopped in my tracks.

"How do you know that?"

He cocked one eyebrow.

"Sorry. I forgot: You know everything."

"Tell me what happened."

"I don't know. Inspector Romero asked me to look into it since he kept hitting a brick wall with the coven sisters. I'm afraid I didn't fare much better."

Aidan took a deep breath in through his nose, his mouth pressed together as though he was straining not to speak. A marionette in an elaborate mahogany box beside us started dancing maniacally, wooden arms waving and legs marching. Though Luna was enjoying the show, the tinny circus music put me in mind of the sound track to a hokey old horror movie—silly yet sinister.

"Inspector Romero again? It really disturbs me that you're so close to the SFPD."

"I wouldn't go that far. I'm friendly with Carlos and his partner, Neil, but that's about it."

"Just don't get *too* close to Carlos."

"He's not all that wild about my relationship to you, either."

"I'd like you to find out who did this to Tarra, what's going on."

"I'm assuming Tarra's death is connected to what happened to Miriam." Aidan nodded. "The night of the ball, you told me to stay out of it."

"Things have changed."

"Anyway, I *am* trying to find out what happened.... That's why I came to you. I was hoping you could help."

He shook his head. "Things have changed and I need you to take this on. I'll do what I can to support you, but I can't be public about my involvement. Sailor can help you."

"Sailor's not happy with me lately."

"Sailor's never happy," Aidan said.

"True enough."

"Take him with you to the Paramount Theater and have him communicate with Miriam's spirit."

"Did you overhear us talking the other night at the Cerulean Bar?"

"My darling Lily, what *are* you accusing me of?" he asked with a slight smile.

"After I left the bar I saw a champagne-colored Jaguar drive by. Complete with personalized license plate."

The grin broke out full force. "It's those darned halogen bulbs they're using these days in the streetlights. Something about the wavelength plays havoc with glamour spells. In the eyes of someone like you, anyway."

"You should have joined Sailor and me at the table," I said. "I'd dearly love to get you two in the same room one of these days. We might be able to hash out a few things."

Aidan turned his attention to a glass-encased scenario from the Wild West, complete with blacksmith shop and a bordello. When he touched the metal coin slot, the little painted dolls in the saloon started to dance, a cowboy rode up on a black horse, and the blacksmith swung his mallet onto a tiny anvil.

"Anyway, if you were eavesdropping, you must have heard him refuse to help me."

"I have the feeling he'll be more amenable now."

"I take it you spoke with him?" I asked, but Aidan remained silent. "When are you going to talk to me about freeing him from his obligation to you?"

"Never."

"I promised him—"

"You should learn not to make promises you can't keep. Do *not* meddle in my bond with Sailor, Lily. It's not your place, and it's futile."

"But—"

"*Enough.*"

I startled at the anger in his voice and the Old West scene jangled until it smoked, until an ugly crack ran along our side of the glass case.

Chapter 16

Luna started to cry.

"I apologize," Aidan said. "I—"

Just then three laughing boys jostled past us, coins jingling in their pockets, excitement shining in their eyes. Aidan stepped back to let their mothers pass, smiling; they smiled shyly in return, tittering among themselves. It was stunning how easily and quickly Aidan put up his façade around other people. With me, increasingly, he was showing another side. I wondered whether I should take it as a compliment that he felt free to show his true feelings around me . . . or as a danger sign that I was dancing ever nearer the hungry lion.

After the people passed, Aidan continued. "I'm . . . frustrated. I should have intervened earlier in this matter, should have perceived what was going on. Unfortunately, now my hands are tied. I can make sure that Miriam's body remains healthy, ready for her spirit to return. But as to the who, what, and how . . . you'll have to handle it."

I nodded. I dearly wanted more of an explanation, but I knew, as a witch, that not everything could, or even should, be explained.

Aidan squeezed the baby's thigh. "She looks happy enough."

"She likes to be held. But she's not well. I believe she's got a mild case of whatever happened to her mother."

"She'll be fine. You'll make sure of it. Anyway, here's what I can tell you: I let someone down. Now I owe her."

"Who?"

"She's a . . . well, let's just say she's an old friend."

"An 'old friend'? Why do I think there's more to that story?"

Aidan graced me with his crooked grin, his blue eyes sparkling once again. "Because you are a very perceptive witch? I'll tell you about it one day. Over wine, perhaps?"

I took a deep breath and watched the folks milling around the arcade, dropping coins into slots and laughing at the historic machinations that still functioned, decades — even a century — after they had been created. There were ghosts in these machines. I thought of the video games for sale at MJ's and wondered whether they would be functioning a century from now.

Aidan handed Luna back to me, his hands brushing against my arms as he did so. I felt sparks between us shivering along my skin, as I increasingly did when he touched me. Or looked at me.

The machines around us came to life all at once, and several children ran over to watch the spectacle, milling about us. Baby Luna kicked her legs and reached out, a drooly smile on her face. So now I knew the secret to keeping her happy — I should move into the arcade. I wasn't sure our needs were compatible, however; my headache was blossoming from the cacophony.

Over the tops of the children's heads, Aidan held my gaze for a long moment, his blue eyes sad. But then he looked down at the children with a genuine smile on his face. Who would have guessed that Aidan was a sucker for kids? It made me wonder: Had he ever been married? Might he have children of his own? It dawned on me how little I really knew about the man and his past.

Luna and I turned to watch the dancing girls in the Wild West scene for a moment. The glass had magically repaired itself, and other than a few wisps of smoke there was no sign that the machine had broken a few moments ago.

Something else occurred to me.

"Aidan, how can I get in touch with Calypso Caf—"

He was gone.

I searched the crowds but, with all these arcade games and people milling about, could see no trace of him.

And I still carried his mandragora in my satchel.

After returning Luna to her grandfather, I stopped by my apartment to drop off Oscar—who was under strict orders to babysit the mandragora, despite his loud protestations—and to pick up a few supplies. Chief among them was my Hand of Glory, a gruesome artifact that worked like a magical skeleton key.

Then I went in search of Sailor.

First stop: the Cerulean Bar. No luck there, so I headed to my second—and last—stop, his apartment. Sailor's regular hangouts, at least the ones I was privy to, made for a very short list.

Calling him wasn't an option. Like a lot of magical folk, Sailor didn't carry a cell phone. I could probably send him a psychic SOS, but, Sailor being Sailor, he might just run in the opposite direction. Better to track him down in person.

Sailor lived on Hang Ah Alley in Chinatown. As I walked down the narrow, brick-walled passageway, I enjoyed the subtle, ghostly whiffs of perfume. Hang Ah Alley had been the site of a perfumery years ago, and for the sensitive the scent still lingered. It clung to Sailor as well. Even though he often looked like he'd slept in his clothes, the man always managed to smell good.

I found the small entrance to Sailor's apartment building and tried the door. Locked.

This was not the kind of building that had remote buzzers or indeed any obvious way to let its inhabitants know they had visitors. I glanced around for possible witnesses, but the alley was empty save for an orange tabby that watched me from a distance. I held out the Hand of Glory, muttered a quick incantation, heard a click, and opened the door. I glanced over my shoulder as I slipped in, but the cat had disappeared.

The dark foyer and stairwell of Sailor's apartment building reeked of cabbage, pine-scented disinfectant, and spices I could not name. As I mounted the old, dark wooden stairs, the sounds of television sets and the staccato rhythm of conversations held in Cantonese floated through the thin walls. At the landing in front of Sailor's door I sensed a hopeless, desperate emotion, traces of energy left over from a long-ago murder over a gambling debt. Sailor claimed it didn't bother him, but surely it couldn't help his mood.

I knocked. No response. Knocked again and called out to him. Nothing.

I could use the Hand again to get in, but that seemed like too much. I sank down onto the top step to wait.

And wait.

I am not by nature a patient person, and mastering the waiting game had been one of my greatest challenges as a witch. *Paciencia es una virtud*, my grandmother Graciela used to lecture me. *Patience is a virtue,* especially where witchcraft is concerned. After much struggle, I had learned to remain serene while spell casting: There was no sense in trying to rush, since the methodical rhythm of the preparations played a role in getting me into the meditative frame of mind. Experience had taught me that an impatient witch was likely to conjure something she hadn't intended, which could pose no small danger to herself and others. Not to mention break a lot of crockery.

Still, except when it came to spell casting, I had a hard time being patient. As I waited, I tapped my foot and reviewed what I knew: Miriam had been sickened, and Tarra killed, presumably by the same person. Witchcraft was involved. Rex might have been jealous of Tarra and Wolfgang, but why would he have struck out against Miriam? Then there was Jonathan and Jonquil and Anise and the other coven sisters . . . and the elusive Calypso Cafaro.

I reached into my shoulder bag and pulled out the tiny black mirror I had started to carry around with the goal of practicing my scrying. A good scryer has the ability to see the future, or the answers to secrets, in a reflective surface, such as a crystal ball or a mirror. I didn't like the idea of being locked out of an entire plane of perception, so I was determined to improve. A while back I was trying to train with Aidan, but certain events took place that made our working together . . . awkward. I needed to ask someone else for instruction. Maybe Sailor's aunt, a witch in the Rom tradition, could train me. Then again, I still owed her from last time she helped me out. Hmm, I should probably follow up on that, the sooner, the better. If her grudges looked anything like my grandmother Graciela's, I had some 'splainin' to do.

For the next half an hour I focused on blocking out the sounds and smells of the building, trying to concentrate yet not think. It was quite a trick, and I was no better at it than I was with eighth-grade algebra. More than anything right now, I wished I were a powerful seer. Apparently, that gene had skipped my generation.

I was about to give up on my scrying homework for the day when the sound of the front door opening and closing echoed up the stairwell, followed by heavy clomping of motorcycle boots upon the wooden stair treads.

As he turned the corner on the landing below, Sailor spotted me and let out an audible sigh.

"I need your help," I said.

He shook his head.

"I won't go away." I stood, blocking his path up the stairs. "I can't. This is a young mother we're talking about. She has a baby, a father, friends. She's loved, and needed. You have to help me help her."

His dark eyes met mine. I stroked my medicine bag and tried to exert some control over him, though I knew it would be fruitless.

"I have the Hand of Glory. I can get us into the theater, no problem. It'll take us an hour, maybe an hour and a half, tops."

He sighed once more, turned, and started downstairs.

"Is that a yes?" I asked as I hurried after him.

"It's not a no," he replied.

"Don't you need your things? Séance things?"

"I've got what I need. You brought the Mustang?"

"Yes."

"Good. I'm driving."

"How long is this gonna take?" Sailor growled in a low whisper an hour later.

We were in a crowded storage nook behind a curtain at the Paramount. After using magic to let ourselves in a side door to the stage area, we had headed for the lobby, only to be forced into hiding by the sudden appearance of a security guard. Rather than making his rounds, the paunchy, asthmatic fellow had taken up residence in one of the plush red velvet theater seats, propped his feet on the back of the chair in front of him, whipped out a cell phone, and proceeded to complain bitterly about his mother-in-law to whoever was on the other end of the line.

"How should I know?" I whispered, irrationally annoyed at the security guard for interfering in my plans for breaking and entering.

"Can't you speed this up?" Sailor asked.

"How would you suggest I do that?"

"*You're* the witch. Figure it out."

I checked my vintage Tinker Bell watch, whose hands glowed green in the darkness. It had been five minutes. Surely the guard would have to return to his post soon?

I was as antsy as Sailor. Not only because I wanted to hear what Miriam had to say, but because ... standing this close to Sailor was unnerving. There was something about him ... As my mother used to say, I could eat him up with a spoon.

It must be pheromones, I thought. I had romance on the brain lately—every male I ran into was looking good to me.

Get a grip, Lily.

In order to distract myself, I tried to make out the jumbled contents crowding the closet behind us.

"What is all this stuff, do you suppose?" I whispered.

"Leftover props, I imagine. Or stuff they shoved in here decades ago and forgot about."

"Is that a Victrola behind you?"

"Looks like it."

"Huh."

So much for *that* conversational gambit. The guard was still chatting and so involved in his conversation, I imagined he wouldn't notice if we spoke in regular voices, but caution nonetheless seemed advisable. I blew out a breath, checked my watch again, and tapped my foot. Anything to distract me from the impatient man sharing this cramped space.

"Feeling anything yet?" I whispered after another few moments.

Sailor shifted a little closer, until his thighs were touching mine. "Mmm-hmmm," he murmured.

"Sailor!"

"It's not my fault. You're a woman, I'm a man, and this is a very small nook."

"I *meant*, did you feel any spirits yet?"

"You have to be more spec—"

"Sssh." I heard steps approach, then pass by, and realized I no longer heard the guard speaking on the phone. The slam of a door reverberated through the silence.

I peeked though a gap in the curtains. As I'd hoped, the security guard had left.

Slowly, we emerged from our hiding place. The dim golden light cast by the sconces made the theater's plush red velvets and sumptuous gold and silver gilt seem oppressive, even sinister. The intricate plaster decorations were not meant to be paired with a tomblike silence. All old buildings retain energy traces of what has gone before, but this was ridiculous. The theater felt as though it was itself generating ghostly chatter, eerie music, and ethereal energy.

The back of my neck prickled, and I chided myself for letting my imagination run away with me. But I stroked my medicine bag, just in case.

"Let's go," I said to Sailor, who was watching me with a trace of amusement. I started to lead the way up one aisle toward the rear of the theater.

"Good," said Sailor as he joined me. "For a moment

there I thought you were going to ask me to take that old Victrola with us."

"Why would I want a Victrola?" I stopped and looked at him.

"To backmask. What've you got, a small device? Or are you fluent?"

"I don't . . . I don't understand anything you're saying," I said, feeling a sense of déjà vu. Why was I having trouble understanding people lately? First Miriam, then Sailor . . .

"You said you needed to speak to Miriam."

"I said I needed to *communicate* with her. The speaking part doesn't seem to be working. It's garbled."

"You mean reversed."

"Reversed?"

"She's in the mirror world. Everything she says is reversed. You're saying you don't understand backward talk?"

"Apparently not."

He shook his head. "And you call yourself a witch. Aleister Crowley, the man some call the father of American witchcraft, advocated learning to backmask to all his disciples."

I blew out an exasperated breath. There was so very much to learn.

"So you're saying you didn't bring a recording device of any kind? Something you could play backward afterward?"

"It never occurred to me."

Sailor went back into the little closet and rooted around. He handed me a disc that had grooves on only one side; the other was smooth. Then he hoisted up the heavy-looking Victrola and held it awkwardly, the horn blocking part of his sight.

"Can't believe I'm doing this," he muttered as he walked

unsteadily up the aisle. "But then, what did I expect? Following a crazy witch into dark theaters at night . . ."

"What exactly are we doing?" I asked as I scooted along after him, record in hand.

"Old Victrolas record as well as play. My aunt has one, plays it backward to scare the hell out of her clients."

"Really?" I remembered the story Carlos told me, of the DOM members who claimed records held secret messages. Perhaps they weren't quite as wacky as I'd thought.

We passed through a set of doors at the back of the main theater and emerged on the second-floor landing. A sweeping stairway led down to the grand lobby; from there a smaller set of steps led to the ground floor and the ladies' lounge. I hesitated.

"What about the security guard?" I asked.

"Don't worry—he's back in his post at the ticket booth."

Before letting ourselves in tonight, Sailor and I had waited outside the theater for a long time, watching. There seemed to be only one guard, and he did his rounds at the top of the hour, then returned to sit in the ticket booth out front.

In fact, Sailor had seemed so sure of his ability to case the joint that it made me a little suspicious. He told me once he used to study architecture, but an interest in home design didn't preclude a career in, say, thievery.

"How about now?" I whispered, mostly just to hear my own voice. I yearned to drown out the sounds and sensations swirling about me. "Feel anything?"

"I'm feeling all sorts of things. This place is lousy with spirits. All those souls coming and going over all those years? Besides, theatrical types are good at projecting. They tend to hang around whether they died in the building or elsewhere."

"People died here?"

"It's an old building. Lily. Over the years, yes, people have died here. Surely you can feel it."

"I'm all jangly. There ... there are too many sensations."

"Like I said, it's jammed in here." He shook his head and let out a mirthless chuckle. "These folks never want to leave."

"Really? You mean they stay here on purpose?"

"A bunch of hammy actors with all of eternity to strut upon the stage? Why would they leave?"

We arrived at the grand lobby with its soaring green sculptures, moving quickly in case anyone was looking through the front doors.

"Are the ghosts tormented?"

"More like they torment each other."

"I thought ghosts stuck around because they were unhappy." I led the way down the hall to the final flight of stairs, which would take us to the ladies' lounge, where, I presumed, Miriam was waiting.

"Not always. Sometimes they're content to hang out for a while. From what I can tell, time doesn't pass the same way in the next dimension. A century might seem like a single afternoon. Ghosts live very much in the present."

"Zen ghosts?"

"Zen drama queens, maybe. Anyway, they're everywhere."

I shuddered. I couldn't "see" ghosts, but I often sensed them as one felt cool air on a hot day, passing over one's skin with a shivery rush, filling me with angst or fear or hope. And I seemed to attract them, like my own spectral entourage.

We hurried down the last flight of stairs. As always when I'm with Sailor, I felt a strong kinship. Sailor seemed to be as awkward navigating his way through the world as I was, and though our talents were very different, we complemented each other. Too bad he didn't seem to like anybody . . . including me.

We paused at the doorway to the ladies' lounge. There were no lights on in the outer lounge, but sconces from the marble-tiled lavatory beyond cast a subtle yellow glow. The room was just as I'd remembered it: ringed with gold-framed mirrors, with little metal chairs and a shallow shelf inviting women to sit and attend to their makeup. A crystal-and-mirror chandelier hung from the ceiling, and the deep red carpet gave the room a sumptuous feeling.

"Are all ladies' rooms this nice?" Sailor asked, looking impressed.

"Sure," I teased. "Aren't men's rooms?"

"Not really, no."

"Do you sense Miriam?"

"No, but since I have no idea who she is, I'm not sure I would know if she were reaching out among this crowd." He blew out a breath. "Let's get this over with."

Sailor set the record on the turntable, smooth side up. He then started up the machine and set the needle down on the disc.

I extracted a jar of the brew I made last night and drew a circle around us.

Sailor and I sat cross-legged within the circle, facing each other. We had done this once before, used our combined energies to tease out a ghost from a demon. At least this time we weren't dealing with demons.

But in some ways, the stakes were higher—the fate of a young mother was in our hands. I thought of Luna's reluctant smile, the way she tucked her golden head under my chin. Every maternal instinct I would have sworn I didn't have surged up, urging me on.

Luna needed her mother. We had to figure out a way to help Miriam, get her to tell us who had cast the spell on her.

"When I go into the trance," said Sailor, "call to Miriam with all the strength of your mind. I'll be doing the same, but since you've met her . . . she's more likely to come to a familiar voice."

We held our arms out in front of us, horizontal to the floor, one palm facing up, one palm facing down, my hand on his, his hand on mine.

Sailor rolled his shoulders, exhaled, dropped his head back until he faced the ceiling. After a few moments, I saw his eyes roll slightly in his head. I concentrated on allowing myself to be a conduit for the powers of my ancestors, sharing my energy with Sailor, feeling it pass from my cold fingers to his warm ones. The heat built, our palms itching and burning, as our powers merged and blended.

I called out to Miriam with my mind. Not knowing how much she might sense, I kept the picture of Luna in my head, hoping she would be able to see it and be motivated by it to appear.

After a moment, I could have sworn I heard far-off music surging and waning. It was a male tenor, backed by a Jazz Age orchestra. It reminded me of being here with Aidan the night of the Art Deco Ball.

I opened my eyes and searched the mirrors, waiting.

Finally, Miriam flickered in the mirrored chandelier high above us. Then disappeared.

Sailor's head whipped from side to side, then stilled.

That ethereal, barely there music grew louder.

I glanced in the full gold-framed wall mirror, and there she was, as clear as though she were standing in the room, looking at herself in the glass.

She raised her hand, placing her palm to the mirror,

holding my gaze. Her hazel eyes shone bright, her color high, flushed. She licked at her chapped lips.

"Ohs eetsirth. Pleh eeem," Miriam whispered. Then louder, she repeated: "Pleh eeem!"

Help me. I finally got that part. I strained to understand her, but as before, the words seemed foreign. She kept talking, faster now, but though I concentrated, trying to connect with her on other levels, it was no use. The babbling continued, and she banged on the mirror in frustration, her palms flat against the surface of the glass, trying to break through, to break free.

I pulled away from Sailor so I could hold my hands up to the mirror, my palms to hers. If only we could make physical contact, then surely I could communicate with her on a different level.

But the moment I pulled free of Sailor's grasp, he came out of the trance.

Miriam flickered, looking about as though in fear, and faded away. Her handprints were the last to leave, their foggy trace slowly evaporating from the surface of the mirror.

Something grabbed at the top of my head, pulling my hair. I felt something else skitter up one leg and the sound of rodents scratching overhead.

"Let's get the hell out of here," said Sailor. *"Run!"*

Chapter 17

I grabbed the disc from the Victrola as Sailor took my hand, yanking me out of the lounge and down the hallway toward the green glow of an EXIT sign. As we ran, the lights blinked and went out, casting us into pitch-darkness.

"This way!" he yelled.

I could sense Sailor next to me, but not see him as we stumbled along in the darkness.

An ice-cold blast slammed into me from behind, and something yanked my hair again.

The noise around us grew in intensity, until it sounded like a freight train rumbling through the basement corridors of the theater.

"What is going *on*?" I yelled.

"Apparently we woke something up," Sailor replied.

"You think?" Something pinched my arm. "Ow!"

"You okay?"

"So far. What do you think it is?"

"Something not good. Something *really* not good."

"I'm getting that feeling."

"Now'd be the time to be proactive, Lily."

"I'll try," I said, and grabbed my medicine bag. I started to chant, which proved difficult to do while running. We were in the bowels of the theater now, running toward EXIT signs that disappeared whenever we neared.

Something snagged my hair, and I felt another ice-cold hand on my shoulder. As I ducked and pulled away, I heard the laughter of ghosts—not real, human laughter, but a chilly undercurrent of perceptible not-noise. I flashed on a sudden memory of being in second grade, accidentally making my diorama of the American West come to life. The other children were laughing at me, picking on me, teasing and making fun of me until I burst into tears and ran away to hide.

I was no longer seven years old, and I was no longer powerless. The ghostly bullies weren't going to push us around.

I yanked away from Sailor and stopped, standing stock-still.

"Lily! What are you doing?"

"Trust me," I said calmly. Ignoring the spirits that surrounded me, wanting, needing, clutching at my clothes and hair, laughing and jeering, I took a deep breath, held up my right hand, and envisioned power flowing through the top of my head, down through my body to the tips of my toes, and out my right hand.

"What is dark be filled with light; remove these spirits from my sight."

An orangey red glow emanated from the palm of my right hand, dispelling the ghosts and illuminating a panting, frowning Sailor.

He looked me up and down. "You couldn't have done that earlier, maybe?"

"I didn't think of it."

"Some master witch you are."

"Hey, you were the one who started running and

dragging me along. I'm surprised you didn't start screaming like a little girl."

"A few more minutes of those ghosts and I probably
would have."

"Besides, it's not like a magical flashlight, you know.
It takes effort. Hold on. Speaking of magical flashlights,
we left the Hand of Glory with my other things in the
ladies' lounge. We have to go back."

He shook his head. "I don't think so."

"Wait here for me, then. I'll be right back."

"You'll do no such thing, Lily. Dammit, you might not
be able to feel it, but those things are building in strength.
They're—"

The light from my palm dimmed, remaining bright
enough to see only the bare outlines of objects.

"What the hell just happened?" asked Sailor.

"I don't know. This has never happened before."

"That seems . . . bad."

"Yep."

The word had no sooner left my mouth than the spirits descended on us once more, swirling and jabbing, the
laughing and moaning and shrieking all the more unnerving for being just barely perceptible. And now I was
seeing things, too: lights and mist and barely there faces;
eyes and mouths distorted by theatrical greasepaint, as a
chorus of music whirled about us.

Sailor tried to shield me from them by placing himself
in front of me, holding his arms out and slightly back in
a protective gesture. Something grabbed him by the
front of his shirt, dragged him, and tossed him into a corner like a rag doll. He landed with a thud and a grunt.

"Sailor!"

I stumbled toward him, but something kept getting in
my way, keeping me from reaching him. It was nightmarish: I felt like I was moving, but never got nearer to him.

Finally I stopped, let the light from my hand die out completely, put my head down, and gave my all to concentrating. I mumbled a potent incantation I remembered my grandmother Graciela using years ago, when she was fighting my father face-to-face. I recited the words exactly as she had taught me: in a smattering of English, Spanish, and Nahuatl, the language of the Aztecs.

Once again I held my hand up and out away from my body. I twirled around, focusing my anger on blasting my energy at . . . whatever it was all around me.

An arm settled on my shoulders, and in my fury I almost unleashed my energy on it. I stopped myself in the nick of time: It was Sailor.

He urged me down the hall toward the door we had seen earlier. We ran up a short flight of stairs and felt our way along a hall. I didn't dare look behind us, but whatever it was seemed to let us go. Finally we emerged onto the landing overlooking the grand lobby, which was lit by amber sconces.

We stopped short. There, laid out before us, was a grand party reminiscent of the Art Deco Ball, but with more authentic clothing.

Had I not been so freaked out, I might have enjoyed the novel experience of actually seeing ghosts. As it was, I clutched Sailor's hand and savored the warmth and strength of the arm around my shoulders.

"Keep chanting," he mumbled in my ear.

We started down the sweeping stairs as if we were just another pair of partygoers. The music played; couples danced. If it weren't for the fact that they were transparent when backlit, it would be hard to tell that they were spirits. Had we slipped into another dimension?

I continued stroking my bag and chanting for all I was worth.

Halfway down the stairs, the ghosts began to notice

us. One by one they stopped talking and turned to watch us pass. At long last we reached the bottom of the stairs. We started for the theater's front doors when a tuxedoed man with slicked-back hair, rosy lips, and shadowed eyes blocked our path.

"Do join our party," said the ghost.

"'Fraid not, pal," said Sailor in a surprisingly strong voice. "Step aside."

Sailor and the apparition stared at each other until the ghost disappeared, then reappeared behind us.

"Another time, perhaps," he hissed.

"Don't hold your breath," said Sailor. "We ain't Jack Nicholson."

"Who?" the ghost asked.

"Back off *now*."

And as quickly as that, the ghosts faded away, leaving only the murmured sounds of their party, faraway music that grew fainter and at last disappeared, leaving only a deafening silence.

We jogged across the lobby and through a set of interior doors that opened onto a small foyer. Only a few feet of carpet and one last set of doors stood between us and the safety of the street. Unfortunately, without the Hand of Glory we had no way of unlocking the final set of doors to the outside. Sailor pushed and banged, but they didn't give. We turned around, but the interior doors had shut—and locked—behind us with a quiet *snick*.

Trapped in the foyer. On display to the street like mannequins in a shop window.

Sailor cursed a blue streak, pulling me over to the side wall so a casual observer wouldn't notice us. Still, we were easy prey. There was nowhere to hide.

Sailor took a phone from his pocket and flipped it open.

"You have a cell phone?" I asked, surprised.

"Everybody has a cell phone." Sailor ducked his head and engaged in a brief conversation that consisted of: "*It's me. Busted . . . I know. Oakland . . . Good.*"

He snapped the telephone closed.

"Who was that?" I asked.

"None of your business."

"You never told me you had a phone."

"Why would I tell you? You'd call me, and I don't like people to call me."

"Could I have your number?"

"I just said, I don't want people calling me."

"I'm not 'people.'"

"No, you're worse. Look what you just put me through."

That gave me pause. "Are you all right? Were you hurt?"

He shrugged. "What those SOBs do to my head is a lot more destructive than what they do to my body. You know, it takes a hell of a lot of power to manifest like they did, not to mention the power that's required to throw a human around. You might want to keep that in mind."

"Is there . . . a demon in the theater?"

He shook his head. "It's not a demon. More like an outside force, an out-of-control rage."

"Like a spirit that has been invoked and brought down upon someone? Upon Miriam? Could it be loose in the theater?"

"Not in the sense that it will be haunting the theater. It might be serving to separate us from her, though. Lily, you're dealing with more than a cursed corsage here. I think whoever it is left a part of themselves here, to keep Miriam from escaping. Someone who is naturally gifted, but out of control. Like you, but mean, without any moral code."

Moral code reminded me of DOM. Whose morality was it? It was all relative.

"What did she say? Could you understand?"

He shook his head. "I don't understand backward talk, since the thoughts are backward as well. But at least you have the recording."

I still clutched the record to my chest.

"There's clearly a displacement of some sort. The others are ostracizing her."

"How do you mean?"

"The other spirits. They recognize something's wrong with Miriam, that she's not complete. She's still tied to her body."

"That's something I'd like to encourage," I said. "So how do I get her back to her body?"

"You have to figure out who put the curse on her and why. And then figure out how to undo it."

We were back to that.

"Anyway, if we can hold tight my buddy'll . . . Aw, *hell*." Sailor swore in a low voice. I followed the direction of his gaze through the glass of the theater's front doors.

"What is it?" Looking out at the street, I saw nothing.

"It must be the top of the hour; guard's making his rounds."

The security guard stood on the other side of the interior glass doors, shining the beam of his flashlight straight at us, his mouth open and goggle-eyed.

And then he lifted his radio to speak into it.

"Hope you brought bail money," muttered Sailor.

"Oh, Sailor, I'm so sorry I got you into this."

"I'll just add it to your considerable debt to me. Though this time . . ." He shook his head. "It's really gonna cost you."

Chapter 18

As it turns out, a large vinyl record is hard to hide from the police. I was relieved of it immediately, and was left wondering what the police would think, if and when they tried to play it.

Considering we'd been caught in a locked theater where we had no place being in the first place, there was no easy manner of talking our way out of this mess. I needed someone to intervene, and I knew only one official well enough to ask such a favor. I used my phone call to contact Carlos Romero.

Sailor and I were separated, and I spent the night in jail. Actually, by the time we were booked it was four a.m., so it was more like spending the morning in jail. I slept all of an hour.

"Thanks for helping us out," I said to Carlos as we finished up the release paperwork.

His silence reverberated with anger.

"Where's Sailor?"

"Already released—I guess a friend posted bail."

I hadn't realized Sailor *had* any friends.

"Abandoned you. Such a gentleman," Carlos said as

he yanked open the front door and held it for me. I blinked in the bright sunshine of the late morning.

"Lily, want to tell me what you were doing breaking and entering, and with Sailor, of all people?"

"Do you know everyone in San Francisco?"

"I know the ones who specialize in milking hardworking citizens of their money. Seriously, Lily, the fact that you think of *me* as a friend is beginning to worry me. First Aidan Rhodes, now this guy? I thought you were going to keep a low profile. That antiwitch group is just the tip of the iceberg—you know that?"

I nodded. "You're right. I'll keep my head down."

"You do that."

"There are just a couple of things . . ."

Carlos sighed. "What is it now?"

"I left some items in the theater, personal items that I need back." What would I do without the Hand of Glory? As gruesome as it was, it came in handy.

"Personal items?"

"Of a witchy caliber."

"Super. Anything else?"

"I need the record that was confiscated when we were arrested."

"A record?"

"Yes, an old vinyl LP. It's not valuable or anything, but I need it."

"Did you steal it from the theater?"

"It's more like I borrowed it. I just need to listen to it; then I'll give it back. It's not a regular record. It's special."

We had arrived at his car, a beat-up blue Subaru. He looked at me over the roof of the car like I had a screw loose. I wasn't doing a very good job of explaining this. I tried again.

"It's the recording of . . . a spirit."

"You mean a ghost?"

"No, a spirit. She's not dead."

"Who's not dead?"

"Miriam Demeter. Her spirit is trapped in the mirror of the ladies' lounge at the theater."

"A spirit in the mirror."

"You know I don't make this stuff up."

We climbed in the car. Carlos put the key in the ignition but paused. Rather than starting the engine, he sighed and pinched the bridge of his nose. "Does this have something to do with my case?"

I nodded.

"Tanya Kolchek?"

"Otherwise known as Tarragon Dark Moon. And her coven sister Miriam Demeter. Miriam's the woman who fell ill at the ball I attended."

He started up the car and pulled into traffic, nimbly finding a hidden entrance to the freeway and heading toward the Bay Bridge.

"Do I want to know more details?"

"Probably not."

"Fine. I'll look into getting the record released, but it was theater property. You don't happen to know anyone associated with the theater. Do you?"

"I don't think so."

"What about that woman, what's her name? Owns a vintage clothes store. Surely you know her?"

"What woman? What store?"

"Over on Union Street. She's pretty influential; I think she sits on the board. That's how I knew about the Art Deco Ball; she was going on about it at the policeman's fund-raiser. She was at the dance. Didn't you see her?"

I tried to think. Wait—the petite woman in the beautiful ruby gown who had addressed the crowd—was that

Greta? I had been so distracted at the time that I hadn't remembered where I had seen her.

"Maybe you could talk to her, one vintage clothes dealer to another. She probably has some pull with the theater's owners, maybe even could get them to drop the case against you. If the record isn't valuable, as you say, no one should care."

"Thanks, Carlos. I really appreciate your help."

Later that morning, I was trying to forget that I had spent the night in jail. I didn't even tell Bronwyn and Maya. I explained away my haggard appearance by claiming insomnia, and tried to lose myself in the minutiae of running a busy retail establishment in San Francisco.

But my carefully constructed façade fell when Max Carmichael walked in. Our brief relationship had ended because Max couldn't handle the witchy side of me, and I wasn't willing to change to please him. Supposedly we were "friends," though that sort of arrangement had been easier to agree to than to live up to. My stomach still did funny things when I saw him . . . or heard him. He had an amazing voice.

"Lily," he said, in that voice. "Good to see you. You look wonderful, as always."

After the night I'd had, it was evident to all that the man was lying. But I appreciated it. "Thank you. You too."

Maya and Bronwyn both greeted Max briefly, then pretended to be absorbed in their task of sorting new acquisitions for repair and washing.

"What brings you here?" I asked. "Looking for a vintage outfit?"

"Actually, I'm here in an official capacity. I'm following a story."

"No comment."

"I haven't asked you anything."

"Is your story about vintage clothing?"

"No."

"Then no comment."

"It's about ghosts."

"I'm not a necromancer. I can't see . . ." I trailed off. Except maybe now I could. I saw them at the theater, after all. Did that mean that I was developing a new skill, or was it just a quirk?

"You can't see?" Max asked.

"Sorry. I'm not really a ghost gal."

"There's a rumor that there's a spirit in the ladies' room at the Paramount Theater in Oakland."

"I . . . uh . . . really?" Was Max here to ask me about last night? Did he know I'd been arrested?

"You were there for the Art Deco Ball, right? Did you notice anything?"

"Mmm," I said, shaking my head. I really was a bad liar.

"Hmm," he responded. "I take it that means you're not going to tell me about it."

"What do you think you know?"

"That there's some sort of apparition in the mirrors there. It's scared the heck out of a few women the last couple times they've had events."

"There are always a lot of ghosts in theaters, or so I hear. Have *you* seen anything?"

"No . . ." he said, fixing me with a gaze. "But then, as you know, I'm skeptical about these things."

"One might even say bullheaded," I said lightly.

Max symbolized what I had always wanted: someone steady and normal, someone at ease in the regular world. He was the sort of man who might marry a person and honor the commitment, love her and stand by her. A non-witchy person, that is. He thought of himself as a tough guy, but Max was dewy with the innocence of those untouched by the sorts of things I knew, had witnessed, the supernatural powers that coursed through my veins, that sang to me through the generations. He tugged at my heart, at a part of myself I didn't even know existed. At the same time, I was never fully myself with him; I held back, held my tongue, held my breath.

Which was why we could never work.

I knew it, but it still made me sad.

The mail carrier arrived, bringing bills and one padded manila envelope with a Paramount Theater return address. The overly curious Max cocked one eyebrow. I hesitated, but decided that there was no harm in him seeing it—he would have no way to connect the contents to his story.

I opened it. Inside was a rather smooshed corsage, as though it had been stepped on. I imagined it had been kicked aside on the night of the ball, trod upon by innumerable high heels. The limp flowers were partially shredded and gone.

But I wasn't interested in the flowers. I wanted to inspect the needles beneath. The curse.

"Your corsage from the other night?"

"How did you even know I went to the ball?"

"Bronwyn mentioned it. We're still in touch."

It figured. Bronwyn wasn't one for dropping friends.

"That looks like an uncomfortable corsage," Max continued. "What's with the needles? It takes that many to keep it attached?"

I didn't respond, caught up in what I was seeing. There was one in particular that didn't look like the other rusty needles. It was like a very thin wooden spool with a spike at the end. What *was* that?

"Why would anyone put a spindle in a corsage?" said Maya over my shoulder.

"A spindle?"

"Looks like a miniature one, from a spinning machine."

"As in spinning cotton into cloth?"

"Or straw into gold, yeah," Maya said. "Wasn't it Sleeping Beauty who was pricked with a spindle?"

"I think so. Sleeping Beauty is the same as Briar Rose, right?" Maybe I should brush up on my fairy tales.

Maya nodded. "More or less, yes. My mom has an antique spinning wheel she keeps threatening to put back into service. So, lest the house be even more covered in fuzz, I'd appreciate you keeping her busy with her dressmaking project here. My father might just leave her if she gets involved in yet another hobby."

I smiled. "After thirty-five years, I can't imagine he'd leave over a new hobby. Besides, he's nuts about her." The last time Maya's father came into the shop, he and Lucille had stood giggling over the gauzy negligees. And every time I had seen them together, he gazed at his wife with open adoration. It was enough to give a cynic like me pause.

Not to be left out, Bronwyn joined us at the counter. "Speaking of Sleeping Beauty, I spoke with Duke again this morning. He tells me Miriam's boyfriend, Jonathan, came over to the hospital. They had a long talk, came to a new understanding. Looks like he's not willing to get out of Miriam's life and wants to be there to help."

"That's wonderful news, Bronwyn. Thank you for telling me. You just made my day."

Max, snooping, read the return address on the package. "I know this woman—she's a docent at the theater. Very sweet. Gave me a tour."

"Just how close are you two?"

He gave me a questioning look. "She said I reminded her of her son. Why?"

"I wonder if you could do me a favor. I left a few things at the theater that I need to get back."

"Things? Like another corsage?"

"Not exactly. More like . . . things I used to cast a spell. One of them is a kind of candleholder, looks like a hand. It's pretty important I get it back."

"This wouldn't have been in the ladies' lounge, by any chance?"

"The very place. And if you get the items for me and promise to keep my identity anonymous, I'll give you an exclusive scoop on what's up with the mirror."

He took a deep breath through his nose, lips pressed together in what looked a lot like annoyance. Then he nodded and held out his hand.

"You've got yourself a deal."

Getting those spell craft supplies back was one thing, but I needed the record most of all. Which was in police custody. Better follow up on Carlos's suggestion to speak with Greta. Couldn't hurt, right? I told Maya and Bronwyn I was headed to Vintage Chic to check out the competition, then offered to pick up lunch on the way back. There were a lot of great-looking restaurants along Union Street.

I spent a few minutes petting the yappy dog while Greta finished up with a refined-looking mother and daughter who had just found "the *perfect* gown for the cotillion."

They have cotillions in San Francisco? This town never ceased to amaze me.

When we were alone, I approached Greta and told her what I wanted.

"I don't understand," she said, a tiny frown marring her

forehead, her fingers tapping on the glass counter. "Why were you in the theater after hours, without permission?"

She wore an incongruous-looking Garfield Band-Aid on her pointer finger, making me think of Miriam.

"It's a little hard to explain," I said. "I guess that's obvious. . . ."

She shook her head. I tried to use my power to will her to agree with me, but she wasn't having any of it. Greta had a wall up around her feelings, rare among regular humans. I wondered what her background was: abused, abandoned, traumatized?

"You can't have it," she said. "Why would I reward you for being a thief?"

"It wasn't thievery exactly. It's very important for me to get some information from that record."

The phone rang, and Greta answered in a singsong: "*Vintage Chic.*" She looked up at me with a sour look on her face, her lips pulling back in irritation. "Yes, she is. Here."

She handed the phone to me.

"Hello?"

"Lily, I'm glad I caught you," said Maya. "Carlos just called to tell you that someone attacked your friend's voodoo store. Herve's place."

"Herve?" My heart leaped to my throat. Herve was a good friend and an important magical ally. "Was anyone hurt? Is he okay?"

"I don't know anything else. Carlos said he heard it up at the station, but it's not his department."

"Thanks. I'll go straight over."

I hung up, then noticed that Greta was holding her dog, stroking him while she stared at me. Her words dripped with saccharine-sweet sarcasm.

"Any other calls you'd like to make? Or receive? Any other police evidence I can obtain for you?"

"I'm sorry about the phone call. But I really do need that record back. It's not valuable or anything— wouldn't mean anything to anyone but me. And I can return it to the theater soon. Maybe I could repay the favor by—I don't know—helping with costumes for upcoming theater productions, something like that?"

"I'll think about it." Greta pursed her lips, remaining silent for a long moment. Then she asked, "And how is poor Herve? Will he have to close the store?"

"I'm on my way there now," I said as I headed toward the door. "You're friends with Herve?"

"I know him. I know a lot of people."

Chapter 19

"Herve, I'm so sorry this happened to you."

We stood on busy Valencia Street, looking at the smashed windows, the colorful graffiti claiming that "Magick is Murder," the chaos of broken pottery and shredded cloth inside the shop called Detalier's. Curious onlookers stood around the section of the sidewalk that was roped off with bright yellow crime scene tape, and a uniformed officer was filling out forms on a clipboard while another was taking photos.

"At least no one was hurt." Herve shook his head. About my age, Herve was a powerfully built man with dark skin and a commanding air. In front of customers he spoke with a deep Caribbean lilt, but in private his accent was pure California, which made sense since he'd grown up in LA. He had explained that people didn't give his magic much credence unless he seemed exotic. Their mistake.

"Madame Detalier would be rolling in her grave," he continued, referring to his patroness and the namesake of the store. "So. Did you come here for a social call, or did you need something?"

"I heard what happened, so I came to see if I could help. Is there anything I can do?"

He shook his head. "Not at the moment. Caterina took the kids to her mother's until this blows over. Police say they want to keep the store undisturbed for a day or two to see if they could find any trace evidence—looks like they're trying to have all their ducks in a row in case they catch the culprits and can prosecute. Since it's a string of crimes that seems to be ratcheting up, they're being particularly thorough."

"I'm happy to help with the cleanup, when you're ready."

"Thank you. I'll take you up on that."

"Hey . . . now that I think about it, could you tell me what you think about this salve?" I brought Miriam's jar of homemade salve out of my satchel.

Herve brought it to his nose cautiously and sniffed. He clicked his tongue against the roof of his mouth, as though tasting something at the back of his throat. His eyes were closed in concentration.

"Does it contain henbane?"

He nodded and handed the jar back to me. "But there's more. There's a curse involved. Witchcraft. Your ilk, not mine."

I always felt vaguely insulted when Herve did that, drew the line in the sand between his tradition and mine. It made me feel insecure, knowing that our normally collegial relationship was limited. He was familiar with a whole world that I was not, and vice versa.

"That's some wicked stuff you got there, my friend. If I were you I wouldn't hang out with folks playing with things like that."

"I'm not. Not exactly. Or not knowingly, anyway."

"Sounds like there's a story there. Were you going to go track down the maker of said cursed salve?"

I nodded.

"Mind if I tag along?" Herve asked, with one final pained look at his shop. "I'd love to get out of here for a couple of hours, get my mind on other things. And you always seem to land in . . . interesting situations."

I smiled. "I'd love some company. Thanks."

As we drove across town I filled Herve in on Miriam, Tarra, and the various goings-on.

"So where are we headed now?" asked Herve.

"I may be grasping at straws, but there are two people in this mix that I haven't spoken to yet: Calypso Cafaro, a botanicals worker who was running a class that included both Miriam and Tarra; and Rex, Tarra's boyfriend."

"What does Tarra's boyfriend have to do with what happened to Miriam?"

"I don't know. Maybe nothing. Probably nothing, but . . . isn't it usually a loved one or family member who's ultimately responsible for a person's murder?"

"That's a terrible thought." He looked at me askance. Herve prized family above all.

"Sorry," I said, feeling like quite the cynic. "That's what I hear from the SFPD. Anyway, Rex works at Randi's Café over near the ballpark. I just want to talk with him, feel him out."

Randi's Café was one of those understated places I still couldn't get used to: The decor was exposed pipes and metal beams with rivets, and the tables were simple bistro-style metal. You ordered up at the counter, then took a number and the food was delivered to you. But the prices were more like a nice sit-down restaurant. There were lots of complicated, organic concoctions on the menu, perhaps justifying the cost. I found it all confusing—but the place was clearly popular, packed and bustling this lunch hour. Good thing I was in retail and not the restaurant business.

I asked the harried young woman at the register for Rex Theroux and she waved me toward the back of the restaurant, where I saw a man walking through the rear door with a sack of organic coffee beans thrown over one shoulder.

"Rex?" I asked.

"'Sup?" he said with a nod.

Rex was tall and buff, with a shaved head and multiple tattoos visible on the backs of his hands. He wore a hoodie sweatshirt with a leather jacket over it, even though it was warm in here. Thick-framed black glasses, à la Buddy Holly, looked so out of place as to be stylish. Around his neck was a black leather strap with a tiny little burlap sack hanging from it.

"I'm Lily Ivory. A friend of Miriam's. I wondered if I could ask you about Tarra?"

"Dude, I'm, like, I can't even believe it, you know?" He was multitasking, arranging the sacks of coffee that lined the back wall of the restaurant. "The police have asked me about it already, a lot. I told them that like any couple we had some problems, but violence isn't the solution to anything. Know what I mean? I would never do anything like that."

"I'm looking into what happened with Miriam. You all were friends?"

"This is, like, so weird. First my girlfriend, like, totally dies, and now Miriam's in the hospital? Jonathan's pretty messed up over it." A shadow passed over his eyes. He shook his head. "I can't even . . . I still can't wrap my head around that. Know what I'm sayin'?"

I nodded. "I know it was sudden. Could you tell me what happened with Tarra? Was she sick, anything like that?"

"You a sister?"

He meant coven sister. I took a deep breath and de-cided to lie: I nodded. "I'm just trying to figure this out."

"You and me both." His eyes shifted to Herve. "I know you, right?"

Herve just shrugged.

Rex nodded. "Anyway, I talked to the cops and I was, like, I don't even know. She seemed fine, kind of run-down. But that morning . . . she felt stabbing pains, the sensation that she couldn't breathe, then passed out. I totally called nine-one-one, but I sort of freaked out."

"How come?"

He shrugged. "She was into herbs—know what I mean? We both were. But I'm into a particular kind of herb, if you get what I'm saying. I started thinking if the author-ities were snooping around the place . . . I'm just saying, weed's practically legal, but I don't exactly have my med-ical marijuana growers' license and the feds are still busting people . . . so I ran."

"You ran?"

"I left the door open for the ambulance, but I took off."

"Very gallant," said Herve.

"Look, they said the autopsy showed she'd been poi-soned, like, twelve hours before. But I totally had an al-ibi."

"What was that?"

"I was with my drumming group until real late. Didn't get home till after two."

"Is this the coven drumming group, the one with Wolf-gang?"

"Yeah. You know Wolf?"

"I've met him. What can you tell me about him?"

"Well, he and Tarra were having an affair."

"Really." I wasn't sure I'd heard what I thought I

heard. If Rex was telling me Tarra and Wolfgang were seeing each other, wouldn't it be more traumatic? He had announced it like it was no big deal.

"They had a thing."

"You don't seem very upset."

"I'm trying to overcome jealousy. Jealousy is at base just fear of loss. We can't allow ourselves to be ruled by fear. Humans can't avoid loss, but we like to think we can."

As I thanked him for speaking with us, I realized I had forgotten to tell Carlos this little tidbit about the relationship between Tarra and Wolfgang.

As we left, I looked around at the new construction, the ballpark, took in the scents off the bay, the call of the seagulls. The massive base of the Bay Bridge was nearby, and I could see that traffic was already starting to get heavy.

"What do you think?" I asked Herve. "You think we need to overcome jealousy?"

He gave a humorless laugh. "I guess we do; it would certainly bring down everybody's blood pressure. But if you're asking me whether I could handle knowing my woman was with some other guy?" He shook his head. "Never."

I nodded. "It does seem like quite a feat, to remain unaffected by something like that."

"On the other hand, you never know. Maybe they were into threesomes. Maybe Rex is secretly into guys, so that's how he gets his kicks. Maybe—"

"Yeah, thanks. I think I've got enough information for the moment, not to mention visuals."

Herve gave me a deep, sonorous chuckle. "You do get yourself into some interesting fixes, my friend. I should mention to you that I gave Rex some help a week or two ago."

"What kind of help?"

"A talisman to keep someone away. I see he's still wearing it, the bag around his neck."

"That seems awfully coincidental."

"Not really. He's a pagan. I supply a lot of those people. In fact, these coven sisters? Seems to me that I've met some of them. Rex was with a woman when he came into my shop. I wonder if that was this poor Tarra. She seemed . . . a bit out of it. Dazed. But she refused my help."

"Any idea who Rex was trying to keep at bay?"

He shook his head. "Not really. But I got the sense it was female. Someone powerful. After what's happened, I would assume it was whoever attacked Tarra and Miriam."

There was one female associated with everything that had happened. One I dearly wanted to speak with: Calypso Cafaro.

And then I remembered why the name Randi's Café had sounded so familiar—Anise had told me a chef who worked here took lessons with Calypso. Probably heard of her through Rex.

I went back in, but Rex had gone. Still, I barged into the kitchen without asking and inquired whether any of the workers knew Calypso Cafaro.

"*Please* remove yourself from my kitchen," yelled a small, officious man wearing wire-rimmed glasses. He moved to escort me out. "What's this about?"

"I'm sorry for barging in—"

"I should hope so," he cut me off. "Who do you think you are?"

"Do you know her? Calypso Cafaro?"

"I've been attending a series of workshops she teaches about herbs," he said. "Not that it's any of your concern."

"Rex wanted me to get her address from you?"

He hesitated.

"It has to do with a murder investigation," I said, my voice rising so that all the customers couldn't help but hear. "Regarding your employee's girlfriend who was found dead in their apartment last week?"

His eyes shifted, looking out over his clientele. Then he took a business card from the counter, wrote on the back of it, and handed it to me. "She's a very private person. I would appreciate you not mentioning where you got that address from."

"You got it," I said. And then, just to annoy him: "Oh, before I go, do you suppose we could have two lattes?"

"I enjoy seeing your mean streak," said Herve as he sipped his latte. We were back in the car headed toward the Golden Gate Bridge.

"I'm not mean, just caffeine-deprived," I said with a smile. "Besides, I don't cotton to snooty."

"Says here Calypso Cafaro lives in Bolinas. It's about half an hour up the coast," Herve said as he tapped the address into his smartphone. First I find out Sailor has a cell phone, and now Herve has a smartphone. . . . I guess *I* was the only magical type who didn't use such things. I thought it was common to steer clear of such technology. Once again, I was out of step.

"She lives a little outside of town, actually," Herve continued "Ooh, looks *secluded*."

He said the last in a spooky voice. Herve was teasing me for being nervous about going to see Calypso on my own. A middle-aged botanicals worker didn't strike him as scary.

"I really appreciate you coming with me."

"No problem. Not much to do while the shop's closed, anyway."

"I have to say, Herve, you're remaining awfully calm in the face of all this."

"I'm a skilled practitioner of hoodoo magic. You think the perpetrators won't be properly punished?"

I glanced over at him. Herve fixed me with a stare as I drove onto the Golden Gate Bridge. He started to smile very slowly, and then chuckled. I laughed along with him, but there was something in the intensity of the deep rumble of his laugh that was . . . unsettling.

We exited the freeway when we passed Sausalito, then headed toward Mill Valley and beyond to Highway One. The highway was famous for its intense twists and turns and the beautiful scenery: thick groves of redwoods, dramatic hillsides, babbling creeks, the Pacific Ocean. We passed Muir Woods and Stinson Beach, and still we drove on.

"Have we hit Bolinas yet?" I asked after nearly half an hour.

"Hard to tell," said Herve. "You never know about Bolinas. The residents are famous for taking down all road signs leading to their village."

"Why would they do that?"

He shrugged. "Guess they don't want visitors."

"That seems . . . kind of creepy."

He laughed. "I imagine we can hold our own. Anyway, our quarry doesn't live in town. It looks like . . ." He studied the device. "Yes, up here about half a mile, take a left."

I turned on to a small, unmarked dirt road.

"Is this right?"

"Looks like it. If not, it's an adventure, right?"

I had never spent much time with Herve outside of his shop. He had quite the *joie de vivre*. I wasn't sure if he was reckless, or if I should take a page from his book.

"Either that, or we'll be met 'round the bend by someone with a shotgun."

"I think these are mostly aging hippie folk out here. Probably not big into guns."

"How reassuring."

He chuckled again.

"Why are you so *happy*?"

"I'm relishing what's going to happen to the DOM folks who tried to destroy my shop. As soon as I get back into my workshop ..." He rubbed his hands together and waggled his eyebrows at me. "I do adore helping a bit with karmic payback. Don't you?"

I had to laugh. "Not particularly, no. I'd rather people just acted decently toward one another from the start."

"Where's the fun in that? I didn't start this battle, but I'm sure going to enjoy finishing it."

"Maybe it's a guy thing."

"I thought it was more a magick thing. You are an odd one; you know that?"

I nodded. "How are you planning on tracking them down?"

He waggled his eyebrows again and smiled like the proverbial cat with a canary. "I have blood."

"Blood?"

"One of them cut themselves on a ceremonial knife. Just a few drops, but I found it. I've got it. And I'll use it."

Blood was powerful, no doubt about that.

"So, what are you planning on doing?"

"Haven't decided yet," he said, clearly relishing the possibilities. "There's always a Capsicum Curse, but that seems so ... banal, somehow. I might have to go with something more inventive. Maybe something dermatological—ugly rashes are so wonderfully public and annoying."

"Remind me never to get on your bad side, Herve."

He chuckled, reached out and ruffled my hair. "You and I ever go up against each other in a battle, my friend, and no one comes out alive."

I guessed that was supposed to be reassuring.

A hedge obscured the road in front of us, so thick it looked as though we couldn't pass. But as we approached, we could see glimpses of the house beyond. The car barely managed to squeeze through, thorny branches scratching the sides as we drove past. I cringed as I heard the scraping, thinking of my red paint job.

Once through the hedge, we pulled into a clearing. It was picture-postcard perfect: The house before us was an old white-and-yellow farmhouse, with a wraparound porch and a large glass conservatory to one side. Hanging baskets brimmed over with colorful trailing flowers. A dozen wind chimes sent out a delicate music, and a whirligig weather vane swung on the roof's peak. The walk to the front door was lined with trained rose trees, full of red blossoms. Only one was full of white.

Herve and I climbed out of the car, looking around and taking it all in.

To the right side of the house was a huge, verdant vegetable garden, an herb garden, and something that looked a lot like a witch's garden. There were rabbit hutches and a chicken coop, and beehives buzzed to the far end of the land, right up against the woods.

The porch was full of white wicker furniture and ferns. A black-and-white tuxedo cat lay curled up on a porch swing.

"Hell's bells," I breathed.

"You can say that again," Herve echoed. "It's as though the maker of calendars set the whole place up for a photo shoot."

"Right? Except it's not fussy . . . just inviting."

"*Now* I'm worried," said Herve, though he smiled when he looked at me. "It's just a little too perfect. We should be on our toes."

And with that, a woman appeared in the doorway.

Tall, strong-looking, wearing a flowing white vest over

some sort of red leotard and brightly flowered leggings. Long silver hair fell in soft waves over her shoulders, and silver cuffs outlined her ears.

She smiled, her gentle brown eyes crinkling at the corners.

"You must be Lily. And you've brought a friend. Welcome."

She stepped back to allow us to enter, and I felt a wild tangle of emotions. How did she know who I was and that I was coming? What had she been teaching her botanicals group? So many people in Miriam's life seemed tied to Calypso's class. And given what was going on . . . could Calypso be responsible for the poisonings?

But on the heel of those thoughts came jealousy. Here was a woman with obvious power, but she was grounded and calm and confident. Next to her tall, angular body I felt like a shadowy little gremlin. I envied her this home, the greenhouse, the gardens.

Inside the house, the jealousy grew. Bundles of herbs— hundreds of them—hung from the rafters, drying. The scent was incredible: lavender and rosemary and sage, thick wafting breezes full of exotic dried spices.

"Make yourself at home. You're welcome here," she said as she led the way into the kitchen, a cream symphony of bead board, with a stained-glass transom over the door leading to the hall. It was a fantasy kitchen. An assortment of old-fashioned glass cylinders and mason jars stood on rustic wooden shelves, gouged and blackened with age. There were several stone and ceramic mortar and pestles, an electric grinder, even an old-fashioned hand-turned meat grinder screwed to the wall. Kitchen utensils of all kinds hung from pegs along the top of the bead board wainscoting, many of which, I would bet, were used less for cooking food than for working with botanicals.

"It's chilly out. Would you like hot tea? The kettle's already boiling. All my teas are my own infusions, from my garden. Organic, planted during the full moon. Or planter's punch? Something alcoholic?"

"Hot tea would be lovely, thank you," I said.

"I'll have the same," said Herve.

"Calypso, are you a member of the Unspoken coven?" I asked. No sense in beating around the bush.

"Oh no, not at all."

"No? You're not part of the coven?"

"I'm not a witch," she said as she poured hot water over tea leaves. "I'm just an old lady who knows far too much about plants and botanicals. I started years ago, with a copy of *Sunset* magazine that taught housewives how to plant their own kitchen garden. I put in a little four-by-five raised bed, and somehow I just couldn't stop. Now I manufacture all sorts of salves and soaps, that sort of thing."

"But you advise witches?"

She smiled. "I advise anyone who would like to learn about herbs and botanicals. A lot of those people are witches or natural healers, but I hold workshops for chefs as well. I advise several local restaurants, and supply them with organic herbs. You'd be shocked to know how much restaurants will pay for such things. I've done very well."

She handed mugs of fragrant tea to Herve and me and led the way into a front parlor. I noticed that Herve set his tea down on a side table without drinking it—I did the same. Better safe than sorry. The fireplace mantle and every table were covered with framed photographs, mostly of young women. But then I spotted a silver-framed picture of Calypso Cafaro standing arm in arm with Aidan Rhodes.

I picked it up and studied it. She looked at least a

decade younger than she did now; Aidan appeared just the same. He also looked uncommonly happy, displaying a genuine, artless smile the likes of which I had never seen.

"Aidan and I have history," she said before I was able to form a question.

"A lot of history?" I asked.

Another smile, her eyes crinkling adorably at their corners. "I assumed he was the one who gave you my name."

"No. No, he didn't."

"Ah. Well, no matter. I think we both know that Aidan often knows things he has no business knowing."

Ain't that the truth.

"And the young women in the pictures—are these your daughters?"

"Foster daughters," she said, her tone wistful. "I used to take in teenage foster kids—young people in need of a steady home so they could stay in high school and graduate. My sister and I grew up in foster care, so I know the value of having a steady, safe place to live."

"You say you 'used to'—you don't do it anymore?"

"I couldn't . . . no. Not anymore. Oh, let me show you my greenhouse." Calypso abandoned her own tea and led us out to the gorgeous conservatory, crowded with thriving plants and flowers. The space was huge, jungle-like with walls of green.

"This is amazing," I said.

Herve remained mute, but started pinching bits of earth from pots and bringing them up to his nose to smell.

Calypso looked at him approvingly. "It's my own compost. I make it outside, all the scraps from my gardens, the rabbit manure, the work of the worms . . . makes for potent potting soil."

Picking up pruning shears, Calypso reached out to snip off a trailing arm of morning glory. I stopped in my tracks.

I could have sworn I saw several flowers turn in her direction and the plant's twining strands reaching out toward her.

Chapter 20

Calypso met my gaze in silent challenge. Slowly, almost imperceptibly, a delicate green tendril wrapped lovingly around her upper arm.

I looked away. "I'd love to take one of your workshops. How much do you charge?"

"I do the trainings for free."

"Why would you do that?"

"There was a terrible incident some years back, when a young Wiccan initiate miscalculated the amount of belladonna she used in a draft. She nearly killed herself."

"I remember that," said Herve.

Calypso nodded. "I read about it in the paper and decided I could help. I contacted the coven and offered my services. If you're familiar with botanicals, you know how important it is to have proper training."

"That's very generous of you."

"I enjoy being around young people. Otherwise I'd just be an old woman in this big old house, banging around alone."

"Who all's in the training group now?"

"You must know Miriam, Jonquil, Anise, and Tarra,

from the Unspoken coven, and there are two others from other covens. So all in all, six initiates. Plus one botany student from UC Berkeley and a couple of chefs."

"Is anyone else sick?"

"Sick?"

"Tarra passed away, and Miriam appears to be in a coma."

Calypso turned ashen. She stumbled and Herve caught her, then helped her to a bench by the doors.

"I take it you didn't know?"

"No, I . . . What on earth happened?"

I exchanged glances with Herve. Was she telling the truth, or was she simply a really good actor? I didn't trust her. There was something about her . . . But I couldn't claim that I'd felt any odd vibrations, nothing of the sort. I feared I might be reacting more to her relationship to Aidan than anything else. That and the fact that, in some ways, she was who I would like to see myself as in the future . . . or who I feared. Living alone, seemingly content but still . . . Though I didn't spend a lot of time thinking about it, I guess there was a part of me that longed for a future that included children, a family of my own.

"It looks as though henbane was involved, and mandrake."

"Are you sure?"

I nodded.

"There's no way one of my students would have made that kind of mistake. I've been very clear about the dangers of poisonous plants."

"Anise told me that she came here and gathered some henbane flowers to include in a corsage."

Calypso's jaw dropped. "Why on earth would she do *that*?"

"How well do you know Anise? She mentioned that she lived here for a while?"

"She's a sweet girl. It's taken her some time to get her feet under her, but she's making progress, doing well in her job. She has a real way with flowers."

"Does she always seem a little"—how should I put this?—"vague? Confused?"

"Anise? No, not at all. She's young, but she's quite focused and energetic."

"When's the last time you saw her?"

"The group was here a week ago last Saturday."

Two days before Tarra was found dead.

"And what did you do in the class?"

"We went over salves, made our own lip balm from olive oil, beeswax, and essential oils."

Once again, Herve and I exchanged glances. We were both thinking of the lip balm I found in Miriam's house.

"The four of them—Jonquil, Miriam, Anise, and Tarra—they're inseparable. They . . . they always giggled like little girls, their heads together over the counter while they worked." She looked up at us, tears in her eyes. "I can't believe what you say, that Tarra's gone, that Miriam . . . There must be some kind of mistake."

"I'm sorry to say, there isn't. Right now I'm trying to figure out who would want to harm them. It may be the only way to save Miriam."

"I wish I knew what to say." She was slowly weeping now, tears streaming down her face. "Tarra . . . gone? I can't believe it. Why wasn't I told?"

I had no answer for that. Calypso excused herself for a moment and went back into the main house to pull herself together.

"What do you think?" I whispered to Herve.

"She seemed genuinely shocked by the news. On the other hand, she certainly has the skill set to poison folks, if she so desired."

"So do I."

"Good point. Remind me not to get on *your* bad side," he said with a smile.

Calypso returned a few minutes later, more composed though red-eyed. She offered to show us the gardens on our way out. I recognized wolfsbane and mugwort, foxglove and datura. Medicinal herbs all, but like most medicines, they were poisons in the wrong hands or taken in the wrong dose.

Looking out toward the edge of the woods, I noticed a grouping of immensely tall redwood trees that formed a nearly perfect ring, dotted with ferns and moss-covered boulders.

Calypso followed my line of sight.

"Faery circles are common in the redwood forest. If a tree dies, the babies come up from the still-live roots and form a circle around the mother." She gave a sad smile. "They say the faeries meet there for their dances during the full moon."

I nodded, the mention of babies making me think of little Luna. And Miriam. My visit to Calypso hadn't actually answered any of my questions.

Herve and I climbed into the Mustang and pulled away from the house, Calypso standing in her garden, watching us leave.

"Well, *that* was something of a water haul," I said as we passed by the thick, thorny hedge.

"What's a water haul?"

"Frustrating. No fish. We didn't catch anything."

"Ah. In LA we'd call it a wild-goose chase."

I smiled. "I guess we say that too."

"But I'm not so certain it was a wasted trip," Herve continued. "I take it you're ruling Calypso out as the killer?"

"Not necessarily. But I can't imagine what kind of motive she would have. Why would she kill off her students?"

"Good question. So, are you going to give her name to your friend Carlos Romero?"

That was a tough one. Seriously, pretty soon people would learn they couldn't talk to me, and I'd be even more of an outcast than I already was.

"I guess I'd better."

What did I do now? I shouldn't make the mistake of attributing witchy attributes and talents only to women. Could Wolfgang have cast a spell of some sort to get Tarra away from Rex? Could it have gone terribly wrong?

"Anyway, you should feel happy that your instincts were correct. You were right to be wary of her."

"Really? She seemed like a kind person. What did you sense?"

"Much more than that. I'm not saying she's not kind. But she's powerful. Surely you noticed the way the plants turned their faces to her?"

"I thought it might be my imagination. Why would she claim not to be a witch?"

Herve chuckled. "Not all who are powerful are witches, my little chauvinist. She appears to have a powerful link to the earth, a kind of symbiotic energy. I've met a few women with that sort of plant magic in the Caribbean. They don't call themselves witches or priestesses because they don't manifest. Rather, they express the energy of the earth."

"I've never heard of such a thing."

"But you understand the power of the earth, so you can imagine."

I nodded. In the tradition of witchcraft I was raised in, root workers were among the most powerful, because of their connection to the primordial powers of the earth.

I dropped Herve back at his apartment, then headed home. Before losing my nerve, I called Carlos and gave him Calypso Cafaro's address. I told him her current profession, and that she used to be a foster mother.

"And what did you get from her? Do you think she's involved in either of these poisonings?"

"I really don't know. Oh, here's another thing. It seems Tarra—Tanya Kolchek—was having an affair with a guy named Wolfgang, who is connected to the Unspoken coven. I don't have a last name, but it shouldn't be too hard to find him with that first name, right?"

"An affair? And I'm only learning this now?"

"I just found out myself."

"All right. Good work. Thanks."

"Carlos, if you dig up any unusual background on Calypso, would you let me know? I have a whole lot of unanswered questions."

"I'm a cop, Lily, not your own personal private eye. But I'll see what I can do."

"Thanks."

Jonquil had told me that the twice-weekly drumming circle was meeting tonight in Sibley Park. Rex would be there, along with Wolfgang and maybe even Jonathan.

But it didn't make sense for me to go. What could I hope to learn, anyway? Herve was no longer with me, and I really shouldn't go by myself.

Besides, I could use a nice quiet evening at home. I would practice backward talk for a while in case, just in case. Also, I should keep up my admittedly clumsy scrying efforts and go to bed early.

After sharing leftovers with Oscar I looked up back-masking on the Internet and even listened to some audio examples over and over, trying to decipher the odd sounds. Then I wrote out a few lines I would like to say to Miriam and painstakingly repeated them backward. The sounds felt foreign and nightmarish on my tongue.

Afterward, I set myself up at the coffee table trunk in my living room, my stones on one side, a pentagram on the other, and the ornate crystal ball Graciela had given me in the middle. I breathed in deeply through my nose, let it out very slowly through my mouth, and concentrated on clearing my mind. During brewing, I reached out to my ancestors, but scrying was more . . . passive. Contemplative. It was a neat trick to keep the mind concentrated while allowing one's thoughts to wander. Aidan told me the reason I hadn't been able to master this skill was that I tried too hard to keep control over the situation in front of me; I needed to release control.

I had done everything I could to make the situation conducive to sight. I had taken a ritual bath with olive oil and lemon verbena soap, dressed in black, and set out my stones. I sat cross-legged and breathed. I looked into my crystal ball.

In my mind, I saw Wolfgang, imagined him drumming among the trees. Sibley was sandwiched between Tilden and Redwood Regional Parks. I knew from my research that there were thousands of acres of state and regional lands that linked together, crowning the East Bay Mountains the entire length of Oakland and Berkeley. It must be gorgeous over there. All those redwoods.

Get your mind back on your work, I told myself. Literally trying to shake off my errant thoughts, I stared once again into the murky crystal. *Clear the mind.*

Nothing.

I glanced at my grandfather clock, newly purchased from a roadside junk store in Benicia. According to its hands, I'd been attempting to scry for only five minutes. Felt like half an hour. Outside, strong orangey light came in my kitchen window, signaling late afternoon.

Dusk wasn't far away. Rex and Wolfgang would both be at the drumming circle when day met night, according to Jonquil.

Drumming was the most elemental form of music and could sometimes be magical. If it *were* magical, I might be able to read vibrations or something from it, get a sense of both men and how they interacted. If Rex had acted out of jealousy, how would he be drumming side by side with his rival? I would love to see that.

I blew out another breath. *You are* not *going to Sibley Park tonight by yourself,* I told myself. That would be stupid.

I looked into the crystal once again. If I got good at this, maybe I wouldn't have to traipse around haunted theaters or regional parks anymore, looking for murderers. I could just divine the guilty parties and have done with it.

But I knew only too well that seeing didn't work that way. It was far more subtle than that.

I glanced at the clock again. Another two minutes had passed. This was ridiculous.

I wiped at the table. It was a little bit sticky, no doubt from some concoction of Oscar's. Besides, there was a piece of popcorn under the couch.

I couldn't possibly concentrate with the place all grotty like this. I got up, grabbed the vacuum. Then dusted. I remembered my mama saying to always dust *after* vacuuming, since the machine kicks up more dirt.

Then I noticed the overhead lamp hadn't been dusted in who knows how long. Probably since I moved in. I dragged a kitchen chair over and stood on tiptoe to reach the top of the fixture.

"Watcha doin'?" Oscar asked.

I jumped at the sound. Teetered for a moment, but regained my balance.

"I thought you were asleep."

"Catnap. *Heh!* Like I'm a cat. Get it?"

I wasn't sure that I did, but I smiled.

"Anyhoo, couldn't sleep with all this racket."

That was a lie. Oscar could sleep through a nuclear explosion. I finished cleaning the lamp and stepped down onto solid ground.

"I thought you were scrying. You said that's why you couldn't watch *The Terminator* with me."

"I *am* scrying. I was scrying. I was *trying* to scry," I clarified. "But then I couldn't stand how icky it was in here. You have to start cleaning up after yourself, Oscar. I'm not your maid."

"Yes, mistress." He went into the kitchen to make himself a sandwich. Munching, he came back into the front room, trailing crumbs, and spoke with his mouth full. "Can we watch *The Terminator* now?"

"I have work to do. But you can go in my room and watch if you want. And get yourself a plate; you're dropping crumbs."

Sandwich still clutched in one hand, he made a big production about wheeling the TV into my bedroom. The cart squeaked, only partially masking his grumbled comments. It was an old TV, good for nothing but watching DVDs. I refused to pay for cable.

I sat back down and resumed gazing into my crystal ball. And failed, once again. And now the sounds of explosions and screaming from the other room were making concentration impossible.

This was ridiculous. Who was I fooling? Since when did Lily Ivory do the sensible thing? Besides, I'm a powerful witch. What could possibly harm me in Sibley Park, really? Though I couldn't exactly *zap* anyone, if I took an extra amulet for protection and kept my senses on high alert, I should be all right. Still . . . I considered asking

Bronwyn to come with me. Though I wasn't afraid of the dark—my gifts included increased ability to see at night, and I had no fear of the woodscreatures—it still wasn't smart to go snooping around alone. I was mortal, after all, as Sailor would happily tell me.

Sailor . . . My mind wandered to the recalcitrant psychic. He was such an enigma. He seemed to despise me on the one hand, but then he would come through for me at the oddest moments. I thought of how he shielded me down in the bowels of the Paramount. He seemed to do it without thought, no doubt as a holdover from the lessons of childhood, when his mama taught him to be a gentleman. Long before he had turned into the cynical fellow he had become. I bet he was a darling child, with dark mischievous eyes and—

Good Lord in heaven, Lily, you start thinking about the man with tenderness in your heart and you're doomed. After all, I hadn't heard from him since I got him tossed in the hoosegow.

Was there anyone to take with me to Sibley? Bronwyn would be game, but I worried about her ability to take care of herself. There were many Wiccans with true magical abilities, but she wasn't among them. What I'd really like was to have someone powerful with me. After our little outing to the Paramount and my own recent traitorous tender thoughts toward him, Sailor wasn't the best bet. Aidan would be ideal, of course, but given his limited abilities outside of his sanctuary, I doubted he'd come if I asked him. Too bad I had already dropped Herve off at his place. He had mentioned he was going to turn in early.

I was wasting time.

"Oscar, want to come on a little trip?"

He jumped up, doglike, bat ears standing up and quivering. "Where we going, mistress?"

"Sibley Park."

His green eyes widened. "To the labyrinths? Are you going to do a ritual?"

"You know about the labyrinths?"

He rolled his eyes. "That's a good place for rituals. Your kind like it."

"My kind . . . as in witches?"

He nodded as he packed cookies into a bandanna and wrapped it up like a little package. "Snacks," he explained. "In case we miss dinner."

Oscar had just polished off a sandwich, but if there was one thing the little guy didn't care for, it was hunger.

The trip across the Bay Bridge toward Oakland was uneventful; the bay was placid and blue-green, dotted with ships and sailboats headed toward harbor; the late-afternoon casting the Oakland hills in an orangey light, sun glinting off the windows of the houses studding the slopes. Following the directions I had downloaded off the Internet, I made my way to the impossibly twisty Skyline Boulevard, and finally to the entrance to Sibley Regional Park.

There were half a dozen cars in the small parking lot; several hikers were packing up to leave. Officially the park closed at dusk, but though there was a small house for a forest ranger, no one appeared to be guarding the entrances or the parking lot. Oscar and I got out—he in his potbellied pig guise, and me carrying his cookies in my woven Pilipino backpack along with jars of herbs and a *paket kongo*, a special kind of Congolese medicine bag. I stroked the medicine bundle that hung from my waist, the braided belt made of silk in the colors of red, yellow, orange, and blue.

Sibley was an off-leash park for dogs; I hoped the same might apply to pigs. Oscar was downright insulted by the notion that he should wear a leash.

As we started to walk, I found myself thinking of the faery circle I had seen at Calypso's place. The creatures of the wood—faeries, brownies, goblins, and imps among others—were traditionally aligned with witches. In fact, we were among the few humans that they were willing to deal with at all. Given their histories of exploitation and violence, it was no wonder that they kept to themselves, content to have their stories fade into the collective memory as fables rather than reality. That way they were left alone, by and large.

But I had left Texas, and my witchcraft training, before Graciela helped me to establish a relationship with the woodspeople. We had no explicit pact, so they were wary of me. And since I wasn't entirely trusted, I couldn't speak to them directly. It was a faery thing. The custom reminded me of the Jane Austen novel I was reading about aristocratic society in the old days, when one wasn't supposed to speak with new people until making their acquaintance formally, through a third party.

"Hey, Oscar, would you be willing to introduce me to the woodscreatures?"

"What?"

"The woodspeople. I need a formal introduction."

He let loose with a loud cackle, as though I'd made a joke. He shook his head, muttering "woodspeople" under his breath and chuckling as he hiked on ahead. I made a mental note to address this issue another time.

In some spots the ground was rocky and steep. Sibley looked unlike the other nearby forests, certainly distinct from the woods I'd seen in San Francisco's Golden Gate Park and Presidio. Here there was a lot of low brush and rugged rock formations and grass that reminded me more of the Scottish Highlands than the lush redwood forests I was coming to associate with this area of California.

I consulted the map I had picked up in the parking

lot. Apparently, we were trodding upon an ancient volcano.

No wonder the vibrations were so strong here; no wonder someone felt compelled to build labyrinths. Forced up through the crust of the earth by the stunning forces of nature, stones were full of history and magic. They were primordial, primeval. Here the stones lay not far below the dirt, preventing tall trees from taking root and thriving.

"How much longer?" Oscar whined. "I thought this would be fun."

"Enjoy the beautiful nature surrounding you."

"I'm bo-o-ored. Hey! I know! Let's go to the mall."

"We are not going to the *mall*. Lord, what an idea." I thought it moot to point out that a pet pig, much less Oscar in his current form, would not be welcome in the average American mall.

We walked a bit farther, Oscar kicking at the small rocks. No one was around so he felt safe in his half-goblin, half-gargoyle guise. He picked up some pea-sized pebbles and pitched them toward a stunted, twisted pine, which stubbornly insisted on eking out a living in the scant soil above hard volcanic rock.

"You like malls?" I asked. I had never thought of Oscar as a shopper, but then I'd never really thought about what Oscar might do for fun, if he weren't hanging around me.

"I hear tell they got food courts."

Oscar often mimicked my Texas accent and phrasing, on purpose or not I wasn't sure.

"Why, yes, I do believe they have food courts," I said, taking the cue and pulling the package of cookies out of my backpack. "Have you ever even been in a mall?"

He shook his head, jamming half a cookie in his wide mouth.

"They're full of *cowans*," I teased, dropping my voice dramatically. The sun was nearly gone, filling the strangely stunted landscape with an ethereal red-tinged light. I pulled the flashlight out of my pack, just in case.

"Whole *place* is full of cowans." He shook his head. "I 'member back when the hills were full of brownies and dwarves, halflings and unicorns."

"How old are you?"

"Not polite to ask."

"You're my familiar, Oscar. We don't keep such secrets."

"How old are *you*?"

"Thirty-one, almost thirty-two."

"How come you're scared of Aidan?"

"I'm not 'scared' of Aidan." Okay, maybe a little discretion between mistress and familiar wasn't the worst thing in the world. "I'm—"

"Sssh," he said, stopping in his tracks. "Hear that?"

I paused beside him. Once our feet weren't kicking up stones, the night sounds surrounded us. Crickets chirped. Something skittered in the underbrush. There was a faint *vroom* of an aircraft overhead. But nothing out of the ordinary.

"What is it?" I asked.

He gaped at me. "You don't hear that? That . . . thumping sound?"

I shook my head. He rolled his eyes and let out a dramatic sigh. "I don't know how you got along without me all those years."

"It was no easy feat," I said with a smile. "So tell me about this alleged thumping sound."

"That way." He gestured to a small path off the main footpath.

I consulted the map. It was the direction we were headed anyway, the old quarry that held the labyrinths.

At long last we approached a ledge that overlooked a great teardrop-shaped bowl of a canyon. In the fading light I could make out two huge labyrinths, the lines marked with large stones. In between the labyrinths was a group of men forming a circle around a huge fire. They sat on the ground with their legs crossed, most of them shirtless, all of them drumming.

It was hard to tell from this distance, but I could make out bongos, men hitting pots with sticks, and various other drums.

"Hear it now?" Oscar whispered.

I nodded. "What's it all about?"

Oscar looked at me as though I'd either lost my mind or didn't know where it was in the first place. It was disconcerting to be looked at thusly by such an odd little critter.

"You don't know about drumming?"

"I wouldn't go that far. . . . I mean, I know it can be powerful and useful. . . ." Drumming was the most elemental form of music, the mimicry of our own heartbeats. How long had we been human before the first person picked up a stick and started hitting a rock in a rhythmic beat, signifying life?

"They use it to gather power."

"Who are they?"

"The male supporters of the Feri group. The Unspoken coven."

"You know about the Unspoken coven?"

"Sure I do."

I've been running around town asking questions, and here my own familiar knew about this group. That'll teach me to ignore the guy.

"Could you tell me about them?"

"Not here, I can't. Sound travels in places like this. I think we should go back to the car."

"I want to get closer. I want to see what it's all about." More precisely, I wanted to feel what kind of magic they were working up down there.

"Mistress . . ." Oscar whined, wringing his large hands.

"You stay here, behind that shrub. You've got your talisman? You'll be fine." He rubbed the new talisman I had carved for him during the last full moon.

I stroked my own medicine bag for good measure.

A road led down to the bottom of the canyon, but there was little shelter. The steep, rocky sides of the quarry, however, weren't an option. Anyway, in the dim light of the moon, with the men absorbed in what they were doing, I doubted they'd notice one lone figure coming down the path. And even if they did . . . ? They were men like Jonathan getting together and drumming, for solidarity and perhaps for the strength of their sister coven. Nothing to be scared of.

Nonetheless, I scrounged around until I found a large, tumbleweedlike bush. I took a hunting knife out of my knapsack and cut its sinewy stem, then held it at my side, between me and the men. If one of them looked my way, I imagined they'd see what looked like a large tumbleweed rolling down the path, rather than a lone witch. Or so I hoped.

As I descended the path and came closer to them, I noticed how the flickering light from the fire fell upon their bare chests, ranging in hue from pale white to dark brown, all painted golden by the firelight. Many had tattoos, and most were young and fit enough that I could imagine coming across the scene generations ago, during summer solstice in Scotland, or on Easter Island, or any other place where people have gathered together to worship over the course of human history. It was strikingly male, and beautiful in its own way. I had been prepared for a coven of women, was at least somewhat familiar with that kind of feminine energy. But such a masculine assembly was still an enigma to me.

I drew to a halt when I reached the canyon floor and continued to crouch behind my shrub, listening and feeling. The men's drumming energy swelled, wrapping around me. I opened myself up to its sensations. There was no evil here. Power, yes, but it was the communal, caring power of a group coming together for good.

Rex arose and said something unintelligible. Then he placed a little white sailor hat upon the fire. I remembered seeing the hat in the picture of Tarra. Rex lifted his face to the skies and cried out, the sound sending a chill through me. It was full of raw anguish.

"Lily."

I jumped. The voice sounded right behind me.

Wolfgang.

Chapter 21

"What are you doing here?"

Large and imposing, he stood above me. It was full night now, and Wolfgang loomed dark against the moonlit sky. Now I could feel his power. Strong vibrations emanated off of him.

I stroked my medicine bag and glanced around to assess my chances of escape. He was taller than me by several inches and no doubt stronger physically. But for all the power I felt coming from him, I sensed I was more in control of my abilities. And if all else failed, I had a surprisingly strong and brave familiar somewhere nearby, who had intervened on my behalf more than once before.

"Hello," I said. It was all I could think of in the moment.

"What are you doing here? This is a men's event."

"I wasn't trying to join you. I . . . I was just checking out the labyrinths and heard the drums."

As though looking for accomplices, his eyes searched the perimeter, clearly not believing me. "Okay . . . so, what's with the tumbleweed camouflage?"

I felt my cheeks burn and hoped it was too dark for him to notice. "I . . . um . . . I'm sorry. I certainly didn't mean to disturb you. You're saying farewell to Tarra?"

Even in the soft moonlight I could see the shine of tears gather in his eyes.

He nodded and cleared his throat, then squeezed his eyes shut. Hands on his hips, he was a man trying to get himself together.

Suddenly he opened his eyes and met my gaze.

"I loved her."

"I know."

He watched me for a long moment, then nodded and held his hand up as though in a signal to his group, which was still drumming.

"I'll walk you back to your car."

"There's no need . . ."

"We went through this before, remember? I'll walk you back."

Oscar joined us as we reached the rim of the gulch.

"You brought your pig?"

"He sort of goes everywhere with me. Thinks he's a dog."

Oscar glared at me. He hated being compared to canines, despite my repeated assurances it was a compliment.

Wolfgang and I walked in silence, but when I glanced over at him I could see tears streaming down his face.

"I'm so sorry for your loss," I said, wishing there were more to say.

"Tarra wasn't afraid of death. Used to speak to me about passing on to the next dimension; she was excited to see what was next for us. I just . . . I never imagined it would come upon her so soon. Come upon *us*."

"Is Rex a friend of yours?"

"He's a brother," he said, then stopped himself before

adding: "I think ... well, I'd say he's a circle brother more than a friend."

"And he ... never threatened you, anything like that?"

"No, he understands that monogamy doesn't work in today's society, that it's an unnatural patriarchal tradition forced upon us."

"And you? Were you okay with Tarra being with both of you?"

We had arrived at the parking lot, and in the light of the streetlamps I could see a muscle move in his cheek, as though he were clenching his teeth.

"I was ... working on it. I wanted her to leave him, and she said she would. But she was devoted to the idea of loving freely."

"That must have been hard for you."

"Like I said, I was working on it. Life is a journey made of single steps."

I unlocked my car and opened the back for Oscar to climb in. He was rather clumsy in his porcine guise, so I was in the ignominious position of hoisting him from the rear.

"Let me do that," Wolfgang said, ever the gentleman.

"Thanks." I stood back and let him help Oscar. When he was done, I held out my hand to shake, wanting the skin-on-skin contact.

I was surprised to feel that his guard was up. But it was more: Wolfgang was being protected by something, or someone, stronger than himself.

When I pulled out of the parking lot, I looked back to see him standing and watching me go, his hands upon his hips. His bare torso gleamed, his long hair and black tattoos lending him an exotic air.

On the way home, Oscar filled me in on what he knew about the Unspoken coven. Unfortunately, it wasn't anything beyond what Wendy had told me, except that Oscar added his own commentary and thoughts, which made the description of ecstatic worship much spicier.

Along the entire route, something tugged at the edges of my consciousness. Finally, just as I was pulling up to a rare parking spot right outside Aunt Cora's Closet, it dawned on me.

When I had looked back at Wolfgang, standing in the light from the halogen parking lot lamps, I had seen some of Aidan's distinctive shimmer. Just as I had seen it on his Jaguar after leaving Cerulean Bar.

First he was protecting Miriam, now Wolfgang. The man was getting around lately. Plus, he had some nerve asking me to dig into Tarra's death and yet not telling me how deeply he was involved.

I was loath to give up such a good parking spot, but I needed to talk with Aidan again. I had one or two questions about Calypso and about why he was meddling in something he had claimed he couldn't get involved in. Last time he did something like that, there turned out to be a kind of paranormal conspiracy it would have been helpful to know about ahead of time.

"Where we going?" Oscar asked as I started to pull away from the curb.

"To talk to Aidan."

"But I'm *hungry*," he whined.

"Why don't you hop out, then, go on upstairs and fix yourself something?"

Oscar hesitated, clearly weighing whether he could cajole me into cooking for him.

"*I* know what let's do," he said. "We could get take-out on the way to Aidan's! Chinese? Sushi?"

"No, sorry. I'm not in the mood, Oscar. Stay here, eat some leftover *étouffée*, and watch the end of your movie. I've got business to attend to."

"Yes, mistress," he grumbled, shifting into his piggy guise.

When we got out of the car, I noticed Conrad sitting on the curb.

"Hi there. You're here late," I said.

"Dude, just watching over things," he said, tipping back his head to look at the stars. "Beautiful night, right?"

"Yes, it is. Just stopped by to drop off my pig." I let Oscar into the store, locked the door behind him, and headed back to the car. "I appreciate you keeping an eye on the place, Conrad, but I didn't mean you had to be a full-time guard. You should go enjoy your evening."

"*Dude.*"

Talking with Conrad was a little like talking with Oscar. Sometimes it was best not to push the conversational envelope.

I made it to the Wax Museum in twenty minutes. I no longer dealt with the young woman in the ticket booth, Clarinda, who maintained an inexplicable animosity toward me. Still, I did get a perverse pleasure out of hearing her yell at me while I walked straight into the museum without paying, then proceeded up the central stairs, past the macabre Chamber of Horrors, and to Aidan's dark walnut door situated behind the seldom-visited European Explorers exhibit.

Aidan opened the door just as I was about to knock.

"Lily. What an unexpected pleasure. Twice in as many days . . . I'm honored." He stepped back and made a sweeping gesture, inviting me in.

Aidan's inner sanctum seemed almost like a stereotype of what a witch's chamber should look like: heavy Victorian-era furnishings, plush upholstered chairs, velvet drapes. Bookcases lining one wall were crammed with musty tomes full of esoteric, arcane knowledge. His familiar, a long-haired white cat named Noctemus, glared at me from a high shelf of the bookcase. The cat and I don't much care for each other.

I flopped down in a soft leather chair, while Aidan hitched one leg up on the desk and clasped his hands together, as though eager to hear what I had to say.

"Why are you protecting Miriam and Wolfgang?"

"You asked me to look after Miriam, remember?"

"That's true. But"—what was I thinking?—"I think you have more of a connection to her than you're admitting. I think that's why you ditched me at the ball."

"I didn't *ditch* you, Lily."

"You most certainly did. And I didn't appreciate it. But what I want to talk about now is: What is Miriam to you? How is she related to the 'friend' you let down? And is that friend Calypso Cafaro?"

Aidan got up and strolled over to the bookcases, reaching up to scratch Noctemus behind the ears.

"Calypso and I . . . used to be friends. More than friends, to tell the truth. Because of her involvement with me, she suffered. I owe her."

"I'm going to assume you don't want to share the intimate details with me." Frankly, I was glad. "But . . . how does your debt to her involve Miriam or Wolfgang?"

"Stay out of that."

"You just told me to look into it."

"Not with Wolfgang. He's not involved in this."

"I beg to differ."

"All right . . . you're correct that he knows some of the players."

"He was Tarra's lover."

"But he's not the one who killed her. "

"You're sure about that?"

"Very. He was with me when the poisoning occurred. Unfortunately, using me as an alibi to the police is just slightly worse than saying you were home alone watching TV."

"And why did you place an active protection charm over him? Is he in danger himself?"

"Not directly, but I'm not taking any chances. He . . . he's a natural intuitive."

"A psychic?"

"Not exactly. But he's smart, and with proper training, might be able to grow his abilities. I've been working with him a little. Suffice it to say that he's under my watch. You don't have to worry about him."

"Okay . . . so back to Miriam and Tarra. Let me ask you directly: Do you know who assaulted them?"

"No."

"But . . . ?"

"But I'm afraid it has to do with Calypso somehow. I recognized her hand that night at the ball, in the corsage."

"You're saying she made the corsage?"

"No. But she grew the flowers."

"Anise admitted to me that she made the corsage with flowers from Calypso's garden, but I'm sure the needles and thread—the curse—must have been added later. There was even a tiny spindle . . ." I remembered Miriam had a Band-Aid on her finger. Had she been pricked by a spindle, just like Sleeping Beauty?

"A Sleeping Beauty curse isn't an easy one to pull off," said Aidan, as though reading my thoughts.

"Maybe . . . maybe it wasn't meant to be a full sleeping curse. Tarra was killed, Miriam put in a coma, and Anise seems half awake. . . . What if whoever cast the spells isn't aware of his or her own strength? What if they aren't really in control?"

"Remind you of anyone?"

"I might not know my own strength when it comes to

things like coven circles, but I'm measured when I cast. What about . . . Calypso says she's not a witch, but clearly she's powerful. Could she have inadvertently—"

"*No.*"

"O-kaaay," I said, drawing out the word. I got the distinct impression that Aidan's perspective might be a little out of whack where Calypso was concerned. I remembered the photograph I saw of the two of them together; Aidan's expression was open and happy, guileless. I had never seen him that way. Perhaps he and Calypso shared something much deeper than I had first assumed. I wasn't sure how I felt about that notion.

"Listen," said Aidan, sounding impatient. "It's very important that Calypso isn't publicly seen to be involved in any of this. She's been through enough because of me—I owe her my protection and my discretion, at the very least. But if I muck around in this directly . . . well, she'll know it, and that's the last thing she wants. Do this for me, Lily. Figure out who did this and why, and lay this to rest before Calypso gets tarred with the same brush."

Yeah, no problem. Because I was so clear on how to do that.

I was distracted, still pondering Aidan's words as I parked my car around the corner from Aunt Cora's Closet. As I walked toward the store, an uneasy sensation started to grow.

Something is wrong.

Unease blossomed into fear. I ran the rest of the block until coming to stand before Aunt Cora's Closet. My home. My refuge. My haven.

Desecrated.

The front door was ajar, its glass pane shattered and lying in ugly shards upon the mosaic entry. One of the large display windows had been smashed as well, pieces glinting amid the jumble of merchandise inside.

Clothes had been yanked off of hangers and scattered everywhere, entire rods knocked over. Hats, gloves, parasols, and purses were tossed willy-nilly. Satins, silks, and cotton pooled on the floor. In one corner were the torn and shattered one-of-a-kind silk pieces I had found last weekend at the Oakland Museum white elephant sale; beside them were a few military uniforms I had salvaged from "big trash pickup day" in Daly City. The beautiful walnut antique jewelry cabinet had been tipped on its side, and the main display counter bashed in, its velvet trays full of costume jewelry and talismans thrown to the floor. Every single spirit bottle had been smashed, their contents lying in wet puddles.

And scrawled in ugly red spray paint on the back wall, right over the hanging antique dresses on display: *Suffer Not a Witch to Live.*

I had heard the ugly phrase before, many times. Its hateful, vicious tone always made me cringe.

My heart wept at the violation. Bad juju. Bad energy. Whatever you wanted to call it, it now permeated this place. This place I had called home, a haven from the world, from destructive forces. The trespassers had pierced my peaceful bubble. It was ironic—I had been careful about being at the labyrinths at night, but never gave much thought to anyone coming for me here.

The muted sound of explosions drifted down from overhead. The television.

Oscar.

I ran, noting as I went that the back room was intact, the table still set with a china teapot and two delicate eggshell porcelain teacups, evidence of Bronwyn's afternoon chamomile tea break.

Before reaching the top of the stairs, I could see that

my wreath of stinging nettles, superb guardian plants, was untouched. The protective charm I had put on the door was intact. I couldn't use such a strong spell on the shop because it would keep everyone out unless I escorted them, a major flaw in the retail business.

"Mistress?" Oscar opened the door and came out onto the landing.

I felt a wave of relief so strong that I sank onto the top step, scooping Oscar into my arms.

"You're okay?" I asked, though I could see that he was.

"Sure. Why?" He pulled away. He wasn't much of one for overt physical displays of affection. Normally, neither was I.

"Someone ransacked the place. The store's a disaster."

"Really?"

"You didn't hear anything?"

He shook his head. "I was watching *Terminator 2*. The governor's in it!"

"*Ex*-governor."

"Whatever. It was sort of loud." He peered over my shoulder, down the stairs. "So, what happened?"

"Come on; see if you can tell me anything."

I led the way down the stairs.

"I told you cowans were no good," hissed Oscar when we emerged from the back room.

"This isn't the work of cowans in general," I said. "Just one or two really awful ones."

Cowan was a derogatory word for non-witchy folk, handed down from the burning times. I understood the anger behind the word—perhaps never better than today—but in general I disapproved of its use. There was never any point to ascribing to a group the actions of a few.

Crouching, I gathered together random pieces that had been ripped and shredded—they had been handled by the perpetrators. I held to my cheek the softest cottons, scratchy wools, crinkly crinolines. I felt anger, rage, fear . . . and an out-of-control defensiveness.

"Whoever did this was disturbed," I said. "They're dangerous."

As the words were coming out of my mouth, I heard an odd sound. Was that a moan? Was someone here?

I started flinging clothes around, digging through the rubble.

Then I heard it again: another moan. And . . . a giggle?

Conrad.

I found him in the dressing room, eyes closed, his head cradled on a fluffy white petticoat.

I fell to my knees beside him. When I laid hands upon him I sensed the same strange vibration I had when I felt the clothes. There was something . . . not natural. Could the DOM group have magic? That was crazy, though, wasn't it? They were dead set against magic.

"Conrad, can you hear me?"

There was a crashing noise from the front of the store.

I surged up, full of rage. I thrust out my hand and sent a blast of energy that hurled the newcomer back against the door.

"Lily, *stop*! It's me!"

I caught myself. It was Sailor.

"*Great balls of fire!* You like to scare me half to death! Did I hurt you?"

He shook his head, though he rubbed at his chest with one large hand. A smile hovered on his lips. "Did you just say 'great balls of fire'?"

"I don't recall. I guess."

"People *say* that? For real?"

"What would you prefer? That I adopt the regional tendency to use the 'F' word every time I turn around?"

"*Some*body's grumpy this evening," he said.

"In case it escaped your notice, my store was ransacked. And you just scared the living you-know-what out of me." My hand still on my chest, I willed my heart to slow. "I'll be surprised if I don't suffer from *susto* tomorrow."

"That's a Mexican folk illness, right? It's not real, is it?"

"Real enough to those who suffer from it. Anyway, I'm glad you're here. I need your help."

"What happened?" The amusement left his face as he saw Conrad on the floor. He rushed down the clothes-strewn aisle to join us. "Is he hurt?"

"Whoever broke in here . . . I don't know. Help me get him upstairs."

"Shouldn't we call an ambulance?"

Just then Conrad started laughing and burst out singing Lady Gaga's "Bad Romance."

"I don't know. Not yet. I don't think so. He's got a bump on his head, but . . ."

"Looks more drunk than hurt," Sailor said, picking up a half-empty bottle of vodka and handing it to me. I sniffed the contents, relieved to smell nothing more sinister than the alcohol itself.

Sailor crouched down next to Conrad and gently shook his shoulder. "Hey, bud. C'mon, now. Tell us what happened. Are you hurt?"

"Duuude, they totally overpowered the Con." He laughed again. "But they brought gifts! Enough to share." With much effort he pulled a couple of dime bags and pills out of his pants and gestured to the vodka.

"Who were they? Did you recognize them?"

"Nah, dude. They were, like, wearing robes with hoods. Like your people, Lily." He frowned, as though the thought was hurting his brain. "But you never wear a robe. How come?"

I ignored his question, feeling unreasonably angry toward him for putting himself in harm's way and then giving in to his addictions.

"You said 'they.' How many were there?"

"Couple, at least," he said, gesturing to the vodka bottle. "Have a drink. It's time to party!"

"How about you?" I asked Sailor. "Do you sense anything? Can you tell me anything about what happened?"

He shrugged, looking around at the mess. "As you know, this psychic business isn't like calling up an article on the Internet. Things are vague, unfocused images or flashes of insight."

He hesitated.

"What?"

"What what?"

"You were about to say something more."

"You the psychic now?"

"Just perceptive. What is it?"

"There's something else. Something . . . magical, for lack of a better word. But off-kilter. Similar to what was present at the theater. You don't feel it?"

I tried to calm myself, center myself, call on exterior forces. I shook my head.

"You're not a scryer, right?"

"Aidan tell you that?"

He nodded. "Maybe that's it. These things run along planes; maybe you aren't tuned in to this one."

Conrad started singing again, and I felt like smacking him. Sailor looked at me with some amusement.

"What do you want me to do with our friend here?"

"Can you help me get him upstairs? I'll make a draft for him for his head and the inevitable aftereffects of whatever he's on. I think . . . I think he's high as well as drunk. Maybe he'll be able to tell us more when he's sober."

We pulled Conrad to his feet.

"Good thing he's skinny," said Sailor. He flung the young man over his shoulder in a fireman's clutch, hoisted him up the stairs and into my apartment, then laid him down on the couch.

Sailor and Oscar watched me closely while I brewed. I wasn't used to an audience—it had taken me a while to get used to Oscar, even—but for some reason I didn't feel self-conscious in front of Sailor. Not with my magic, at least.

Conrad drank the brew dutifully, then curled onto one side and drifted off, singing softly to himself.

"I'll be right back," I said. I went into my bedroom, washed up, then called Carlos and told him what had happened. Though he was homicide, not burglary, he said he would notify the proper authorities.

I emerged to find Sailor rooting around in the kitchen. Again, I felt surprisingly comfortable with his intrusion.

"Found it." He filled two water glasses with a splash of rum, handed one to me and held his own up in salute.

"Here's to surviving the witch hunt."

We clinked glasses and drank.

I sat at the table while Sailor leaned up against the kitchen counter. The warmth of the liquid seared through me, and I realized I had felt chilly since wandering the East Bay hills of Sibley.

For the first time since he'd arrived, I took a moment to study him. He was only half dressed.

"Sailor, what are you doing here?"

Chapter 22

He looked at me a long moment without speaking.

"Where's your motorcycle jacket and helmet?"

He shrugged. His hair was wet, and he smelled of soap. I read ... embarrassment?

"Did you come straight out of the shower?"

"I pulled on pants, so let's not get picky."

"Did Aidan send you?"

He shook his head. "I ... felt something."

"Felt something? Like what?"

He shrugged. "Back when I spent some time in Aunt Cora's Closet, I put a sort of psychic tracer on it. I can't follow you from afar, but I can track things at the store."

"You mean like a remote alarm system?"

"Sort of."

I smiled.

"What?"

"You came to rescue me?"

He shrugged again.

"You-ou li-ike me," I singsonged.

"Okay, okay. Enough. I admit it. You're not that bad.

In moments of weakness, I worry about what sort of damn-fool trouble you might get yourself into."

"Stop with the flattery or I'll swoon."

He finally smiled in response and took another swig of the rum. He held up the bottle and studied the label. "Flor de Cana, from Nicaragua? Good stuff."

His words barely registered. Sailor had been worried about me. He had rushed over here half dressed in his haste. The hair at his nape was curling softly as it dried, and I found myself jealous of the way it touched his neck.

Our eyes met. Held. For too long.

He pushed away from the counter. "Well, now that I see you're okay and have witnessed your strange magical curing ceremony, I should go."

"You have more strange magical ceremonies to witness, do you?"

He gave a reluctant chuckle as he headed for the door. With one hand on the knob, he turned back and fixed me with an intense gaze.

"You'll be okay, then."

I smiled and nodded. "Thank you for coming to my rescue."

"It wasn't that, exactly."

"How would you describe it?"

"An uncharacteristic impulse."

"You ran out of the shower, Sailor."

He seemed suddenly serious. He released the knob and took a step toward me. The breath caught in my throat.

"*Lily*?" A voice came from downstairs.

Sailor and I both startled at the sound.

It was Carlos. His voice was accompanied by the crackle of police radios. I had been so caught up with Sailor that I hadn't noticed they'd arrived.

"Be right down," I called.

"Oh, goodie, it's your friends from the SFPD," Sailor said, the sardonic tone back in his voice. "Is there a back way out?"

Conrad started singing again, and rolled off the couch onto the floor with a loud thump.

"Listen, Conrad is in no shape to talk to the authorities. Maybe when he's sober, but not yet . . ." I said in a low voice. I wasn't sure what drugs Conrad was on, exactly, and I couldn't bear to have him thrown in the slammer when he had tried to help save Aunt Cora's Closet. "Do me a huge favor and stay with him up here, make sure he's quiet until I finish with Carlos?"

Sailor gave me a pained look.

"You could watch the rest of *Terminator 2* with Oscar." As I said it, I realized it wasn't the best enticement. "Please?"

I could see the muscle work in his jaw, but he blew out a breath and said, "C'mon, pig. Let's go finish up *Terminator*."

"Thank you."

"You owe me. Yet again."

I hurried down the stairs and out onto the main floor of Aunt Cora's Closet, my heart lurching once again as I saw the chaos with fresh eyes.

Carlos was standing by the smashed display counter, braving the broken glass to pick up my carved talismans. He looked like he had just climbed out of bed—his hair was uncombed, there was a day's growth of black beard, and he had circles under his eyes.

"Be careful," I said. "You'll cut yourself."

He shook his head. "This is a damned shame. I'm sorry about this, Lily."

"Me too. But it could have been worse. These are only things," I lied. It was a violation of my safe place, an injury to my soul. But at least Conrad—and Oscar—hadn't been seriously hurt.

A uniformed officer started taking the robbery report, while another looked around and took notes. It was soon apparent, however, that nothing obvious had been stolen: The jewelry was left scattered on the floor; even the highest-value vintage dresses were strewn about or torn, but not taken. The cash register, which I emptied every night anyway, hadn't been opened.

"Looks more like vandalism than robbery," said the young officer. I nodded.

"No shit, Sherlock," said Carlos. "We need the DOM guys on this. It's clearly one of their actions."

I gave them my statement but omitted the part about Conrad, hoping I was doing the right thing. But I imagined I would get more information out of him once he sobered up than the authorities would ever hope to. I would share whatever I learned with Carlos.

After the officers had cordoned off the scene, taken photos, and departed, Carlos helped me to nail boards up over the broken windows.

"I hate like hell that this happened to you, Lily," Carlos said. "You're a vintage clothing store, for heaven's sake. Other than Bronwyn's herbal stand, you've got nothing witchy in here."

"Except for the pentacles."

"Right."

"And the talismans and the spirit bottles."

He smiled. "Okay, I guess you're pretty out there. That's why I was warning you about these whack jobs. Anyway, it's a damned shame. At least no one got hurt, right?"

I nodded. As I surveyed the damage, I wondered what sort of progress Herve might have made with his vengeance against the perpetrators. Though I tried to rise above, I understood the impulse. It wasn't the lost inventory that pained me. It was the sensation of being violated, the nasty energy that now pervaded the store in place of the beautiful vibrations of friends and joy and herbs.

"Is there someone upstairs?" Carlos asked as the muted sound of a series of explosions drifted down to us.

"I left the television on. Felt disconcerted being alone after coming home to this, so I turned on the TV."

"Maybe you should sleep at a friend's house."

"I might. I'll be fine. I've got a pig upstairs to snuggle with." He opened his mouth as though he were going to say something but changed his mind. "Really, Carlos, I'll be fine."

"The DOM task force will be here first thing tomorrow to go over the scene and talk with you. You want me to call a twenty-four-hour glass service?"

"No, thanks. I'll call someone in the morning. I think right now we could all use some sleep. This'll look less bleak in the morning."

Carlos's dark eyes glanced around the store, and he raised his eyebrows. "You sure about that?"

I reached out and gave him a hug. This was unusual behavior for me—I'm not really a hugger. Carlos returned my squeeze.

"Hey, I wanted to tell you. I spoke to Calypso Cafaro," said Carlos. "Get this: She was indeed a licensed foster home for several years. She lost it when she was accused of witchcraft by one of the girls in her care."

"Witchcraft? You're sure?"

He nodded. "That was the accusation. Whether or not it was real . . . who knows? I looked her up—it seems Cafaro was vilified in the local press and wound up pulling something of a hermit number. Bowed out of foster care altogether."

"Do you know the name of her accuser?"

"It was anonymous, since all the girls were underage. I don't know her name, and if I did I wouldn't be able to give it to you."

"Okay, thanks for telling me."

"You sure you're okay?"

I nodded. "I really am. Thanks for coming. Thanks for everything."

"You're welcome," he said as he picked through the tossed inventory on the way to the front door. "By the way, the theater isn't going to press trespassing charges. You just have to pay a court fine and you're off the hook."

"Thanks, Carlos."

"You're welcome. Turns out, I have a second cousin who's married to the brother of one of the board big-wigs."

"You really *do* know everyone."

"Benefit of a big family that's been in this area for generations—sooner or later, I'm related to just about everybody. Plus, I called it wrong when I suggested you speak with that vintage clothes store owner...." He pulled a pad out of his back pocket and consulted his notes. "Greta Cafaro. She can't stand you. She's been spending a lot of time on the phone trying to convince folks to lock you up and throw away the key."

"Greta Cafaro?"

"She's a real piece of work. Suppose she's a relation to your botanical specialist?"

"That's a good question.... I don't suppose you got hold of the record from the Victrola?"

He shook his head. "She got the police to release it to her, and she's not interested in giving it up."

"Thanks for trying, anyway. Good night."

"'Night. And for what it's worth, lock this door after I leave."

"Yes, sir."

As I locked up, as best I could, and picked my way through the mess toward the back room, my mind was buzzing. Calypso had mentioned a sister in passing, when she was telling me about being a foster mother. Could that sister be Greta? The two women looked nothing alike, but then I looked nothing like my mother. Or, for all I knew, they were foster sisters rather than blood relatives. And they certainly *acted* nothing alike.

And how would it be significant, anyway? I wondered.

I entered my apartment to find Sailor grumpy and pacing. *Super.* I had known the reasonable, almost kind version of Sailor had been temporary, too good to last.

"You and Carlos really are chummy lately, aren't you?"

"He's a friend of mine. You know that."

"Uh-huh. I gotta get the hell out of here." He strode toward the door.

"Sailor, *wait.*" I grabbed his arm as he went past. He yanked it away.

"*What?* What is it you want now?"

"You don't have to rush off. I mean . . ." I was at a loss. What *did* I want from him? All I knew was that after he ran over here in the middle of the night, ready to rescue me, I couldn't stand to have him storm off angry. Still, my hostess skills were limited. "Could I get you anything? Another drink, maybe? A beer? Or something to eat?"

He gave a mirthless chuckle. He was breathing hard and scowling, the picture of belligerence.

"Can you '*get me* anything'? Is that what you asked?

I want one thing from you, and you know what it is. You promised."

"I told you I'm working on it."

He snorted. "I'll believe it when I see it."

"Why are you being so nasty all of a sudden? What have I ever done to you?"

"First, you made me confront a demon. I *hate* demons." He held out his hand and extended one finger with each count. "Then you dragged me around town while you got into business you weren't supposed to be in; then you made me introduce you to my crazy aunt; then you broke into my apartment and went through my things. Then I get thrown around in a haunted theater, tossed in *jail*, thank you very much, and before I know it I'm stuck up here babysitting a drunk and a pig while you're making cozy with the cops."

"Like you're an innocent in all of this? You've spied on *me*. And my breaking into your apartment, well, that was only the one time, and it was a misunderstanding."

"Uh-huh. Well, that misunderstanding has my aunt furious. And just in case you weren't aware, it's not generally a good idea to have a Rom witch angry at you. I had to talk her out of casting a hex on you."

"Why bother? If you dislike me so much, why not let her at me?"

"I don't hold with any of that kind of crap. You *or* my aunt. I just want you all to leave me the hell alone."

"I don't believe you. We're friends, and I get the sense you could use all the friends you can get."

"I sure as hell don't need you, princess, and don't go thinking I do."

"We all need someone."

"I don't."

"You're psychic, Sailor, not inhuman."

"I'm outta here, is what I am."

I stood in front of the door, blocking his way. I didn't know what had gotten into me ... but I was determined not to let this already wretched night end this way.

"I'm warning you, Lily. This is one of those times it's best to let sleeping dogs lie."

"I think you like to think of yourself as some terrible sort, an awful kind of loner. But the truth is, I think you're a kind man."

He snorted.

"Noble, even. You've certainly come through for me when I needed you."

"Are you *serious*? I've never been noble in my life."

"Oh, I think you are. You gave your soul for your wife."

"*Ex*-wife. And look where that landed me."

"Why don't you like anyone thinking well of you? I think you're sort of ... great."

"Stop it."

"I like you, Sailor. A lot."

"*That does it.*"

Before I knew what was happening, he was holding me firmly by the shoulders, drawing me to him, and his mouth came down on mine. At first my mind went blank with shock, but the searing heat of his lips demanded a response. I opened to him, all thoughts fleeing as a whirl of sensations swept over me.

Warmth. Everywhere he touched—with his mouth, his hands—left a trail of sizzling heat. His tongue delved into my mouth, demanding, sparring with my own. His arms encircled me, holding me to him, tighter, practically lifting me off the ground. My own arms wound around his neck, accepting him, giving him my all.

He pushed me up against the wall. The kiss went from hot to on fire, almost out of control.

This wasn't the electricity I felt with Aidan—there

was no collateral damage, nothing crashing about or melting. But it was the kind of chemistry between people who fit together, a kind of awareness beyond the norm. Any sense of myself dissipated in the overwhelming, sweet insistence of our bodies, a connection beyond thought.

Sailor broke away, looking down at me with confusion in his eyes, as though he'd never seen me before. Then he stepped back so suddenly, I might have fallen over if not for the wall holding me up.

He ran one hand through his hair. "Ah, *heellll*."

I just stared at him, trying to catch my breath.

"I can't believe I just did that. . . ." He reached out to touch my swollen lips, a vulnerable look on his face.

I put my hand up to his whiskery cheek, relishing the raspy feeling against my palm.

"Kiss me again."

"I . . . This isn't one of your damned spells, is it?" he said. "Promise me."

I shook my head. "I would never do that."

And he kissed me again.

The scent of roses surrounded me, inundated me. It mixed with Sailor's subtle scent of exotic spices to form a heady combination.

At some point we wound up in my bed. Somehow in Sailor's arms I felt able, capable, the vestiges of insecurity sliding away under the ardor of his kisses, the envelopment of his energy. For the first time in days, I felt thoroughly warm.

I slept the sleep of the dead, dreaming of Miriam asleep in a rose garden, saw her prick her finger, blood flowing onto the single white rosebush among the crimson, like the funny fellows in *Alice in Wonderland* painting the roses red.

Chapter 23

When I awoke, there were rose petals scattered on the bed.

I lifted Sailor's heavy arm off of me and glanced around the room.

Like a fragrant pink-and-red blanket, rose petals were strewn on my bureau and vanity, atop my lace curtains, on the windowsill, and sprinkled inches deep upon the floor.

Could this be Oscar's doing? Or was it some kind of accidental magic? I had been thinking about roses when I was with Sailor. . . . Had I unconsciously conjured? Focusing energy was one thing; even animating the inanimate was within my magical realm. But manifesting something concrete like this was beyond my powers.

Or at least it always had been.

My first impulse was to try to cover it up somehow, to hide what I had done. But on second thought . . . I'd be damned if I gave in to insecurity at this point.

Sailor was a big boy. He could handle it. And I was done with hiding myself from people I cared for.

"Sailor, wake up. We need to talk."

He groaned but didn't open his eyes.

"Sailor."

"Anyone ever tell you you talk too much?"

"I believe you've mentioned it once or twice."

He hugged me closer and smiled, the skin at the corners of his eyes crinkling adorably. Finally, he opened his eyes.

"I've got to warn you: I'm not great before coffee. In fact, my own *mother* called me an ogre before coffee. And according to rumor, she *likes* me."

I smiled.

"So if we're going to have one of those 'talks,' for both of our sakes, I should get some caffeine into me before . . ." He trailed off as his hand landed on soft rose petals. He held them up and looked at them quizzically. "What the hell . . . ?"

I avoided his eyes.

"Did you do this?" he asked, his gaze sweeping around the room. "Is this . . . Is this something you do?"

"No. I mean, it's not something I've ever done before. It's . . . I don't really know what it is."

He gazed at me. I thought I noted more worry than anger in his expression, but it was hard to tell. I was still trying to get a handle on Sailor's emotions, most of which seemed to manifest as out-and-out irritation.

"So you're saying this doesn't happen every time?"

"Rose petals have never appeared before."

"What *does* happen?"

My cheeks were burning. I hadn't had all that much experience with this sort of thing; nor was I the kind of person who went around flaunting such things. I was still a small-town girl from Texas, after all.

"One time . . . once before, there was something strange." Sailor gazed at me, clearly not about to let this subject drop. I took a deep breath and went on. "The clothes downstairs, they were sort of . . . enchanted?"

"Enchanted." He scootched back to sit up against the brass bedstead, the white sheet riding low around his hips. "Would you care to elaborate on that?"

"They danced."

"And that was it? They didn't lead into any other transformations, nothing like that?"

I shook my head.

"Is this the first time something's actually manifested?"

I nodded. "It's sort of pretty, don't you think?"

As though deciding something, he paused, then relaxed an infinitesimal amount, his lids falling closed a bit, his mouth relaxing. "Very pretty. Smells good, too."

I smiled. He responded with a half smile that was more seductive than amused.

"Come here."

When we kissed, the petals swirled up and around us like fragrant pink butterflies.

I pulled away. If we felt that magic between us again, I would be off to a late start. And I had to go. The dream I had—the image of Miriam's blood soaking the roses—was it a sign? I had never experienced reliable visions before. But I had seen what must have been a premonition in the theater before Miriam fell ill, when I viewed the woman lying amid thorns in the mirror. And then in the hospital when I laid hands on Miriam, I saw a similar sight. Was it possible that all the work I'd been doing on scrying was starting to pay off?

In any case, whether the dream was merely a random message from my subconscious or a vision of some kind, it compelled me to act—quickly.

I had to go back to Calypso's place. We needed to

chat, and I needed something very particular from her garden. Something she, herself, had grown.

Sailor groused, but I finally coaxed him out of bed with the promise of coffee and the threat of a murderer on the loose. Also, he seemed to savor the idea that Aidan might be blind where his old friend Calypso was concerned—I wasn't convinced she was innocent in all of this. On the contrary.

I put on coffee, then called Maya and Bronwyn and let them know what had happened with the store. I suggested they each take the morning off, and we would get together later in the afternoon to start the cleanup. Then I came out to the front room to find that Conrad had already gone, leaving behind a note of thanks for the use of my couch and apology for having been under the influence and for letting the store be ransacked. Poor guy. I needed to track him down, let him know I didn't blame him for what happened, and see whether he could tell me anything further about the vandals.

Downstairs I put up a sign on the broken window of the front door, telling the public that Aunt Cora's Closet would reopen just as soon as we could.

When I returned to the kitchen and started whipping up a batch of biscuits, Oscar came to join me.

"Be careful, mistress," he said.

"Careful?"

"You and Sailor . . ."

"He's a good man, Oscar. You're sweet to worry, but I feel really good about this."

He wouldn't meet my eyes.

"Oscar?"

"Master Aidan . . . he's not going to like this."

I hoisted Oscar up on the counter so I could speak to him eye to eye.

"Master Aidan doesn't have to find out, now, does he?

He's not your master, remember? I'm your mistress now, and have been ever since he gave you to me. Oscar, you're a very special creature. But a witch's familiar can't be loyal to two masters."

He folded skinny arms over his scaly chest.

"Do you understand me?"

After a long pause, he nodded. "I won't tell, mistress. I promise."

"Good," I said, relieved. I buttered a hot biscuit, fresh out of the oven, added a dollop of my own strawberry preserves, and handed it to him. "Thank you for your discretion."

He nodded again, and bit into the biscuit. I heard Sailor coming out of the bedroom and turned to hand him a cup of coffee.

"I won't tell, but Aidan has a way of finding things out," came Oscar's quiet growl behind me.

Sailor insisted on accompanying me to Calypso's house, and though I put up a symbolic protest I was happy to have him along. Not only for safety concerns, but because it was just plain fun to be with him—his companionship nearly made me forget the mess someone had made of my store. On the long drive up the coast, whether we chatted or sat in silence, it felt good. Exciting, a little nerve-racking, yet at the same time somehow . . . comfortable.

I turned off at the dirt road, and we squeezed through the hedge.

"This is quite a place," said Sailor as I drove up to the house.

"Isn't it, though? I used to dream of having a place like this."

"You don't anymore?"

"Lately I find myself pretty happy in the city. Guess I like the action."

He gave an ironic smile. "Plenty of that, lately."

I half expected Calypso to come out to the porch and greet us as she did last time, but when the house remained silent I went up and rang the doorbell, then knocked loudly.

"Guess she's not home," I said.

I looked at Sailor. He shrugged. Together, we started around the back, searching for an open window.

There were plenty in my life who would accuse me of thinking I'm above the law. Thing is, I was sure of my own motives, and it seemed to me that a woman who didn't adhere to the natural laws of physics or the universe didn't need to worry much about human-made rules and regulations.

I considered how Carlos Romero would respond to that. Not well, I imagined.

The exterior door to the greenhouse was ajar. I pushed it open.

Inside was a gruesome tableau. Several dead birds: a dove, a swallow, a crow. And a hare. A jar with a liquid that looked a whole lot like blood, almost black in the dim light.

"What in the world is all this about?" asked Sailor.

"A love spell," I said, then shook my head. "Not real love, but a way to force someone to feel something they wouldn't otherwise."

On the table was a fat book of spells not like my Book of Shadows, but a real, published book of medieval incantations and recitations. This sort of thing scared me: trying to duplicate spells from long ago without the training and knowledge that had been lost, save for by a few of us.

I read the spell: "*Black dust of tomb, venom of toad, bile of ox, blood of brigand . . .*"

A thief's blood? Perhaps she used her own. At least it

wasn't a chunk of flesh or fat, something that required death beyond the poor birds. A piece of wool soaked in this mixture, then placed under the pillow of the romantic interest—or worse, ingested—would lead to a blind sort of devotion that passed for obsessive love.

Calypso seemed so sure of herself. Why would she need such a strong love charm? I associated this sort of thing with self-doubt, lack of confidence. Or could her apparent charms be due to just such practices as these?

"We should get out of here," Sailor said. He had that look I was coming to recognize, when he sensed something.

I looked around and noticed the flowers and plants seeming to turn toward us, their movements almost imperceptible, but threatening.

Out in the garden, I quickly harvested the special herbs I needed for casting my spell. I would rather have taken a sample of her hair, but it wasn't worth breaking into the house. And in any case, witch or no witch, Calypso was too clever to leave hair lying around, I would wager.

Sailor offered to drive home. The hedge seemed to have closed in on us, but we squeaked through. While Sailor handled the twists and turns of the highway with ease, I asked to borrow his cell phone to call Carlos.

"I think Calypso Cafaro might have killed Tarra," I told him.

"What motive would she have?"

"Could Tarra have been the foster daughter who turned her into authorities?"

"I'll see if I can find out."

"Anyway, there's . . . stuff in her house you might want to see."

"Stuff? Like what?" Carlos asked.

"Evidence of a spell—the kind that involves animal

sacrifice." There is energy in spilling the blood of a living being, a glint of power that cannot be replicated with any other kind of sacrifice, however dear. But anyone who would use it to cast a love spell . . . well, I don't hold with that.

"She showed this to you?"

"Not exactly. I sort of saw it."

"But she invited you into her home, is what I'm saying." At my lack of immediate response, Carlos added: "You can't go into someone's home without an invitation, Lily."

"That only works on vampires, not witches."

I thought I heard a reluctant chuckle. "Unlike some people I can name, *I* can't barge into homes without reason. I need a warrant. I questioned her after you gave me her information, but didn't come up with probable cause. Can you think of any other evidence that would point to her?"

"You mean besides the fact that two—maybe three— of her seven pupils were poisoned?"

"Have the doctors determined Miriam was poisoned?"

"No," I admitted. "They can't figure it out. But there were henbane flowers in her corsage that night at the ball."

"This would be the corsage we don't have, that the emergency personnel don't remember seeing."

"I have the corsage now. You're welcome to it."

"And if this corsage has poisonous flowers in it, we would blame it on some woman up in Bolinas rather than the boyfriend or the florist . . . why, exactly?"

Sometimes I hated the criminal justice system. It seemed enough for me to just determine who might be guilty of wrongdoing. Then again, I reminded myself, I had been wrong too many times to count. I supposed that's why there was a process for such things, to try to avoid such wild accusations.

"Wait—I also have lip balm of Miriam's that contains henbane, I believe. I can get that to you."

"And do you know who supplied Miriam with this lip balm?"

"Not exactly."

"I've done some research into poisonous plants. Apparently a very small dose of Hyoscyamus, aka henbane, does a world of good for motion sickness. Who's to say Miriam wasn't dosing herself, using organic materials?"

I sighed audibly and studied the scenery as we whizzed by. Now that I knew what to look for, I kept spotting rings of redwoods like the one at the edge of the forest near Calypso's house.

"Look, you know I trust your instincts on this sort of thing," Carlos said. "And I'm trying to be flexible, which is evidenced by the fact that I'm not accusing you of criminal trespassing after you just admitted to me that you broke into someone's house. But unless you have something more concrete, the most I can do is conduct an independent investigation of Cafaro based on her involvement with the botanicals group and see if I can get to the same conclusions in a legal manner."

"You're right. Thanks. Let me know when you find anything out, will you?"

"Sure thing. Oh, by the way: We made an arrest in the DOM case. You're not going to believe who."

"Greta Cafaro."

"How did you know?"

"Instinct." Greta had mentioned "knowing" my neighbor Sandra's store right after Sandra found a warning from DOM. And later, she asked whether Herve would reopen his store, though from my side of the conversation she couldn't have known what I was talking about that day in Vintage Chic. Thinking back on her words at the Art Deco Ball, when she spoke of "preserving our way of life"—that was the exact phrase on the DOM flyers and the billboard. And finally, as Calypso's sister . . . there was something about the DOM's fervent messages that made me think someone involved was very familiar with the world of magic.

I felt a surge of sympathy for Calypso. Raised in foster care, with a sister from whom, I presumed, she was now estranged, she had endured some mysterious negative history with Aidan, and then was accused of wrongdoing by a young person she was trying to help . . . Maybe she had simply gone 'round the bend, living out there in that big, beautiful house all alone.

"Anyway . . . Greta and her cronies have an airtight alibi for that night at your place. Across town, at Ghirardelli Square at a fund-raiser. Oh, and by the way? I asked about that record for you. She says it had satanic messages on it, so she smashed it."

My heart fell. "Oh, thanks for trying."

"I felt sort of sorry for her when they brought her into the station. She's got some kind of terrible rash all over her body, even on her face. Almost didn't recognize her."

I guess Herve got his revenge.

But according to Carlos, Greta hadn't been the one who'd torn up Aunt Cora's Closet last night. I wasn't too surprised. . . . I had a feeling the culpable party wasn't DOM, but someone with magical abilities. I didn't care what Calypso said about not practicing magic. What I just saw in her greenhouse was clear: She was casting. But would she go after my store? Was she trying to scare me off?

I had a sneaking fear . . . Could that love charm have been meant for someone like . . . me and Sailor? Was there a reason last night happened?

I could still feel him, the sensation of his whiskers on my neck, his scent and warmth enveloping me. I sighed again. Closed my eyes and tried to get myself together. This was ridiculous.

I opened them to see Sailor glancing over at me. We had emerged from the winding highway and were now on the freeway that skirted the bay to the north.

The look he gave me was one of yearning and desire, unspoken need.

Great. Now I had to worry about whether my most intimate feelings were being manipulated by a third party. But why? To keep me busy and out of people's hair?

"You okay?" Sailor asked, his voice low and gruff.

I nodded. "But Carlos can't do anything about what we saw."

"Chain of evidence."

"Guess so."

"So how do we track down this woman? Any of the people you've been talking to seem open to a friendly conversation, maybe one in which you use your mind-control skills?"

"It's not *mind* control," I insisted, punching him lightly in the ribs. "As you very well know."

He grinned. "Your persuasive skills, then?"

"One of the girls, maybe." I thought of Anise and Jonquil, but I didn't know where to find them. I wished I had asked them more questions. "Or . . . maybe Jonathan?"

"Who's that?"

"Miriam's boyfriend. He's so worried about her—according to Bronwyn, he's made amends. He's been helping with her baby and spending time with Miriam at the hospital. But he mentioned he'd be in his shop today. Maybe he could tell us where to find the women, and they could tell us more about Calypso."

"Worth a shot. Let's go."

I told him the location, and we headed across the Richmond-San Rafael Bridge, past Berkeley, to Oakland. When we arrived, Sailor found a parking space not far from MJ's Games.

"Jonathan's perfectly nice," I said. "You could just drop me off. You don't have to go in with me."

He rolled his eyes. "Yeah. Right."

"I'm serious. I'm sure you have other things to do, and this is probably just another of my harebrained schemes...."

"Why are you trying to get rid of me?"

I felt my cheeks burning. "I'm not trying to get *rid* of you. I just . . . I imagine you have other things to do, and you never used to enjoy following me around."

We looked at each other a long time. The top was down on the convertible, the sun was shining down on us, a soft breeze blowing. After a few moments, I noticed we were both breathing fast.

Great balls of fire, please make this not be the result of a spell.

Finally he lifted his hand to cup my cheek. "This isn't a game, Lily. I . . . I don't really do this sort of thing."

I nodded and took a deep, shaky breath. "I have to tell you something. I'm afraid that we . . . that what happened . . . that it might not be coming from us. There might be magic involved."

He grinned. "I'd say it was magic, all right. And the rose petals were a nice touch."

"No . . . I mean literally, magic. I think the things we just saw in Calypso's greenhouse . . . they were evidence of a powerful love spell. I think she might have cast on us."

"You're saying what we're feeling isn't real?"

"Real, of course. But manipulated."

"Bullshit."

"I'm not—"

"You're scared, and now you're blaming what happened on an outside force. What happened to that overly confident, reckless witch I know and . . . like very much?"

"I'm not making this up, Sailor."

"What possible reason would she have for doing it?"

"To distract me."

"And are you that easily swayed?"

"Not . . . normally." But if I were already falling in love with him, unbeknownst even to myself . . . ? Then such a spell might make for a powerful potion.

"Come here," he said. He pulled me across the seat into his embrace, didn't try to kiss me but simply hugged me to his strong chest. He breathed deeply, as though taking in my scent. Finally he pulled back, not letting me go but looking down into my eyes. "You are a witch with a pretty strong guard up, twenty-four-seven. I'm an exceedingly cranky psychic, also carefully guarded. You think this woman is capable, of—what?—slipping ground-up bird hearts into our food, overcoming our natural barriers, and convincing us of something that wasn't there?"

"You were ready to accuse *me* of casting a spell on you."

"Yes, well, that would make sense. You've already proved yourself capable of getting past my very manly defenses."

I smiled.

"Anyway," I continued, "Calypso has some sort of connection with Aidan. She could be more powerful than I thought."

He shook his head and gave me a crooked smile. "And what explains the feelings I've had for you from the first moment you disturbed my peace at the bar?"

"What feelings?"

"Oh, wouldn't you like to know?" he teased. Then his voice dropped. "The feeling that I wanted to wrap my hand in your hair. That I wanted to kiss every bit of you, *everywhere*. That you scared the hell out of me because I couldn't remain as cold to you as I wanted?"

The breath left my body, leaving me speechless.

"I've thought of you, Lily."

He kissed me. This time it was so very sweet, searching but not pushy, beckoning. I leaned into him.

"Get a room," I heard. It was Jonathan, walking down the sidewalk with the baby in a sling close to his chest and Duke right beside him.

"Oh, I, uh . . ." My cheeks burned as I stammered. Sailor and I climbed out of the convertible. I introduced the men and little Luna, who was cooing, smiling and happy in Jonathan's arms. I raised questioning eyes to Duke. He grinned.

"You believe this? She's cured. I don't know if it was the egg thing you did, or the crazy spell that other gal cast, but she woke up bright and smiley yesterday morning."

"What 'other gal'? Was it an older woman?"

He shook his head. "Nah, about Miriam's age. I thought you sent her—I saw her at your shop once. Real nice, long reddish hair?"

"Jonquil?" I looked at Jonathan.

He shook his head. "I wasn't there."

"What kind of spell was it, do you know?"

Duke shrugged. "She massaged her with some kind of salve she made herself, she said, and then she said a bunch of words over her. Sort of like what you did with the egg. It didn't hurt her. Luna slept the whole night through, and woke up happy for the first time in ages."

"Jonathan," I asked, "how well do you know Jonquil? Was she one of Calypso's foster daughters?"

"Oh, I don't know anything about that. All I know about Calypso is that she ran that botanicals class. Miriam really adored her; they all did."

"But you've never met her yourself?"

"No. I guess she usually stayed pretty close to home. The drive out there is kind of long."

I nodded. "I'm looking for Anise and Jonquil. I don't suppose you know where I could find them?"

"Actually, I do. I mean, not right this second, but they were talking about going to the movies tonight. They invited me, but I'm babysitting my little buddy here."

"The movies?"

"Yeah, right here at the Paramount. They show old movies on Thursday. Tonight's *The Philadelphia Story*, with Cary Grant and Katharine Hepburn. They're taking Rex, trying to get his mind off of what happened with Tarra. I think Wolf's going, too."

The whole gang. It could be handy to have them all in the same place.

Chapter 24

Sailor asked if he could borrow my car to run some errands, and we agreed he would pick me up later and accompany me to the Paramount. Then he dropped me off at Aunt Cora's Closet. I had a lot of concentrating to do, so I was just as happy Sailor wouldn't be hanging around, distracting me.

First, I had to decide between a binding spell and a banishing spell. A banishing spell would keep the target out of my hair, but would simply redirect their anger on another unsuspecting soul. A binding spell would tie us together, enmesh my life with theirs, but give me a modicum of control over what kinds of actions they carried out.

I took a deep breath and pondered my options. What I wanted to do was a banishing spell, but I knew what I *had* to do. I brought out the ingredients for the binding spell.

Using her home grown herbs, which Calypso had tended with her own hands, would help. When nurturing plants, we bless them with a bit of ourselves. These plants had a connection to Calypso, and though it wasn't as powerful as using her nail clippings or hair, they would provide a link.

I ground the herbs, brewed them in my cauldron, cut my palm and dropped in some of my own blood as a sacrifice. And with Oscar by my side, I called on my guiding spirit.

Finally, I chanted while letting three drops of the brew fall on my trusty medicine bag.

"It is done, so mote it be," I intoned.

For better or worse, Calypso Cafaro and I were now bound.

We spent the rest of the day cleaning up Aunt Cora's Closet. Bronwyn's coven sisters came by to help, and even Wendy showed up, bringing pastries from the café to share with the workers and giving me a hug in silent apology. Several of the women from the shelter came to lend a hand as well, and though Conrad refused to talk about the other night, claiming amnesia, he pitched right in. With so many working together, the work went quickly.

"Want to order pizza and work all night till we get this done?" asked Bronwyn after several hours.

"I can't, I'm afraid. I've got a thing tonight."

"Oh! Do tell! A date?"

"Um, kind of. I'm going to the movies."

"With a date?"

"Sort of."

Maya's head swung around. "A date? Is Max back?"

"What? *No.*"

"Aidan, then? I thought he ditched you last time?" said Maya.

"No, not Aidan."

"Tell you what, Lily. You do go through some men," Bronwyn said.

"Very funny. It's ... Sailor."

"Sailor? Seriously?" Bronwyn and Maya exchanged looks.

"Why not?"

"He's a little . . . dark."

"Dark?"

"It's just that you have a few tendencies toward the gloomy, yourself," said Maya. "We were thinking you might do well with someone a little . . . sunnier."

"Sunnier. You're saying Aidan is 'sunny'?"

"He always seems to be happy," Bronwyn said. "An optimist."

"You don't know him as well as I do," I said, still reeling a bit at the idea that my friends had been discussing my love life. "Trust me on this: The man is not particularly sunny, at least not around me."

"Be that as it may," said Bronwyn, "we all know Sailor's not exactly a carefree soul."

"I do like him, though," said Maya.

"So do I," said Bronwyn. "But whether he's right for you . . ."

Maybe they were right; maybe he wasn't the best man for me. It was still so new, the jury was out. But there was something powerful between us. Still, I supposed it was possible Sailor was only with me for magical reasons, which was just too depressing to think about.

Just then Sailor pulled up outside in the Mustang, the top down so he could enjoy the pleasant evening. Through the newly replaced plate-glass window, I could see him chatting with Conrad. I liked that the two men were friendly. My heart leaped at the sight of him.

"Anyway, I appreciate y'all's concern. But I have to go to the movies now."

"Come on, Oscar, want to go for a ride?" My potbellied pig practically sailed over the debris to join us.

I had wondered, after binding Calypso, whether the

love spell might fall away and I would see Sailor as just a man again. But the chemistry was still there. He greeted me with a long, deep kiss.

Once we arrived and found parking, I let Oscar out to go search for gargoyles. Sailor didn't ask why I was permitting my pet pig to wander the streets of downtown Oakland. One of the many things I adored about the man.

Sailor and I both eyed the Paramount Theater with some trepidation. As we approached the ticket booth, I looked up at the tall mosaic façade of the theater and repressed a shiver. I hoped Sailor was correct when he told me that the crowds here tonight—the *live* crowds—would keep at bay the angry ghosts we encountered last time.

We bought our tickets and walked in. I couldn't help remembering being here with Aidan on the night of the ball. Oscar was right—I'd better take some pains to keep Aidan from finding out about my new romantic interest, for my sake, and especially for Sailor's.

The lobby was crowded with moviegoers, chatting and sipping on drinks. One unusual feature of the Paramount was the full bar. While patrons weren't allowed to take drinks into the theater itself, apparently the bar served before events and during intermissions, in the style of opera houses. It lent itself to more social interaction than was seen with the standard multiplex audience.

After a brief search of the crowd, I spied Wolfgang and Jonquil off in a secluded corner of the lobby, their heads close together, smiling and speaking in soft tones. Canoodling, my mother always called it. The way Sailor and I had been acting all day.

Well . . . *that* was interesting.

The lights overhead must have been halogen. . . . I noticed that distinctive shimmer of Aidan's glamour. But it wasn't covering Wolfgang as I had seen it before; now it lay like dust on the floor around him. He was no longer protected.

A witch's spell might have been powerful enough to do that, particularly if Wolfgang ingested something. Something from a spell involving blood sacrifice, perhaps?

"Whoa," said Anise from behind me. She balanced three glasses of wine in her hands and was headed toward the couple. "I remember you. What are you doing here?"

"Just came to see the movie," I lied. "Anise, who is your messenger at the florist shop? Who delivered the corsage to Miriam last weekend? Do you remember?"

She frowned as though it hurt to think. Then she finally met my eyes and blinked. "It used to be Tarra, but then she . . . died. Jonquil took over. Just started last weekend."

I couldn't believe I didn't think to ask that question before. It wasn't Calypso at all.

As though I had called her, Calypso wound her way through the crowd toward me, with Rex close on her heels. She seemed to understand right away that my presence at the Paramount was no coincidence.

"What's going on?" she asked me as she approached, her voice hushed.

Sailor stood right behind me, a support in more ways than one. I felt myself leaning back into his strength.

"I . . . When's the last time you were home?" I asked, glancing over at Jonquil and Wolf. They seemed impervious to everything around them, paying attention only to each other.

"Not since last night. After hearing about Tarra, I came down and stayed with friends from the Unspoken coven. I wanted to offer them my support."

"Someone's been spell casting in your greenhouse."

"No, I . . . It's impossible. The plants wouldn't allow that."

"Unless they knew her, were familiar with her from your classes, maybe?"

I looked back at the happy couple, and Calypso followed my gaze.

"Jonquil?" she said, her voice shaky. "You're saying Jonquil was casting in my greenhouse, with my plants? I've tried so hard to . . . to forgive her, to bring her back into my life. I can't believe she'd—"

"She did," I said, cutting her off.

Jonquil. Of course. Who else might have had a desperate, needy crush on Wolfgang, who was himself so in love with Tarra? Who else might have texted a confused, sedated Anise to put henbane into a corsage and then added a curse before delivering it? Who didn't know her own strength, much less how to control it? And who'd been upset at accidentally poisoning a baby and gone to help her?

I was about to head toward the corner to confront her when I realized Jonquil and Wolfgang were no longer there.

"Look, I think Jonquil's gone after Miriam's spirit. I don't have time to explain, but will you help me? We need to follow her downstairs."

"I'll do anything I can," Calypso said.

"Wait," said Anise. "What's going on?"

"Stay here," I said. "Rex, stay with her, will you?"

He nodded and wrapped his arm around her protectively.

Calypso, Sailor, and I rushed to the back of the lobby and down the stairs. We found Jonquil in the ladies' lounge, on her knees, chanting. Even from the doorway we could see Miriam's image in the mirror. She was yelling, crying, banging her fists against the reverse surface of the mirror.

Jonquil answered her, eyes narrowing, whispering and mumbling.

Wolfgang barred the entrance.

"Let us in," I said.

Wolfgang shook his head. "Sorry, Lily. You can't be here. This is a coven issue."

"It's not the coven, Wolf; it's Jonquil. She's out of control."

"Jonquil *is* the coven."

"Listen to me, Wolf. You're suffering under a spell—"

"Stand aside," Sailor ordered, accurately sensing that logic was futile.

"In your dreams," sneered Wolfgang.

Sailor shoved Wolf, and the men started wrestling. Calypso and I squeezed past them.

"Liqunoj vague eem pil mawb," said Miriam. I understood her now, though it was a little late: *Jonquil gave me lip balm.* It wasn't a pill she was trying to tell me about. "Pil mawb" meant "lip balm." Miriam had been trying to tell me all along that it was Jonquil.

"Muheereem M'ai reeh ute pleh," I responded with the few words I'd practiced: *I'm here to help.*

I tried to keep up with what Miriam was saying, but despite my recent studies, her rapid backward talk was still beyond me.

Unfortunately, I could decipher what Jonquil was muttering about: She was casting a curse.

I started incanting against her, holding my medicine bag in my left hand and rolling my eyes back in my head, concentrating. Calypso circled around to the other side of her, and though she wasn't casting, I could feel her reflecting my power. Intensifying it.

Jonquil stopped abruptly, looking at both of us. Miriam continued to protest, but her anger had given way to anguish. She was crying, still pounding against the mirror but now with hands flat against the surface, defeated.

"Stop it!" Jonquil yelled at us. "You can't help her now."

"Release her, Jonquil, sweetheart," implored Calypso. "Miriam has nothing to do with any of this."

"I didn't want to hurt her. I didn't mean to," Jonquil said, tears running down her face. "I just wanted her to forget what she saw, but she's trying to tell on me!"

"Think about it, Jonquil. Think about what you're doing. You can stop this," Calypso continued in a soothing, motherly tone. "Miriam is a good person. She wouldn't hurt you. And she has a baby who needs her."

"I never meant to hurt anyone. . . . I went back and helped the baby—tell her, Lily."

"You did help her, Jonquil. That was really good of you. Now we have to help Miriam—"

"It's not my fault. I just wanted Tarra out of the way so Wolf would realize I was the right woman for him. I don't know what happened. I cast the spell but"—she lowered her voice to a whisper and glared at Calypso—"then Tarra *died*. It must have been your fault—something about those plants you grow. They were too powerful for the spell."

Calypso was shaking her head, a woman enveloped in sadness. "Jonquil, please—"

"Miriam and Anise saw me gather the plants. I had to keep them from talking, or Wolf would never forgive me."

"And my store?" I asked. "Why did you trash it?"

"I was only trying to scare you, so—"

Jonquil cut herself off as a theater guest poked her head into the lounge: "Hey, there's two guys fighting out here," she said.

"Go!" I shouted at her.

She went. But the interruption ruined our shared moment. There was no more talking.

Jonquil started mumbling again, and so did I. But I dropped to my knees to intensify my power, yelling psychically as loud as I could for Oscar.

He showed up seconds later.

The mumbling continued, but I was much stronger than Jonquil. Her magic was disconnected, not based in skill and training but in anger and need. I could take her, easily, especially with Calypso acting as backup.

Still, her restless, out-of-control energy was stirring up the ghosts in the theater. I recognized the live-wire sensation from the last time I was here with Sailor. If I didn't get control of the situation soon, there was no telling what might happen.

Finally, Jonquil's magic failing, she reverted to decidedly human tactics. She hurled one of the wrought-iron chairs in my direction.

I ducked, but she launched herself at me. We tumbled on the floor. Jonquil was stronger than she looked, quickly gaining the upper hand and pulling my long hair. I grabbed for hers, but it slipped from my hands. Calypso tried to help but couldn't get hold of anything as we rolled around, grunting and shrieking. Jonquil managed one good sock to the eye, making me see stars. Before I could recover, Oscar butted her from behind and then, transforming into his real self, grabbed her with surprising strength and tossed her against the wall.

Jonquil shrank in the corner, petrified.

I called Oscar off as he moved toward her, growling. But the second we relented, Jonquil threw another chair at the mirror containing Miriam. It crashed into the reflective surface, shattering it in an ear-piercing explosion of glass.

Thousands of glittering shards rained down upon the carpeted floor.

Theater security took both Jonquil and Wolfgang—whom Sailor had managed to subdue—into custody. I called Carlos and told him Jonquil was the culprit behind the poisonings, that they should question her carefully and check out her place for toxins. Obviously, there was witchcraft involved, as well, but I imagine that would be hard to sell in a court of law.

Sailor brought us a broom, a dustpan, and a vacuum, and somehow managed to convince the theater staff to permit Calypso and me to clean up the lounge, at least until the police arrived. Before taking Oscar—back in his piggy guise—out to the car, Sailor lingered in the doorway, met my eyes, and gave me a warm smile and a reassuring wink.

He was confident I knew what I was doing. But I didn't.

I sat on the carpeted floor, hand over my aching eye, looking at the damage, feeling stunned. It was one thing to figure out Jonquil was the culprit, quite another to fail Miriam.

Breaking a mirror is said to bring bad luck, because the soul's reflection is fragmented and takes seven years to recover on its own. Miriam didn't have seven years to wait.

I felt a warm hand on my head and looked up into Calypso's kind eyes.

"You can do this," she said, her voice quiet and calm.

"I . . ." I trailed off, shaking my head. I had witnessed my grandmother conduct such a spell once, but she had the backing of a coven, not to mention her seventy-something years of experience. I still recalled the shiny, confettilike look of the mirror shards swirling up around her before reconstituting themselves.

I might be strong enough to do it. Or I might do it wrong, failing Miriam forever.

Calypso crouched down before me. "You are stronger than you know. I'll help you."

"I thought you said you weren't a witch," I said.

She gave a sad smile and shook her head. Her soft brown eyes took in the scene; then she closed them and let out a sigh. "I'm not. I once was, but I'm not now."

"Then . . ."

"You'll do the magic. I'll help focus your power."

"I don't have my Book of Shadows. I don't know—"

"You have no choice, Lily. You're the only one here who can do this, and Miriam needs you. Now, let's get to work."

Her matter-of-fact attitude finally roused me out of my self-doubting stupor. She was right. I had no choice.

"Do you carry a cell phone?" I asked her. "Could I borrow it?"

Calypso nodded and handed me a sleek smartphone. I dialed a number I knew by heart.

To my surprise, my grandmother Graciela was awake and, apparently, drinking with friends. I heard loud voices and raucous laughter in the background. How was it that I was starting to feel ancient, but Graciela seemed to be growing younger with each passing year?

She grew serious when I told her what I needed. She looked up the words to the spell in her own Book of Shadows, ran through the procedures available to me, given that brewing was not an option, and reminded me—once again—how essential it was for me to finish my training.

Before hanging up, she also warned me that a bad wind was blowing in from the east.

Oh, goodie.

No time to think about that now. It was essential to

pick up every shard of mirror. Calypso and I worked as quickly as we could, gathering the largest pieces first, placing them all in a pile in the center of the room.

"You said you were once a witch but no longer?" I asked Calypso as we used wet paper towels to wipe down the hard surfaces like the glass shelf and the chairs. "I didn't realize that was a choice a person could make."

"Not for someone like you, certainly. But for me . . . ? I came to my abilities through sheer practice and grit. They weren't innate talents. I could walk away. And I did."

"Why would you do that?"

"Magic cost me. I lost my license to provide foster care. And my relationship to Aidan . . . It nearly killed me. I'm not exaggerating."

"What . . . what happened?" I couldn't seem to stop myself.

She shook her head. "I made a pledge long ago. I won't talk about it. You'd better ask him."

Great. That wouldn't be awkward at all.

"So what's with the botanicals?"

"My love of plants—and theirs for me—was something I could not walk away from. And, as I told you when I first met you, I was trying to help, to train people to deal with poisonous plants without hurting themselves." The sadness washed over her again. The scent was piercing and strong, not the bright green of spring growth, but the knifelike pain of grief. "I can't believe Jonquil would do this. . . . She lived with me for six months, many years ago. She was the one who turned me in with the foster service. She was angry at me for refusing to train her in hexes. When she joined the Unspoken coven and asked to join my botanicals class, I thought she had grown, changed. But she was never . . . right."

"And Greta? She's your sister?"

She smiled and shook her head, looking chagrined. "Can you believe that? We were so close as kids, but she really hated it when I started studying nature, especially when I told her I was going to become a witch. I'm just so sorry to hear that she really took off with it, decided to go after others. I don't know what to say about that. She's still my sister, for better or worse."

Finally, Calypso vacuumed the carpet, adding the entire contents of the vacuum bag to our growing pile. When we'd gathered all the pieces we could, I performed a quick extraction spell to force the rest. I feared the police would be interrupting us anytime now.

I started circling the pile, stroking my medicine bag and chanting to center myself. Calypso circled opposite me, reflecting my energy. Her calm, confident presence helped me to focus. I reminded myself that I had support and focused on my magic. Then I intoned the words Graciela had given me, repeating them, dancing around the pile, Calypso mimicking my movements.

Slowly, the shards began to quiver, then to lift, then to swirl. Like a mini-cyclone, they gathered and whirled up over our heads. A bright light shone briefly, and though it let off no sound, the impact felt like an explosion. I looked up to see the face of my helping spirit take shape in the swirling dust, almost there but not, gone in an instant. And then Miriam's face, calling out. Also disappearing in a flash.

The shards fell to the floor, fused into a misshapen hunk of dark glass.

I guessed this was the best I could do. When Graciela had performed this spell, the mirror shards reconstituted themselves into their original shape as a mirror. But at least I had seen glimpses of my helping spirit as well as of Miriam; I was very nearly sure the spell had been successful, that I had freed Miriam's soul.

If she survived, I would be more than happy to buy the Paramount Theater a new mirror.

Luckily, the police didn't need much from us, since Jonquil was the one responsible for shattering the mirror. And once Carlos got involved, she would be up on charges far more serious than vandalism.

Calypso and I stood in the lobby. I cradled the ugly hunk of glass in my arms, just in case I hadn't succeeded and Miriam's spirit still wasn't reunited with her body. The faint voices of Cary Grant and Jimmy Stewart drifted through the double doors of the auditorium, along with occasional laughter from the audience.

I used Calypso's phone to call Duke. He was at Miriam's bedside, with Jonathan.

"It's a miracle," Duke choked out. "About ten minutes ago she just opened her eyes and started talking! I—I can't . . ." His voice cracked, and he started to sob. Jonathan came on the line and told me the doctors were checking Miriam out, but that she appeared to be whole and healthy.

When I told Calypso the news, she hugged me for a long time and stroked my hair.

"You poor thing," Calypso said, finally pulling away. "Your eye's swelling. I wish I had my herbs here. I'd fix you right up."

"I've got mugwort at home," I said. "I'll be fine."

She nodded, studying me for a moment. "Well, the movie's still playing. I think I'll go find my friends. I'll take care of Anise, now that I understand how Jonquil dosed her."

"She poisoned Miriam's lip balm. Have Anise put aside anything at all suspect, certainly anything she made with Jonquil. The police might want it all as evidence. Inspector Romero will probably be following up on all that."

She nodded, then turned toward the auditorium doors. "Would you like to join us?"

"Thanks, but I don't think I'm up for it at the moment." I had the depleted, hangover feeling I got after performing very strong spells. All I wanted was to have Sailor wrap his strong arms around me, all night long.

"Miriam is lucky to have you on her side. As for Jonquil ..." Calypso trailed off with a shrug, tears in her eyes.

"Maybe ... maybe when things settle down we could get together and talk? Lunch, maybe?"

Her face lit up with a warm, sad smile. "I would love that. And I'd like to visit your shop."

"Yes, please do." I had a feeling Calypso might become a good friend. One thing was certain: She would fit in just fine at Aunt Cora's Closet.

I watched Calypso duck into the darkened theater, then looked around for Sailor. The bartender told me a man fitting his description, and accompanied by a pig, no less, had headed out some time ago. The bartender didn't remember seeing the man return.

Where could he be? Was he all right? And had I been ditched, yet again, at the Paramount?

I sent out as loud a psychic shout as I could, to no avail. I thought of borrowing someone's phone to call him, but realized—with a trace of bitterness—that Sailor still hadn't given me his supersecret phone number.

As I headed toward the front doors I heard a commotion outside and saw my Vietnamese potbellied pig trying to evade capture on the sidewalk.

I hurried out.

"I'm so sorry! He must have gotten out of my car."

The harried security guard seemed to recognize me from the ladies' lounge, as well as from the other night with Sailor. Before he could speak, I jumped in.

"How about I take him and go home and promise not to come back?" I offered.

"I'd really appreciate that," he said, shaking his head and muttering, "Geesh, this job's a lot harder than it used to be."

I gestured to Oscar and we trotted down the street and around the corner to the Mustang. We climbed in. The street was quiet, so I waited for Oscar to transform. He didn't.

"Oscar? I need to talk to you."

He blinked up at me with his pink piggy eyes.

"What's wrong? Where's Sailor? Is he all right?"

He curled up on the seat as if to go to sleep.

"Oscar, this is ridiculous. *Talk* to me."

He wiggled his corkscrew tail and pretended to snore. I banged the steering wheel and blew out a frustrated breath, feeling my injured eye throb. At moments like these, I thought, what I wouldn't give to have a real witch's familiar. On the other hand, most familiars can't talk. And they don't intervene when a person is rolling around the floor with a murderer.

Count your blessings, Lily.

Miriam was well on her way to recovery; Duke had his daughter, Luna had her mommy, and Jonathan had his beloved back. Jonquil hadn't hurt anyone else, and now that we knew what had happened Calypso would take care of Anise. Carlos should have plenty of evidence to put a case together against Jonquil.

So really, being ditched by Sailor was a small thing. And he probably had a good reason. Or . . . could he be in trouble? Surely I would have felt something, wouldn't I? Or Oscar would tell me if I needed to intervene, wouldn't he?

I drove straight to San Francisco's Chinatown and drove down Hang Ah alley, where cars weren't allowed.

There was something wrong. I felt it as soon as I opened my car door. The alley now carried the typical stench of urban grime, rather than the fragrant, ghostly scent I had come to associate with it.

The door to Sailor's apartment building was locked, as usual. After plenty of banging and yelling, the landlord finally emerged, angry and clad only in sweatpants and a dirty undershirt.

"I'm sorry to disturb you," I said. "I need to see my friend Sailor."

"No cars here; move car," he said in broken English.

"I know. I'm sorry. I'll move it. But I have to talk to Sailor."

"Sailor gone."

"Gone? As in ... *gone*? Are you sure?" I tried to peer past him, up the stairs.

"He give me no notice. You go see if you want. Then move car." He stepped back to let me enter and waved toward the stairs. "Sailor gone."

I climbed the stairs and found the door to his apartment unlocked. The sparse furniture remained: the bed, a nightstand, a small couch and a chair; but his clothes and other few possessions had been emptied out, including his many books.

I remained for a moment, hoping to sense something, anything, to explain what had happened. I placed my hand on the bare mattress, on the mirror in the bathroom. Was he all right? Did he just run away because ... well, because I was too much for him? How many times had he told me that he didn't like witches, after all? But ... that couldn't be it, could it? Sailor, of all people, understood my sometimes difficult relationship to my own magic.

Much more likely was that Aidan had found out about us. And Sailor was under Aidan's influence....

Could Aidan have threatened Sailor somehow? Driven him away?

My heart pounded. I felt my blood rise in anger. A lamp fell over as I ran out of the apartment.

I hurried down the stairs and jumped into my car. Oscar, still in piggy mode, hid in the footwell behind the front seats.

No doubt about it. The perfume had lifted.

Chapter 25

A week later, a newly tidy Aunt Cora's Closet was full of more customers than ever. People had turned out in droves to support the store.

Conrad had brought in a few friends who worked all day in exchange for nothing more than breakfast and lunch—they refused to take my proffered payment. With their help, and Maya and Bronwyn and several coven members and women from the shelter, the shop was put to rights in a matter of days. A few members of the Unspoken coven showed up as well, offering to help, and more important, offering friendship. They had played no part in Jonquil's attacks, and were still reeling from the knowledge that someone they thought they knew had been capable of inflicting harm on another.

Clothing damaged beyond repair had been salvaged for their materials and for use in patternmaking for the new dress venture.

Meanwhile, Lucille's designs were selling out faster than she could produce them. Maya's Web site was pulling in even more custom orders, and there was talk of hiring seamstresses to help keep up with demand. Bronwyn suggested training some of the women from the shelter who were seeking jobs, and Lucille was taking names.

Today Maya and Lucille conferred at the counter, while Bronwyn played with Luna, who was cooing and sweet and no longer preferred my arms to any others. Duke had stopped by to take Bronwyn to lunch, and Oscar was running about with Imogen, who had arrived with Beowulf the cat.

True to his word, Max had used his connections to recover my Hand of Glory from the ladies' room of the Paramount Theater, so I gave him an exclusive interview about the spirit in the mirror—without naming names, of course. I didn't hold back, though, making my peace with whatever he thought of me. He took it surprisingly well. Still, his final article included lots of scientific information about ocular flashes and mass hallucinations, in an attempt to offer a "rational" explanation for the visions of a woman in the mirror.

That woman, Miriam, now sat on the velvet bench by the dressing rooms, holding hands with Jonathan. The doctors still had no explanation for her ordeal, but she seemed to suffer no ill aftereffects, other than tiring easily. Happily, she had no memory of her time in the backward world.

As for me . . . well, Bronwyn was worried about me, I knew. I tried my best to get involved in the new clothing venture with Maya and Lucille, but the truth was . . . my heart ached. I felt as though something precious had been within my grasp, but had slipped away.

After finding Sailor's apartment abandoned, I headed straight for Aidan's office. This time the entire museum was closed to me, not just his door. I called to him psychically as hard as I could and even cast a spell to try to force Aidan to contact me, but I was met with nothing but silence. Oscar had maintained his pig guise for several days, and even after resuming his natural shape adamantly refused to talk about anything other than food and zombie movies.

I kept replaying Sailor's last looks, last words, in my mind. His smile as he stood in the doorway, the wink he gave me, letting me know he was confident in my abilities to help Miriam, that I would succeed. And before that, the way he followed me into that haunted theater and backed me up, every step of the way, even fighting with Wolfgang outside the ladies' room.

I was almost certain Aidan was responsible for Sailor's disappearing act. What could have happened? Where had Sailor gone, and why? Was he all right? Should I chase after him?

I was so mad I could spit. And most of all, I missed Sailor's presence in my life. But as my mother used to say, it looked like I was going to have to get happy in the same pants I got mad in. In other words, it was up to me to deal with the situation. No one was going to fix it for me.

Filling Aunt Cora's Closet, I reminded myself, were good friends. Closer than family. I was very lucky. And perhaps I should surround myself with nonmagical folks from now on. Perhaps it was best I return to my solo-witch ways. I used to vow not to involve myself in local witchy politics, and now I remembered why. It was too confusing, too fraught, too painful.

So I would grow old alone and eccentric, like Calypso. There were worse things. Much worse.

"Careful, Oscar!" I cried. A rack of crinolines teetered as my potbellied pig chased Beowulf under the stiff petticoats.

No matter what path I chose, I'd have to make room in my life for Oscar. Whether he told me what happened to Sailor or not. If he was close-muzzled, it was because he felt he had to be. It drove me crazy, but I still loved him. As proof, I'd agreed to watch *Night of the Living Dead* with Oscar tonight. We were planning on popping popcorn and snuggling on the couch, just the two of us.

The phone rang, and Maya answered.

"No, but she's right here," said Maya. "I'll pass the phone to— What? I— Hello? Hello?"

Maya hung up, looking at me with a frown.

"Was that for me?" I asked, my heart skipping a beat. *Let it be Sailor.*

"Yes, but the connection was terrible, and then she was cut off. She said her name was Pilar."

"Pilar? You're sure?" I felt a tingling sensation at the nape of my neck. The only Pilar I knew well was a powerful witch from Mexico, a friend of Graciela's. The last time I had seen her was when I finally tracked down my father. But . . . surely she was calling for some other reason. Surely Pilar wasn't calling to warn me about—

"She said to tell you your father was coming for a visit," said Maya, interrupting my thoughts. "I didn't even know you *had* a father."

"Oh, Lily," said Bronwyn, her eyes bright. "Your father's coming? That's wonderful news. You need family around you right now."

Oscar let out a muffled squeal and came to stand next to me. He understood who—or what—my father was.

"The weird thing was," added Maya, "Pilar said she called to *warn* you that your father was coming. Maybe something was lost in translation. She had a heavy accent."

I swallowed hard and tried to ignore the the harsh pounding of my heart. If my father were coming to town, it signaled trouble. I would need help.

I took back everything I'd just thought about shunning my magical friends. Aidan once told me he didn't worry about angering me, because I'd forgive him at just the moment I needed his assistance. I still had his mandragora; I could use it as an excuse to arrange a meeting.

And yet . . . I would have to find a way to deal with my anger before meeting with Aidan, presuming I could find him. And in order to secure his aide, I had the uncomfortable feeling that groveling would be required—and probably a heap of promises I didn't want to make.

It was either that, or get the hell out of Dodge.

And that wasn't an option. As much as a part of me wanted to hit the road and look for Sailor, San Francisco was my home now.

Luckily I had friends at my back, and plenty more tricks up my proverbial sleeve. All of which, I imagined, I was going to need. After all, I had been warned: Dad was paying me a visit.

Continue reading for a special preview of

MURDER ON THE HOUSE

A Haunted Home Renovation Mystery
by Juliet Blackwell
Coming in December from Obsidian.

What makes a house look haunted?

Is it enough to appear abandoned, run-down, bleak? To creak and groan when long fingers of fog creep down the nearby hills?

Or is it something else? A whisper of a tragic past, a distinct but unsettling impression that dwelling within is something indescribable — and perhaps not human?

Beats me. I'm a general contractor, with a well-earned reputation for restoring and renovating historic homes, and an abiding desire to chuck all my responsibilities in San Francisco and run off to Paris. Reconciling those two imperatives was hard enough, but my life was made even more complicated when the most recent edition of *Haunted House Quarterly* named me "California's most promising up-and-coming Ghost Buster."

A misleading moniker if ever there was one. When it comes to ghosts, I'm pretty clueless. Not that I let that stop me.

At the moment I was standing on the front stoop of a once-grand house in San Francisco's vibrant Castro District. The home appeared lived-in, what with the cars

parked out front, the cluster of red clay pots planted with
marigolds on the porch, ecru lace curtains in the front
windows, and a folded newspaper on the sisal doormat.

It sure didn't *look* haunted. But the current residents
were certain it was—in fact, they wanted my help to transform the place into a haunted bed-and-breakfast.

As usual, when I was facing a magnificent structure, my
heart swelled at its history, its artistry . . . and its needs.

My practiced eye noted a host of problems: One corner under the roof overhang gaped open, inviting ver-
min. The gutter had become detached in a few spots, and
the roof displayed long streaks of bright green moss that
hinted at water issues. Window sashes sagged, indicat-
ing rot. Such obvious signs of neglect meant a thousand
other problems would be uncovered once the walls were
opened.

And then there were the alleged ghosts.

I took a deep breath and blew it out slowly. *Here goes.*
Looking around for a bell or knocker, I found an ancient
intercom system to the right of the front door. A quick
press of the button was greeted by a burst of static.

I had just reached out to knock on the door when it
swung open.

I squeaked and jumped in surprise, my hands flailing.

This was another glitch in any of my ghost buster career aspirations: I'm not what you'd call cool in the face
of . . . well, much of anything. At the moment, for instance, I appeared to be at a total loss when faced with a
rosy-cheeked little girl, with long chestnut hair and big
eyes the deep, soft brown of milk chocolate.

As I tried to pull myself together, she giggled.

"Sorry," I said, taking a deep breath and striving to
regain my composure. "My mind was somewhere else."

"My mama does that all the time," the girl said with
an understanding little shrug, displaying the preadoles-

cent sweetness of a child who was oh so familiar—and patient—with the mysterious ways of adults. Though she held herself with great poise, I pegged her age at ten or eleven. Give her a couple more years, I thought, and she'd be as snarky and sullen as my teenage stepson.

She stepped back. "Do you want to come in?"

"Yes, thank you. I'm Mel Turner, with Turner Construction. I have an appointment with Mrs. Bernini. . . . Is she your grandmother?"

The girl laughed and shook her head. "No, of course not. I'm Anabelle. Anabelle Bowles. I'll take you to the parlor. Follow me."

I stepped into the front foyer and paused, savoring the moment.

In the old days, all buildings were custom-designed and custom-built, so each historic house was unique. My favorite part of my job, bar none, is stepping into an old structure for the first time; one never knows what to expect.

Although the lines of this house were neoclassical, the interior details were eclectic, drawing on a range of Federal, Greek Revival, Italianate and even baroque influences.

The front entry was airy and open, the intricate woodwork painted a creamy white throughout, rather than stained or shellacked. The brightness was a welcome change from the dark woods so characteristic of the Victorian style, as in the house I was finishing up across town. The walls were lined in high bead board wainscoting. Tall sash windows allowed sunlight to pour in, giving the home an airy, sunny feel. An enormous fireplace, missing several of its glazed blue-green tiles, was flanked by built-in display cases. Each newel post on the banister leading upstairs was carved in a different pattern: One was a series of different-sized balls, another was geometric boxes, yet another sported a face carved into the lintel.

In marked contrast to the home's exquisite bones, the interior design was appalling. Everywhere I looked, there was a pile of clutter. Newspapers were piled in one corner, and flyers from local merchants littered a scarred maple coffee table from the 1960s. Shreds of discarded paper and a pair of scissors suggested someone had been clipping coupons. And it got worse as I looked up at the walls and ceiling. Rather than strip the faded wallpaper above the old wainscoting, someone had simply painted over it; it was pulling away from the walls and hanging in crazy quilt patches. Rusty water stains bloomed in several spots on the peeling ceiling, and the broad-planked oak flooring was warped and discolored in patches.

And there was a distinct chill to the air, so it felt almost colder than the winter afternoon outside. It must have cost a fortune to heat a place this big.

Beneath the papers and layers of grime that had settled across everything, I thought I spied a marble-topped antique credenza near the massive fireplace, as well as a few light fixtures that appeared to be original handblown glass. In general, though, the turn-of-the-century home's ambience was, by and large, twenty-first-century Frat Boy. It would require a lot of work, both structural and cosmetic, to transform this historic home into a welcoming B and B.

"This way," said Anabelle as she led the way down the hall to the left.

Several broad corridors spiraled off the central foyer. The hallway we walked down was lined with so many identical cream-colored doors, the place felt a little more like a hotel than a private home. We passed a formal dining room with a built-in china hutch, a carved marble fireplace, and two impressive crystal chandeliers hanging from the coffered ceiling.

"I like your dress," said Anabelle, glancing over her

shoulder. "You look like you could be in Ringling Brothers. We saw them when they came to town. They say it's the greatest show on earth."

I looked down at myself. It's true: I have a tendency to wear offbeat clothing. Nothing inappropriate, mind you, just ... unexpected. I chalk this up to the years I spent in camouflage as I played the role of a respectable faculty wife to a respectable Berkeley professor who turned out to be a not so respectable, cheating slimeball. The minute the ink was dry on my divorce papers, I yanked every scrap of my expensive Faculty Wife Wardrobe out of my closet and drove the whole kit and caboodle over to a women's shelter.

Once freed from my "respectable" constraints, I indulged my fondness for spangles and fringe with the help of my friend Stephen—an aspiring costume designer and the much-loved only son of a Vegas showgirl. It started as a joke, sort of, but soon became a "thing." My unconventional wardrobe inspired good-natured ribbing on the jobsite, where denim rules the day, but I'm serious about my profession: I always wear steel-toed work boots and bring along a pair of coveralls so as to be ready for any construction-related contingency.

But today I was meeting a client for the first time, so I had left the sparkles shut away in my closet in favor of a simple above-the-knee patterned dress topped by a cardigan. Perhaps Anabelle wasn't accustomed to such uninspired attire in this neighborhood.

"I like your dress, as well," I said, "especially the matching ribbons in your hair."

"It's called robin's egg blue," she said, clutching a bit of the skirt in each hand and holding it up as though ready to curtsy. She gave me a big smile and turned down a narrow passage to the right.

It was rare to find a house this massive in the Castro,

which was studded with Victorian row houses built by Scandinavians in the 1910s and 1920s, and populated by Irish working-class families in the 1930s. Known locally as the Bernini house, after the family who had lived here for the past several decades, the structure had survived the massive earthquake and fire of 1906. It was exceptional not only for its square footage but also for its extensive grounds: It took up half a city block, and included a huge courtyard garden and two outbuildings. This house was a stunner as it was; once renovated, it would be a rare gem. A landmark, even.

I wanted this job so much, I could taste it. But there was no guarantee it would be mine.

I knew the clients were also meeting with Avery Builders, one of my competitors. They were good — almost as good as Turner Construction, though it galled me to admit it. Avery and Turner had similar portfolios and track records for keeping on budget and on schedule. When competition for a job was this tight, the decision usually came down to whomever the clients liked more, whom they felt more comfortable having in their homes, day in and day out, for months on end.

Client relations make me nervous. I'm a whiz at construction, and understand the ins and outs of buildings and architectural history as if they were in my blood. But when it comes to dealing with people, well ... I'm fine. Up to a point. Mostly if they let me do what I want and what I know is right for the house. Diplomacy has never been my strong suit.

I did have one distinct advantage over Avery Builders: The new owners of the Bernini estate wanted to turn the place into a haunted B and B. And as far as I knew, Avery Builders didn't have a ghost buster on staff.

Anabelle hummed as she walked, finally breaking out into song: *"Wish me a rainbow, wish me a star ..."* She glanced over her shoulder and smiled, displaying deep dimples. "Do you know that song?"

"I don't. But I'm no good at music."

"You don't play? I'm learning to play the piano."

"I tried my hand at the clarinet in the fifth grade. It wasn't pretty."

Anabelle gave me a withering look, as though I'd suggested she make mud pies in her nice blue dress. Usually I'm good with kids, because I don't take them—or myself—too seriously. My stepson, Caleb, and I had gotten off to a famously good start because I had immediately grasped why he felt compelled to wear his pirate costume and remain in character for more than a year before graduating, in a manner of speaking, to pretending to be the more "grown-up" Darth Vader. But then I have a flair for sword fights and laser battles, if I do say so myself.

"*...These you can give me, wherever you aaarrrrrree...*" Anabelle resumed singing, slightly off-tune, and stopped in front of a door that stood ajar. "Here we are. Have a seat, please, and I'll let them know you're here."

She skipped back down the hall, calling over her shoulder, "Good-bye. It was nice to meet you."

"Nice to meet you, too." I said, watching her go and marveling at the energy of youth. When was the last time I had skipped somewhere?

I pushed open the parlor door.

The room was empty.

Not just empty of people; it was vacant. No furniture, no rugs, no lights, no knickknacks. Nothing but a heavy coating of dust, a few scraps of paper on the floor, and a pair of shredded curtains on the large windows that overlooked a huge courtyard and garden.

The afternoon sun sifting in through the wavy antique

glass illuminated cobwebs in the corners, and a single paneled door I assumed was a closet. I didn't see so much as a footstep—other than my own—in the dust on the floor, and the musty smell indicated the room hadn't been aired out for a very long time.

"Wait, Anabelle! I don't think ..." I poked my head through the open door and peered down the long corridor, but the girl was gone.

Then a sound came from the opposite direction.

Clank, shuffle, clank, scrape.

I caught a glimpse of something passing in front of the arch at the end of the hall.

Someone, I reminded myself. *Get a grip, Mel. The child is playing a joke.*

"Hello?" I called out as I started down the dim corridor. "Anabelle?"

I heard it again: a slow step, a shuffle, a clank. My mind's eye conjured a picture of a ghost in chains. But that was an old Hollywood convention, not reality. I hoped.

And if this truly was a restless spirit, why should I have been so surprised? I had been asked to the Bernini house to help broker a deal with ghosts, after all. I just hadn't expected to see anything right off the bat, much less in the middle of a sunny afternoon.

Slowly, cautiously, I continued down the hallway to where it ended in a T, the sound growing louder with each step. *Clank, shuffle, clank, scrape. Clank, shuffle, clank, scrape.*

I screwed up my courage, took a deep breath, and peeked around the corner.

An old woman hunched over an aluminum walker, slowly making her way down the corridor. An orange-and-yellow crochet afghan was draped over her narrow shoulders, and her hair was a blue-gray mass of stiff-set curls. With each laborious step-push-step she made, her slippered feet and the walker sounded off: *Clank, shuffle, clank, scrape.*

"Hello?" I said.

"Oh!" she let out a surprised yelp, one blue-veined hand fluttering up to her chest. "My word, you gave me a fright!"

"I'm so sorry," I said, still basking in relief at the sight of a flesh-and-blood woman instead of a spectral presence. "I'm Mel Turner, from Turner Construction?"

"Oh, yes, of course. How do you do? I'm Betty Bernini."

"It's so nice to meet you. You have an amazing place here."

"Thank you. Come, we've been expecting you. The Propaks are in the front room." She resumed her slow progress, and I fell in step, resisting the urge to offer to help. "I'm afraid I didn't hear the doorbell. Who let you in?"

"Anabelle answered the door, but she showed me to the parlor—the wrong room, I take it."

The clanking stopped as Mrs. Bernini straightened and fixed me with a steady gaze. "Anabelle?"

"Yes, she's a sweetheart."

"Anabelle let you in."

I nodded, suddenly feeling guilty. Was Anabelle not supposed to answer the door? Had I gotten the girl in trouble?

"Let me show you something." Mrs. Bernini shuffled a little farther down the hall and opened the door to a bookshelf-lined study full of cardboard boxes, stacked furniture, and a cracked old leather couch. She gestured to an oil painting hanging over the fireplace. Done in rich old master hues of blue, red, and burnt sienna, it featured a girl and a slightly younger boy. She stood with one hand on the boy's shoulder, while he held a cocker spaniel puppy.

The girl had long chestnut brown curls, tied in blue ribbons.

Robin's egg blue.

A brass plate on the picture frame read:

ANABELLE AND EZEKIEL BOWLES. 1911.

ABOUT THE AUTHOR

Juliet Blackwell is the pseudonym for a mystery author who, together with her sister, wrote the Art Lover's Mystery series. The first in that series, *Feint of Art*, was nominated for an Agatha Award for Best First Novel. She also writes the Haunted Home Renovation mystery series. Juliet's lifelong interest in the paranormal world was triggered when her favorite aunt visited and read her fortune—with startling results. As an anthropologist, the author studied systems of spirituality, magic, and health across cultures and throughout history. She currently resides in a happily haunted house in Oakland, California.